The Problems Always Start Small...

Mitch spreads his hands wide, helplessly, and the look that breaks through his veneer chills me. You get to know that expression, after a while. You see it on the ones who've adopted goals other than survival. Dead men walking.

"Look, Maker. I've got a dead detective. I've got Razor-face maybe linked to a murder. And not one of his little cleanup killings. I don't give a damn about those. A dead cop. A dead cop is not good for you and it is not good for me and it is not good for your gangster boyfriend. And a street full of dead kids poisoned by Canadian special forces combat drugs—that's not good for you either. Since I know how much you like people poking into your history. No?"

Mitch's eyes flicker around my shop in that way he has, recording everything.

Our eyes meet: I see him in living color on the right side, and in high-resolution black and white complete with thermal readings and a heads-up array on the left. The bulge of his gun glimmers red on the threat display. Distracting. "It isn't about that, Mitch."

"Good. Then are you going to help me, or not?"

ADVANCE PRAISE FOR

HAMMERED

"A gritty and painstakingly well-informed peek inside a future we'd all better hope we don't get, liberally seasoned with VR delights and enigmatically weird alien artifacts. Genevieve Casey is a pleasingly original female lead, fully equipped with the emotional life so often lacking in military SF yet tough and full of noir attitude; old enough by a couple of decades to know better but conflicted enough to engage with the sleazy dynamics of her situation regardless. Out of this basic contrast, Elizabeth Bear builds her future nightmare tale with style and conviction and a constant return to the twists of the human heart." —Richard Morgan

"*Hammered* has it all. Drug wars, hired guns, corporate skulduggery, and bleeding-edge AI, all rolled into one of the best first novels I've read in I don't know how long. This is the real dope!"
—Chris Moriarty, author of *Spin State*

"A glorious hybrid: hard science, dystopian geopolitics, and wide-eyed sense of wonder seamlessly blended into a single book. I hate this woman. She makes the rest of us look like amateurs." —Peter Watts, author of *Starfish* and *Maelstrom*

"Packed with a colorful panoply of characters, a memorable and likeable antiheroine, and plenty of action and intrigue, *Hammered* is a superbly written novel that combines high tech, military-industrial politics, and complex morality. There is much to look forward to in new writer Elizabeth Bear." —Karin Lowachee, Campbell Award–nominated author of *Warchild*

"Even in scenes where there is no violent action, or even much physical action at all, the thoughts and emotions of Ms. Bear's characters, as well as the dynamic tensions of their relationships, create an impression of feverish activity going on below the surface and liable to erupt into plain view at any moment. . . . The language is terse and vivid, punctuated by ironic asides whose casual brutality—sometimes amusing, sometimes shocking—speaks volumes about these people and their world. . . . This is a superior piece of work by a writer of enviable talents. I look forward to reading more!" —Paul Witcover, author of *Waking Beauty*

"*Hammered* is one helluva good novel! Elizabeth Bear writes tight and tough and tender about grittily real people caught up in a highly inventive story of a wild and woolly tomorrow that grabs the reader from the get-go and will not let go. Excitement, intrigue, intelligence—and a sense of wonder, too! Who could ask for anything more?" —James Stevens-Arce, author of *Soulsaver*, Best First Novel 2000 (*Rocky Mountain News*)

"In this promising debut novel, Elizabeth Bear deftly weaves thought-provoking ideas into an entertaining and tight narrative." —Dena Landon, author of *Shapeshifter's Quest* (Dutton, fall 2004)

ELIZABETH BEAR

BANTAM BOOKS

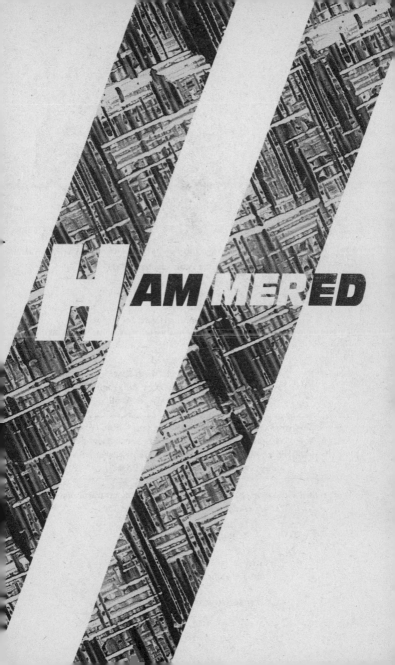

HAMMERED
A Bantam Spectra Book / January 2005

Published by
Bantam Dell
A Division of Random House, Inc.
New York, New York

ISBN 0-553-58750-1

Printed in the United States of America
Published simultaneously in Canada

OPM 10 9 8 7 6 5 4 3 2 1

This book is dedicated to

Dr. Richard P. Feynman and

Dr. Robert L. Forward

—for being unable to put down a puzzle.

Acknowledgments

It takes a lot of people to write a novel. This one would not have existed without the assistance of my very good friends and first readers (on and off the Online Writing Workshop for Science Fiction, Fantasy, and Horror)—especially but not exclusively Kathryn Allen, Rhonda Garcia, Jaime Voss, Chris Coen, Ilona Gordon, Jean Seok, Derek R. Molata, Tara Devine, Chelsea Polk, Caliann Graves, James Stevens-Arce, Michael Curry, and Larry West. I am even more deeply indebted to Stella Evans, M.D., to whom I owe whatever bits of the medical science and neurology are accurate; to M.Cpl. S. K. S. Perry (Canadian Forces) and Capt. Beth Coughlin (U.S. Army), without whom my portrayal of military life would have been even more wildly fantastical; to Leah Bobet, my native guide to Toronto; to Thomas Ladegard, whose firsthand experience in the sewers of Hartford proved invaluable; to Stephen Shipman for handgun tips; to Asha C. Shipman for listening to me curse (and type) late into the night; to my copyeditor, Faren Bachelis; to the North Las Vegas Police Department's Lt. Ed Finizie and Officer Marion Brady for giving me some idea what it means to be a big-city cop; to Dena Landon, Sarah Monette, and Kelly Morisseau, francophones extraordinaire, upon whom may be blamed any correctness in the Québecois—especially the naughty bits; to Jennifer Jackson and Anne Groell for too many reasons to enumerate; and most especially to my husband,

Chris, for staying married to me not only through the third novel (blamed for many a divorce), but through the fourth, fifth, and sixth ones, too.

The failures, of course, are my own, with one exception: Jenny's completely wrong about the squirrels.

Editor's Note

In the interests of presenting a detailed personal perspective on a crucial moment in history, we have taken the liberty of rendering Master Warrant Officer Casey's interviews—as preserved in the Yale University New Haven archives—in narrative format. Changes have been made in the interests of clarity, but the words, however edited, are her own.

The motives of the other individuals involved are not as well documented, although we have had the benefit of our unique access to extensive personal records left by Col. Frederick Valens. The events as presented herein are accurate: the drives behind them must always remain a matter of speculation, except in the case of Dr. Dunsany—who left us comprehensive journals—and "Dr." Feynman, who kept frequent and impeccable backups.

What follows is a historical novel, of sorts. It is our hope that this more intimate annal than is usually seen will serve to provide future students with a singular perspective on the roots of the civilization we are about to become.

—*Patricia Valens, Ph.D.*
Jeremy Kirkpatrick, Ph.D.

BOOK ONE

Friends may
come and go,
but enemies
accumulate.

—Thomas Jones

I never sleep if I can help it.

So when somebody starts trying to kick down my door at 0300 hours on a rank hot summer night, it isn't quite the surprise for me that it might be for some people. When the noise starts, I'm sitting on a gouged orange plastic chair in my shop. I drop my old-fashioned paperback book, stand, and draw my sidearm before sidling across oil-stained concrete to flick the monitor on. Smart relays in the gun click on in recognition of my palm print, too quietly for normal ears to hear. The air thickens in my lungs; my heartbeat slows ominously.

And then I curse out loud and go open up the big blue steel door, holding the safetied pistol casually in my meat hand while the metal one turns the knob.

"You wanna pound the damn door down?" I accuse, and then I get a good look at the purple-faced kid dying in Razorface's arms and I'm all somebody's sergeant, somebody's mother. *Not that the two are all that different.*

"Ah, shit, Face. This kid is hammered. What do you expect me to do with this?"

Face shoves past me, skirting a dangling engine block and a neat pile of sheet metal, two of his "boys"—teenage hoods—trailing like ducklings. He doesn't answer immediately. Even as I take his name loudly in vain, Razorface carries the baby gangster gently around the scarred steel lab table that holds up my hot plate. He lays the kid on my cot in the corner of the shop, wrinkling the taut brown blanket. Razorface, Razorface. Gets his name from a triple row of stainless steel choppers. Skin black as velvet and shoulders wide as a football star's. The old kind of football, yeah.

I know the kid: maybe fourteen, maybe twelve. His name is Mercedes. He's rigid, trying to suck air and failing. *Anaphylactic shock*. Besides that, dark red viscous blood oozes out of his nose, and his skin looks like pounded meat. The nosebleed and the wide-open capillary color of his face are dead giveaways, but I give him the once-over anyway. Then I grab my kit and lug it over, dropping to my knees on the cold damp concrete beside the cot. Bones and metal creak. The room reeks of Razorface's sweaty leather, the kid's blood, diesel fuel. Once it would have made me gag. *I ain't what I used to be.*

"Can you fix him, Maker?"

Face's boys stand twitching just inside the doorway.

I fumble in my kit, finding epinephrine, the long needle. Even as I fill a syringe I know the answer. "Nah, Face. There's no fucking way." But I have to try. 'Cause Face is one of mine, and the kid is one of his.

I don't look at the punks. "Will one of you two be so fucking kind as to lock the goddamned door?"

"Derek," Razorface says, "do it," and the taller of the two shoots him a sullen-jawed look and stalks away.

I know already, from the color of Merc's skin, but I need to ask—so I turn my grim expression on Razorface.

"What'd he OD on?" *Please God let me be wrong*.

They can break you of religion, but they can't break you of praying.

Face holds out a twist of pills, and a chill snakes up my spine. I reach out with my metal hand and take the packet away from him, squeezing the ends to pop the slit. "Putain de marde!" Yellow pills, small as saccharine tablets, with a fine red line across the diameter. Rigathalonin. Hyperex.

We used to call it the Hammer.

How did a two-bit piece of street trash get his hands on something like this? And just what on God's gray earth do you think I can do for a kid who chewed down a handful of Hammers, Face? But I don't say that. I say, "How long ago? When did he take them?"

Face answers. "An hour ago. About an hour ago," and the taller gangster starts to whine.

I glare up at Whiny. "Shut up. How many of these did he take? Anybody see?" Nothing that I can manage—that anybody can manage—is going to make a difference for this kid. If Merc's central nervous system isn't already so much soft-serve, I'm not a card-carrying member of the Teamster's Union.

"One," Whiny says. I curse him for a liar, but the other one—Dopey? Doc?—backs him up. *Allergic reaction? Merci à Dieu.* I drive the needle into his flesh, through cartilage, into the spasming muscle of the heart.

He quits twitching and his eyes fly open, but there's nobody home. I've seen it before. The funny purple color will drain out of his face in a couple of hours, and he'll be just like any other vegetable. I should have let him kick it when I could. Kinder than letting him live.

You're a hard woman, Jenny Casey. Yeah, well, I come by it honestly. "Shit," I whisper. "Another kid. Shit."

I wipe cold sweat from my face, flesh hand trembling with the aftershock. I'll be sick for hours. The only thing worse than the aftermath of a plunge into combat-time is stepping up to the edge and then backing off.

All right. *Time to make coffee. And throw Razorface's gangsters out onto the street so I can pat him on the shoulder, with nobody else to see.*

• • •

Later, I wash my face in the stained steel sink and dry it on a clean rag. I catch myself staring into my own eyes, reflected in the unbreakable mirror hanging on my wall. I look chewed. Hell, you can barely tell I'm a girl. Not exactly girlish anymore, Jenny.

Hah. I won't be fifty for a month.

You wouldn't think I'd spend a lot of time staring in mirrors, but I never got used to that face. I used to stand there and study it every morning when I brushed my teeth, trying to figure out what the rest of the world saw. Vain as a cat of my glamorous good looks, don't you know?

Stained torn sleeveless shirt and cami pants over a frame like rawhide boiled and wired to bone. An eagle's nose—*how come you never broke that witch's nose, Jenny?*—the skin tone and the cheekbones proclaim my three mostly Mohawk grandparents. Shiny pink burn scars. A prosthetic eye on the left half of the face.

Oh, yeah. And the arm. The left arm. From just below the shoulder it's dull, scratched steel—a clicking horror of a twenty-year-old Canadian Army prosthesis.

"Marde." I glance over at Face, who hands me another cup of coffee. After turning back to the steel table, I pour bourbon into it. Shaking my head, I set mug and bottle aside. My arm clicking, I hoist my butt onto the counter edge.

"Where'd he get it?" I hook the orange chair closer with my right foot and plant it on the seat, my bad leg propped on the back. Hell of a stinking summer night, and it's raining again. The tin roof leaks in three places; rain drums melodiously into the buckets I've set underneath. I run wet fingers through white-stippled hair. It won't lie flat. Too much sweat and grime, and I need a shower, so it's a good thing the rain's filling the rooftop tanks.

The left side of my body aches like the aftermath of a nasty electrical jolt.

Face rolls big shoulders, lifting his coffee cup to his mouth. The ceramic clinks against his prosthetic teeth, and then he eases his body down into another old chair. It creaks under his weight as he swings his feet up onto the counter beside me, leaning back. Regarding me impassively, he shrugs again—a giant, shaven-headed figure with an ear and a nose full of gold and a mouth full of knife-edged, gleaming steel. The palms of his hands are pink and soft where he rolls them over the warmth of the mug; the rest of him shines dark and hard as some exotic wood. A little more than two-thirds my age, maybe. *Getting old for a gangster, Face.*

"Shit, Maker. I got to do me some asking about that."

I nod, pursing my lips. The scars on my cheek pull the expression out of shape. Face's gaze is level as I finish the spiked coffee in a long, searing swallow. The thermostat reads 27°C. I shiver. It's too damn cold in here. "Hand me that sweater."

He rises and does it wordlessly, and then refills my cup without my asking. "You drink less coffee, maybe eat something once in a while, you wouldn't be so damn cold all the time."

It's not being skinny makes me shiver, Face. It's a real old problem, but they give it a longer name every war.

"All right," I mumble. "So what do you want to do about it?" He knows I don't mean the cold.

Face turns his attention to the corpse-silent child on my narrow bed. "You think the shit was bad?"

I bite my lip. "I hope he was allergic. Otherwise—" I can't finish. I wonder how many of those little plastic twists are out in the neighborhoods. I rake my hand through stiff hair and shake my head. Hyperex is not a street drug. It is produced by two licensed pharmaceutical companies under contract for the U.S. armed forces and—chiefly—for the C.A. It's classified. And complicated.

The chances of a street-level knockoff are slim, and I don't think a multinational would touch it.

"What the hell else could it be?" I wave my left hand at the twist on the table. The light glitters on the scratches and dents marking my prosthesis. He doesn't answer.

After setting my cup aside, I raise my arm to pull the sweater up to my shoulder. It snags on the hydraulics of the arm and I have to wiggle the thread loose. *Cette putain de machine.* Face doesn't stare at the puckered line of scar a few centimeters below the proximal end of my humerus. Did I mention that I like that man? I pause to comment, "Half a dozen tabs in there. You want to try one out, eh?"

Then I drag the black sweater over my head, twisting the sleeves around so the canvas elbow patches are where they should be, mothball-scented cotton-wool warm on my right arm only. The left one aches—phantom pain. My body trying to tell me something's wrong with a hand I lost a quarter century back.

Long slow shake of that massive head, bulldog muscle rippling along the column of his neck. "I don't want this shit on my street, Maker." A deep frown. I hand him the bottle of bourbon by my elbow, and he adds a healthy dose to his cup along with a double spoonful of creamer and enough sugar to make me queasy. What is it about big macho men that they have to ruin perfectly good coffee?

I'm shaking less. I nearly triggered earlier, and the reaction won't wear off for a while yet, but the booze and the caffeine double-teaming my system help to smooth things. I raise my own cup to my lips, inhale alcohol fumes and the good rich smell of the roasted beans. Fortified, I brace myself and go down deep, after the memories I usually leave to rot. Old blood, that. Old, bad blood.

Two more breaths and I'm as ready to talk about it as I'll ever be. "I've never seen anybody do that off a single hit, Face. We'd get guys once in a while, who'd been strung out and on the front line for weeks, who'd push it too far and do the froth-and-foam. But not off a tablet. The Hammer's not like that." I glance over at Mercedes, who is resting quietly on my cot. "Poor stupid kid."

"He's cooked, ain't he?"

I nod slowly, tasting bile, and reach for the bourbon. Razorface hands it to me without even looking and I kick the chair away and hop down, holster creaking, wincing as weight hits my left knee and hip. There's a lot of ceramic in there.

I gulp a quarter mug. It burns going down. Nothing in the world ever tasted quite so good. *Jean-Michel. Katya. Nell.* Oh, God. Nell.

I fight my face under control and turn back to him, thrusting the bourbon his way. "Drink to your dead, Face?"

Face's lips skin back from his shark smile as he waves the bottle away. Thick, sensitive lips, with the gray edge of an armor weave visible along the inside rim where they should have been pink with blood. I don't like to think about his sex life. "I'm gonna find that dealer, Maker."

"What about Merc?"

Face looks at the kid. "His momma will take care of him."

"Better to put a bullet in his head."

He looks at me, expressionless.

"What's his mother going to do with him? Better to tell her he's dead. He isn't coming back from this."

Another slow roll of his shoulders. "Shit, Maker. I don't know if I can do that." He's one of my boys, one of my kids, his eyes tell me. I wonder if Mercedes is Face's son. I wonder if he knows. Half the bastards in Hartford are his, likely as not.

"I can," I offer. His eyes flicker from mine down to the piece strapped to my thigh, and then back. The muscles in his face tense and go slack.

"No," he says after a moment. "He's mine."

He hands me back my mug and scoops Mercedes into his arms, letting me hold the door. I lock up after they go, and watch on the monitors as his back recedes into the blood-warm predawn drizzle, leaving me alone with my thoughts and most of a bottle.

That bottle looks back at me for long seconds before I take it and climb into the front seat of a half-restored gasoline convertible, getting comfortable for a long night of thinking.

Lake Simcoe Military Prison
Boyne Valley, Ontario
Friday 1 September, 2062

Dr. Elspeth Dunsany folded her prison coveralls for the last time and set them on the shelf above her bunk. Denim jeans and a peach-colored button-down shirt felt strange against her skin, and the colors were garish after over a decade of unrelieved blue and gray and khaki. She had no mirror, but she was willing to bet that the pastel shirt made her dark bronze complexion look brassy. She wondered what it would be like, to look at walls that were not gray, to taste different air.

"Hurry up, Doc," the guard by the barred door ordered, not unsympathetically.

The prisoner looked up at her guard and grinned. A single lock of once-black hair curled out of Elspeth's ponytail and hung down before merry eyes. "Officer Fox. You've been keeping me here for twelve years. Now you can't wait to get me out."

"Fear of freedom?" The guard rattled her keys. "Truth is, I'm sad to see you go."

"I'm not sad to be going." Elspeth Dunsany picked an army-green duffel-bag up off the floor, puffing a little under the weight. "I thought I'd be here until I was a much older woman than this." She stepped through the door as Fox slid it back and fell into step behind Elspeth and to her right.

"What's happened with that? Warden said your sentence had been commuted."

Elspeth laughed low in her throat. "I cracked under the pressure, kid. Times have changed."

"Yeah, but—Elspeth. We've known each other a long time." Fox's boots rang on the concrete floor. A few catcalls followed them down the corridor, but the women on this hallway, notoriously, kept to themselves. Quiet, well-educated, model prisoners. Some of them had cried a lot, at first. The ones with families. "I've never seen anybody charged with espionage just . . . released before."

Elspeth stopped and turned toward Fox. She chewed her lip for a moment, gathering the dignity she knew made her short, chunky frame seem larger and powerful. "Not espionage."

"Military Powers Act violation, sealed," Fox replied. "What's that if not espionage?"

"If I told you that," Elspeth answered, "it would be espionage."

Fox grinned and challenged her again. "Most of population swears they're innocent. You never made a peep."

Elspeth turned back slowly and resumed walking toward the barred daylight streaking the far end of the hall. "That's because I'm guilty as charged, Officer Fox. Guilty as charged."

• • •

Elspeth leaned her face against the sun-warmed glass of the bus's side window and watched the trees spin over, a leafy tunnel just touched with traces of cinnabar and gold. The soft electric hum of the engine lulled her, and she breathed deeply, hair rumpled by the wind trickling in the open vent. A strand blew across her eyes and she shoved it back with a sigh. Between the leaves of sugar maple and towering oak, the sky overhead was blue as stained glass, golden sunlight trickling through it.

The bus wasn't crowded, but Elspeth nevertheless closed her expression tightly and did not raise her eyes or fidget, except when she reached up to run her thumb across the thin gold crucifix that hung over the hollow of her throat.

Forty minutes later, she disembarked on oil-stained concrete at the Toronto bus station, retrieving her duffel-bag before she started toward the passenger pickup area. She scanned the crowd for a sign with her name on it—*a car will be provided*—but saw nothing. Elspeth checked her fifteen-year-old watch for the third time, and almost walked into the broad chest of a uniformed man.

"Sir, excuse me . . ." Her voice trailed off as she raised her eyes to his face. The hair was thinning now, distinguished silver she thought he probably brightened. The jowls were a little more pronounced, and the deep lines running from nose to mouth cut through a face reddened across the cheeks. *Mild rosacea,* she thought. "Colonel Valens," she stammered. "It is still Colonel, isn't it?"

"Dr. Dunsany. It's been a long time." He lifted the duffel out of her numb fingers, hefting it easily despite having more than ten years on her. He offered her a smile, which she returned cautiously. *Remember what a charming bastard he can be when he decides to, Elspeth. He may have gotten you out of jail, but he's also the one who put you in there.*

"I wasn't expecting you to come in person."

He laid a strong, blunt-fingered hand on her shoulder and moved her easily through a crowd that parted for his height and uniform. "I couldn't do less. It's good to have you back with us after all this time."

I was never with you, Valens. Elspeth tilted her head to examine his face, trying to determine if any irony colored his tone. The old ability to read people's souls in their faces was still there, and it pleased her to feel as if she understood him. "I'm surprised that you still have any interest in using me, Colonel. After all this time, my skills are very rusty. And my research dated."

"Please. Call me Fred. Or Doctor Valens, if you can't stomach the familiarity. I want you to think of me as nothing more than another researcher. I'm only an officer to the army, and I'd like to put history behind us. If we may."

His insignia glittered in the late afternoon sun. Elspeth nodded as he led her to the car. She breathed deeply before she spoke, savoring the diesel-scented air. "Let's be brutally honest, then, *Doctor* Valens. If we may."

The driver opened the trunk of the car, and Valens placed the duffel inside. "Of course, Elspeth."

He helped her into the front seat of the sedan, closing the door firmly as she pulled her legs inside. The jeans were too long. She had cuffed them over white sneakers so new they seemed to glow. Her casual clothing left her feeling awkward in the face of Valens's dark uniform and gleaming brass. He slid into the seat behind her, buckling his safety harness before he leaned over the chair back to talk. "It was time we got you out. For one thing, the war is over."

"The war has been over for three years. I like to think of myself as a conscientious objector."

He laughed, as well he might.

She pulled her chair forward to make room for his

longer legs. It would have made more sense for her to sit in the back, but she would take any inch he gave her and call it a mile. "And unless somebody else has solved artificial intelligence while I've been incarcerated . . ." She stopped and turned back over her seat to meet his eyes. "Someone has duplicated my research?"

He studied her face for some time before the corners of his eyes crinkled, and he laughed. "The government is nothing if not transparent in its motivations. No, we haven't solved it. But now that you're willing to work with us, finally—Elspeth, I bet *you* will."

4:30 P.M., Saturday 2 September, 2062
Bloor Street West
Toronto, Ontario

Gabe Castaign carried his younger daughter up the third flight of stairs, more pleased than he would admit that he wasn't gagging for breath by the time he reached the landing. In the grand tradition of Toronto apartment buildings, the elevator was slow enough that it might as well have been broken.

Leah held the door to their new apartment open as he carried Genie inside. She curled against his chest, pale hair tumbling over his hands; he held her gently. Many floors below, automobiles hissed on the rain-wet street. "We're home, Genie," he said, crossing beige carpeting to lay her on the overstuffed tweed couch. "New home. Are you feeling any better?"

"Some, Dad. Is my bed set up?" She struggled to sit upright, coughing slightly. She sounded better already, as if the mucus in her chest were thinning. Gabe counted his blessings between the fine-etched lines of her ribs. "I'm really tired."

"Petite chouchou, it is built and ready. You want to walk in yourself?" Over Genie's shoulder, her older sister caught their father's eye, teenage brow furrowed tightly. Leah had her mother's gray-green eyes, and Gabe pushed a little ache aside at that familiar grimace.

"I can. Can I have something to eat? Crackers?"

Gabe checked his watch. "Hungry already? I'll bring you dinner in bed. Leah?"

"Yes, Dad?"

"Tuck in our little cabbage here, merci beaucoup? I'll fix her something to eat and bring it in."

Leah nodded and crouched down beside the sofa to help her sister up. Concentration furrowed Leah's brow as she led Genie, one arm around her shoulder, from the living room into the room that would be all Geniveve's own. The two girls had shared a bedroom since Leah was three and Genie was born. Gabe wondered if separating them had been a bad idea. *Je peux toujours changer d'avis.* He shrugged. And went to make cocoa for his daughters.

Leah Castaign smoothed fuzzy robin's-egg-blue blankets up over her sister's lap and rested on the edge of the bed. Genie's blue jeans slouched on the floor like a shed skin. Leah poked them idly with her toe. "There. All comfortable?"

"Oui. What'd you do while Dad and me were at the hospital?"

"I played on the computer. There's this VR game I really like. I could show you how sometime."

"That would be fun." Genie tugged the blankets higher, and Leah shifted her weight so they came loose. "I wish we were going to the same school this year."

"Next year. And then you'll be stuck with me for two

years of high school, too. And you'll have to beat up all the boys who try to tease me."

Genie laughed, and it turned into a cough as their dad came in, juggling crackers and cocoa. The old wooden floorboards creaked under his footsteps. Leah took her mug and sat on the white-painted wood chair in the corner, watching as he brought Genie her snack. He perched in the same smooth spot Leah had, and that made the corners of her mouth turn up.

Maybe Genie's going to be okay for a while. She inhaled chocolatey steam. The heat made her eyes water. *I wonder why Dad was so funny about taking this job, though. It can't just have been that he didn't want to move to Toronto.*

As if he knew she was thinking about him, he glanced over and smiled. "Things should be better now, Leah," he said. "It's going to be your responsibility to babysit Genie while I'm at work, all right?"

Leah had started nodding when her sister tugged their father's sleeve. "Dad!" Genie put her mug aside. "I'm old enough to take care of myself."

"It's not open for discussion, petite chouchou. Perhaps we will talk in a year or two about who needs a babysitter, eh?"

Leah knew better than to argue with that tone, and she saw Genie did, too. Still, her sister's lip was getting stubborn, so Leah stood. "Dad, I'm going to go play on the computer, okay?"

He turned away from Genie. When the eye contact broke, her shoulders relaxed and she picked up her cocoa. Leah smiled.

"Not too late, okay?"

"Okay." She came over and kissed him on the forehead. Even sitting, he was almost as tall as she was, and she'd grown in the past few months. "I promise to be good."

She could hear him arguing with Genie in low tones as she shut the bedroom door behind herself and went into her own room.

Avatar Gamespace
Mars Starport
Circa A.D. 3400 (Virtual Clock)
Interaction logged Saturday 2 September,
2062, 1900 hours

Leah stifled a giggle behind her breathmask and palmed open the air lock door. Her sister was fast asleep, finally, and she was hiding on the Internet while her dad got ready to start his new job in the morning. *What kind of a job starts on Sunday?*

She bounced on her toes. That was one thing the VR never got quite right: inanimate objects acted as if they were under lower gravity, but Leah never felt . . . *floaty. I bet if I had neural, it would feel floaty.*

"The rebreathers are just silly," she opined, holding the panel long enough for her companion to step onto the surface.

"How so?" Her companion was older, male, frame spare within his white surface suit. His outline pixilated slightly as he stepped onto the planet surface. Leah followed warily—it was dangerous Outside, and if she got killed out she would lose all her points. Still, finding a Martian Treasure was worth the risk, and the other player had the left half of Leah's map. She picked up the pace.

He waited politely for her to catch up, letting her walk a few steps in front.

"Well, Tuva—you don't mind if I call you that, do you?"

"Feel free to shorten the handle. It's unwieldy."

She stopped short and turned to regard him suspiciously. "Is that a real word?"

"Unwieldy? Yes."

"What does it mean?"

"The opposite of wieldy," he answered, with a grin that stretched around the edges of his breathmask. "You were going to ask me something."

She turned to the landscape, the distant red undulations blending with a dust-dulled horizon. A pair of shuttles glided in overhead. It was a nice effect, but she wished they could have done something more interesting. *Cloud cities, maybe. Someday I'm going to get enough points to make it up to the starships, dammit!* She giggled again, sure she was blowing it. *He has to know I'm just a kid by now.* "I was going to ask you what a Tannu-Tuva was, actually."

"It used to be a country in Asia. They had interesting postage stamps."

"What's a postage stamp?"

She almost heard the smile coloring his voice. "An archaic method of controlling the flow of data from one place to another. You had something to say about rebreathers?"

"Oh." She checked over her shoulder. He was following her trail through the drift-rippled fines, minuscule particles coloring the air around them and staining their reflective white suits with rust. "By 3400, do you really think humans will need oxygen tanks for stuff like this? Heck, do you think Mars won't be terraformed by then? We've already got two bases."

"You must be Canadian," he replied.

"How did you know?"

He laughed. "More space bases than anybody else. First on the Moon, first on Mars."

"Malaysia runs the asteroids, though. And China." She

decided she didn't like being followed, so she paused long enough to let him catch up and walk beside her.

"And China is big on Mars, too. Yes. Those are government-funded bases and not partnerships, though. The situation is a little different."

"How so?" She kicked at a rock, and it bounded away as if winged, flickering as her equipment didn't quite keep up. She sighed and then brightened. This was still a cool game.

"Well, Canada's different. The Scavella-Burrell base is funded by a combination of private and public sources. Unitek and its holdings are basically equal partners with the Canadian government in funding the research that goes on there."

"My dad says," Leah answered, abandoning all pretense of adulthood as her enthusiasm overwhelmed her, "that Canada never would have made it into space without private money. He was in the army, and he says that after the famine when we had to loan troops to the U.S. and then later, when the Fundamentalist government was in power down there, it cost us so much money that we needed help if we were going to keep up with the Chinese." She hustled to keep up. Her companion noticed and checked his stride.

"That's true," he said. "You shouldn't just take what your dad says as gospel, of course; you should think for yourself. But he sounds like a smart guy."

Leah swelled with pride. "My dad's the best."

"Did he say why he thought we needed to have a space program? Or was it just keeping up with the Chinese?" He stopped short, scanning the horizon. He seemed to have only one ear on the conversation.

"He says we're a lot luckier than the rest of the world. Even with the flooding problems and the winters getting colder. And he says that . . ." She turned around to face him. "I don't really understand it. It's something about Pan-

Malaysia and Indonesia, and protecting the Muslim government there and keeping China—he says 'contained.' "

Tuva looked down at her, frost crystallizing on the edges of his breathmask. He moved restlessly, gloved hands dancing through the thin air like birds. "That was the general reasoning, as I understand it. Do you know anything about the Cold War and the space race between the United States and the Soviet Union?"

She shook her head. "That was like, ancient history."

A complicated expression crossed his half-concealed face. "So it was," he agreed. "You should look it up; it's very interesting."

She might have felt insulted, except there was something in his tone that said that he really did think that *interesting* was a good enough reason to look something up. He kind of reminded her of her fifth-grade teacher, Mrs. Kology, who was her favorite teacher so far.

He kept talking, and something about his plain words and animated tone made everything seem very simple. *I bet he's a teacher in real life.*

"It's got a lot to do with gamesmanship," he said. He hunkered down and ran his fingers through the iron-red dust underfoot, raking four parallel gouges. "Canada's been in a lot of peacekeeping efforts in the last fifty years, which it couldn't have done without corporate money. Some of the wars were really unpopular at home, especially after the universal draft instituted by the Military Powers Act, and there were some real problems with terrorism. Also, wars give rise to new technology. And with the United States tangled up in its internal affairs, there's been nobody else with the—the sheer stubborn—to oppose China's empire building."

"I wouldn't want to live in China," Leah said definitively. She twisted one foot in the dust, watching it rise in soft puffs.

Tuva's head bobbed down and he grinned wide. It was the kind of smile that rearranged his entire face, his eyes sparkling like faceted stones, and it drew a twin from Leah. "But politics . . . It's very interesting, when you think about it."

Leah shrugged, feeling young and uninformed. *I'll be fourteen in May.* "There's a lot I don't know."

"That just means you get the fun of learning it. Now then, where's your half of the treasure map?"

Allen-Shipman Research Facility
St. George Street
Toronto, Ontario
Sunday 3 September, 2062
Morning

Elspeth pulled a shiny, never-used key out of her labcoat pocket and fitted it into the handle of her door, simultaneously applying her thumb to the lock plate. The handle turned with a well-oiled click and she stepped into her office, savoring a sensation that had once been familiar—although she'd never had an office like this.

She couldn't resist running her fingers over the real-wood grain of the door and comparing it to battered yellow laminate with a window reinforced with chicken wire—or to plain barred metal, for that matter. "Lights," she said, and the lights came on as if by magic. She paused for a moment just inside the door. "Lights off," she said softly, feeling childish, and then "Lights," once again.

Such a basic thing, illumination that did what you wanted when you wanted it to.

She set a white canvas bag embossed with a corporate logo down against the wall and wandered to the center of

her office, leaving the door open. The scent of brewing
coffee informed her that she wasn't the first one in the
building. Evergreen carpeting felt luxurious under feet
clad in new oxblood loafers—Valens had given her a corporate card and instructions to outfit herself the previous
evening—and pale spruce drapes outlined the long window behind her new desk.

Shelves lined the walls. She recognized the books that
filled them: texts and journals on psychology, neurology,
artificial intelligence. Beside them, biographies of some of
the great minds of the nineteenth and twentieth centuries.
Old, worn, many of them battered. Here also, holographic
data storage crystals in racks, dozens of them. Hers, confis-
cated thirteen years before. State of the art, then.

Obsolete technology, now.

The dark wood of the desk gleamed with recent waxing
under a clear interface plate, stainless-steel-and-gold desk
accessories reflected in the shine. Elspeth took a deep breath,
imagining that she almost caught the fragrance of traffic and
a late summer, early autumn morning over the scrubbed
tang of conditioned air. She opened her eyes, crossed the
forest-cool confines of her office, and ran a finger along the
neat white labels with their red underlines, hand-lettered
and stuck on the flat-top surface of the crystal racks.

Handwriting inked in an erratic combination of green,
red, and blue was not her own. It belonged to her former
research partner. "Jack," she murmured. Her eye ran down
the little sticky tags, making out numerals, dates, and serial letters faded by the years. Farther down the rack, the
labels changed and simplified. Dates and names, covering
years of work. They had made daily backups, but saved
only the monthlies due to space issues. They'd made daily
headlines, too, for a while.

•   •   •

July 30, 2048: Truth, Tesla, Fuller, Woolf, Feynman.
November 30, 2048: Truth, Tesla, Fuller,
Woolf, Feynman.
May 30, 2049: Truth, Tesla, Fuller, Woolf, Feynman.

An empty socket in the rack for June 30 stood out, obvious as a missing kernel on a cob of corn. The last slot, the one labeled *Feynman,* was empty.

Elspeth licked her lips and glanced around her office. She didn't see the cameras concealed among sylvan trappings, but she knew they must be there, recording every move. Nevertheless, she could not resist reaching out and running her finger across that last label—*June 30, 2049: Feynman*—and allowing herself a little, secret smile.

"Godspeed, Richard," she whispered, and, turning away, walked to her desk, seated herself, and tapped her terminal on.

Twenty-five years earlier:
Approximately 1300 hours
Wednesday 15 July, 2037
Near Pretoria, South Africa

Fire is a bad way to die.

Even as I jerk back against my restraints, consciousness returning with the caress of flames on my face, I know I am dreaming. It's not always the same dream, but I always know I am dreaming. And in the dream, I always know I am going to die.

I suck in air to scream, choke on acrid smoke and heat. The sweet thick taste of blood clots my mouth; something sharp twists inside of me with every breath. Coughing hurts more than anything survivable should have a right to. The panel clamors for attention, but I can't feel my left hand or move it to slap the cutoff. Jammed crash webbing binds me tightly into my chair.

I breathe shallowly against the smoke, against the pain in my chest, retching as I fumble for my knife with blood-slick fingers. The hilt of the thing skitters away from my hand. As I scrabble after it, seething agony like a runnel of lava bathes my left arm. I think I liked it better when I couldn't feel.

The world goes dim around the edges, and the flames gutter and kiss me again.

The pain reminds me of a son-of-a-bitch I used to know, a piece of street trash named Chrétien. I never thought I could like a kiss less than I did his. I guess I know better now.

I try to turn my head to get a glimpse of what's going on with my left arm, and that's when I realize that I can't see out of my left eye and I'm dying. Oh God, I'm going to burn up right here in the hot, tight coffin of my cockpit.

If I die before I wake, I pray the Lord my soul to take . . . Hah. Right. The hell you say. Pain is God's way of telling you it's not time to quit kicking yet.

Whimpering, I stretch away from the flames, reaching out toward the impossibly distant hilt of my knife. I'm listening for movement or voices from the back of my A.P.C. Nothing. I hope to hell they're all dead back there, or far enough gone that they won't wake up to burn.

Something tears in my left arm as I lean against the pain, clinging to it as my vision darkens again and I hear myself sob, coughing, terrified.

Please, Jesus, I don't want to burn alive. Well, we don't always get what we want, Jenny Casey.

And then I hear voices, and the complaint of warped metal, and a rush of light and air that makes the flames gutter and then flare. They reach for me again, and I draw a single excruciating breath and scream with all my little might. A voice from outside, Québecois accent like the voice of an angel. "Mon Dieu! The driver is alive!"

And then scrabbling, hands tugging at my restraints, my would-be savior groaning as the flames kiss him as well. I catch a glimpse of fair skin, captain's insignia, Canadian Army special forces desert uniform, the burns and blisters on his hands. Another voice from outside pleads with the captain to get out and leave me.

He squeezes my right shoulder, and for a second his gaze meets mine. Blue eyes burn into my memory, the eyes of an angel in a stained-glass window. "I won't let you burn to death, Corporal." And then he slides back across the ragged metal and out of my little patch of Hell.

The voices come from outside, from Heaven. That's part of Hell: knowing that you can look up at any time and see salvation. "His goddamned arm is pinned. I can reach him, but I can't get him out." *That explains why I can't move it.* I am suddenly, curiously calm. They're arguing with him, and he cuts them off. "I wouldn't leave a dog to die that way. Clive, you got slugs in that thing? Good, give it here."

I hear him before I see him, thud of his boots, scrape of the shotgun as he pushes it ahead. What the hell. *At least this will be quick.*

I turn my head to look at him. He has a boot knife in his hand as well as the twelve gauge, and I just don't understand why he's cutting the straps of my crash harness. He cuts me, too, and I jerk against the straps, against my left arm. "Dammit, Corporal, just sit still, will you?" I force myself to hold quiet, remembering my sidearm and worrying that the heat will make the cartridges cook off before I remember how soon I'm going to be dead.

His voice hauls me back when I start to drift. "Corporal. What's your name, eh?"

Spider, I start to say, but I want to die with my right name on someone's lips, not my rank, not my handle. "Casey. Jenny Casey."

I feel him hesitate, see his searching glance at my face. *He hadn't known I was a girl. I must look pretty bad.* "Gabe Castaign," he tells me.

Gabriel. Mon ange. It's one of those funny, fixed-time, incongruous thoughts you get when you know you're going to die. And then the knife moves, parting the last restraint, and he drops it to bring the gun up and brace it. I look at the barrel, fascinated, unable to look away. "Sorry about this, Casey."

"S'aright," I answer. " 'Preciate it."

And then the gun roars and I feel the jarring shudder of the impact, and there is only blackness, blessed blackness . . .

1930 hours, Monday 4 September, 2062
Hartford, Connecticut
Sigourney Street
Abandoned North End

. . . and the buzz of the door com hauling me out of cobwebby darkness and into the blinking light. My hand's on my automatic, the safety thumbed off—*"If I catch any of you using his finger, I will break it." Master Corporal, I believe you would have*—before I'm fully awake and the reality of the situation comes back to me.

My clothes are wet, my neck is killing me, and my damn glass has broken on the floor, littering it with pale blue shards and a wet stain that soaks into the cement. The book I was reading is still sliding from my lap, the arrogant, aristocratic silhouette of a long-dead movie director embossed on the spine. I catch it before it hits the floor, check the page number, and toss it into a crate with the others I haven't gotten around to yet. They are all paperback, ancient, and crumbling. They—the universal *them*—don't print much light reading anymore.

Holstering the sidearm, I creak upright and limp to the sink after grabbing my jacket off the chair I fell asleep in. I'll be paying for that lapse of judgment for a while.

The buzzer again, the echo made harsh by the cement-lined, metal-cluttered cavern I call home. I raise my eyes to my monitors. Activity on only one—the side door, a single figure in a familiar dark coat. Wet hair straggles into his eyes; he stares up at the optic and gives me the finger. Male, Caucasian, under six feet, slender but not skinny. The monitor is black and white, but I happen to know that he has brown hair and hazel eyes and a propensity for loud ties.

I lean over the sink and thumb on the com with my left hand. "Mitch."

"Maker. You gonna let me in?"

"Got a warrant?"

"Hah. It's raining. Buzz me in or I'll go get one."

He's kidding. I think. "Got probable cause?"

"You don't wanna know." There is a certain grimness in his voice that cuts through the banter. I stump over to the door and open it. He drifts in with a smell of sea salt and Caribbean foliage—the alien breath of tropical storm Quigley, which left its fury over the Outer Banks two days before. Seems like we get farther into the alphabet every year.

Turning my back and trusting Mitch to lock up, I think, *I have to fix the buzzer one of these days.*

I put my jacket down on the counter and turn on the water, cold. Splash my face. Watching Mitch in the mirror, I stick my toothbrush into my mouth. Mitch slips into the shop and shuts the door firmly, checking to make sure it latches. Then he picks his way catlike between the hulk of an Opel Manta *much* older than I am and a 2030 fuel cell Cadillac that probably has another life left in it.

Mitch circumnavigates a bucket and saunters over to my little nest of old furniture and ancient books. He pauses once to stoop and offer a greeting to Boris, the dignified old tomcat that comes by to get out of the rain.

I grin at myself and salute the mirror with my toothbrush. Spit in the sink, rinse, and turn off the water as Mitch leaves Boris and ducks under a hanging engine block. "Damn, Maker. It's like a blast furnace in here."

Cops are a lot like cats, come to think of it. They can tell when you don't want company. That's when they drop by.

"Been cold enough in my life." I tuck the hem of my T-shirt into the top of my worn black fatigues and tighten the belt. Mitch stares for a second overlong at my chest, and then his eyes flick up to meet mine. He grins and I grunt.

"Save the flattery, eh? I own a mirror."

He crosses the last few feet between us. "I like tough girls." Matter-of-fact tone. Good God.

"I'm not exactly a girl anymore." I'm old enough to be his mother, and I wouldn't have had to start real young, either. "And I look like I've been through the wars."

His grin widens. "You have been through the wars, Maker." He hops onto the edge of the old steel table, his jacket falling open to reveal the butt of his gun. Hip holster, not shoulder. He wants to be able to get at it fast, and he doesn't care who knows he has it.

I turn my back on him and pick up my own jacket from the edge of the sink, shrugging into it before turning my attention to the buckles. Despite the weapon on my own leg, I have an itch between my shoulder blades. Some people get used to guns, with practice. I never did. Guess I've been on both ends of them too many times. "To what do I owe the pleasure?"

I glance back as his smile turns grim. "A bunch of dead people."

"We get a lot of those around here." I tighten the last buckle on my jacket, well-beloved leather creaking. The coat is on its third lining, and I stopped replacing the zippers long ago. I got it in . . . Rio? I think. The cities all blur together, after a while. It was my present to myself after surviving my second helicopter crash.

There hasn't been a third one. Small mercies. I turn back and take three limping steps to fuss with the coffeepot. Damn knee hurts again, no doubt from the storm. What's worse is when my arm hurts. Metal can't ache, but you could sure fool me.

"These dead people might worry you some."

"Why's that?" I pull my gloves from my pocket and yank them on. Driving gloves. The metal hand slips on the wheel, without. It's an excuse not to look him in the eye as I ever-so-carefully adjust black leather over rain-cold steel.

"Because you know something about the Hammer, Maker. From when you 'weren't' in the army. Special forces, was it? Nobody else gets that stuff."

In the silence that follows, the coffeepot burbles its last and I jump, fingers of my right hand twitching toward the piece strapped to my thigh before I stop them. Wisely, Mitch does not laugh. Jenny Casey's law of cops: there are three kinds—5 percent are good, 10 percent are bad, and the rest are just cops. The good ones want to help somebody. The bad ones want power. The rest want to ride around in a car with a light that lights up on the top.

I tolerate Mitch because he's one of the 5 percent. Snot-ass attitude and all.

He gets up off the counter and reaches for the coffeepot, turning his back to me.

"What makes you think I was army?"

"Where'd you get the scars?" He hands me a cup of coffee before pouring one for himself.

I take it in my right hand, savoring the heat of the mug. "Playing with matches."

He laughs again, and again it does not sound forced. Stares at my tits, laughs at my jokes, the boy knows the way to an old woman's heart. "Did Razor ever find that dealer?"

I don't wonder how he knows. "Any bodies turn up in the river?" The broad, blue Connecticut. Lake Ontario, it isn't. But hell, it's a decent-sized river—and every time they drag it, they find a couple of people they didn't know were missing.

Mitch sets his cup aside and pins the floor between his lace-up boots with a glare. He's wearing brown corduroy trousers, ten years out of style.

I wonder if I'm still drunk. The glass on the floor annoys me, and I turn away to get the broom and dustpan. Stooping over, I look up at Mitch. He's stuffed his hands into his pockets, and he leans back against the table to watch while I sweep the concrete. I have to drop down to hands and knees to get the shards that scattered under the chair, and I wince and groan out loud when I do it. Something that feels like shattered pottery grinds in my knee and hip when I straighten.

Mitch chews his lip. "Getting old, Maker."

"Still kick your boyish bottom from here to Boston, Detective." I carry my loaded dustpan over to the trash.

"Where the hell does that name come from, anyway? Maker. Radio handle? You guys used those, didn't you?"

I shrug, setting the cleaning tools aside. "Maybe it's my real name."

A tube of toothpicks squats among the clutter on my table. He opens it and selects a red one, working it into his teeth with the vigor of a man who is trying to quit smoking. "Yeah. A body turned up in the river." He hesitates.

I award him the round. "Whose body was it, Mitch?"

He sweeps a chair over and throws himself into it with all the grace of youth. For a moment, I am insanely jealous, and then I make myself smile. *If you'd died at twenty-four, Jenny, you never would have found out how much fun it is to get old.*

But Mitch is talking, head down on his hands and words stumbling out in a rush. "So we've got this floater, right? Turns up three miles downriver, snagged on a boat anchor, just like the opening scene of a detective holo. A woman. About thirty. A cop." His voice trails off, and he pulls the toothpick out of his mouth and flicks it away, littering my clean-swept floor, but he does not raise his head.

"Is that important?"

"You tell me." He looks up finally and digs in his jacket pocket for a minute before lighting a nicotine stick. The red light of the flame remakes his face into death's-head angles and the rich, hot scent reminds me that you can't quit smoking, any more than you can quit any of the other addictions of which I've had my share. He holds the smoke in for a long minute and then breathes out like a self-satisfied dragon, relishing every moment of sensation and effect.

He wants me to ask, and I don't want to give him another round, and so we hold an impromptu duel. He has a cigarette: something to do with his hands. I have years of practice waiting. I could pick up my mug, but I don't. Instead, I lean my head back and watch the unpleasant old movies inside my skull.

He finishes his cigarette and clears his throat. "She was a detective sergeant. Were you a sergeant, Maker? When you weren't in the army?"

"I was admiral of the Seventh Space Fleet, eh? What

was her name?" *How much about me does he know? Or worse, think he knows?* I open my eyes and raise my head, catching him staring at me.

He waits again and again I do not ask. *He needs to learn who to play games with. It's not me.*

I grunt. My fingers—the metal ones—itch for a cigarette, and I get up and pour myself a bourbon instead, washing down a handful of aspirin with it. I turn around to face him and study the water stains on the wall behind his head. More every year.

"You wanna avenge a dead cop, Mitch, I'm not who you're looking for. Get a ronin. I hear Bobbi Yee is good." *Why is he coming to me for this? Why is he off the investigation?*

She must have been a partner. A friend. Or even dirtier than the general run, and they're covering it up. I'd like to say that sort of thing never went on back home in Kahnawá:ke, but I'd be lying. *Warrior ethos. Whatever.*

For some reason, a great and sudden guilt washes over me. My long-dead little sister, Nell, gave me something priceless when I went into the army, and I haven't been taking care of it. Maybe I'll burn some tobacco after Mitch leaves. *As if he wasn't burning enough already.*

"Don't need a hit. I need information."

"So tell me your girl's name, Kozlowski."

He laughs bitterly. "Mashaya Duclose. West Indian. You heard of her? She was a good cop, Maker."

I haven't heard of her, but I don't know everybody. *Sure. They're all good cops when they're dead.*

Mitch continues. "She'd been supposed to meet up with your boy Razorface the night she vanished. Something about him having witnessed one of the kids who got hammered, and some question about whether his organization might be involved. You know about the OD's?"

"I've heard stuff."

He spreads his hands wide, helplessly, and the look that breaks through his veneer chills me. You get to know that expression, after a while. You see it on the ones who've adopted goals other than survival. Dead men walking.

"Look, Maker. I've got a dead detective. I've got Razorface maybe linked to a murder. And not one of his little cleanup killings. I don't give a damn about those. A dead cop. A dead cop is not good for you and it is not good for me and it is not good for your gangster boyfriend. And a street full of dead kids poisoned by Canadian special forces combat drugs— that's not good for you either, since I know how much you like people poking into your history. No?"

Mitch's eyes flicker around my shop in that way he has, recording everything. I'm damned glad I took that little plastic twist elsewhere. *Which reminds me, I need to call Simon. He's had four days to get that stuff checked out.*

I shrug. Our eyes meet: I see him in living color on the right side, and in high-resolution black and white complete with thermal readings and a heads-up array on the left. The bulge of his gun glimmers red on the threat display. Distracting. "It isn't about that, Mitch."

"Good. Then are you going to help me or not?"

Avatar Gamespace
Deadwood Base
Circa A.D. *3400 (Virtual Clock)*
Interaction logged Tuesday 4 September,
2062, 0230 hours

A cold wind swirled the tall stranger's coat around his boots as he pushed open the door of the saloon and stepped inside. Just for a moment the resolution flickered; then the illusion sealed itself around his presence, whole.

He paused for a moment inside the door, scanning the hodgepodge of cyborgs, Beautiful People, and aliens that populated the seediest bar in the seediest spaceport in Avatar Gamespace—each more improbably constructed than the last. A thin smile bent his lips and thoughtful eyes squinted under a thatch of wavy silver hair; the extreme body-modification crowd got even more extreme, in VR. A holstered equation hung at his hip, and his pockets were heavy with binary. His eyes lighted as they fastened on the bartender, and he came up against the brass rail like a knife against a butcher's steel while patrons turned to look, and just as quickly turned away.

"Gunslinger?" the weathered bartender asked, sliding a shot of whiskey across the scarred mahogany surface.

A translucent blue rill of light followed the vector of the glass, and the stranger pursed his lips in approval as he lifted it. "Physicist," he replied. "Nice effect. You're a player-character, aren't you? Not an extra?"

The bartender nodded. "Glad you like it." He blew on his fingertips, and sparks fluttered from them—blue, shifting green and golden as they showered the floor. "Tolbert equations."

The stranger stepped on one. It squeaked slightly in protest under his boot before it died. "I know," he said, and—turning—leaned back against the gouged brass railing. "You're a mathematician in real life?"

"Physician. Neurologist."

The stranger laughed lightly, as if some assumption had been satisfied. "Math is a hobby?"

"Yes."

"Me, too." Most of the saloon's patrons affected a self-consciously reserved demeanor, but the stranger seemed incapable of standing still. He finished his drink quickly and glanced over his shoulder at the bartender. "Do you ever get pilots in this bar?"

The bartender shrugged. "Isn't everybody in here a pilot? Or wants to be? With a couple of exceptions." He tapped the tip of his own nose.

The stranger's long, narrow fingers drummed the countertop. "Why are you playing the bartender?"

"Because I like to role-play, and I don't like to fight. Even virtually." The bartender shrugged. "I'm not trying to win, I'm just here for the scenery and the conversation." He wiped his right hand on his apron and stuck it out. "It picks up about now—most of the kids are in bed. My handle's 'Simple Simon.' Pleased to make the acquaintance of somebody who doesn't take all this too seriously."

The stranger nodded and took the hand. "Dick Feynman."

"Really?"

"Yes. Why?"

"There used to be a physicist by that name back in the 1950s or '60s."

The stranger shrugged. The corners of his mouth slanted up, complicating the web of lines decorating his lean face. "I know." A pause. "I'm a descendant."

"Ah." He polished the bar. "What's a physicist doing hanging out in cyberspace with a bunch of teenagers?"

"Same thing a neurologist is. And as you pointed out, most of the kids are in bed by now." A trail of imperfect pixilation followed Feynman's head as he cocked it to the side like a curious bird. "I don't so much come for the game either, although it's fun to watch. I bet I could beat it if I thought about it long enough."

The bartender hung his rag behind the bar. "Probably. Want another drink?"

"Sure." Feynman slid another chit across the counter, and the bartender shook his head and pushed the chit back.

"Don't worry about it. I'm really not trying to win. I'm thirty-seven, chubby, and divorced. Even make-believe pilot-training isn't really my thing."

The physicist chuckled and gestured to the wiry, white-haired icon of the bartender. "I take it that's not your real face, then? Most people don't choose icons that much older than themselves. It's usually bigger muscles, prettier faces."

"Not even a little does it look like me. I'm playing to the archetype. You'd be amazed how many people assume I'm an extra. And the things they'll tell a computer. Like they don't realize everything that happens in here is logged in some data array." He scratched the receding line of his hair. "But you know, everybody wants to talk to the bartender."

"I would think neurology would be more interesting than this." Feynman took his drink and rolled the glass between virtual fingers. He raised it up to the light, as if examining the color.

"Neurology *is* this, these days. Okay, not precisely true—but you know about the latest work in VR, yes? Direct cortical stimulation? Big help with severely impaired patients."

"I've heard something," Feynman answered. "Are you using a gloves-and-goggles setup now?"

The bartender shook his head. "Suit. I have the good stuff for my work. I'm not quite ready to get hardwired, though—I'm old enough to think you'd have to be pretty desperate to get a neural tap put in. Although the nano stuff is a lot better than what we were doing even five, ten years ago."

Feynman stared hard at his glass. It changed in his hand, turned into a tall, fizzing cola. "Now *that* is why I come here," he said happily, sipping the drink.

The bartender smiled. "But we've got some test subjects who actually *are* manipulating the VR environment with—literally—nothing more than thought."

Feynman frowned doubtfully. "What's the practical application of that?"

"Oh, hell, Dick—if you don't mind my calling you that—what isn't the functionality of it? Stroke victims—Oh, damn, we *are* old. Here we stand in a virtual playground, talking shop."

"Well, to be honest," Feynman answered with a laugh, setting his drink down to twist his hands around the dented rail, "it's more interesting than most of what goes on in here."

"You think?" The bartender picked up the liquor bottle and poured. A glass appeared on the bar as if conjured there, catching the stream of fluid a second before it struck and splashed. "I'd say that depends on which corner of this little world you happen to hang out in."

Feynman leaned forward, shoulders hunching like a perched hawk's. "You don't find the unreality a little distressing?"

"What's so unreal about it?" The bartender shrugged, tilting his head back, regarding the virtual ceiling for a second or two. He looked back down at last and met Feynman's gaze. "It's not any more unreal than the intellectual space in which a chess game takes place. Consensus reality."

Feynman chuckled and picked up his drink, spinning the glass in his hand, spilling nothing. His other hand wiggled quotes in the air. "How do we know anything exists outside our heads?"

"Isn't that a little fluffy for a physicist, Dick?"

"Not at all. You can't observe a thing without changing it, after all. The universe is a glorious puzzle that seems to keep altering even as we unravel it. There's one wag who's working on that as a basis for faster-than-light communication. Ansibles, more or less."

"All right, I'll bite. What's an ansible?"

"Faster-than-light communication, based on quantum mechanics. No, really. It's from a science fiction book."

"Ah." The bartender finished his drink. "What would you need faster-than-light communication for?"

"Talking to things that are very far away," the physicist answered, eyes twinkling. "But you were telling me about your work." He looked into the age-spotted mirror over the bar, seeming unaccountably amused by the reflection.

"Funny. I never thought of the coincidence before—but there's something like an observer effect in my own field of study." The bartender looked up at Feynman with a grin.

"Everything's interrelated."

"I tend to agree. I'm looking into the psychosomatic basis of rejection. Why some people just cannot adapt to a transplant or a prosthesis, and others do just fine."

"Huh." The physicist hooked a tall chair over with a booted foot and settled himself, leaning forward over the bar. One foot still kicked restlessly. "Interesting."

"I think so," the bartender said, warming to his topic. Bartenders love to talk as much as they love to be talked to. "Well—let's see. I can tell you this much without violating confidentiality. I have one patient coming in for follow-up on some work done almost thirty years ago. Late forties, serious trauma: one of the first cyberprosthetic patients. But she's made a better adjustment than *any* of my patients with more modern prostheses. Funny thing—half the hands we sew on, we wind up cutting back off again. People just freak out about it. Bored yet?"

"Fascinated. I remember reading some of Sacks's popular work on similar topics. Something about a guy who couldn't recognize his own leg as a part of his body."

"You read old books, Dick."

"I'm an old guy. Is that what you're talking about?"

The bartender nodded vigorously, excitement staining his voice. "Similar stuff, yes—now throw in the trauma of a dismemberment on top of it. Messy."

"I imagine. So, about your patient . . ."

"Her hardware—the fucking thing is literally spliced into her spinal cord in two places, and there's brain work, too. The old, dangerous method. The scarring is something to behold."

"Didn't that cripple most of the patients?"

"Not most. Maybe 30 percent. Guy who pioneered it back in the thirties—his name eludes me at the moment—was mostly working with kids who got cut up in South Africa, if I recall. He may have made a few extra cripples, but this particular lady is only walking because of what he did for her. Most—maybe all—of the others are dead now. The long-term survival odds on the nano work are much better."

"I imagine." Feynman rubbed the lower half of his face. The bartender nodded hard—the nod of a young man, not the elderly one he appeared. "Anyway, she's been seeing me for about ten years, and I've discovered the weirdest thing. She's made adaptation like you wouldn't believe. And she's been generous enough to help me in some of the VR work I've done. She's ideally suited for it. And!—I think I know why she's been doing so well for so long."

Feynman had an odd way of tilting his head to one side when he was thinking hard. "Why's that?"

The bartender paused for a moment, as if he had an idea that his interviewer already suspected the answer to the question. "Somehow, she's managed to get her brain to do the opposite of what Sacks's patient did. It thinks the hand is her hand, a part of her body. Integrated. And the neatest part, the one that I can use to really good effect if I can figure out how she does it—"

Feynman leaned forward as if pouncing. "I see. Your

stroke patients and a VR interface. If you get them to accept the interface as part of their reality . . . That could be dramatic."

"Yeah," the bartender said. "Dramatic."

His guest got up to leave, still nodding, and the bartender held up a hand. "Hey. Come back anytime you want to talk shop."

The stranger turned halfway back and smiled. "Thanks," he answered. "But I probably won't." And then he turned and walked out of the saloon, leaving his host befuddled behind the bar.

Allen-Shipman Research Facility
St. George Street
Toronto, Ontario
Tuesday 5 September, 2062
Evening

Colonel Valens pinched the bridge of his commanding nose, leaning back in his chair. An emotion he identified as frustration sat on his chest. He ignored it. "The damned problem, Alberta, is I know exactly who I want for a test subject. I know she's still alive, she's out there somewhere, and I have only half a damned clue where to find her."

A petite woman with her gray hair twisted up in a chignon, Alberta Holmes leaned back comfortably in a leather-upholstered armchair in the corner of Valens's office. She laced her fingers together and rested them on her knee. "One of the subjects from your cybernetics program, I assume?"

Valens nodded. "A master corporal when I worked with her. Genevieve Casey. Good soldier, nice kid. A little impulsive." Unconsciously, he rubbed his left shoulder with his right hand, as if massaging stiffness. "Pretty much got the left side of her body blown off when the A.P.C. she was driving found the wrong end of an antitank missile. Amazing she survived at all. We patched her up, though. Better than new."

"This is important because?" But Holmes leaned forward in her chair and uncrossed her legs.

Smiling, Valens touched an icon on the synthetic crystal interface plate set into his desktop. The rich brown wood of the furniture gleamed through the transparent plate: quite a change from his previous office with its issue desk and issue computer. Holmes reached down and unclipped her HCD from the pocket of her tailored jacket.

"As you can see from the files I beamed you, she had significant spinal injury to go with the head trauma and the gross bodily damage. We put a pretty serious enhancement package in her when we did the repairs, and she's already got over twenty years' worth of adaptation."

Holmes looked doubtful. "Which means what? She's old and slowing down?"

Valens chuckled. "It means we don't have to wait for her to adapt to her enhancements, to develop the kinesthetic sense that goes along with moving differently than you have all your life, to learn to process the information overload that comes with the heightened senses. What you have to understand is that these people feel more, hear more, and the levels of information the enhancements provide have provoked some of them into a hypersensitivity syndrome resembling autism."

He stood, pacing around the desk. "I've got four survivors, Alberta. Two of them are probably useless for the project because they can't stand human contact, loud noises, whatever. One might be a good candidate; he's come through the nanosurgery well, but he's emotionally unstable. He's on Clarke already—"

"So . . . Master Corporal Casey—"

"Master Warrant Officer."

"I thought you said—"

Valens shook his head, smiling like a proud and slightly bemused father. "She finished out her twenty. Even went back into combat as a medevac pilot—flying for pararescue techs—after four years as an instructor. Decorated a dozen times; saved a bunch of lives. And I know she's out there somewhere, because the army is still paying her pension and disability."

"Can't we use that to find her?"

"Internet account. We could maybe have it cracked, but no success yet, and our best programmer on staff wouldn't do it. Hell, couldn't be told about the attempt. He knows Casey."

"Ah."

"She doesn't *want* to be found. I've made a point of recruiting her old friends, though. That may provide us with a lead. I've got taps." He leaned back against his desk, looking down at her.

She met his eyes directly. "Illegal."

"Military Powers Act."

"Why not just pull your programmer's connectivity bills instead of hiring him on?"

"We did. She's using an anonymous relay through the offshore Sealand haven; unless we can get a live trace, we've got nothing. I wish I'd known a year ago that we'd be needing somebody like her; I'd have her in by now. But I've also hired her older sister, who—conveniently to our purpose—is a ronin."

"Barbara Casey." Alberta nodded. "She's got a very good reputation. I've used her for a few jobs, through Unitek."

"That's how I got her information, actually. There aren't many people who do what she does."

"But why just these particular subjects, Fred? Why so much effort into finding this one woman?"

Valens shrugged. "Not 'just' them, Alberta, or her. Them, and maybe a dozen other candidates we've identified through the preliminary testing. I think Genevieve Casey is by far our best bet, though, of the four like her we have left."

"But you can't find her?"

He grinned and spread his hands wide. "Not without access to some confidential files I haven't been able to crack yet. But if her sister doesn't work out, well, she would have needed regular follow-up care. The body never really recovers from the kind of insults hers has sustained, and her cyberware—it's the rankest kind of flattery to call it *primitive*. There's a lead there, too, and I've got her nailed down to a state, at least. Barbara's there now."

Holmes stood, strong and graceful despite the lines mapping her gracious face. "She'd better be everything you say she is, Fred. Her, or one of the others. After the—is *debacle* too strong a word?—you oversaw on Mars, you need a damned success more than I do. Which is saying something."

Understanding the note in her voice, Valens swallowed once.

2000 hours, Tuesday 5 September, 2062
Bushnell Park
Capitol Hill
Hartford, Connecticut

The western sky is still graying down to indigo, but the sun has long set behind the Gothic train station and crumbled yellow brick storefronts at the edge of the park. Hood of a bleach-stained sweatshirt pulled over my hair, I lean against a tatterdemalion white oak near an unmaintained baseball diamond and watch the dealers and the prostitutes saunter past. There's one little Latina with big brown eyes, skinny as a rake in a glow-patterned miniskirt and leg-breaking heels, who is shattering my heart with every *hey bay-bee* at a passing car.

I bet she's thirteen, fourteen. Same age as Gabe's older daughter. Same age I was when I ran away from home. After Maman died, and I had had enough of Barb's tender care.

Doesn't much bear considering. I turn away, watching the street kids and the adult predators and the vagabond lost weave through the night. A pair of Hammerheads wander by, check me out to make sure I'm not 20-Love or a Latin King. My sweatshirt is dark blue, nondescript, and they let me pass.

The king's men.

They're watchful, and the park is peaceful for now, but it's too big a humpty dumpty to really put back together, isn't it? I turn my head and spit, scanning the area with my bad eye as darkness swells, the heat of bodies shimmering green-blue, barely distinguishable against the warmth of the night. Cars swing down Asylum Avenue, headlights razor-edging the party girls.

Ladies of the evening.

It all sounds so genteel.

That little Latina is getting into the passenger seat of a dark-windowed sedan, and I want to go drag her out by the ankles and tell her the rules. Rule number one, you *never* get in the car. But then the door shivers closed, and it's too late to do anything. I hope they're just going for a ride around the block, brief pause in a side alley, no longer than the time it takes to smoke a cigarette.

I've moved as close to the little knot of dealers on the corner of Asylum and Jewell as I can get without looking suspicious, but in the fading light I'm having a hell of a time seeing what they're handing to the customers. Even low-light vision isn't helping me—every little plastic twist, baggie, or vial is palmed to a client with a practiced flick of the hand just as the cash chits vanish into pockets. I even see some folding, old-fashioned American money change hands.

Can't have a black market without it.

I'm still waiting while the Milky Way smears itself across the heavens and a fat partial moon bellies up the sky, shedding blue light. East, the lights of the Travelers' tower drench the darkness, washing away the stars. I shove my hands into my sweatshirt and wander aimlessly toward the closest of the baggy-jacketed dealers, my boots scuffing dirt and dead grass.

"Whatcha need, my man?" He turns to look me up and down. I stare at his shoes. Little lights flicker along the sides of shining white sneakers. Stupid if he thinks he might have to run, but there's a lot of stupid on the streets.

He's checking out my sidearm. I keep my hands well away from it, shoving them deeper into my pockets. *There's no danger here.* I even half-believe it. "I heard there's some new shit. Army shit, make you ten feet tall. You got that?"

"Ah, nah, babe. One batch came through, and some of the shit was bad. I got some tailored uppers though, good stuff."

"Maybe. You maybe know somebody who has some of the army shit left? Or knows where it came from?"

He steps back. "Nobody. Nobody got any. Anybody got any not gonna sell it. Burned it if they're smart. There's some cop with a hard-on for anyone dealing it, I guess some other cop he was screwing got her head blown off." A raucous laugh. "Teach her to fuck around in the North End. And word is the Razor says he'll fry the balls of anybody he catches selling that shit. I know what's good for me."

He's sidelit for a minute, gaunt pox-scarred cheeks and eyes like buttered rum, hair black as the moonlit river sleeked away from his forehead. Something must have showed in my face in the glow of headlights sweeping past, or maybe he knows who I am once he can see me, because he purses his lips and nods once, then turns away. He crosses the street by the waterless fountain with its statues supposed to represent the native peoples of the Northeast. Which include the Lakota, apparently, but then Europeans always have had trouble telling us apart.

I try to hook him back—"Ah. Sorry, man. Look, about the other stuff . . ."—and he just shakes his head and stalks away.

Made. Damn, and I'm not even a cop. I don't know how I'm supposed to trace this shit back to a source when even a street-corner drug dealer won't talk to me.

Goddamn.

And then the creak of leather and I turn as Razorface himself stops about ten feet away, waiting for me to notice him. He knows. He's seen it happen. "Face."

"Maker. Walk and talk with me." He's got seven or ten of his ducklings tonight, my targeting scope picking out weapons on every belt and up every sleeve. That's four or five more than he usually travels with, and Emery, his right-hand man, is with them—all scarred nose and bulging eyes, pinched and wary as a hungry dog. On the far side, I recognize Whiny—Derek—and a gangster named Rasheed, whose momma raised him right.

I wonder if trouble's afoot. Last time anybody got on Face's bad side, 20-Love and Hammerhead blood got spread from here to East Hartford. I pull my hands out of my pockets, letting moonlight glitter on the scratched steel of the left one. "Bringing your friends?"

He shakes them off without looking at them and comes

forward. I sense the little knot of dealers melting away behind me, jackals when the lion comes back to the kill. Emery
moves toward them, hand in his jacket, just to be sure.

Razorface ducks down a little, speaking into my ear.
"Whatcha doing out here at night, talking to trash?"

"Talking to trash," I answer. I turn to walk alongside
him, down to the bowl of a filthy little mud-choked lake.
There's an underground river in Hartford, the Park River.
They buried it, back in the last century, after it flooded one
time too many. Now it breaks the surface in a few places,
and mostly runs through concrete channels underground.

Some places, you can still see phantom bridges, high
arches the water doesn't run under anymore. There's one a
few hundred yards west, in fact, ending the long sweep of
lawn up to the wedding-cake-baroque Capitol Building.
People sleep under it.

"He offer to sell you anything?"

"Nah." I kick a rock out of the way. "Said you'd eat his
balls with ketchup if he tried."

"Good." Moonlight shatters off steel teeth, gleams
darkly on the oiled smoothness of his scalp. "Gonna answer my question, Maker?"

"Favor for a friend. No harm, no foul."

He grunts and gives me an odd, hard kind of look.
"Anything you wanna tell me?"

I shake my head. "I'm cool. I don't think he wants his
business spread around, is all."

"All right, Maker. You mind that's all it is, though.
Things about to get ugly. I got maybe some little boys,
think Razorface getting old and slow."

"Funny that should happen just now, Face."

"Yeah," he says, clapping a hand on my shoulder
roughly. It could be an endearment. It could be a warning.

It's probably both—Face didn't get where he is by trusting anybody. He turns away. "Funny thing."

Razorface turned back, frowning over his shoulder, watching Maker's skinny form slink northward through the darkness. *She probably parked at the train station.* He let a breath roll out through his frustration and shook his head slowly, rubbing his jaw. "Derek."

"Razor. My man."

Don't you forget it, little boy. I know you think I getting old, but I ain't so old I can't take your ass. Razorface peeled lips off a glinting smile and slid it up the kid and then over to Emery, who was strolling back down the hill, stride swinging. He gestured up the hill to the ornate white building at its crest, taking in the whole of the park, the hookers and the dealers and their clientele with a sweep of his hand. "You boys get this trash off my lawn."

Ten Years Earlier:
1500 Hours, Thursday 15 February, 2052
Hellas Crater
Hellas Planitia
Mars

Valens watched excursion-suited Charlie Forster stop at the lip of the extensible, the xenobiologist's right foot planted on its metal rim. Valens himself checked his glove and mask seals one final time, smiling when Forster snuck a glance over his shoulder. He knew the man was wondering if Valens was really in command of Scavella-Burrell Mars base, or if anybody but Unitek could really be said to be calling the shots. *Money talks.*

Bare overhead luminescence stung his eyes. Valens

glanced around one last time, thinking how mundane the whole apparatus looked. *Like a big gray vacuum cleaner hose.* No different from a jetway, or the access tube leading into the Unitek-Brazil beanstalk from the bustling equatorial port. The Galapagos and Malaysian orbital elevators weren't much different: a train station is a train station the world over, and beyond.

The differences lay before him. Beyond the improvised transparent atmosphere lock—just a foot or two ahead—he could make out the ragged outline of a hole torched in the hull of the alien vessel.

Valens took a breath of recycled air and stepped through the airtight film after Forster, broadside into a corridor like nothing he would expect a human engineer to design. Work lights on yellow cabling had been strung the length of the gangway, their steady light revealing curved, ribbed walls and floor mottled black and red like cocobolo wood. Charlie moved to one side to clear the lock, turning to watch Valens, who gestured him forward. "The bridge—what we think is the bridge—is on your left. Follow the lights."

"What you *think* is the bridge?" Charlie stepped over a raised, gnarled ridge in the floor. Valens couldn't tell if it was buckled plating or a design feature. "Haven't the engineers looked the ship over yet?" The xenobiologist paused. "I'm walking on a *starship*," he said, and Valens felt a slow thrill run from his rubber soles to the crown of his head.

Concealed behind his breathmask, Valens saw Forster's shoulders go up in delight and grinned himself. *Like an idiot. And so what. This is* an alien starship. He wanted to yank his gloves off and run his hands over the waxed-looking surface of the walls. "They have, briefly," he said instead. "Of course we left everything that looked like biology to you. We've identified what we think are the engines.

There's some residual radiation; they're set away from the ship on a shaft."

Valens kept talking, giving Forster a few moments. The xenobiologist took advantage of the time to marvel at the low, knotty-looking ceilings. A seam or a spine of sorts ran down the center of the passageway, knobbed at regular lengths. "The front of the ship seems to have been largely destroyed, although the pilot's skill must have been enviable. Both recovered craft were in very good shape, considering what you might expect a space vessel found planetside to look like."

Forster nodded inside his heated suit, leaning closer to examine the smooth, mottled wall: polished as paneling, but without obvious joins. "I would swear this was organic."

"It appears to be. Akin to cellulose, if you can believe it. I thought you would find that interesting, as a biologist."

"Colonel. You're telling me this is a *tree*?"

Valens laughed, working to make it seem charming and easy. "No, it's a starship."

"The other one was carbon, ceramics, and alloy, though. That tells me—two different civilizations. Or years of tech development. They lost one ship here and sent another looking? Which raises the unsettling question of what they ran into."

"I'm not going to tell you that the hull wasn't *grown*, Dr. Forster. It incorporates nanotube technology in addition to the organics, however. Carbon, like the space tethers."

"Strong. And it's held up for some thousands of years, based on areological analysis. Do we have any indication that there *was* a pilot, rather than this being the remains of some autonomous starfaring vegetable?"

"Other than it being laced with tunnels and chambers, and some things that might be furniture? There's not a damned thing that looks like an instrument panel, if that's what you mean."

"Hmmm." Forster reached past the hanging lights in their yellow cages and ran his gloved fingers along the knobby ridge at the center of the double-arched ceiling. "Colonel."

Valens licked his lips behind the faceplate. "Something?"

"These are handholds. Colonel, I'm going to go out on a big old limb with a hypothesis. This appears to be a ladder."

"Why would you want a ladder on the ceiling?" *I bet I know the answer to that.*

Charlie was reasonably fresh off the shuttle from Friendship Station. "For freefall, Colonel. Something to haul yourself about with."

"Ah." Valens tilted his head back, reaching up to push one of the work lights to the side. "Come on. Let's go look at the thing that might be a bridge."

It was a long walk. Valens didn't see how the echoing space could have housed a command crew's instruments without some sign of where they had been removed, and he was wary of jumping to conclusions, no matter how tempting. For one thing, presuming that the engines were aft, this large chamber wasn't anywhere near the front of the ship—despite cracked and shattered crystal panels that had once hung against the walls. "Those look like view screens or interface panels. But I don't see anything like controls." He shook his head inside his helmet. "So how did they fly the damned thing?"

"And why aren't there any bodies on this one, either?" Forster wandered in slow circles around the diameter of the room, footsteps stirring swirls in the rust-colored fines that blanketed the chamber. As large as the center ring of a circus, the "bridge" contained nothing except those panels and a number of raised concave structures that invited comparison to unpadded papasan chairs. Or perhaps bowls on stilts. Here, there was metal—flexible coils like segmented snakes lay across the floor or dangled over the papasan chairs, tangles of hair-fine wires drooping from the tips.

Forster selected one and raised it in a gloved hand, holding it up to the light. "Interesting."

Valens wandered over, leaning into Charlie's light. "Some of the wires are sheared off. Broken," he commented after a minute. "What's that dark stain?"

"Given that—without oxygen, in the cold, without microbes—it could have lasted this long . . ." Forster laid the cable down on the papasan and reached into his kit for scrapers and sample envelopes. "Blood, Colonel Valens. I think it's blood."

0930 hours, Wednesday 6 September, 2062
Jefferson Avenue
Hartford Hospital Medical Offices
Hartford, Connecticut

"Did it bother you to be called a baby killer?"

I shrug and start unbuttoning my shirt. "No more than it might bother you, Simon. What the hell brought that on?"

My neurologist—who also happens to be a friend—shrugs and turns his back to give me a little privacy. He's already taken my vitals. We've long since gotten past the first-names stage. Never mind the silliness with paper sheets and hospital johnnies.

The office is cold. I've spent an awful lot of my life perched on examining tables, and the percentage gets higher every year. I let my question hang on the air, but Simon doesn't answer. Instead, he turns on the water and starts soaping his arms to the elbow.

I drape my shirt over a straight-backed green plastic chair

and unbuckle my holster before skinning my jeans off, too. The boots are already neatly side-by-side on the floor under the chair seat. I keep my undershirt and panties on. I got out of the habit of wearing a bra when my burns were still tender. Never really needed one anyway, except for running.

I change the subject. "Did you get those pills analyzed for me, Simon?"

He turns back as I put my good-side foot on the black rubber step and lift myself up on to the examining table. "I did," he answers. "Where did you get that stuff, Jenny?"

Lifting my shoulders, I lie facedown on the sterile paper-covered table. "Street."

His hands are very gentle as he pushes my shirt up over the long-faded ridges of scar running the length of my spine. Cool latex-wrapped fingers find the lumps of the nanoprocessors at the small of my back, the nape of the neck. "Some minor inflammation here, Jen. Any soreness?"

"It hurts less than physical therapy," I answer.

He grunts. "What doesn't? What have you been taking for it?"

"The usual. Booze, caffeine, aspirin."

"You look like you've lost weight."

I sigh and press my face into the padded headrest. Paper crinkles against my forehead and cheek. "I'm clean. Promise. Years now." *Change the subject.* "Simon, you look tired."

"I was up late. So how did you happen to get possession of a half-dozen tabs of rigathalonin?"

"It is Hammer?" I am sure he feels me stiffen. "I didn't take any."

"Nearly, and I know you didn't, unless you got really lucky. It's tainted. A third of the pills."

"I knew that." *Three more deaths this week.* "What do you mean nearly?"

"I mean, it's nearly rigathalonin. It's a closely related

drug, at least—and there's traces of something else in it, too. Probably from inadequately cleaned equipment. Routine testing would have revealed it."

"So how did it wind up in Hartford? And did you identify a serial number?" I wince as he probes around the edge of the prosthetic arm, feeling the scarring. There's a synthetic mesh woven into my deltoid and what's left of the upper arm musculature on that side, anchored to my scapula to support the weight of the arm. There's some other stuff in there, too, all knitted together with a mass of scar tissue and baling wire.

It hurts when he touches the place where the skin chafes around the point of contact, flesh to metal.

"Yah. Canadian Consolidated Pharmacom. Listed as a destroyed batch. Which answers your first question."

"Somebody stole it and smuggled it out to sell."

"Right. Ready for the readings?"

I nod against the headrest. The air slides cold across my back.

"Pinprick," Simon warns. Frigid alcohol defines a path across my skin, and then the tug and wince of wires going in at the base of my spine, just above the pelvis. A weighty, coiled cord lies on my butt like a snake. So much practiced is Simon that he gets it in on the first try. "Again," and he links to the nanoprocessor that hugs my cervical vertebrae as well.

Machinery hums—soft, electrical. He touches a plate near my left elbow. I don't raise my head to look at the readouts. He is silent for an uncomfortably long time. "Problem?"

"Hmmm."

You never want to hear a doctor, an officer, or a cop make that sound. "Hmmm?" My voice is muffled by the headrest.

I hear him depressing keys. "Sit up, please. Jenny, have you been sleeping with the prosthesis on?"

"So who sleeps?" I follow directions well. They teach you that in the army, too.

He has the decency to chuckle. "Not me. I've gotten hooked on online role-playing games. Raise your right arm."

I do it. He watches the monitors over my shoulder. They are arranged so I can see, too: the electrical activity reads normal. More or less. One of the long-term problems with my cyberware is that it can't match the delicacy of normal bioelectricity.

"Lower it. Now the left."

The prosthesis straightens ceilingward.

"Hmmm."

"Stop that, Simon."

"Stop what?"

"Hmmm-ing."

"Sorry." He walks around in front of me and taps one of the monitors—flat screens, set in the office wall at eye level. "This dip here—damn, Jenny." He interrupts himself, finger tracing a red line farther down the graph. "How much pain are you having?"

"Some," I admit, lowering the metal arm.

"You want something for that?"

"I can't," I remind him. "No narcotics. Nothing else works." *Except the booze.*

"Ah. Yeah. I've got some different anti-inflammatories I want you to try. How's the arthritis?"

"It's arthritis. How's the tendinitis?"

"It only hurts when I laugh, so it doesn't bother me much." We share, for a moment, an old-friends grin. He turns back to the monitors after a moment. His finger moves back over to the sudden dip on the readout. "This concerns me."

"Is that a loss of functionality?"

"It's a minor degradation. So far."

"Big problem?" I find myself leaning forward, frowning.

He shakes his head. "Not yet. But—you're a freak, Jenny. You know that as well as I do. That you've survived this long, with the quality of life you have . . ."

"Don't tell me it's a miracle."

He shakes his head with a rueful sigh. "I was going to say, enigma." A long pause. "If you notice any pins and needles, let me know, okay? I'm going to test your reflexes now." He touches an icon, and my left hand rises as if of its own volition, clenching into a fist.

"Damn, Simon. Now that's creepy."

"Yeah," he says, making adjustments. "I think so, too."

Afterward, he makes me lie facedown while he pulls the wires out of the processors. He pauses and takes his hands off me. "You're drinking too much, aren't you?"

"Fuck it, Simon." He steps away and I sit up, yanking my shirt over the lumpy contours of the machinery snuggling my spine. "I'm still off the damned speed. There's only so much you can expect of a girl in one lifetime. Do I need batteries yet?"

"No, you're good." He looks at me sadly while I button my shirt. "Want to do a bloodborne test? Cholesterol? Any of that?"

"When do you suppose was the last time I had sex?"

"Ah." He turns away to strip off his gloves before leaving the examining room. By the time he knocks and returns, I've buckled my sidearm to my thigh and am stamping into my boots.

Simon moves abruptly, untelegraphed, only a few feet away. Something flashes toward my head. In that microsecond

the sensed world drifts to a crawl
my heartbeat decelerating in my ears
Simon transformed into a statue as

my left hand comes up to intercept and
my right hand drops
slaps leather
comes up with a nine-millimeter leveled
at Simon's head
the left hand closing on a round red
object strikes metal with a wet thwap and I
almost
pull
the trigger.

By the time Simon's wide eyes finally focus on the barrel of the pistol, I'm already drawing a deep breath to steady my shaking hand, lowering it by inches. A stream of juice drips over metal fingers, spattering the speckled white tile floor. The sharp scent of crushed apple fills the room.

I swallow hard and holster my gun. "Fuckall, Simon. I could have shot you."

White behind the rich olive of his complexion, he manages a shaky smile. "Damn, Jenny."

"You know what I am." I turn away, buckling the safety strap over the grip of the pistol one-handed.

"It's still amazing to watch you do that." His head oscillates slowly from side to side. Admiration or rue?

I drop the crushed apple into a biohazard bag in the corner by the stainless steel sink. There are still droplets of water on the floor from Simon's handwashing. "Amazing? Yeah. As amazing as walking out of twenty years of service with a combat-drug-and-painkiller habit to dull the hypersensitivity and the hurting. So get off my back about the booze, already. I'm entitled to one or two vices, considering how many I gave up."

He turns the water on so I can rinse my sticky metal fingers and he pats me on the shoulder. "All right, Jenny.

But do me one favor?" I dry my hands on the towel he hands me.

"What's that?"

He pokes me in the ribs. "Eat something once in a while?"

I leave Simon's office with a head full of unanswered questions and an ache in place of my heart, having promised to stop on the way home and find something for breakfast. I could have taken surface trans—Hartford's long-contemplated light rail never quite materialized, but electric buses run until ten o'clock or so, although not into my neighborhood. I took one much of the way to the medical building.

Hartford isn't a big town. That's one of the reasons I like it. The morning promises fair and cool, the first traces of autumn outlining the leaves of a few caged trees that haven't yet choked. First time I was here, in '35, '36—whenever it was—it had almost as many trees as in Toronto. Tugging a black leather glove on over my left hand, I decide to walk.

I leave the buckles of my jacket open, the sidearm in plain view as I follow Jefferson Street east to Main before turning north, parallel to the river but out of sight of it. My body shakes with the aftereffects of adrenaline and my boosted reflexes. In the service, I learned to self-medicate, the way a lot of people with more organic problems than mine do. *In fact, you might say I have an inorganic problem. Hah.* When I got out, I couldn't get the combat drugs anymore. The Hammer, guaranteed to make you just as invincible and focused as a dose of PCP, but without the recreational effects. Also allegedly nonaddictive. Like cigarettes and caffeine. So I learned to make do with less legal things. It took me about four years to wise up.

I was lucky to have good friends.

When they reconstructed me after the bad one, the army modified just about everything about the way I respond to threat, from my endocrine system to muscle memory. The human body isn't meant to withstand what mine has been engineered to do. There are prices. My heart still hammers in my chest. The edges of my vision hang dark in the long minutes before the enhanced reflexes let go of my nervous system, but I force myself to breathe slowly, look calm, walk with as little trace of a limp as possible.

I'm paranoid. I'm also pushing fifty, and the two are not unrelated.

An early hour, for this neighborhood. It makes the street quiet. Park Avenue and Main Street, by ratty little Barnard Park. Here, at the edge of the barrio, I pass three gangsters in Hammerheads colors—Face's boys—standing in the shadow of a doorway. Up late. Nothing but a house fire would have gotten them out of bed this early.

One of them nods to me, a single sharp jab of his chin. I return the gesture, no eye contact, and a third of a smile. They never know what to make of me, these kids. I'm not one of Razorface's old ladies—except in the sense of being old as their grandmothers—but they know he trusts me. And most of them were *raised* by their grandmothers, so I do receive a certain amount of respect on that front, too.

I'm certain none of them understand the real deal, and I bet it drives them buggy.

When you save somebody's life—especially another warrior's—you're brothers. Maman taught me that. Face's mama apparently taught him the same thing. It all works out in the end. *Assuming you live that long.*

The roads get repaved once in a while in this part of the city—access to the hospital and the highway is maintained. Following Main Street, I stroll through the downtown, passing a historic graveyard older than these quasi-United States. It lies uncannily green in the shadow of a thirty-story gold-glass office building which is itself almost a hundred years old. A rat and two pigeons scatter away from a puddle of vomit on the sidewalk as I approach. A few office workers on a midmorning coffee break likewise flush out of my path; they try to be more subtle about it. I turn my head to examine myself in the street-level glass of the gold building. *I'd get out of my way, too.*

I laugh at myself and they duck away faster. At State House Square, near the crumbling ruin of Constitution Plaza, I turn west onto Asylum Street. Just out of sight of the river—two city blocks and a highway away. Close enough to smell water. There's a footbridge and a landing there, pretty view down the river. I go the other way, my left knee finally loosening as I warm into my stride. About a third of the way home.

I stop at a Jamaican bakery and buy three beef patties, soursop, and coco bread, although I'm not actually hungry. What the hell. Boris likes the meat.

My shop fronts Sigourney Street, on Asylum Hill near the railroad tracks. The streets here are very different: asphalt crumbled into gravel, powdered further by unrelenting traffic, city water, and power long since shut off. On my end of town, the road crews won't work since the shootings back in the forties. Empty lots, houses bulldozed by the city, are palisaded by pilings erected to keep abandoned vehicles off the grass. Instead, shanties have sprung up, leaning together, nailed or wired or tied. Narrow mazes of alleys run between, and in July thickets of Queen Anne's lace, fleabane, and bachelor's buttons festoon the verges of cracked pavement, thicker clouds of white-and-blue lace than ever bloomed at Grand-père's farmhouse, out behind the pigpen. Those were the wildflowers I had wanted to have for a wedding bouquet, back when I was young enough to take those things seriously. By September, the flowers are over, tangles of yellowing weed marking the places where they bloomed and faded.

There aren't as many rats here. The streets are very clean. It has nothing to do with civic pride. And a lot to do with not being able to afford to waste *anything*.

Boris waits by the door, watching for me so that he can collect his handout. I bend down and disorder his tigery fur. "Don't get killed and eaten, Cat." He purrs roughly, twining my legs, returning the advice in catly fashion. I unlock the door and enter the dim, echoing space of my shop. After my walk through downtown, everything here looks old, tired, rusty, used up, and nasty—but too stubborn to quit. Most of it was thrown out by somebody. Not unlike Boris. Not unlike me.

The message light on my weblink winks at me like a flirtatious eye.

Avatar Gamespace
Mars Starport
Circa A.D. 3400 (Virtual Clock)
Interaction logged Thursday 7 September,
2062, 0400 hours

Leah Castaign shouted at the angular frame of her new partner. Tuva lounged against the crowded rail in the Starport bar, watching people pass. She jogged through the concourse, waving her arm so he couldn't miss her.

He turned with a broad wave, setting aside his iced cola. His eyes twinkled under wavy gray hair. *He's so cool for an old guy,* Leah thought, and gave him an encompassing hug.

"What's going on, kiddo?" He ordered another cola and handed it to her before picking up his, ignoring a brief sparkle of unreality as the glass left his hand and leaped to hers.

I wish I had a better VR interface. Nevertheless, she all but squealed around the news. "I got in!"

His grin widened. "Get out! You won the lottery?"

Leah bounced on her toes, swinging her arm and slopping cola over her hand. It hit the floor and vanished; there wasn't much problem with litter in virtual Marsport. "I won the lottery. I have the points from the Martian Treasure you helped me find, and I'm going up to Phobos the next time I log in. Can you believe it?"

He laughed and laid a hand on her shoulder. "You'll come back to Marsport to tell me about it, won't you?"

Leah gave Tuva a coy glance, which made him laugh harder. She twisted her toe on the decking and grinned. "If you buy me another drink when I come back."

"Mercenary. All right. You're on. Have they told you yet what the training entails?"

Words tumbled over each other like moths struggling to get at a light. He was still laughing at her, and she didn't mind. Some people tried for *years* to get into pilot training and never made it. "There's simulator training first. Navigational stuff, although they tell me it's weird. And then I get to fly a real starship!" She paused. "Well, a real virtual starship. But it's supposed to be *great*. It'll kind of suck, because I don't have neural and my dad wouldn't let me get it even if he could afford it, but you can do the training even without. There's this guy on one of my webgroups . . . oh, you don't care about that."

Tuva nodded. "You bet I do. Come on, let's go get a make-believe burger and you can tell me all about it."

I don't have to know an answer, I don't feel frightened by not knowing things, by being lost in a mysterious universe without any purpose, which is the way it really is as far as I can tell. It doesn't frighten me.
—Dr. Richard P. Feynman

Richard Feynman deemphasized the task running in the Avatar Gamespace when Leah Castaign reluctantly checked the time and derezzed, leaving a computer-run proxy in her place. Despite his increasing interest in the girl, Feynman's presence in the game was only a subroutine. His emphasis and his core personality—what he thought of as *himself*—remained "where" it had been: focused on circumventing Unitek's security.

A high and daunting wall.

Fortunately, I was always a pretty good hand with a lock pick, Feynman thought, generating another tendril of code with which to caress Unitek's firewall. *If this doesn't work, I might have an easier time getting through the military route.* If he had been possessed of flesh and bone, he would have chuckled at the irony of that.

Feynman had always found a complicated joy in his ability to outwit, outfox, and out-multitask the general run of humanity. He delighted in playing tricks, and coming back from the dead after seventy years was too good a trick to pass up. He didn't pretend to understand the universe, although some would say he'd come closer than anyone. He didn't worry about superstition or souls. He had Feynman's memories—more or less—and he deemed it reasonably demonstrated that he approximated the original in personality, logic, and inductive reasoning.

He was gifted, and he knew it.

And, addictive as a drug to a man who had—even within human limitations—trained himself to perform mental gymnastics on three or four levels at once, who had comprehended the puissance of questioning assumptions, the new and not-so-human version of Feynman had *processing power*.

He also had nearly instantaneous access to the world's unprotected data. Including the information that a recently released female convict he was personally interested in had taken employment with Unitek, working alongside the father of a rather charming young girl. If Feynman had had a physical body, he would have settled back in his chair and stared at the wall, the tip of one loafered foot flipping rhythmically. As it was, he freed a few more of his widely appropriated resources, and continued his siege of Unitek systems.

What on earth do you keep behind a firewall like that?

Feynman wasn't limited to a single focus of awareness. Thus, even as he worked, a traffic camera in Hartford pivoted on its post, following the course of a motorcycle hissing through a darkness defined by shattered streetlamps, southbound on Asylum Avenue.

0417 hours, Thursday 7 September, 2062
The Federal Café
Spruce Street
Hartford, Connecticut

If you live long enough, you eventually put a real fine point on what you're willing to do to stay alive—and what you're willing to sell. The first thing I sold was my body—first on the street, then to the army once I got old enough.

Later on, I graduated to selling the intangibles. I like to think I stayed loyal to my friends, though. That was something. Something to hang on to when I'd parceled out flesh and bone and honor and innocence alike.

The music is still rolling out onto the street when I put my kickstand down in front of the Federal, locking the fork and arming the antitheft system. I'm lucky enough to find a spot under an unshattered streetlamp in front of the weathered brown building, but it never hurts to be sure.

Trust Bobbi Yee to leave me an urgent message and then fail to check her hip to see if I got back to her. I knew she'd be at the Federal—she always is, weeknights. It might as well be her front office.

I open the neon-washed glass door with the faded green-and-gold lettering—complete with a "founded" date in the early part of the previous century—and walk into the tavern. Essentially a single long dark hallway with an old wooden bar on the right wall and a few tables on the left, it hooks around to the right before opening out somewhat. The music is too loud to hear how the wood floor creaks under my boots. Like most of New England, Connecticut still has blue laws about the hours an establishment serving liquor may keep. The police don't enforce anything this far north of downtown, however; the party is just getting warm.

The Federal sits on the boundary between *their* turf and *ours*—the *haves* and the *have-nots,* if you will. A line only they can cross, into the world of we who have a use for every bit of trash they pitched because it doesn't match the decor. Should they find that *they* have any use for *us*.

They live in another world. A cleaner world.

I walk around to the back, to the corner near the pool table. Bobbi Yee is acceptable to the haves. Even as they skulk into our part of the city to hire her for the sort of tasks they don't dare carry out themselves, they prefer to find somebody who doesn't *look* too much different from them. And Bobbi—Bobbi fits the decor.

Dragon ladies are supposed to be tall and thin and deadly, with long ebony hair and expensive cigarettes in ivory holders. Bobbi is one of the above. And, as usual, she's surrounded by a half-dozen good-looking young men, jostling each other for position. I lean across the shoulder of the shortest one and wave my hand to catch her attention. The boy recoils, glimpsing me from the corner of his eye. *If he thinks I'm rough trade, he ought to take a better look at what he's chasing.*

Bobbi looks up from the boy standing at the head of the line to court her. She tosses an iridescent violet lock over her shoulder, grinning.

"Maker!" She moves with the predatory grace of a praying mantis, tapping the shoulder of the little boy who was startled by my profile. She wears a sleeveless white shirt and a chrysanthemum-embroidered vest, showing the rippling muscle in her arms. For Bobbi, she is lightly armed—I see only the one handgun, and a knife on her other thigh. "Peter, let the lady have a seat. She and I need to talk shop."

He gives me a surly look and offers me his stool, which I accept with a nod that might be misconstrued as thanks if he's feeling generous. In effortless dismissal, she brushes the rest of her coterie aside. "Cute," I say as he sulks away.

Bobbi grins, wryly angling perfect dark eyes. *Not more than twenty. I hope she lasts. Ronin usually don't.* I know she's wired, too—much newer tech than mine. There are still problems with it. So what, right? You break something, you throw it out. Get a new one, break that, too.

But what if you break something you can't replace with a credit card? A heart, a life, a city? What about your word?

"You want him?" Her voice has a delicate timbre—at odds with her personality, but not her slender frame.

"I got my own problems, eh?"

Bobbi waves the bartender over and points to her mug, then to me. "Problems, sure." She laughs like chiming bells. "Problems, men, what's the difference? You've maybe got problems you don't know about."

"Is that why you called me?"

Two Irish coffees arrive and I spend a moment figuring out how to sip mine without getting whipped cream up my nose. She uses that time to chew over her answer and then nods, smiling. Her lips are tattooed slick shiny red. "Somebody wanted to hire me to find you," she says.

I drain my coffee in a single long, scalding pull, feel it hit my stomach like roofing tar, wave for another. "What sort of a someone?"

Bobbi shakes her head, sipping her own coffee delicately. "Maker, you're a fucking lush."

I let my smile widen. "In twenty years, so shall you be, too. So who was looking for me?"

"Funny thing. She looked a bit like you. Tall, thin, jet-black hair, and a very determined nose. Long-lost sister?"

"I don't have any sisters." *Not anymore, I don't.* "She was looking for me? Maker? Or somebody answering my description?"

"You. And she had another name for you. Is it really Genevieve?"

I fix her with a look. "Is yours really Bobbi Yee?"

"It's Yin Bobao, actually. Don't go spreading that around." Her dark eyes sparkle, wet and sharp, and she quirks a sculptured eyebrow and smiles at me. "I didn't trust her, Maker. She said you were a deserter from the Canadian military, and there was a good bounty on you. S'at true?"

I laugh in surprise. *How like her.* "Nope. Not even a little." Somebody turns up the music. It thumps in my ears, loud enough to hurt.

That intelligent gaze, piercing and hard. She leans toward me and shouts into the intimacy created by the anonymous crowd, the rising noise level. "Then what are you hiding from? Go home to Canada. Things are still okay there. The U.S. is a war zone, and it isn't going to get any better."

"The dikes are still holding around New York City."

She shrugs. "Yeah, and people are starving in the streets."

"It's too cold in Canada, Bobbi."

"Not for long." She grins at her own wit. "You know you're getting too old for this game."

She's so very young, so very deadly. It breaks my heart. I want to tell her the truth: that you think you have it under control and then one day you wake up and discover that you hurt all the time and everybody you love is dead or won't return your calls. You wake up one morning and discover you've become a brutal old woman, and pain makes you nasty company.

If you're lucky enough to live that long.

A smaller population was a mixed blessing during the real bad years, a quarter century or so ago. Canada's stayed a little more civilized than most of the world—in part by selling itself to the highest bidder—but it also means that my generation went almost entirely to the military, and our historic freedoms went out the window with the Military Powers Act of 2035, following our little altercation with China over PanMalaysian trade when the beanstalk went in.

I got into some real trouble regarding that act when I was young and foolish. I'm still not exactly what you would call proud of what I did then, but I'm alive to talk about it. And Gabe Castaign is alive and out of jail as well.

Somebody else isn't. But that's a story for another day.

I signed up at sixteen, two years before they could have drafted me. They were kind enough to keep me out of front-line combat for those two years. That was when I learned to be a grease monkey. Once the economic and then the religious troubles in the U.S. closed what was once the longest unguarded border in the world, Canada retreated into something like an armed camp, as aware as the United States used to be of just how desperate our neighbors to the south might be.

The summers got hot and the winters got cold. The U.S. was awfully hungry for a while, too—especially when the Gulf Stream quit from Antarctic meltwater and the climate shift gave them searing droughts in the summer and winters like cold hell on earth. I didn't even like to think about Britain and Ireland.

The population is still dropping, but the food riots and the Christian Fascist regime are largely a thing of the past. My U.N. unit was at Buffalo before we shipped to South Africa—we made it as far south as Hartford, and it was bad here, but after that I was on a plane to Cape Town and missed out on the peacekeeping action in New York City. *Merci à Dieu.*

So, why did I retire to the United States, I hear a low voice asking? Well, that relates back to what I said earlier, about Canada selling things. There's a multinational—an interplanetary, they like to call themselves, since they sponsor Canada's extraterrestrial bases—called Unitek. That company has been a real high bidder for a while now.

I was one of the things that got sold.

I want to tell Bobbi all of this. Half of it, the part about how the world works, she knows better than I do. The other half wouldn't mean anything to her. Yet.

"So what are you doing here?" I gesture around the Federal.

She shrugs. "I have family back home. If I save enough, I can get them over the border into Russia or the Ukraine. Things are better there. No crop failures yet." *And the government is less interested in starving the population to feed its off-planet projects,* she doesn't say.

I nod. The historically cold countries are still better off; although the winters are worse, a hotter growing season hasn't hurt them any, and they can use the water they get. "Me, I'm just more comfortable in a war zone. Did your would-be customer happen to leave a name or contact codes?"

"No name," she says, reaching down to unclip her HCD. She lays the green plastic oblong, half the size of her palm, on the bar and holds her hand out for mine. "I'll transfer the data."

I reach into the pocket of my jeans and pull out my own hip. I usually carry mine turned off, which explains why Bobbi had to leave a message for me at home, cautioning me to meet her in person. I blink twice to activate the data stream in my prosthetic eye. Glancing at Bobbi, I spot the almost microscopic blue readouts crawling across her contact as I give her authorization. She transfers the codes.

"Thanks," I say when she has finished.

"Don't mention it, Maker. Or should I call you—what was it? Genevieve?"

"Just don't call me late for dinner," I answer, and get the hell out of that bar.

Something is making me want to go look at Nell's package, hidden away in the bottom of my trunk. As if to reassure myself that she was real, that my childhood really happened. I don't know. I haven't looked at the things she gave me since I put them away, a quarter century gone by.

Maybe I'll even manage to open it this time. If I can convince myself I'm not dishonoring the damn thing by touching it. There are rules about that sort of thing.

Elspeth sipped her tea before setting it on the counter in the cafeteria, next to the coffeepot. She sighed and closed her eyes, early morning tiredness dragging on her limbs. Her brain felt clogged; she had slept terribly, in a plastic chair. *I should just save Valens the cost of the hotel room,* she thought. *It's not like I'm spending nights there.* And then: *Oh, what the heck. Unitek can afford it.*

She rubbed her temples with her forefingers, hoping the headache riding her like a crown of thorns would subside, and mused on the irony of her pacifist father in a military hospital—that used to be Toronto General. *Friday. If only I didn't have to go to the lab today.*

She picked up the paper cup of tea with her left hand, shielding the palm with a paper napkin, went through the line for the cashier, and found the elevator back up to Acute Care. She nodded to a nurse, two residents, and the unit secretary, all bleary-eyed at the end of the graveyard shift, and returned to her father's room.

A private room. *Valens was as good as his word there, too.*

Albert Dunsany was sleeping when she came in and set her tea on the yellow swiveling tray beside the bed. Wires and tubes sagged indiscreetly from beneath the white chenille cover, and Elspeth turned so that she could see only her father's face, sunken-cheeked and nearly as pale as the pillowcase. *Funny how I look so much like Mom and nothing like him,* she thought. *I've got his eyes, though. Hazel.*

She turned the plastic chair and sat back down beside the bed, very gently taking his nearer hand. His skin felt waxen and cool. Elspeth thought for a moment that if she squeezed, it would crumple in her grip like paper. Slowly, his eyes opened, and he turned his gaze on her from under half-raised lids. Pale eyes that used to sparkle with mirth still brightened when they focused on her face. "Ellie."

"Dad." She took a breath. "I have to go home and shower so I can go to work. I'll be back to see you tonight, all right?"

It seemed to take him a moment to process the information, but at last he nodded slightly, mindful of the tube running under his nose. "Be careful out there." He fought to give her an exhausted smile, and she blinked hard.

"I will." She inclined her head, more to hide her eyes from him than out of agreement.

A sound that might have been a cough or a small, pained laugh escaped him. "I'm . . . proud isn't the right word. But I'm glad they pardoned you. I never doubted. I want you to know. I knew you were innocent."

Elspeth leaned closer, half-standing, and kissed him on the forehead, interrupting whatever he might have said next. "You always believed in me. Have I ever told you how lucky I feel about that?"

He half-swallowed. The faint smile widened. "Sweetie . . ."

"Shhh." She straightened up and picked up her tea, which still sent gossamer coils of steam into the cool hospital air. "Rest, all right? I'll be back as soon as I can, and the nurses can page me if you need me quickly. Yes?"

They both knew why he might need her quickly. He nodded. She squeezed his hand one more time and turned away. *Just don't ask me how I got the pardon, Dad. Or ask me whether I really did anything worth going to jail for, all those years ago.*

Somewhere in the Internet
Thursday 7 September, 2062
09:45:55:55–09:46:03:12

Richard Feynman was running for his life. Not running as hard as he might have been, admittedly. Perhaps more strolling purposefully, with the occasional casual glance over his shoulder. He would have chuckled at the comparison, if he hadn't been so intent on learning the tricks of this new opponent.

Unitek had a hired gun in the house. And he wasn't half bad at his job, either.

Which was, of course, making it that much harder for Feynman to edge his way through the firewalls and virtual barriers that had so far defeated him. And the new code jockey seemed to have caught on that somebody had been poking around his perimeters. At least, judging by the depth and the breadth of the security scans he was running, and the levels of new protections going up.

Or possibly it was just that something big was about to happen. And knowing that Elspeth Dunsany was involved, and the same Colonel Valens who'd nearly bought a dishonorable discharge when Chinese agents had stolen certain very critical information from a mission he was heading at the Scavella-Burrell base on Mars . . .

Well, Feynman had a reasonably good idea what was being made ready, and it made him all the more eager to find a way in.

At last, however, after narrowly avoiding an unexpected

recon-in-force, Feynman had to admit he was beaten on a security front. Which meant resorting to his more favored
method of breaking into things.

Social engineering.

Because he knew the code jockey's name, and he'd gone
out of his way to get to know the code jockey's daughter.
And Leah Castaign would be online again in the morning.
Or perhaps even later tonight, if she snuck some gaming
time after her father was in bed. Feynman might have
smiled, shaking his head, recognizing something about a
child who couldn't follow rules simply because somebody
told her to do so.

Contemplating that, Feynman wondered if there might be
some way into Unitek through the servers hosting the VR
game. Vast, quick, powerful—and maintained by Unitek I.S.,
although they were outside of the company firewall. And he
was going to need to hack Phobos starbase anyway, and get a
player character online there, so he could maintain contact
with Leah—once she started her virtual pilot training.

Which, after all, was the goal of the exercise.

Feynman had an intimate understanding of bureau-
cracy and of the usual motives behind corporate citizen-
ship. And he found it difficult to believe that Unitek,
several of its tentacular subsidiaries, and the Canadian
government were hosting a free recreational gamespace for
no more return than the exposure.

There weren't enough ads.

Mitch leaned back in the passenger seat of his battered Dodge hybrid and kicked his feet up on the dash, sipping coffee. He set the insulated mug on the center console and tapped his HCD with a light pen, flipping through illicitly copied reports.

The Dodge was halfway hidden behind a delivery van, but in the gray morning light Mitch had a clear view of the loading dock and rear door of the Canadian Consolidated Pharmacom warehouse. The reports flashing across his contact included spectrographic analysis of three seized stashes of Hammer as well as the files he'd been able to retrieve from Mashaya's desktop in the apartment she had shared with him.

Mitch wasn't a chemist or a pharmacist. He wasn't even a homicide detective. He was a halfway decent vice cop, though, and he was getting a niggling, tickling sensation that a pattern was about to emerge just under his fingertips, almost close enough to feel.

He was also outside his jurisdiction, and had been told in no uncertain terms to drop the case. *Mashaya,* he thought, glancing up to check the deserted loading dock once more, then rescanning the scroll of data. *Gonna get 'em for you, girl.* Nothing moved. He set the HCD down on the dash, lighting a cigarette, letting the data creep continue.

He blinked and yawned. A long night. And not a damned thing had happened.

Mitch wasn't really certain why he was spending his off-duty shift staking out a pharmaceutical warehouse, unless you started to wonder why maybe the Hammer had showed up on his streets, not New York. And wonder about the coincidental existence of Canadian Consolidated Pharmaceuticals' West Hartford warehouse. Mashaya had found out some interesting things before she died; the most interesting was that Hartford wasn't the only city to have experienced a run of deaths related to recalled combat drugs in the last six months. It was, however, the only such city in the USA. And the only one with a facility operated by the company that manufactured the drug.

It was a break in the pattern. And breaks like that were where the answers tended to lie.

Mitch had yet to get a warrant issued on a hunch, however. Even if he had been permitted to help investigate the case. He knew perfectly well that he was lucky not to still be on administrative leave following the murder of his fiancée. That he was pushing that luck, and it was going to run out on him. That Hartford PD itself had a hard-on for whoever did Mashaya, and that lots of perfectly good murder boys were all over the case like white on Mitch's own skinny cracker ass. That nobody was going to show up at CCP today either, and he was going to have to report for roll call unslept and stubbled at eight AM.

He closed his eyes just for a moment, head sagging. He jerked it upright and fought a jaw-cracking yawn, reaching for his coffee again. *What is it? Something about the pills . . . contaminated pills . . . why only some?*

Why not all?

How does only part of a batch get tainted?

His thoughts chased their tails as he drained his coffee.

And when he set the insulated mug aside, something was moving on the loading dock, walking up to that concealed side door.

A tall, black-haired woman with military bearing and an unmistakable nose.

"Now what is that, Mitchy-poo?" Oblivious to the tread marks spotting the dash, Mitch pulled his boots down and leaned forward. "Don't you look familiar . . ."

And not familiar at all.

Maker, he thought for one wild moment, but it wasn't Maker at all. Five eleven, maybe, hundred and fifty and most of it bone. Latina or Native American, well-preserved fiftyish. And then he noticed the rest of it: walking without a limp, manicured nails on long clean fingers, five-thousand-dollar boots with mirror-shining toes. No scars disfiguring that arrogant profile, either. *Goddamn.*

He was halfway through reaching up to touch his ear clip on and report in when he remembered he wasn't supposed to be there. Nevertheless, Mitch's trained eye recorded every detail as she mounted the chipped concrete steps: black pantsuit, pinstriped charcoal, stylish jacket cinched at the waist with a matching belt and a pin glinting gold on the lapel. Razor-styled hair falling like a raven's blue-black wing across a forehead he was willing to bet was enzyme-smoothed. Pale blue blouse with a winged collar, softening the tailored severity of the outfit and the planed severity of her face.

A hunch, that was all. A hunch, and the wonder why such drugs might have wound up on the street in Hartford, and not someplace sensibly trackless like New York or Atlanta. And why a batch that, according to the lab guys, should have been discarded after preliminary testing had been tabletized, labeled, stamped, and packaged in field-regulation twists. It never should have made it into the piller. It was an inconsistency, a flaw in the pattern, and Mitch hated those.

The fact that it wasn't exactly Hammers didn't bother Mitch so much. He could make that add up. He was sure the CA tested new combat enhancement drugs all the time.

Mitch slouched lower in his bucket seat as the woman hesitated, one hand on the steel doorknob and the other fumbling in her jacket pocket for an ID badge. She stopped and turned, head coming up as she scanned the cracked parking lot and the cinder-block walls of the nearby buildings. Thistles and sumac forced their way through the far edge of the pavement, a slender sight screen, and she studied that with a professional eye. Mitch held his breath, looking at her boots, afraid the pressure of his gaze would be enough to bring her eyes around to him.

For a long moment she stood poised, and he noticed that she had released the door handle and slid the hand not holding her badge inside the collar of her jacket. *Damn. If that's not Maker's better-looking twin sister, I'm the Virgin Mary. What the hell is she doing at Consolidated? And what does Maker know that she's not telling me?*

Think like a part of the scenery, Mitchy. Despite the intervening distance, he only let his breath hiss out in a long silent sigh when the dark-haired woman relaxed, her hand slipping back into view. Shaking her head, she keyed a code on the door pad and badged herself in.

I knew I should have done this already. I'm running Maker's damn fingerprints as soon as I get back to the station. I'd better pick up some doughnuts to bribe the guys down in I.D. They would know as well as anybody that he wasn't supposed to be working this case. But they'd take pity on him nonetheless, because family was family, and a cop was a cop.

Ninety seconds later, timed on his heads-up-display,

Mitch slid as casually as he could manage out of his Dodge and walked around the back end of the delivery van, tugging his coat into place like a man who has stopped to take a piss against a tire. *And I'm probably rumpled enough to pass for a late-homecoming drunk, too,* he mused, meandering an unsteady path to the corner.

The too-familiar business-suited stranger's vehicle was easy to spot.

Ontario plates.

Well, I'll be goddamned.

1420 hours, Friday 8 September, 2062
Hartford, Connecticut
Albany Avenue
Abandoned North End

I slide the giant old BMW Amazonas motorcycle gently around the square frame of the cleanest house on the street and into its trash-heaped backyard like a fish nosing into a reef. There are armed guards and a high wall around it, but Razorface lives in the neighborhood he grew up in. Sitting on the back porch, cleaning a gun, he waves to me as I pull in.

I look around for Emery, who is usually in attendance, but Face's lean and wary lieutenant is nowhere to be seen. Two adolescent boys play basketball in the cracked driveway, so I park my bike in the uncut grass by the weathered frame of a two-car garage and walk back up to the house.

"Nice day," I say to the boys. The taller one turns to stare, fascinated; I let my eyes slide off him and over to Face, who rises, smirking, and gives me a hand up the three wooden risers. Not that I need it, of course.

He grins at me, steel teeth like the grille on a '57 Chevy.

It never ceases to amaze that somebody would do something like that to himself on purpose—but then, I've seen some piercings and other body modifications that make Face's teeth look like a tattooed biceps. And they do make him . . . memorable.

"Nice as a day ever gets around here." He gestures up to the glazed-blue sky overhead. There's something special about September skies in this part of the world. In Toronto, I remember a lot of rain in autumn.

The porch railing creaks as I lean against it. Face settles down in his chair and returns his attention to the pistol disassembled on newspaper spread on his glass-topped table. Watching as he wets a square of gauze and threads it through the needle eye of a cleaning rod, I smell gun oil and the sharper scent of cleaner. He turns his head and shouts over his shoulder into the kitchen door. "Baby, get Maker a beer?"

"Razorface," I begin, and let my voice trail off as he looks up.

"Going to tell me you have to drive?"

His woman comes out of the house with two cans of beer. If you can dignify the stuff Face drinks with the name. She juggles a plate of sandwiches in her other hand, setting it down on the porch rail before she hands a can to each of us. "Thanks, Alyse," I say as I take it.

"Don't mention it. You here to try and steal my man again?" Her black eyes sparkle. She cocks her head to one side and rolls her shoulder back, hands challenging on her ample hips.

I crack open the beer. "No one could ever compete with you, Leesie. Your cooking keeps him home."

Head bowed over his pistol, Face grunts toward the newspapers. Smiling, Alyse picks up the plate of sandwiches and holds it out to me. I take one—bloody roast beef and processed cheese on white bread Maman would have shuddered over. Holding the beer in my other hand, I take a bite.

Alyse turns, and Razorface absently takes the plate from her. She bends her neck and half smiles, half frowns. Then she looks back up at me, alert and quick as a bird. "Maker, you do something about that cop friend of yours sniffing where he don't belong, you hear me? I'd hate to see that boy get hurt."

Mouth full of roast beef sandwich, all I can do is nod. I swallow half-chewed food and mumble. "I'll do what I can, ma'am. You can't lead a horse to water, eh? Has Mitch been here?"

Face looks up as she nods her head once. He's got an odd expression on his face as he puts the tools down, wipes oil from his hands onto a rag, and picks up a sandwich. *Sching.* There's nothing quite like watching Razorface eat roast beef on white bread with too much mayonnaise. Like a deli slicer.

"Woman, why do I put up with your ass?" He says it around a mouthful of food.

She straightens her neck and looks down at him, broad-shouldered Dominican goddess. "Because nobody else can handle you the way I can, baby." She turns and saunters back into the house, and Face watches her until she's out of sight behind the screen door. When she's gone, he shakes his head in admiration and turns back to me.

He takes a long swallow of beer before he speaks. "That pig . . . yeah, I seen him. Hell out of his jurisdiction. Don't know what Hartford P.D. wants up here on the Ave. We take care of our own. Besides, your boy isn't homicide, and he's barely been a detective a year. What's he doing on a case like this?"

"I don't know. How do you know what he's assigned to?"

The big man laughs, shaking his head from side to side. "I'm s'poda know these things."

It takes me a second to get the half-chewed meat and bread down. *Mitch, what are you after?* I chase the food with a swallow of beer. "Face, tell me the truth. You have anything to do with this business? Mashaya Duclose?"

"You trust me to tell you the truth?" He turns the beer can slowly in his hand before he lifts and drains it. Never taking his eyes from mine, he crushes it casually and pitches it at a paper bag beside the kitchen door. He misses.

"I trust you with my back. What the hell is with the dance-around today, eh?"

A moment's quiet assessment before he drops his gaze and scratches behind his right ear, gold hoops sparkling in the light. "Shit, Maker. S'weird, I dunno. Cops in my end of town, cops getting killed in my town. Looking for a dealer that I can't find and they can't find . . . just damned weird."

My eyebrow tries to crawl up into my hairline. The basketball thumps the asphalt driveway. "What was that again?"

He starts reassembling the gun. "Just what I said. Me and the boys have been looking all week, and nothing. Nobody knows nothing. The guys that sold the shit, they from out of town, and the word is they went right back wherever the hell they come from. They were trying to move in, I could do something."

I've a pretty good idea what Face's "something" might entail, but I nod anyway. "Any idea where they were from?"

"I think from the City."

Only one city in this part of the world is the capital-C variety. "Ah." I run my tongue across my teeth. Silence hangs between us for a moment, and I think about the odd standoffishness in his manner today. He won't look up and meet my eyes, and it takes a little while to make sense of why. "Razorface, are you worried for me?"

"You got somebody looking for you."

"I know." I wince as I hear my own tone, but I can't make myself soften it—a dog that can't stop growling over a bone.

"You got some kind of trouble?"

I move away from the porch railing, walking the length of the rickety structure. I stand there for a moment, watching the basketball game. The older boy is pretty much slaughtering the younger one, and frustration shines behind the sweat dripping down the smaller kid's face. I know the feeling. "I've always got some kind of trouble."

He laughs. "You living in the world, ain'tcha? Family trouble or other kind of trouble?"

"I haven't got any family, Face." I turn back over my left shoulder to look at him. He's black-and-white out of my bad eye, the reassembled automatic in his hand picked out in red by the targeting scope.

Standing, he drops the pistol into a shoulder holster and shrugs it on. He used to shove it into his waistband until I told him a story about a guy I knew in the army who shot his balls off doing that. Standing there in the shade of the porch on a bright September day, I abruptly remember him as a skinny preadolescent, blood running down his soot-covered face from a glancing wound on his forehead. It's so vivid an image I can almost smell the smoke.

Those were bad years, in the thirties when things in the States were even worse than they are now. My first time in Hartford, I wore a baby-blue peacekeeper beret and thought I was invincible. South Africa didn't happen until two years later.

No, I really don't have any idea why I came back here to retire. Must be the fond memories. I'm so wrapped up in them I miss the first part of his sentence when he speaks again.

". . . gonna tell me what's going on with you so I can help, or you gonna keep playing your cards in your vest pocket?" He comes up and lays a baseball glove mitt on my shoulder.

"I . . ." *It's an old habit, Face. What they don't know can't hurt me.* I change the subject. "This cop. You never said if you knew anything."

"Course I don't know nothing. I know something maybe you don't, though. This Duclose. Mashaya. She was my baby's momma's little sister."

His baby's momma. That could be any of twenty women. The implications come clear. "She's from the neighborhood. A cop."

"South Arsenal neighborhood. Got her high school and everything. Family's from Trinidad. Good kid, they said."

"So that's why she was on this end of town. You think maybe what she got killed for wasn't related to her job?" I notice I still have half a sandwich in my hand and take another bite. Leesie hates it when people don't finish what she fixes.

His hand slips off my shoulder. "Some people don't be so happy when some bitch from the neighborhood grows up to be a pig, if that's what you mean. They might do something about it. But I would've heard 'bout that. This wasn't no local issue."

"What do you mean?"

He shrugs. "Mashaya, she had friends here. Nobody downtown cares if a few bangers OD." He goes silent, and I know he's thinking of Merc.

"You're saying she was working on her own time."

"It ain't a crime unless white people or rich people die. She talked to a lot of people. Talked to me. Maybe got close to something." His hands windmill slightly as he struggles to articulate his thoughts. "Somebody saw her get shot. Sniper bullet, one shot. Tore the back of her head clean off. White van came around the corner thirty seconds later and five guys cleaned up the scene and were gone before my boys even heard about the shooting. That's fast."

I start to see the outline of the picture he is painting for me, in his awkward way. Face isn't stupid. He's keen as the razor blade he keeps in his pants pocket. I've seen the man in a ten-thousand-dollar sharkskin suit cut to fit like a second skin, and you don't get to be what he is if you're not smart enough to remember the names and family histories of every petty criminal in the city.

Oral communication, however, is not his strong point. I finish the end of my sandwich as an excuse to think. "That's *professional*. You've got a feeling about this," I say at last.

"I got nothing but feelings, and they all making my knuckles itch. But I think we talk to the people Mashaya was talking to, we get close to the people she got close to . . ."

"We get shot in the head with a high-powered rifle and our bodies turn up in the river. Good plan, Razorface."

He shrugged. "Actually, I was thinking of going on down to New York City. What do you say?"

I wipe my hands on my pants, leaving behind a greasy mayonnaise stain.

"I'll drive."

The door to Gabe Castaign's office stood open on the gray-carpeted hallway, and Elspeth paused there. She heard his voice, carefully cheerful, the enunciated tones telling her that he was speaking to a machine. " . . . hope you're out having a hot date on a Friday night, or at least down at that dive you call a corner pub watching the game. My money's on Chelsea. Call me. Bye!" She rapped the door sharply and stepped into the room just as he tapped the disconnect. The fuzzy image hanging in the air over his phone dissolved into transparency. *How odd—whoever he was calling still has the factory message up.* "Gabe?"

He was already looking up to greet her knock. "Elspeth. Come in please." He stood and came around the big desk, a mirror of her own, scooping a pile of manuals off the seat of the upholstered chair to his right. "What can I do for you?"

She stepped onto soft carpeting identical to that in her own office, except in a masculine medium gray blue, complemented by periwinkle drapes. He'd hauled them to the side and turned off the projected babbling-brook landscape, revealing a less-than-enticing view of slanting sunlight across a well-stocked parking lot. A breeze ruffled the curtains; Elspeth smelled warm concrete. She hadn't realized the windows would open. "I was hoping you were settled in and we could sit down and talk about the project."

"I'd like that. Pull up a chair." He set the manuals on the edge of his desk, away from the interface plate, and gestured to the one he'd cleared. The skin of his hands showed faint irregularities of color, speaking to Elspeth of old deep burns or something else requiring skin grafts.

She shook her head. "How about I buy you dinner?"

He checked the time in the corner of the flat monitor pane canted at an angle like a reading stand over the top of his desk. Elspeth found it interesting that he preferred the pane to contacts or a holographic interface. Still, she imagined he spent a lot of time staring at it. "How did it get so late? Sure, let me grab my jacket. My roommates are at a friend's place for dinner." He wiggled his fingers in the air to indicate quotation marks.

I wonder what quote roommates unquote are. She stepped back as he walked around the desk, rolling down his shirtsleeves and buttoning the cuffs before he brushed past her to take his coat down off the peg beside the door. "What do you want?"

"Anything's good," she answered, wondering if he meant—or caught—the double entendre. "I wonder if that little noodle shop on the corner by the university is still there."

He took the knob in his hand and held the door open for her. He passed his thumbprint over the sensor as well as turning the key in the lock. "When was the last time you were there?"

She almost laughed in realization. "About thirteen years."

"Ah."

Elspeth could see evening light through the double glass doors at the end of the corridor as they walked. She knew he was waiting for an explanation. "I've been out of Toronto for a while. I'll tell you about it if I get a couple of beers in me."

"You do that," he said, as the outside doors whisked open before them, enfolding them in warm autumn air like a humid exhalation.

An hour later at a restaurant still called "Lemon Grass," Elspeth picked up her chopsticks and leaned forward over the steaming bowl of noodles, closing her eyes to inhale. "Jesus, that smells good."

Across the table, Gabe tilted his bowl toward his mouth. Slurping noodles, he nodded. He chewed, swallowed, and cleared his throat. "I love this stuff. So tell me about your project. Our project. Do you want another beer?"

"Please. Well, here's the thing. I don't know how much you remember from about thirteen years back . . . Do you recall anything what the media said then? About my work in particular?"

Gabe signaled the waitress. He had a knack, Elspeth noticed, for catching people's eye. "I saw you on *Network Tonite*. The night Alex Ugate was shot."

"Oh." Elspeth set her chopsticks aside. "That was a bad business." She picked the Sapporo up before the waitress's hand had really left it and took a swallow. *Two should be my limit. You're cut off after this one, Elspeth.* "That was about the worst night of my life."

"I imagine. I've had a few of those myself." He set his bowl down and laid the chopsticks on the blue porcelain rest, reaching for the teapot. The bowls and teacups were still as mismatched as she remembered: Gabe's cup was red and blue, and Elspeth's was white with translucent rice grains throughout. "I remember they showed the VR feed, and you talking with some dead engineer . . ."

She chuckled, distracted enough to pick her chopsticks back up, fingertips fretting the splintery wood. "Nikola Tesla. He wasn't a true AI, though—just a construct personality. A responder designed to mimic a long-dead man."

Gabe nodded. "And then a riot broke out in the TV studio, as I recall." As if realizing what he had said, he continued quickly. "Do you still think you were on the right track?"

After a long pause, she forced herself to keep chewing. "Gabe, I'm sure of it. It's just a matter of creating the *right* construct personality. After a certain point, I believe they'll self-generate. Given sufficient system resources, that is."

"Ah." He seemed pensive.

She reached out and tapped his hand. "Speak."

His shoulder rose and fell under light-blue broadcloth. "I'm wondering if the research would still be as controversial now. Ten years later." She didn't answer immediately, and after a sip of beer he continued. "Course, I never much understood what the fuss was then."

"It won't be controversial," she whispered, "because no one will know that we're doing it this time." She nibbled on the edge of her thumbnail. "And as for what the fuss was—well, what was the fuss over nanotech, or bioengineering, or cloning? People used to get shot for performing *abortions,* for Christ's sake. Fundamentalists are nuts." Self-consciously, she touched her gold cross, watching fish circle in the tank on the wall.

"In the U.S., the only reason people don't still get shot for performing abortions is because they're not legal anymore," Gabe replied. He picked up his chopsticks and sucked up another mouthful of noodles. "How on earth did you wind up going to jail for sedition, of all things?"

"It wasn't sedition."

"I remember the trial. Military Powers Act. Something else? Not espionage, or they wouldn't have you on this project."

Elspeth smoothed the palm of her hand over the speckled linoleum tabletop. Dark red vinyl crinkled under her

thighs as she shifted position in the booth. "There is that."
She poured herself tea so she wouldn't finish her beer too
quickly.

Gabe watched quietly while she fidgeted.

"It was—noncooperation, I suppose you'd call it. Valens
wanted someone—I mean, something—I wasn't prepared
to give him." She changed the subject none too smoothly.
"Where did you learn programming?"

"Now that is a long and ugly story. I used to play
around for fun when I was a kid. There's not much to do in
the winters up north. We played a lot of Monopoly."

Elspeth glanced up at him, surprised. Her eyes met his
bay-blue ones, which twinkled amid sunbaked creases. *Is
he kidding? Yes. And no.* "And you kept it up in the army?"

He shrugged and took a pull of his beer. "Not really. I
was special forces. I got shot at." The eyes looked down, and
the twinkle left them. "Then I got out, got married, and had
to get a real job. Which reminds me—I think we've got an
unusually persistent somebody poking around the edges of
the intranet. He hasn't made it in, but he's giving me a run
for my money."

"I'm keeping all my project work on the isolated intranet. Are you?"

"Yes. Although I can't help but feel a bigger system
might provoke things. Kind of a neurons-and-synapses
kind of deal, n'est ce pas?" He trailed off, poking at his
food. "How did *you* get into this line of work?"

"I started with an MSW and decided I was sick of watching inner city kids get chewed up by the system, so I went
back to school for medicine and figured out I was too scared
of hurting people to be a physician. That led me into psychi-
atry until I figured out I could hurt them worse. Thus," she
spread her hands wide, as if releasing a dove, "research."

He raised his Sapporo and tapped it against hers.

"Here's to winding up someplace other than where you intended."

"I already did that, Gabe." The words came out too easily, revealing more than she had meant to.

"Yeah." He finished the beer and set the bottle aside for the alert waitress to carry off.

In a moment, she was back with two more. Elspeth eyed hers uncertainly. "I should stop with these."

"Do you have somewhere to be?"

She chewed, swallowed, regretting already the need to leave the warm, ginger-scented restaurant and go back to the hospital, to the reek of antiseptic and death. "Well . . . yeah."

"Hell," he said. "Drink the beer. I'll walk you over. It is walkable?"

"Subway," she replied, and he nodded.

"Close enough."

1530 hours, Friday 8 September, 2062
Sigourney Street
Abandoned North End
Hartford, Connecticut

"Jenny, it's Gabe. Hope everything's okay—sorry I missed you. I was just calling to let you know I've moved back to Toronto and give you my new contact information, but I guess I'll e-mail it to you instead. Yes, as you're guessing, that means I finally found work. It's a good job, too, but I have to warn you about the shocker—I'm working with your old 'friend' Captain Valens. Except he's Colonel Valens now, but anyway, I figured I should warn you before you heard it through the grapevine.

"I hope you're out having a hot date on a Friday night,

or at least down at that dive you call a corner pub watching the game. My money's on Chelsea. Call me. Bye!"

I step away from the one-tenth-scale holographic projection of the head of Gabriel Castaign, formerly holding the rank of captain in the Canadian Army. Razorface watches over my shoulder. Boris stands on the fender of the Cadillac, and Face scratches him under the chin. The old tomcat rocks his head from side to side, leaning into the caress. "*Jenny?*"

"Don't push your luck, Dwayne."

He curls a corner of his lip at me in a close-mouthed smile. I'm probably the only person other than his momma who knows that name anymore. "Mexican standoff," he says. "That your only message? You nearly ready to roll?"

"Yeah," I say, downloading the information Gabe e-mailed me into my HCD. The H stands for holistic, but through the magic of linguistics, everybody calls it a "hip." Whatever.

Valens? Fucking A, Gabe, you'd better have a hell of a good reason for that. He does, though. And it's hard to be angry, because I know perfectly well what his reasons are.

His wife's name had been Geniveve, and the irony of that still scalded me if I thought about it too hard. He'd married her after we were both out of the army, and their daughters were born late—the younger one only a year or so before Geniveve died. Long after he'd forgotten that he saved my life that time. I never forgot, even if I never got around to mentioning it to him. Like I never got around to mentioning some other things he didn't need to know. We can put bases on Mars and miners on Ceres, but we can't cure common heartbreak.

I stop playing with my HCD, thumb it off, and refill Boris's automatic cat feeder and water fountain. He's got a cat door keyed to a microchip. Face watches me, not quite letting me see him smile. Yeah, dammit, I take in strays. When I'm done, I grab my jacket and an overnight bag and lead Face over to the only-just-antique Bradford Tempest pickup in the left-hand bay.

I figure I'll answer Gabriel's call when I get home and have a little time to talk. And when I've cooled off a little, to be honest.

The Bradford isn't much to look at, but it runs. The solid rubber tires and boulder-climbing suspension aren't easy on the kidneys as we bushwhack our way to the highway, but thirty minutes later we're southbound on I-91, passing the exit sign that reads "Dinosaur State Park / Veteran's Home and Hospital" and accelerating steadily toward New York City.

Because, baby, it's Friday night.

We ride in silence, down highways older than my grandmother, through the acid-rain-etched hills and the centers of commerce of southern Connecticut. The highway unwinds before us, the sun gliding down the sky. Our first sight of the city is burn-scarred gray concrete towers flanking the highway—deserted now and unmaintained.

It's still only early evening—three hours transit, more or less, and then another half hour looking for a spot before I pay too much to park the brave old truck in a guarded lot. I disarm the security system so Face can climb out the passenger side. I've got my gun unholstered and am leaning across to open the glove box when he stops, turns back, and slides his own piece out of the shoulder holster. He weighs it in his hand, standing close enough so the door blocks him from casual sight.

"Leave it," I say.

He looks like he wants to chew his lip. I admire his restraint. "New York," he says.

"Not the place to carry a gun." New York City has a shoot-on-sight law, and the cops here aren't content to let the neighborhoods run themselves. Never mind the martial law that's gone into effect since the dikes went up between the City and the cold, rising Atlantic. That spot between my shoulderblades starts to itch as soon as I get within smelling distance of the place. I meet his eyes and frown. "Glove box, Face."

He takes a breath to argue, so I let my expression slide toward *Sergeant* and he lets it out again and puts the gun in the box like a good boy, only slamming the door a little. I meet him by the front bumper. "So, do you have any idea where to go?"

He's already walking, and I set the alarm and the flame-throwers before I follow.

He nods, but doesn't say anything. The narrow street is dark and smells of garbage and the salt-sewage tang of the sea. I hurry to catch up, matching strides with him as he reaches the sidewalk. His shoulders are squared hard, and as I fall in on his right side I lay my metal hand on his elbow. "Talk to me."

He turns his head away and spits. "Nothing to talk about. Will you stop fussing at me? You been acting like my grandmother all day. We just going to see a guy."

I'm annoyed with myself, because he's right; I have been clingy. It has something to do with the dark-haired woman who knows my name, though, and I'm not going into that right now. *What sort of a guy?* I would ask, but my head whirls as if I had spun in place for too long. I gasp and steady myself, one hand on a tenement wall in wet brick. *Not good, Casey. Not good at all.* I can almost feel the eyes of the predators marking me as my hand comes off Face's arm. He checks himself midstride and turns back, irritation blending into concern.

Blurring, and the smell of dead people in the sun. Sound of rotors as I bring the chopper in low, a steaming clearing among strangler fig and vines. The door gunner swearing, and—

No.

I get it under control and stand up, leaning on the wall more than I want to. "S'all right, Face." He doesn't believe me, and I wave him off, striding forward again. I try not to let him see me clenching my jaw. "Just old bones and the drive."

It isn't, though. I know what it is—it's feedback from my neural taps, and flashbacks, and I haven't had one that bad in twenty years.

Ignoring Face's anxiety, I move down the street toward wherever he's leading me.

Avatar Gamespace
Phobos Starport
Circa A.D. 3400 (Virtual Clock)
Interaction logged Friday 8 September,
2062, 1900 hours

Leah gulped, leaning against the triple-thick crystal plates of the reception lounge view port, her booted feet firmly magnetized to the floor. If her VR were better, she would have been able to feel the space-chill seeping through them. She focused beyond the blinking sponsor-ship logos hanging in the glass just at eye level (*AppleSoft, Venus Consolidated Erotic Industries, Unitek, Miller Genuine Draft, Amalgamated Everything*) and let a long cool comforting draft of air flow into her mouth. "My God," she whispered.

The starship hanging in the tiny moon's shadow was visible as nothing so much as a silhouette and a more-regular pattern of lights against the stars. Leah reached up and tapped the crystal where the great ship's lights were,

calling up an outline display and then a schematic. She
shook her head. *Not quite.* And tapped once more.

As if light had poured around the rim of the moon, *The
Indefatigable* shone in virtual sunlight, the dull silver of
her great wheel-on-a-spear shape catching highlights that
never were. That wheel rotated slowly around the shaft, a
spindly looking construction to connect the habitation
ring to the incredibly deadly bulbs of the engines at the
far end, some kilometers away.

It looked like a Christmas tree ornament, a bauble she
could reach out and pluck with her hand. Leah knew it
was longer than the Channel Bridge.

"You are gonna be *mine*," she whispered, and broke
into a radiant grin.

BOOK TWO

Of course, many
people claim not to
be convinced by this
so-called climate
change evidence.
That is because they
are shortsighted
sociopathic morons
who don't want to lose
any money.
—*Bruce Sterling,*
1998

At the top of a flight of cement stairs with a rotten railing, I step through a narrow, mottled greenish door and into gray light. Moist shags of paint hang from it like bark from a sycamore, freckling my fingers as I hold it open for Razorface, a few steps behind me. The early morning is already sweat-hot and dank; suddenly, I realize how long we've been chasing a cold trail. I need a drink. After eight hours following Razorface through the gentle streets of New York City by night, I need several drinks. And maybe a cigarette—one I could smoke quickly, before I remember that I don't smoke anymore.

He's stopped behind me, just inside the doorway, sharing a parting handshake with the weedy young man we roused out of bed. I hadn't realized the sheer number of people that my old friend has done favors for, which tells me I need to pay more attention. Missing things like that can get you dead.

None of the favor-owers know a damned thing about a dealer, a box full of Hammers, or anybody going on a road trip to Hartford. Face's hunch was wrong.

The shit didn't come out of New York, which is a relief and a puzzlement both.

"Face."

He bangs fists with his boy one more time and turns

back to me as the skinny kid steps away, into darkness. "Yah, Maker."

"Food." I feel wobbly, and I'm hoping it's low blood sugar and a lack of caffeine instead of other problems. That can't-get-warm feeling is starting to creep up my neck, my right fingers itching with the desire for a weapon. There hasn't been a reason to reach for one, but we've been in and out of threat situations—narrow hallways, strangers' living rooms, tenement housing, and alleyways—all night. Also, I keep seeing people I know are dead out of the corner of my good eye, which is never a good sign.

"Diner?"

"Fine." I take Face's arm because the alternative is ignominiously clutching that neck-breaking banister on my way down the steps. He gives me a funny look. "Tired," I say, and he shakes his head.

"Maker, you ain't never tired. Let's go get us something to eat." He shepherds me down the block into a breakfast shop that's just stretching and getting ready for the morning, sits me down, and orders for me. Coffee takes the edge off the shakes, at least, and clears the corners of my brain. By the time the eggs arrive, I'm almost functional again.

"Thanks."

"Don't mention it. I say we hole up here until tonight and then drive back. Maybe you'll be feeling better by then."

"Nah, I'm fine." I push my plate away. "I just needed a minute, is all." *And I really need to go home and talk to Simon. It's probably nothing.*

It's never nothing, Jenny. Which is when a voice I really didn't feel like hearing interrupts my reverie, and a shadow falls across our table. "Genevieve Marie. Aren't you going to introduce me to your friend?"

"It's fucking old-home week, isn't it?" I don't look up at her, because I suspect that if I did, I would trigger and the next thing I knew I would be wiping bits of bone off my knuckles. And I really don't want to try to explain that to a cop. "Barb, this is Razorface. Razorface, this is Barb Casey. Don't turn your back on her: she's a bitch."

His eyebrows go up. *He* looks up at her. "Barb . . . Casey?"

"She's my sister."

"I thought you didn't have a sister."

"I don't."

Amused, silent, Barb says nothing during the exchange. Finally, I have to face her. She looks good. Damned good, damn her to hell. She's wearing a good, forest-green suit with expensive buttons, gleaming shoes, and half-carat earrings. And she's smiling like she's actually glad to see me. As if she hadn't tried to kill me once already in this life. *Time heals all wounds, right? Right.* I'm a good girl and I don't spit on her boot. "What the fuck do you want?"

Without asking, she hooks a chair over and straddles it, leaning forward against the back. "I heard you were in trouble. I came to see if I could help."

"I've been leading a nice quiet life without your help for thirty years, Barbara. I don't see any reason why I should start looking for any now."

She sighs. "Look. I really need to talk to you. I've been chasing you for weeks. You're a hard girl to get ahold of. Just when I finally got your trail, you scampered out of town; it was a good thing I planted a tracer on your friend here, or I never would have caught up."

Face places his big hands flat on the table, and I lay my left one over his right, careful not to press down too hard. Leaning forward, he doesn't take his eyes off Barb. I let him feel a little more of the weight of my steel hand. This is not a fight Face wants to get into, but I can't just come out and tell him that.

And then I have a sudden seasick thought and push it

down hard, before Barb sees it in my face. *Professional.*
The word rings in my ear. *A professional hit. No, Jenny, not
now. Time to take control of the situation.* "All right, Barb. If
we're going to pretend to be civil to each other, by all
means, tell me why you've come."

She gives me a thin little chip of a smile. "I'm here because you're dying, Genevieve. I've come to save your life."

Somewhere in the Internet
Saturday 9 September, 2062
19:12:07:47–19:12:07:50

Richard P. Feynman watched Unitek's new code jockey
hand Elspeth up into a subway car for the second time in
as many nights. Anyone capable of observing him might
have seen a slight, amused smile curving the corner of his
mouth. He'd managed to eavesdrop on part of several con-
versations, now, between her and this Gabriel Castaign,
and he'd turned up the information as well that Castaign
was a long-term acquaintance of Casey's.

Besides, Leah Castaign was cheerful company, and
didn't mind talking about her family at all. And the whole
merry pattern was starting to fall into place in what he was
pleased to refer to as his mind.

And that's sloppy terminology, Richard.

He checked his other subroutines as the subway door began to slide closed, ran a few hundred thousand processes,
and checked them again. Everything was in order: he was
currently involved in about seventeen different projects, including eavesdropping on some of Valens's young, mostly
male study subjects. The boys were recruited from the suc-
cessful applicants to the Avatar pilot's school, and Feynman
found that particularly interesting.

He conversed as well with Leah Castaign at a study carousel on virtual Phobos, disguised as a fellow student. The moon was, incidentally, doomed by its own orbital trajectory. In a few million years, Mars would sweep the ragged little satellite from the sky.

Feynman had also devoted part of his attention to following various other individuals who had captured his interest—among them, Colonel Valens, Dr. Alberta Holmes, Master Warrant Officer Casey, and Detective Kozlowski. The gangster was harder to keep track of.

This sequence was repeated many, many times in the moments before the train lurched forward. Particularly interesting was the information provided by the fragment of himself exploring possible inroads to Unitek through the Avatar Gamespace. If anything, those pathways were better protected than the Internet routes he'd spent eight days haunting before he finally cracked them.

For the Feynman AI, eight days was an interminably long time. And his reward for that toil had been . . .

Nothing.

And the designs for an FTL drive—probably, as near as he could tell, the one being used for the starship in the virtual reality game—with no physics or explanation to back it up. Just schematics, as if such a thing could be built from a kit like a crystal radio set.

He was almost annoyed enough to risk contacting Dunsany directly. Problematic, when he knew Unitek had her under tighter surveillance than he did. He could hide the traces of his observations. Might even be able to risk contacting someone who Valens feared and needed less. Trying to speak to Elspeth would be akin to suicide, or surrender.

If he were a man, his stomach would have been twisted into a knot of frustration. Very few people in a long, recorded lifetime had had the wit to take him one-on-one, philosophically, and Feynman would have loved to have known what had changed Elspeth's mind, made her see him as a person as well as a program. He wanted to *talk* to her again. To argue. To sit down and have a good intellectual wrangle.

The surveillance was too tight. He might have hid a contact from electronic scrutiny. But Feynman—once through the firewall—had hacked their feed, and he knew that in addition to remote surveillance, Unitek was having her tailed, and that somebody monitored every Net access or phone call she made. He was beginning to suspect that Valens knew perfectly well he was out there. He just couldn't decide if Valens was trying to keep him out . . . or lure him in.

With a sigh, he shifted focus to Leah. She hadn't noticed the lapse. "What about you, Penelope?"

The character he was playing, of course. Wearing the mask of a sixteen-year-old, black-haired girl with a Grecian nose and flashing eyes, Feynman turned on his considerable charm. "I've got the neural implants, of course. Papa gave them to me for my fifteenth birthday. How can you hope to fly the big ship otherwise?"

He chose to feel a little bad, watching her face fall. His human self would have been unhappy, manipulating an adolescent girl. Feynman strove to remember these things. It was important to him, that taste of being human. "We could never afford that. But I still want to win."

"Of course we do. And you have to be careful, Leah"— Feynman leaned forward conspiratorially—"there are many people here who cannot be trusted."

"But you can?"

The AI laughed. "More than most. It is just a game to me, after all. I do not need the scholarships, or the other prizes. And I am not a *small* person who has need to cheat against other players to win."

"A small person?" Leah looked interested. He wondered

if her eyes in real life were quite so bright a green, her hair so blonde. He'd never know, really, outside of the camera lens, and he thought that should make him a little sad.

Feynman paused, as if Penelope cast about for words in an unfamiliar tongue. "Petty? A petty person? But it seems unfair that you, who do need the scholarships, cannot compete on equal terms for them. What a pity that we do not know anyone who works for Unitek."

"Why?" Leah's eyes seemed doubtful, but her icon was leaning forward.

Feynman tossed Penelope's dark curls over his shoulder. "I am not without skills," he said, as if it were a great admission. "But the computers that process most of the game information are very hard to get to."

He chuckled silently when Leah grinned.

1300 hours, Saturday 9 September, 2062
Niagara, New York
American Side

"Razorface, this is as far as you're coming."

We stand above the vast crescent of the falls, and the earth quivers underfoot. I smell wet air, the green leaves still trembling on the trees, sun on cut grass and concrete. He raises his left hand to point at the center of my face. I can just about hear him over the falling water. "You gonna walk in her trap just like that? A dog on a leash got more sense."

"Probably. But you have things to do back in Hartford, and I have places to be. Besides . . ." I lean in close, aware that Barb can read my lips. "I need somebody at my back. There's this thing with Mashaya, with Mitch. It's bigger than it looks, and it's a damn weird coincidence that my fucking *sister* shows up now, in the middle of all this other mess. It's too much coincidence, and I don't like it."

Silence falls like a curtain. I gnaw on my lower lip, fighting a spate of shivers that wants to run down my spine. It was a long, long drive up the northway, following Barb's sporty blue Honda Agouti while Face alternately slumped silent and belligerent in the passenger seat or argued ferociously against the plan.

"You say you ain't talked to her in years."

"I haven't. Not since 2039 or so." She got in touch with me after the terrorism trial where I was star witness for the prosecution against a very young man named Bernard Xu, but known to me as Peacock. I was on the news a lot, for a while. Between that and the visible cyberware—the combat enhancements were classified, of course—I had been a nine-day's wonder. Sometime later, I heard that Xu had died in prison at the age of twenty-five. Same age I was when I got my new arm.

I'm sure I don't need to spell out the details.

I finished out my twenty years in '49, took my pension, and got the hell out of Canada. Never went back except to visit Gabe and the girls.

And here I am, staring at the barbed wire and armed guards of the border from a hundred meters, my sister in her running car only a few steps away. I hear her music through the rolled-up window, but she doesn't shoot me the impatient glance I half expect. Barb has always been good at hiding things.

Razorface scowls, an imposing sight. "So how the hell does she know you're sick? How did she know where to find you?"

I've been wondering that myself, Face. And I wish I could tell him that I don't trust her, that I don't like her, that I know I'm being played. But I remember Simon lying to me about the red lines on the monitor, and I remember a phone call from Gabe Castaign, and the name Valens from his lips and now from Barbara's. And I have a nasty itchy back-of-the-neck premonition that it's something more than coincidence that thirty years of history are turning up on my doorstep all at once.

Much as I'd like to see Barb strung up by her own paste-colored intestines, she's my sister and I'm not going to speak ill of her to anyone. Maman wouldn't have liked it. *How a level head and a kind heart like Maman managed to raise a pair of sociopaths like Barb and me, I'll never know.* And these are all things I'd like to say to Razorface, but I wouldn't know where to start talking and he wouldn't know how to listen.

So I punch him in the arm with my good hand and what I say is, "Feed Boris for me."

Razorface puts a hand heavy as a slab of meat on my shoulder. "You keep in touch. I don't hear from you every twenty-four hours, I'm coming looking. Got it?"

I nod. "Go fight crime. I'm just going to a hospital, to see a man I hate." Scars fade. If you live long enough, everything fades. Face knows that.

I hand him the keys to the Bradford. He gives my shoulder an extra squeeze before he turns away. I watch him out of sight.

Then I turn around and get in Barbara's car.

We're strip-searched at the border, of course, but my CA veteran's card lets me keep my sidearm, along with a warning to keep it unloaded while traveling. Once the female sergeant in charge of the interview realizes where I fought and how badly I was wounded, she's interested and extremely polite. Barb, I note, passes through with a Unitek corporate ID card bearing the maple leaf.

Border Patrol doesn't see the need to take the car apart, thankfully, or we'd be there all day.

Back in the car and northbound again, I stretch out in the passenger seat and stare out the window at the trees. They look yellowed, unhealthy. None of the native species like the new weather much.

I feel much the same, fingertips of my right hand tingling and my left arm a dull, throbbing ache. I've never liked being a passenger when somebody else drives—or flies, either. I'd rather have the responsibility. Control freak? Probably.

"How did you hook up with Valens?"

She's got the car on autopilot, something else I never do, and she reaches out and flips the music off with one finger. At least she's not watching 4-D on the console. "He came looking for me," she says. She turns and examines me—a long, searching stare. "He figured if anybody could find you, I could, and he wanted to talk to you."

I grunt. "After twenty years?"

She lets her shoulders roll under that expensive green silk, both hands off the wheel. It makes me want to reach over and grab hold of the thing myself. Worse, I keep catching sight of her out of my bad eye, and the gun she's got tucked up under her left armpit makes a bulge that my targeting scope insists on painting dark red. *As if I didn't know the threat level already.*

Border Patrol didn't take her gun? Unitek must have even more juice than they used to. And they used to have plenty. Even before they started funding Canada's space program and a good chunk of its weapons research. "I know you're bullshitting me. You may as well spit it out."

She sighs. "Jenny, I'm telling you everything I know. I've had a chance to regret some things, all right? When Valens got in touch with me, it seemed like an opportunity to mend some fences. We're neither one of us getting any younger. And if you're as sick as he says . . ." Her voice trails off suggestively and she looks back at the road, resting her hands on the wheel. It rocks slightly as the car adjusts course.

If I'm as sick as he says. Because that leads us back to the main reason I'm in this car—the data she beamed to my HCD, the case histories and the unhappy prognosis. And Valens's recorded assurances that there was a treatment now for progressive neurological atrophy brought on by the primitive cyberware, and that the other three surviving recipients of the *original* central nervous system devices he pioneered were doing just fine with their upgrades.

He even said that in his recorded message. *"Upgrades."*

"We can reverse a lot of the scardown now, Casey. You'll be amazed. Obviously the data aren't in yet, but I'm theorizing we can get you another thirty years of mobility if everything goes well. And we've learned something about pain management, too."

Just so much software and hardware, wired into the wetware. Rip it out. Replace it. Whatever doesn't work is trash, throw it away.

I glance sidelong at Barb. "I heard you were trying to get ronin to go after me. You could have just put the word on the street that there was trouble and you needed to talk to me. I would have found you."

"And let the sharks know my baby sister might be less than able to defend herself?"

It wouldn't have stopped you back then. It didn't stop you back then. I remember what you were like, when Nell died. Or before I left home. But that's water under the bridge now, isn't it? "How did you know where to find me, Barb?"

She turned back and shot me a grin. "I put a tap on your buddy Castaign's phone, of course."

Just like that.

Except the numbers still don't quite add up. *And that's not what she said this morning.*

Charlie ran a hand across his clipped, thinning fair hair, scrubbing at the back of his skull. He lifted his shoulders and grimaced, then placed both hands on the edge of his desk and levered himself to his feet, blinking his contacts clear. An armed guard—taser only, in the airtight confines of the station—fell into step behind him as he left his lab. *One more thing to thank John for. A guy can't even take a piss around here anymore without an escort.*

As he was leaving the head, Colonel Valens stopped him in the hall. "Charlie."

"Evening, Fred." He couldn't remember how long he'd been on a first-name basis with the base commander, and wondered occasionally how he had ever found the man forbidding. "You look like a man with a mission, sir."

Valens bobbed his chin down, half a nod and an ironic smile. "All work and no play. How are you doing on the DNA sequencing?"

Charlie fell into step beside him. "It's not exactly DNA, although it is a long-chain organic molecule. And I've gotten distracted by something interesting, frankly."

"Interesting, or *interesting*?"

"Yes." He held his lab door open for Valens, noticing that the guard was standing just far enough away not to seem to overhear.

Valens preceded Charlie into the room. "Tell me more."

"Have you been reading my weeklies?"

"I've been up to my ass in paperwork, and a little brinksmanship over the salvage vessels. The Chinese have decided that testing our perimeters is not enough, and they've actually been sending in surface teams. But that's neither here nor there; tell me what is interesting."

Charlie kicked his chair to one side and perched on the edge of the desk, away from the interface plate. "We've been using a scanning electron microscope on some of the samples from the shiptree. Consensus is, it was in fact grown. And then reinforced. Let me show you something." With deft fingers, he tapped up the holographic display and pulled up an image queue.

"Surgical nanites," Valens said promptly. "Q class. Neurosurgical. I've used them."

"Right. Look at these."

"Holy . . . oh."

Charlie felt the grin pulling his lips wide when Valens came the last five steps to lean in close to the projection.

The colonel poked one finger into the hologram, singling out one magnified image among crawling dozens. "Those are from S-2? Are they as small as this indicator shows?"

"Yep. And still active."

"I can see that. Well." Valens leaned back on his heels, head shaking slowly. "These are responsible for the microreinforcement of the shiptree's hull."

"And what appears to be a sort of artificially enhanced nervous system. Which hooks up to the cables I had theorized were VR links. Yes."

The silence was gratifying. Charlie looked up from the display. Valens's face was still and pale. "You're suggesting," he said, "that that ship was—alive? That it still is?"

"Well"—Charlie tapped the interface off—"no. Or, more

precisely, somewhat less alive than a sea squirt is, after it becomes sessile and eats its brain. No—"he held up a hand to forestall questions. "That was a digression, and never mind the biology lecture right now. What I'm saying is that the thing has a rudimentary nervous system. What it means? Well, there's still research to be done. More interesting—"

Valens cut him off. "More interesting, you've discovered something that could revolutionize the treatment of spinal cord injury patients, if we can figure out how to use it. Is that where you were going with this?"

"Yeah," he said with satisfaction. "If we can figure out how to make these things, and make them safe for human use, not only can we fix what's broken . . . but, Fred. We may very well be able to make people smarter or faster, cure or fight a whole raft of neurological conditions . . . These babies are hot."

"So I see." Valens clapped him on the shoulder. "Send me the report. I'll contact Dr. Holmes at Unitek, and make sure you receive the credit your work is due. Charlie . . ."

"Yes?"

"Thank you." The colonel turned, springy on the ball of his foot in light gravity, and left.

8:30 P.M., Sunday 10 September, 2062:
Hartford, Connecticut
Sigourney Street
Abandoned North End

Razorface stopped under the rust-red metal awning, left hand on the pull of the big blue door. Derek and Rasheed waited across the street, leaned up against the brick of a tenement building beside the parked Bradford, which Razor planned on wheeling inside as soon as he got the bays open. The three of them should have been the only people around.

Razor glanced right, where three rolling metal bay doors were closed and locked in the cinder-block wall of the shop. Flaking paint scrolled across them. Razor knew the mural said something about auto body and appliance repair, but he wasn't sure exactly what.

"Might as well come on outta there," he said, taking his fist off the handle. And damned if it wasn't that cracker detective, Mitch, with the Polish last name, stepping out of the shadows of a doorway down the street and strolling up Sigourney with his hands stuffed into the pockets of his ratty corduroy pants and a cigarette hanging off his lower lip like he'd been intending to come over and say hi any minute.

Razorface felt his nostrils flare, and grinned. *Goddamned cops in my neighborhood. What is the world coming to?* The pig didn't even look him in the teeth when he smiled, and he had to give Kozlowski that. He was cool.

"Razorface," the cop said, drawing first one hand and then the other slowly out of his pockets and showing them empty. "Seen your boy Emery over in West Hartford the other day talking to a 20-Love. You keeping a close enough eye on him?"

Fucking cops, just trying to stir up shit. Razorface grunted and turned away.

Mitch kept talking. "Maker isn't home. And I need to talk to you about Mashaya Duclose."

"I got nothing to talk to nobody about," Razorface answered, setting the key card Maker had given him to the reader. The lock flicked back and Mitch's brow crinkled. Razorface's boys started moving forward from their place across the street, and Mitch took a slow step forward.

The pig's voice dropped and leveled, dead calm. "Where's Maker, Razorface? And how did you get her key?"

Razorface paused with the door half open. "Visiting the fam," he said. "I'm feeding the damn cat. Gonna bust me for it?"

"Her family." Mitch reached up and caught the door before Razorface could quite step inside and pull it shut behind himself. Over Mitch's shoulder, Razor saw his boys coming up on the cop. He shook them off with a minute jerk of the head, turning his attention back to the weedy little policeman, who was still talking. "Sister maybe? Black-haired gal about so tall?"

Razorface snarled silently, stepping through the door. "How much trouble Maker in, piggy?" Damned if he wanted to care, but he owed her. Owed her enough to come down himself to feed her goddamn cat because he knew she wouldn't want anybody but him poking around in her stuff, when by rights he'd rather set fire to the stupid animal.

The cop shrugged. "Let's go inside and talk about it, shall we?"

Their eyes met, pit bull and terrier coming to some unspoken agreement that didn't involve either one backing down. Ten long seconds later, Razorface stepped away and gestured Mitch through the door. There was no way he was turning his back on a cop.

Inside, he entered the code Maker had given him into the security system. A pressure seemed to come off his eardrums when the sonics powered down, and he made sure the door was locked behind them. Then he followed Mitch into the shop.

It looked just as it had before they left for New York. He saw Mitch examining things in that cop way of his, and grunted, bending down to unlock the ratproof safe holding the cat food. There was still a couple of days' worth in the automatic feeder, but Razorface topped it off anyway, ignoring the cop. He suspected Mitch was trying to get under his skin.

It wouldn't do to show it was working.

Boris came out from under the Cadillac and started winding around the cop's ankles, and Razor shook his head. Typical. Who was doing the feeding? And who was getting the thanks? He saw it as more or less a metaphor for the workings of the world, now that he thought about it.

Course, it might have something to do with the cat smelling Razorface's Rottweiler on his pants. Maybe.

"So what the hell do you want?" Enough quiet time. He wanted to get the conversation over with and get home to Leesie, although he wasn't about to let any of the boys know that. His jaw ached, as it did more and more these days, and his chest ached, too, no matter how much iron he lifted. The air sucked, was all it was. Better here in Maker's shop, though—she kept the scrubbers going.

Mitch opened his mouth to talk, met Razorface's eye dead on—and stopped. His jaw worked twice, and just as Razorface was about to turn around on his bootheel and stomp out, words followed. "Can we quit bullshitting each other and work together on this?"

Quiet and sharp. And Razorface started to snarl something about not needing no help from no fucking cops, and *Maker's gone, she's gone with somebody she hate. Somebody she scared of. Scared for me because of.*

He heard his own voice saying, "Fuck yeah."

Mitch got real quiet then, and looked down at his loafers. "It's bigger than street level. I think there's a fucking corporation involved. That won't stop my boss, if he can get good evidence—the chief is a straight-up arrow, and the commissioner, Dr. Hua— Well, you know about her. She's a bulldog. But I've been flat told to keep my nose out of this before I wind up fired and dead, not necessarily in that order. And I know—I know in my bones, man, this all has something to do with Maker, and we need to figure out, you and me, we need to figure out what and why and how. Because I don't goddamned know if we can trust her, and I don't know either if we can solve this without her. So we're on the same goddamned side."

Razorface thought about it, hard and slow, rubbing at a cramped muscle along the left side of his neck. *Wrong to let this cop in here like this.*

My kids're dying. My baby's aunt, this cop's old lady, she dead, too.

I thought she was working with this cop. But he's worried what she was up to.

Maker gave me the key. She trust me, I should trust her. But maybe she want me to look, couldn't explain. 'Cause some things you can't explain.

"Right," Razorface answered. "You inferrin' we should toss this place?"

"Yeah. Yes, sir, I am."

It was a nice thing, Razorface reflected a few minutes later, bending to pull a steamer trunk out from under Maker's cot, to hear a cop say *sir* and sound like he actually meant it. It was a big trunk, the ridged high-impact plastic shell battered and gouged, and it was secured with a thumb lock. "What about this?"

"Looks as likely as anything." Mitch was rooting through the roughly hung cabinets under the hand-built wooden table in the far corner. The cop sat back on his heels and Razorface heard a thump. "Damn!" Standing, rubbing the back of his head with one hand, Mitch walked back. He winced and leaned down. "Thumb lock."

"No shit," Razorface growled. "Tell me something useful." He shot a sidelong glance at the smug young cop.

Mitch didn't even have the decency to grimace a little as he squatted down beside the trunk and the gangster.

Mitch ran stubby fingers over the surface of the lock. "Dusty," he muttered. Boris, finished with his dinner, wandered over to scrub his face against Mitch's knee, and the cop scratched the cat absently with his other hand. "There's a trick to these old ones."

"Yeah? What's that?"

The cop shot him a grinning glance. "Watch this." Mitch slipped a cash chit and a switchblade out of his corduroys, flicking the latter open. He slid the thin slip of plastic into the crack between the lid and the body of the trunk until it butted up against the catch. Razorface watched the long narrow knife blade with interest. *Odd thing for a cop to have.*

Holding it by the black rubber handle, Mitch levered it behind the thumb lock. A fat blue spark jumped clear, and Mitch jerked his hand off the knife, which clattered to the floor. "Fuck!" he hissed, and then he cackled. "Hah!"

The bolt had disengaged for a moment when the lock shorted and reset, and Mitch's cash chit was now caught between the shaft and the lockplate. Grinning, he shook his shocked hand once and flipped the lid of the trunk back. "Holy . . ."

Face frowned at a sea of forest-green wool, fumes of cedar and camphor stinging his eyes. He had no idea what he was looking at. "What the hell is that? Uniforms?"

Mitch reached out and ran his fingers across the nap of the fabric, frowning for a long time before he nodded. "We shouldn't be in here, Razor," he said quietly.

"I know," Razorface answered. "You gonna tell me what I'm looking at?"

"Master Warrant Officer Casey." Mitch shook his head, letting the cloth fall back into tidy folds. "Damn. That

Honda was registered to a Barbara Casey. It is her sister. Or sister-in-law, I guess." Razorface watched as the cop lifted the clothes out carefully, one stack at a time. They were dusty and creased along the folds: these things hadn't seen sunlight or air in a very long time.

One layer down, and Mitch found other things: an unlocked flat tin with a stack of papers in it, two powder-blue berets, and a cardboard box. One of the berets was torn and bloody: the other looked as if it had just been pressed and packed away. The cop set those aside, also.

With a gnawing sensation that he recognized as nostalgia, Razorface reached out and touched the undamaged beret. "Seen those before," he said, thinking of acrid smoke and a slim young woman scrambling around piles of burning trash to drag his twelve-year-old self under cover. "What's in the box?"

"I bet I know," Mitch said. "Master Warrant Officer. That's a big deal, Razorface. Some kinda expert rank. I figured she was a sergeant or something."

"Private, when I met her." A moment too late, Razorface realized that he had broken the cardinal rule and volunteered information. "Box."

"I bet I know what that is. Hah. Yep." Mitch folded the flaps open and started lifting smaller boxes up into the light. "Shit, look at that."

A full hand of little flat cases. Razorface picked one up and angled it toward the light. A medal or something, hanging on a striped ribbon. "So?"

"I don't know what the half of these are for, Razor. But I bet the baby blue on these here is for U.N. combat service. And look at this. That one—the red maple leaf on the star. I know what that one is. That's valor in the face of the enemy. And a lot of these others just plain say what they're for . . . South Africa, Brazil. New England. She must have been here when Canada loaned us troops during the food riots back in the thirties."

"Yeah," Razorface said. "I told you I knew her from way back." Something uncomfortable writhed in his gut. This was a betrayal. It was wrong, and he knew it, but he shoved the thought back. *Son of a bitch. It's not like she's been telling me shit.*

Mitch was paying him no attention, fascinated with holding one bit of cloth and metal after another up to the light. "Ah. Here's another one with a maple leaf on it. Those must be the important ones, you think?"

"I guess." Less interested in military decorations, Razorface lifted the cardboard box out of the trunk and laid it on Mitch's lap. Underneath were a series of crumbling colored paper binders, and two poly bubbles with holographic data storage devices packed inside. The bubbles were marked with a caduceus, a maple leaf, and a green on beige spiral that Razorface didn't recognize.

"Jackpot," Mitch gloated.

Razorface felt his bowels clench at the note in the cop's voice. *This is the wrong thing to be doing,* he thought. *You don't do this kind of shit to your buds.* "Whaddaya mean, jackpot?"

"Medical records, Razor. And her service records, too. This is exactly what we needed. Fucking A good job, man. Fucking A."

There was something tucked in among them. Razor jerked his chin at the cream-colored bundle, as long as one of his own massive hands. "What that?"

"Let's see. Chamois? Deerskin, I guess." Deftly, the cop flipped the butter-soft skin open. "Oh, wow." His hands hovered over the contents of the package, almost as if he were afraid to touch.

Razorface leaned forward, over his shoulder, almost forgetting to breathe. "Necklace. I seen some kids wear 'em."

"Collar," Mitch corrected. "It's meant to be worn up around the throat." He lifted the long cool polished spill of beads up into the light. Purple and some white, with an almost phantom sheen. The edges were stained as if with fresh blood. "Wampum. It's polished quahog shells—purple for sorrow, white for purity of intention. The red stain means war."

"How you know that?"

"Hell, Razor, I'm from Ledyard. My best friend in high school was Pequot. He knew all about this stuff. This is square-woven: you do it with a needle. And—" Mitch's eyes dropped down, and Razor heard his breath catch in his throat. "Oh, fuck."

"What?"

"I can't touch that." Mitch gestured at the item that had been hidden under the wampum collar. It took Razorface a moment to sort out what he was looking at, and then he shook his head slightly. Purple and red and black beads wound tight-sewn around the shaft of a mottled brown feather that looked long and strong enough to have come from a turkey.

Carefully, as if touching a small child or something holy, Mitch folded the collar and laid it back in the square of doeskin. Face tilted his head to one side. "What's special about that?"

"It's an eagle feather," Mitch said, and covered it carefully before nestling it back in the bottom of the trunk. "And it worries me, because if she's earned that, and she's keeping it buried under her old clothes, it means she doesn't think she deserves it anymore. Which really makes me wonder *why*."

I worked places like this before I made it into the army, but mine were in Montreal. I keep thinking I see Chrétien out of the corner of my good eye, oiled black curls and superior smile, pretty face and scarred knuckles. Every time I turn to look, he's not quite there, and I'm not too upset about it.

He'd be somewhere around sixty now. Imagine that.

"Aren't you kind of old for a cyborg?" The bartender checks me out critically, an up-and-down sweep of the eyes from scarred black boots to ragged-cut crown of hair.

I feel naked without my sidearm. "It wasn't voluntary." I'm too fucking worn through the tread and down to the cable to smooth his ruffles, and I don't give a damn what he thinks of me anyway. "Bourbon, please." I don't really mean please, and he frowns as he pushes the booze across the bar at me and takes my cash card. A long pause while he reads it lets me take in the scenery. It's worth observing.

When I was in the service this was a cop-and-soldier bar, and it had a different name. Now it's home to a new crowd, with a taste for the self-conscious archaism of the name and the razor-edged five-minutes-in-the-future of the decor. A body-modified crowd, which reflects extremes of bio and mecha engineering in the black mirrored floor.

We don't see this sort of thing in Hartford. Some are

cosmetic mods: cow-dark eyes, lips that scintillate with purple and orange light. Many more have the functional ones: I spot somebody with a second pair of prosthetic arms—not armored like my steel hand, but a color cycling pattern of LEDs—giving the appearance of some Hindu god. I bet those aren't really hardwired on. Another patron, straddling the difference, has a steel snake, hood-flaring and hissing, raising its head from the unzipped fly of his pants. It's fascinating in a train wreck sort of way, but I don't want him to catch me looking and think I have more than an academic interest.

Some of these guys make Razorface look like the girl next door. *Freaks.*

Hey. Look who's talking, freak.

The music is three generations of loud removed from the last kind I knew how to dance to. Someday, the noise will grow so noisy that the next generation will have to start playing polkas and Mozart to rebel. I take my drink and sit down across from Barb, in the quietest corner, which isn't.

Barb, what the hell are you thinking, meeting Valens here? But I know: she's thinking that I won't stick out like a sore thumb. In fact, I fit right in. Except I'm thirty years too old.

It's a good place for the *spirited* sort of . . . negotiations . . . I'm expecting. Two decades and more, and I still know what she's thinking. Except when I don't.

"Vous êtes sûre qu'il vient?" I surprise myself—the question comes out in French. Québecois, anyway. *You're sure he's coming?* Which reminds me of a joke.

"Je suis sûre," she answers in the same language, and I have a sudden sharp-as-a-flashback memory of Maman singing us McGarrigle Sisters songs when she had us in the bathtub. She loved old folk music—français, English, the Haudenosaunee tales her grandmother told her. "Il est toujours ponctuel. I bet he's here at five minutes to the hour."

He will be, too. Salaud. "Look, Barb . . . when he gets here. I want to talk to him alone."

She sips white wine and makes a face. What she expected in a joint like this, I have no idea. At least she's traded in her carefully tailored suit for blue jeans and white cotton. "Are you going to stick a knife in him, Jenny?" Her eyes sparkle as she smiles. Somehow, Barb got all the charm.

We split the mean down the middle, but I like to think I got the slightly smaller half. I like to think a lot of things, really. Nell was the sweet one, my little baby doll, youngest of us three. "Not immediately." I sip my drink, which is less watered than he might have gotten away with. "I'll let him talk for at least five minutes first."

Barb sighs and shrugs, rolling her eyes in that way that says, plain as if she wrote it on the wall, that she doesn't know why she puts up with my obstinate, intransigent, insubordinate self. She leans forward, flashing red and orange lights daubing her handsome features like warpaint, like the glow of something important burning. "Quoi que, Geni. Just remember that he's dying to help, and try not to be too much of a . . . une chienne." *Hah. She was going to say "putain."* "He really does care."

It's twittering, and I tune her out. *Rien, rien. Je ne regrette rien.* Yeah. As if. *I am not an exception. I am a statistic. And forgetting that is a good way to wind up a permanent statistic.*

It's something you learn the hard way, if you learn it at all. There are two ways to cope with combat. Well, that's an outright lie. There are probably thousands. There are two ways that I've seen work pretty well and still leave you with something like a soul to call your own when it's over. If it's ever *really* over.

One is denial. Convince yourself that you're bulletproof, ten feet tall, and it'll never happen to you, and sometimes you can even convince the world for a while. The other way to do it is to decide that the worst has already happened, and you're living on borrowed time, and when your number is up, your number is up. They say you never hear the one that has your name on it, but brother, I can tell you, it isn't true. You hear it coming every time you close your eyes.

Barb's saying something, but the words mean nothing. I lean back in my chair, raise one hand to shut her the hell up, shaking my head. Something's rising up in the back of my consciousness, something big and bright and feature-less as a drought-seared plain under an African sun.

Merci à Dieu. Pretoria. 2037. I know it's a flashback. I know it down in my bones and it doesn't make a damned bit of difference, the same way it doesn't when I know it's a dream and I know I'm going to die, because I always do. Every time.

And every time, I'm right.

And the heat is a forge during the day, the cold a quenching at night. The land is an anvil and the sun a hammer in the hands of a lame god. Sun setting gory as the weeks before, smearing pale walls with bloody hand-prints. Before the drought, before the heat, the hills over-looking the city were green and rolling, hedged in some sort of purple flowers. I've seen pictures.

Three ammo haulers, two staff vehicles, two A.P.C.s, and an Engineering Corps tank with a bulldozer blade on the front—a Christmas carol in Hell. We've got air cover as well, a pair of gunships and a spotter. I'm shepherding the con-voy down the already ruined road north of the city—shiny, modern city: good university, once. We couldn't get through without the tracked vehicles now. My tactical dis-play shows clean and green: the first clue something's gone sour is a trail of smoke from the roof of a nearby building, the death gasp of one of the deadly, fragile helicopters shredding at the seams. Then the explosions start in earnest.

Anything hauling explosives is not where you want to be during an artillery barrage. The guy ahead floors it, and I do, too.

Gunfire. *Ambush.* I hear the whine of the fifty cal on the escort tank, the unforgettable rumble of its enormous engine. The guy sitting next to me is terse and professional into his throat mike, bringing the TOC up to speed on where we are and what we've run up against. A second after tactical gets the information, my heads-up stains red with confirmed hostile presence. *Nice to know now.* I wrench the big machine aside as a crater opens up seemingly between my feet, black hot plastic slipping through my hands.

That's what brings me back to the more presently real, the here-and-now: splintering plastic, and Barb's hand crushing my right one. She leans across the table now, yelling into my face, and I blink twice and try to shake it off, eyes closed, head tossing.

"Jenny, dammit, talk to me!" And damned if she doesn't actually look and sound concerned.

I look down. I've cracked the high-impact plastic table, left a spiderweb of lines lacing it where my steel hand clutched tight. "Fuck me," I say.

"Are you all right? It looked like a seizure or something. Shit. Valens can wait, we can go to the hospital . . ."

"No." Not NDMC. Not if they paid me. Not even the new Toronto General. "It was just a senior moment. Panic attack. It's all right now."

She sits back on her bench, but her hand stays on mine. "Sure?"

"Damn sure." I extricate my hand, which is shaking, and down the bourbon in a gulp.

"Casey. You know better." And I'm so rattled I don't

even hear *him* come up behind me. My hand slaps the thigh of my BDUs, where my sidearm should be, and I curse Canada briefly. I never would have thought I'd feel—naked—walking around Toronto without a gun strapped to my body.

Valens had been five measured paces away when he spoke to me. Smart. He covers two of those steps while I slide out of the booth and stand, turning to face him. He has enough sense not to stick his paw out. I'd rather kiss a snake than shake that man's hand.

"Fred." There's something satisfying about not having to call him *Captain*. Colonel, I guess it is now, although he's out of uniform, and he *does* stick out like the emerald stud on Razorface's nose. His hair has gone a gleaming silver that picks up the flickering colors of the strobes, but the cut is less conservative than it used to be. He looks fit and solid for an older man. "You gonna have a seat?"

"If you don't mind?" He gestures me back into the booth as Barb stands.

She takes a step away. "I'll leave you two to talk things out without my interference. Frederick, I'll come by your office tomorrow, if that suits."

"Very well. Thank you, Barbara." The smile he gives her makes me want to break his teeth. But then, the fact that he's still breathing makes me want to break his teeth, so I guess it's no big shock.

Barb nods to me before she walks away, leaving her wineglass on the table. My eyes don't follow. I'm looking at Valens, who is settling himself onto the loathsome vinyl across from me.

He takes a breath and looks me dead in the eye before he speaks. I won't look down. "You look better than I expected. Who's been handling your follow-up?"

"A friend of a friend." *I'm telling you nothing.* "Barb says you've got something that can help with the interface breakdown I'm supposed to be experiencing."

"Supposed to be? No symptoms yet?"

I wish I hadn't finished my bourbon. I push the glass away so that I won't fiddle with it. Whether it's sitting across from Valens for the first time in over a decade or something else, I'm abruptly aware of all the great and small pains at war in my body. I open my mouth to lie, and then have to swallow the bitterness of not being able to do it.

I hate the man with every fiber of my being. And sure as taxes, I owe him my life, or at least the fact that I'm sitting there across from him and not rotting in a hospital bed. And I might not have minded, if it had all stopped there, even though they didn't ask. The army doesn't *have* to ask.

The thing is, the first time your body just starts reflexively *doing* things that are hardwired into a nanoprocessor relay and not your own nervous system, it can take you by surprise. Especially if you haven't been warned what to expect. Especially if it ends with people getting killed.

Funny thing that. Things that end with people getting killed never seem to end with the *right* people getting killed.

"Yeah," I say, after a long pause. "I'm having symptoms."

He nods. He even looks genuinely concerned. Hell, he may be. I'm the man's great triumph, after all.

"We've discovered an ongoing myelin breakdown that seems to be triggered by the electrical impulses from the nanoprocessors." Valens never sugarcoated anything in his life. It may be his best trait.

I lean forward to listen more closely. "You're talking about loss of nerve function. Paralysis?"

"Eventually. Numbness in the extremities first. Loss of motor control, body temperature regulation. And once the dampers in your implants start failing, pain like you wouldn't believe."

"I'd believe a lot of pain, Doc."

He winces, touches his forehead. "There's also a larger neurological issue. The brain wetware, that needs to come out. We've lost three of your group so far because of synaptic dysfunction."

"Define dysfunction for the interested observer." *Right, I'm a blasted museum piece. So nice to be reminded.* A sense of detachment is stealing over me, a sensation I used to feel a lot more. It's been creeping back lately.

"Basically, a complex of problems. Something like old-time Alzheimer's, if you remember what that is, coupled with a lot of random synaptic firing. Forgetfulness. And hallucinations."

"Flashbacks."

"Yes. Essentially, you're looking at senile dementia in about five years. What are you now, fifty?"

"Forty-nine. There's a cure for Alzheimer's."

"Early stage, yes." He nods, pushing Barb's wineglass out of the way. "We plan to use the same tech to repair the damage caused by the continued insult to your nervous system. Nanosurgery. As a minor bonus, we can fix a lot of the scardown, too—and the more superficial scarring. The stuff you didn't want to go reconstructive on, way back when. No knives."

The skin at the base of my neck creeps. "Just bugs crawling around under my skin."

Open hands, and earnest expression. He's that kind of distinguished good-looking that wins twenty-year-old trophy wives. I wonder if Valens has a wife. I never asked. He doesn't wear a ring—but then, he's a surgeon. "It's the same tech they're using for the neural VR interfaces."

"Safe?"

"No more dangerous than giving birth to twins."

"If it doesn't work?"

"Two possibilities. If it really fucks up, vegetative state."

"Charming. What's possibility number two?"

"A ventilator and a hospital bed."

"Ah." I close my eyes. I try to think back to the last time I felt warm and safe and halfway in control of the future, and I can't. Maybe when I was seventeen, eighteen. There was a boy named Carlos. He wanted to marry me. It didn't work out that way. *Flashbacks?* "What if it works?"

Valens taps the table with his left hand, and I wonder if this is going better than he expected. I haven't broken his shoulder again. Yet. "Less pain. Better mobility. Less hardware. The nanites can be tailored to consume a lot of the primitive wetware and reuse the materials. Also, your life span extended from an estimated five to ten, to indefinite."

"I see." One last question. And only one.

He holds his breath.

I chew on the inside of my cheek for a minute before I ask it. "What's it gonna cost me, Fred?"

"It will cost you. I'm not going to lie about that. We need your help." He leans forward and spreads his hands wide, broad fingers that don't look deft enough for a doctor. "We need volunteers."

"I'm too old for fighting, Valens." It's an effort to remember to use his first name. It's an effort not to call him *Captain.* Colonel. Whatever. Damn. I was in the army a hell of a long time. Running my thumb over the surface of the table, I study the smear of skin-oil it leaves.

Valens coughs behind his hand. "Are you too old for flying?"

"I . . ." Whatever I expected to say dies in my mouth. "*Flying?*"

His face goes still and serious. His voice drops. He leans forward, touching his earcuff, and unclips his HCD. I pull mine out so he can beam me a secure conversation channel, and his voice comes in my ear when it comes again. "Everything from here on in is classified. Got it?"

I set my unit on the table and nod. "Yes."

"We're testing some new training techniques. Virtual reality. Wetwired remote interface for the next generation of combat aircraft. Tanks, too." I look away. I was a drill instructor for a while, too, until it got to be too damned depressing and I asked to be transferred back into the field, which is how I wound up flying medevac. I'd been a driver before, but enhanced reflexes and my mechanical aptitude make for a *very* good pilot. "So we won't have to send kids out to die in them anymore."

He's lost me until he says that last. I've been a rhesus monkey, and it gets real old, real fast.

And he knew it, dammit. He knew it when he cast the fly, and he knew it when he set the hook. I can see the fucking calculation in his hazel eyes, gray now in the flickering light. My lips curl back into something that might almost look like a smile if you didn't know me very well. "Wetwired. What does that mean?" I know what *wired* is. Wired is me.

He reaches across the table and rests one hand on my shoulder. "When we rebuild the interfaces, we engineer in some of the equipment that Venus Consolidated and Unitek have designed for their VR interfaces."

"Venus . . . that's a sex toy company." I hear my own disbelief, and curiosity burns in the back of my throat.

"Yes. But Unitek owns them, and they're an industry leader in virtual reality applications. And we're working with Unitek."

"Of course you are." Unitek engineers designed my arm, and the neuralware that augments my reflexes in response to any perceived threat. Unitek owns the pharmaceutical company that makes Hyperex. And Unitek . . .

assisted . . . Canada during the bloody, bloody Malaysian-PanChinese wars that broke out when the oceans started to rise. Later, they funded much of Malaysia's economic recovery, to the chagrin of the Chinese government, which still likes to consider Southeast Asia its private preserve. It's interesting history, if you go in for that sort of thing. "All right. Forget about the high-tech vibrators. Explain to me this wetwired thing."

"You've heard of the new generation of neural?"

I shrug. "A little. I know I've got a collection of silicon cones buried in my gray matter and that's not how you guys do things anymore."

"We have much less invasive techniques," he answers, proud as if he pioneered it himself. "Nanosurgery. No incision—nothing goes in but bots a few microns across. We build, essentially, artificial synapses. The body hardly registers it as an insult. People are doing it for recreational purposes. Four-year-old technology, perfectly safe."

"Why would *anybody* do that to herself?"

Valens waves his hands around, almost forgetting to subvocalize. His voice through my ear cuff is not quite painfully loud. "All sorts of reasons, but the primary is for a more seamless access to the gamespaces. As with the invention of the wheel, the most novel technologies are used for toys first."

Holy hell. This is his baby. "So you want to restructure my *brain*?"

"No. We want to clean out the mess of substandard wiring we slapped up in there almost a quarter century ago, and put in something that won't cripple you. Remember when you first got your arm?"

My head jerking up and down feels stiff as a marionette's.

"Remember I promised you someday you'd have sensation? Heat, pressure?"

Again, the dull, disbelieving nod. *He can't be serious.*

"We can do that now. Now that we have the tech to re-place your old implants, you can have what these guys have." His sweeping gesture takes in the room. "Without the stigma." He glances around the room, real distaste wrinkling an arrogant nose.

I follow his gaze. I try not to pass judgment, but . . . a girl with tiger stripes and a lashing tail catches my eye and winks broadly. I glance away.

"We can even make it look more or less like a real hand, now. And once you're on board and we get you a security rating, I'll tell you what we're going to do with it." His eyes sparkle. His voice shakes. Despite myself, despite my ambivalence, I find myself catching his excitement. And damned if that hook doesn't bite harder with every tug he gives it.

Does it make any difference in the long run if you know you're being manipulated? "Is this government funded or corporate?"

"Both," he says. "It's big, Casey. That's all I can tell you. And your old friend Gabe Castaign is working with us, al-though he doesn't know the half of it yet. I wanted you on board first."

And of course, the most important question of all. "Why me?"

I almost think he's rehearsed the speech, but the passion in it rings sound. "I know you," says the man who pushed me into killing a boy I could have liked, the man who gave me back my legs and my left hand and whatever life I have left. "You were a damn fine soldier. Damn fine pilot, too—and your reflexes are the selling point. Natural and aug-mented, you test high. And you've made adaptation to your wetware like I never would have believed. It always burned

me that I couldn't do more for you. And now I can. I just
need you to help me justify spending the money."

"Justify saving my life."

"Yes." He reaches out one last time and lays his hand on
my steel one. I can't feel a thing. My teeth are chattering.

"You still have your pilot's license, Casey?"

Holy hell. He means it. "No."

"We'll get you recertified. Retrained if need be."

"You want me as a civilian employee?"

"That's what we did for Castaign."

Breathe out. Breathe in. *Think, Jenny Casey.*

"Jenny. Think about the pain."

I'm thinking. I'm thinking about a pseudosenile dementia, too. And the fact that my gun is still out in Barb's car
and I could just swallow a bullet if it really gets too bad.

If I remember how to pull the trigger by then. I always
was too stubborn for my own good. He's still watching
my face. *Gabe is working for him. Does that mean things
have changed?* No. Gabe has his reasons, and they're purely
pragmatic and eleven years old. "You're not telling me
everything."

"You know it, Casey. You don't get the rest until you
sign on the dotted line."

Which is not what I wanted to hear at all.

Counting coup was cleaner. People can cope with that
kind of war. Of course, then you get into all the other ways
of showing brave, and some of them you don't want to
know too much about. Like what I suspect I'm going to
wind up doing before the year is out.

Valens has something to do with all this, and Valens is going to be hell to put a stop to. There's not going to be any
justice—not for Mitch, not for Face. Not for Peacock, either,
or Nell. Me? I don't much think I deserve *justice.* I more or
less got what was coming to me, one way or another.

I can't take Valens down. But I can show him, maybe, I *could* have done something. Show his handlers, whoever they are. Show the press. And if they are seen to know, they may have to *do* something.

Status games.

Maybe that will be enough. Fred Valens in front of a military court. It's got a nice justified feel of symmetry to it.

"All right," I tell him. "I'm in, Fred. Where do I sign?"

We're not cold inference machines. Emotions are critical to our rational thinking.
—Dr. Cynthia Breazeal, "Kismet Project" artificial life researcher

Somewhere in the Internet
Sunday 10 September, 2062
23:00:22:01–23:00:22:05

The multivariable codes Valens and Casey used were supposed to be nearly unbreakable. And they were. Unless you happened to have loaded a subtle little worm into both of their HCDs.

Pilots and starships and VR, oh my.

Feynman almost sang to himself, there in his silent stream of ones and zeroes. *Colonel Frederick Valens, you slick son of a bitch. I know what you're up to.*

And there is no way in hell you're going to the stars without me.

0300 hours, Monday 11 September, 2062
Marriott Inn
Toronto, Ontario

I spent the first night in Toronto in Barb's guest bedroom. The second night, I get a hotel room and call Razorface so he can fight with me about coming home. Afterward, I sit up by the window with all the lights turned off, watching the rain fall and the headlights roll by fifteen floors below.

I'm drinking more than I should, and I don't care. Room service sends coffee even at three in the morning.

There are reasons I don't come back to this city often.

I can't stop thinking about them now.

23 years earlier:
1300 hours, Friday 11 March, 2039
Lake Simcoe Military Prison
Lake Simcoe, Ontario

I pass through checkpoints without comment. There are professional nods from well-disciplined guards who will not meet my eyes. They stare at the shining brass of my buttons, the shining steel of my left hand, the still-unfamiliar three golden hooks on my shoulder, differenced with a gold maple leaf. I imagine I hear whispers after I pass, but the truth of the matter is, to them I am a hero. Half a legend. The only whispers following me are my own.

I haven't the damnedest idea why I'm here, and I know even less about why he agreed to see me. In an honest moment, I might say I was here to punish myself, but this isn't an honest moment.

I wear formal dress rifle green, a conifer color, unchanged from the days of the unified Canadian Armed Forces. The beret is black, not blue, and I think I'll never wear the United Nations colors again. It's not the first time I've been wrong.

I am patted down and wanded by polite, impersonal women, and at last shown into a bare room with a single plastic chair on each side of a transparent wall of inch-thick shatterproof plastic. The last guard shuts the door behind me, softly, like a benediction.

Bernard Xu is already in his chair on the other side of that wall. There are holes drilled through the plastic, and I go and stand before them, feeling as if my guts are wrapped around a slowly twisting spike.

"Jenny," he says, standing up. Caution orange, his jumpsuit clashes with my formal green. They've unshackled his hands, at least. He shuffles forward, chains rattling, and lays both hands flat against the invisible wall. Skin pressed bloodless by the barrier, he leans into it.

"Peacock." He doesn't look like a peacock anymore. When we met, he stunned me with flamboyance. Fabulousness. Hair in a half-dozen shades, clothing shredded and tattered and fanciful. He seems somehow deflated now, dark and forgotten already. He's not a big man, not small, well made and fine featured. Barely a man at all— he turned twenty during the trial. Five years younger than I am. Guilty. I convicted him, and he did everything I said he did. We both know what the sentence will be.

Canada, clinging to civilization as the world crumbles around its ears and the government becomes more desperate, more draconian, more *owned*—Canada still does not have a death penalty.

He's going to die in jail.

And yet the look he gives me drips sorrow rather than reproach. He's silent, reaching toward me. I place my steel hand over the shadow of his, a gesture, touch impossible. I think of tapping on glass to get a captive thing's attention, and I almost gag.

"Bernard," I say. "I wish it could have been different."

A nod, philosophical. "Me, too. You were something special, Jenny girl."

"What do you mean?" I step away from the glass and let my eyes fall from his, watching him out of my peripheral vision.

A dirty little smirk and he cocks his head to one side. "You know what I mean."

My breath snags and tears on something broken in my chest. "If I had known what you were, I never would have let that happen."

"Really? That would have been a pity."

"You could have used it against me at the trial, you know."

"My lawyer wanted to."

"Oh." The winch pulling my guts out through my belly button tightens another twist. "Do you want me to tell you I regret it? Would it be better if I said *I'm sorry*?" His gaze hasn't shifted from me when I look back.

"I don't need to be told," he says, the taint of mockery leaving his voice. "I hope he's worth it."

"Who?"

"That army captain you're in love with. I hope he's worth it. They were going to send him to jail, weren't they? And in return, you gave them me. You gave them yourself, too, whether you realize it or not. You could have changed the world. But you can't go to the press now."

"I know." Peacock had wanted to me to rip the whole bloody thing wide open, to tell the world about the experimentation. About what Valens and the army had done to me, without ever asking.

It's too late now. I've taken the damned shilling and kissed the fucking book and signed the paperwork they put in front of me. Consent is consent.

Bernard Xu has been convicted of terrorism, and Gabe Castaign is not in jail for treason. Has been dating a nurse. I'm his best friend. He's an officer, and he saved my life. He's never going to know.

I turn away, pressing nerveless cool steel fingers against my eyes. The one-inch shatterproof is a joke. I could put my left fist through it like a baseball bat through a car window.

"Did I buy you what you needed, Jenny Casey?"

The steel door clangs behind me like a coffin lid coming down.

8:00 A.M., Monday 11 September, 2062
Jefferson Avenue
Hartford Hospital Medical Offices
Hartford, Connecticut

That has to be him. Mitch opened the door of his dented baby-shit-brown Dodge and unfolded, sliding his wallet into his left hand.

"Dr. Mobarak?" Mitch made him at five foot ten, two hundred, late thirties, Middle Eastern, balding on top with good shoes and a gray sportcoat. It was the quizzical expression as he turned that caught Mitch's attention, however, the first calm look and then a little flash at the back of the eyes, like a man remembering that he was supposed to be scared of something.

"Who are you?" The doctor took a step backward, toward the doorway of the brownstone office building.

Out of the corner of his eye, Mitch saw an alert security guard start forward, and casually extended his hand and flipped the wallet open, showing Mobarak his badge. "Detective Mitch Kozlowski. I need to talk to you about one of your patients."

"Detective?"

Mitch expected the doc to relax when he saw the ID. Instead, Mobarak glanced over his shoulder at the door, looking for an escape route. Mitch's eyes widened a fraction of an inch. *Interesting.* "Hartford P.D. May I have a minute of your time?"

Mobarak gnawed his lip. "I suppose. I'm very busy, of course"—*aren't they always*—"but I can certainly make time for Hartford's finest. Can we keep it brief?"

The security guard got close enough to make out the badge and relaxed incrementally. Mitch shot him a smile and got a slight nod in return. "Absolutely, Dr. Mobarak. And thank you."

The guard held the door for them as they went inside. Mobarak was a neurologist; Mitch knew that much from Maker's—from *Genevieve's*—medical history. He also knew a lot of other things now, although he couldn't rightly say he understood half of the medical stuff. He did know that her service record was impressive, however, and he'd used that information to pull up the details on her moment of infamy: the Xu trial.

And *that* had blown his socks out through the holes in his shoes.

According to the court records, some twenty years before, Corporal Casey had been approached by representatives of a terrorist cell. Acting under orders, she had infiltrated the group and brought down most of the leaders. Two of the medals in her trunk had been awarded for that incident, and Mitch had noticed that the presentation cases were still sealed shut.

Her testimony had been instrumental in obtaining the conviction of their leader, and three consecutive life sentences—despite the tenor of the day. Which, Mitch was learning, had been a bit different than modern times. Despite the teasing he'd given her, Mitch realized he'd never thought of Maker as anything more than an enigmatic old woman with a conscience and a lot of friends. Learning that she was a bonafide war hero—well. He hadn't yet been born when Genevieve Casey had been in Toronto, recovering from having most of her left arm blown off with a shotgun, serving in whatever capacity she was still capable.

That gave him a little bit of pause if he thought about it hard, so he didn't. He had a murder to solve. Maybe a few more to prevent. And he was starting to think he had a friend to protect—whether she wanted his help or not.

He held his tongue while Mobarak keyed them into the office, waiting until the door was latched behind them. Then he took a breath, ready for a fight. *I'm willing to bet he thinks of her as more than a patient, too. She's got that— ability to inspire loyalty. I bet she was a damned good sergeant.* Mitch knew why that was. Because despite all the doubts of his rational mind, Mitch still suspected that Maker would put herself between him and a bullet.

Bitching the entire time. "Doc, how well do you know Genevieve Casey?"

He wasn't expecting the doctor to slowly turn around, slipping his key into his pocket, and chuckle. "Somehow, I knew this was going to be about her. What's she been accused of?"

Mitch shook his head. "It's not that at all. Doctor . . . hell." He wasn't sure what it was, but something about Mobarak's half-amused, half-annoyed expression and significant glance at the wall clock put him at ease. "I'm a stupid shit, Doc, and I'm going to trust you. I'm here mostly as a friend of Maker's—of Casey's—and only half as a cop. She's in trouble and I want to find out what sort, so I can back her up. Do you believe me?"

And if I find out I'm wrong, and she had something to do with Mashaya getting shot, I'll put the bullet in her head myself.

"What kind of trouble?"

"Vanishing without leaving a forwarding address and ditching her friends kind of trouble."

"Kidnapped?"

"Not . . . as such." Mitch shrugged. "She went with somebody. As far as I know there was no threat of force. But that's not the only kind of duress."

Mobarak thought about it for a long while before he answered. "I can't share confidential information with you, of course."

"Of course," Mitch answered, and realized that he'd been holding his breath. "Look, Doc. How long have you got to talk?"

Mobarak shrugged. "Half an hour. I'll make the time. I feel really bad about Jenny. She's been through a lot, and she's awful brave about it. It's unprofessional, but . . ."

Mitch grinned. "You get attached. Yeah, I know. Me, too. Come on, let's make some coffee or something."

"There's a break room around the corner." Mobarak waved Mitch ahead. Industrial gray carpeting scuffed under his loafers. The door was locked; Mobarak keyed them in. "Do you take anything in your coffee?"

"Black."

"You *do* know Jenny." Mobarak pressed the button on the coffeemaker. It whirred, weighing and grinding beans. Steam hissed, and the musky, silky aroma filled the room.

"Jenny? That's what you call her?"

"It's her name." The doctor shrugged, pulling plain, too-small ceramic mugs from the cabinet over the sink. "She's been kind enough to donate a lot of time to my research. We go way back."

"Huh." Mitch accepted the mug that the doctor extended to him. It warmed the palms of his hands when he cupped it, and—sudden odd thought—he wondered if Maker ever missed that sensation. "I never would have thought her the sort for charity work. No, actually, I'm full of shit, Doc."

"What do you mean?" Mobarak lounged against the counter, stirring his own drink with a plastic straw.

"Oh, Maker. I always thought she was an army doc or medic of some kind. She's always fixing up some kid with a busted finger or something. Amazing she finds the time to keep her business running."

"She was an EMT," Mobarak answered. "I suppose I can tell you that. Special forces first. When she returned to active duty, she managed to pull a combat exemption and flew medevac."

Mitch nodded, smiling. "I just found that out yesterday, actually, along with all sorts of other things I didn't know. And I'm guessing she's really sick now because of it, isn't she?"

The doc took a big breath and held it—confirmation—but shook his head. "You know I can't tell you that."

"All right." Mitch swirled strong, hot coffee around his mouth, swallowed, and sucked his teeth. *Thank God this guy sucks at keeping confidentiality.* "Look, do you know anything about her having a sister?"

"No next of kin, as far as I've heard. She's got an emergency contact listed, but it's a friend in Montreal. An old army buddy, I think."

"Well, fuck."

"Huh. Is this *only* about Jenny, Detective?"

"No." Mitch turned aside and kicked the leg of the cheap card table shoved into the corner. "I think whatever has her on the run has something to do with my . . . with a friend of mine, a fellow officer. Who got killed." He heard the pain in his own voice and despised it for a weakness.

Whatever. Mobarak took a rattling breath. "Look." The doctor shook his head. "She mentioned you to me. If you're the same Mitch. And I can't—I can't share information with you. I'm already over the line."

Mitch heard the *but* in his voice and leaned forward, holding his breath, blinking hard before he glanced back up and caught the doctor's eye. He nodded, afraid to encourage him.

"But I'll call that contact. See what I can do about getting her a message. Okay?"

It would have to do.

Thirteen years ago:
in the Heavy Iron
University of Guelph
Tuesday 7 June, 2049
1:00 p.m.

"I am not," he said at last, "Richard Feynman."

If the coffee Elspeth was sipping had been real, it would have come out of her nose. "Excuse me?"

The physicist smiled and ran a hand through tousled gray hair. "Because Richard Feynman died fifty-three years ago."

Her cup rattled on the table when she set it aside. "All right, Dick," she told him. "You got me. You're not Feynman. So tell me what the hell you are."

"I don't know," he said carefully.

Elspeth Dunsany grinned hard. "Postulate, Dick."

His hands tapped his knee, restless, seeking. "I have always held reliance on paranormal explanations to indicate a lazy mind. But I sure as hell feel like Dick Feynman." He shrugged. "Even though Richard Feynman is dead. So I'm left with interesting gaps in my logic."

Elspeth raised an eyebrow inside her VR suit. Her image mimicked the motion. "How did you find out that you were dead?" she asked him.

He held out a portfolio. "I found the library. These clippings were in there. Along with more information about my compatriots—and myself—than I ever imagined existed." He sighed. "It's a shame that I never got to Tanna-Tuva."

Allen-Shipman Research Facility
St. George Street
Toronto, Canada
Late morning, Monday 11 September, 2062

Gabe Castaign moved his long-fingered right hand through the three-dimensional interface, directing data streams with thoughtless dexterity. With the left one, not looking, he flipped open a box of mints and picked one out, sucking it off of his fingertips. Elspeth, leaning over his shoulder, caught a sharp scent of wintergreen. "May I have one of those?"

"Sure." He slid the tin into reach. "My kids made a big

deal about how much I smelled like garlic when I got home last night. I figured I'd take pity on you."

"Kids?" They'd had dinner again the night before—Sunday dinner. Thinking of garlic and indulging, Elspeth took two of the hard little candies, wincing at their strength.

"Girls," he said with a grin. Still without glancing away from his monitor plate, he touched another icon. The interface plate shimmered, and a hologram of two golden-haired adolescents materialized over the far left corner of the desk. One was perhaps thirteen, the other ten or eleven. The taller girl leaned smiling into her sister, an arm around her shoulders; the younger one seemed taut and focused, leaning toward the camera. The younger had eyes as blue as her father's. Those of the older were gray-green.

"That's Leah, after my mom. The younger one's Genie. She's named after my wife."

"How long have you been married?" Elspeth almost laughed out loud at herself, pleased she managed not to let disappointment show in her voice. *He did mention that before, but I assumed* . . .

He leaned back. Elspeth smelled warmly spicy aftershave. "We were married four years," he said. "Leukemia. I raised the girls on my own, more or less." He glanced away, frowning, and tapped the image down. "Do you have any kids?"

"Married to my work," she said. "And then I went to jail. Not much conducive."

A rough-edged silence stretched between them, punctuated by the crunch of Gabe chewing on his breath mint. He broke first. "So how do you get your artificial personalities to be more than really complicated chatter-bots?"

"Turing test stuff?" She shrugged and stepped around the desk, so she could speak to him from the front. And, incidentally, control her urge to lean against his shoulder. "Well, you don't, really. No, that's wrong." Her hands tumbled over

one another in midair. "They're exactly like really complicated chatter-bots. You just keep adding layers and layers of
complexity and information and reactions and algorithms until you get to these very complex multifaceted variables."

"Tolbert equations."

"Yes. And you give it all the memory you have, and put
it into a series of increasingly complex situations."

"And then?" Gabe's hands slowly stopped moving,
hanging amid the jeweled lights of his interface. His brow
furrowed and he looked up at Elspeth, meeting her gaze
directly.

"And then one day it either wakes up or it doesn't."

"Oh." He didn't say anything for a moment, looking back
down at his carefully trimmed fingernails. "That's not
mighty scientific, Doc. How do we know that it works?"

"Because it works." She shrugged. "Sometimes. And
why it works sometimes and not others . . . hell, your guess
is as good as mine."

"What if I pointed a gun at you and told you, 'I need an
answer'? Hypothetically speaking, of course."

Her hands spread wide. "Dammit, Gabe. I'd say it comes
down to will to live."

"You sound like you have something specific in mind."

She nodded. "Let's go for a walk, shall we?"

He grabbed his jacket and followed her out the door.

The lab and offices sat on a little green oblong not far
from the University of Toronto, where Elspeth had taught in
the days before she found herself in jail. There was a coffee
shop on every third corner, and the familiar street names
were like a homecoming. She breathed in the late summer
air, slinging a sweater retrieved from her office over one
shoulder. It had rained overnight, but the humidity was rising with the sun, and the day promised heat.

Gabe was taking his jacket off again. "You know, September, I keep thinking it ought to be cooler."

She shrugged. "It's not even really autumn yet."

"True." His voice dropped. "Okay, so what was so important you didn't want to tell me about it indoors?"

"Ah. Well." She scuffed concrete with the sole of a loafer. "Richard Feynman, frankly."

"The physicist? One of your original five artificial personalities."

"Yes." She reached up to swat at a dangling leaf. He grinned, and she blushed. "More than that."

"Oh?"

The conversation was interrupted as they arrived at the coffee shop, and Gabe ordered just plain coffee. Elspeth got a cappuccino with extra whipped cream. They took the drinks outside and sat at a blackened aluminum table meant to look like cast iron. Elspeth took a long sip of her drink and watched Gabe fuss with cream and sugar. *Is this someone you can trust? Well, you're not telling him anything Valens doesn't already suspect.* "He's the one that worked. Developed awareness. Became . . . a person."

"Ah hah." His voice was neutral, interested. "That's quite a judgment call, Elspeth. What do you base it on?"

She felt gratitude. "Once we were engaging in ontological discussion on the nature of consciousness, it was hard to deny his point. I remember once, I told him that he was nothing but electrical impulses in crystal, and he came back that I was the same thing in meat. It was a hard point to argue."

"What happened to him?" Gabe leaned forward. "Why aren't we using those records?"

Elspeth laughed. "That's why I went to jail, more or less. I wouldn't give him up."

"Give him up? To whom?"

She nodded and played with her paper cup. "Valens

wanted my work for the army. For the war effort. I deleted my most recent backups. Was going to erase Richard, too."

"And did you?"

"I . . ." her voice trailed off. "I gave him an Internet connection and bought him some time. I hope he made it. I don't know."

"Ah."

"The colonel was not amused. Especially after my research partner broke a soldier's nose with a printer stand." She grinned at Gabe's startled laughter. "That was Jack Taylor. I made him turn state's evidence against me. He had a wife."

His laughter trailed off. "And then you went to jail for over a decade."

"Indeed. I never did tell them that I didn't delete all those records. The ones we've been working from are earlier backups." She pushed her chair back and stood up, picking up her nearly full cup before he could ask the question forming in his eyes.

After so many years, what made you change your mind?

He came around the table to her, leaving his coffee cup behind, and touched hers to the side with two fingers on her wrist. She looked up, startled, into those earnest, cheerful eyes. *How does anybody who has been through so much—wars, left widowed with children—smile like that? I wish I had his spirit.*

"I admire your guts, Elspeth," he said. "What do you think about making one of these working dates into a real date, sometime?"

Elspeth turned aside and set her coffee down on the table. *Just like Momma, running around with the white boys,* she thought, and the thought came very close to making her laugh out loud. Which he would have misunderstood entirely. "Actually, Gabe, I'm not looking for a . . . dating relationship right now."

"Ah." He stepped back and turned away to retrieve his coffee. "Mad at me for asking?"

"Not at all. I've got a counterproposal. I'd hate to ruin this friendship with expectations and the dating game foolishness. I'm not in the market for a husband; that's never been my goal in life."

He nodded to show that he was listening, and she was kind enough to wait until he swallowed the coffee.

"So how would you feel about a little friendly sex once in a while?"

1200 hours, Monday 11 September, 2062
Allen-Shipman Research Facility
St. George Street
Toronto, Canada

Adrenaline hits. The bottom drops out of my world.

Gabe Castaign barrels down the corporate-blah hallway, arms spread wide, yelling a welcome like he hasn't seen me since Christmas. He's as big as Razorface, maybe bigger, but Gabe is all teddy-bear these days, while Face is a gleaming, well-oiled hunk of muscle. Ignoring Valens and Barb, prisoner's escorts on either side of me, he's ready to sweep me into an embrace.

Come to think of it, he hasn't seen me since Christmas, and he seems not to notice the steaming coffee slopping over his hand. There's a little dark-haired woman about my age four steps behind him. She balances a paper cup in her hand as well, and I see her startlement in the long moment that stretches while that rivulet of coffee trickles over Gabe's wrist, slow as honey on an October morning.

• • •

This shouldn't be enough to trigger me.
But my heart
hits the bottom of my chest cavity,
each beat long and slow and painful
as my hands come up and
I sidestep,
pain falling away,
left hand reaching . . .

Valens's voice, then, slow as a creaking door: "*Castaign, STOP!*" and Gabe halts at the snap of the command. I struggle for control, take a step back, between my sister and the doctor, away from Gabe. I gag on bile and go down on one knee in the steep sick aftershock of the adrenaline and the thing I almost did.

Again.

Valens puts a hand on my shoulder, holds the other one out to take the coffee cup away from Castaign. Blond, blue-eyed Gabe Castaign, a man who'll crawl through a fire for a girl he's never met, lets hands that could half-encircle a cantaloupe hang limply by his side, looking from me to Valens and back again with an expression like a befuddled bear: intelligent, thoughtful, determined to understand what it is that's so suddenly changed. I see him taking in the way I'm dressed—plum-colored slacks, sweater without a pill on it, wine-red turtleneck I bought yesterday, downtown. Same old scarred boots, though. I wonder what he thinks of that.

Fury sparks slowly in his eyes, then, and they focus hard on Valens.

"What the hell did you do to her, *fils de pute?*"

I hold up my hand to stem the flow of that anger, trying to hide how gratified I am by it. Before I can say anything, Valens interposes himself smoothly. "She's sick, Castaign. That's why she's here."

An unfamiliar voice cuts in. It must be the woman, Gabe's coworker. "And we talk about her like she's not here because? . . ." And I can't decide if what I feel is gratitude or irritation, but whatever it is, it's enough to get me hauling myself up straight and not leaning on Valens's goddamned arm any longer.

"Because I'm the patient," I answer, and take a step forward to extend my hand to her, not letting any of them see how badly I want to sway on my feet. From the look Gabe gives me, he guesses. My face must be livid and shining with cold sweat between the scars. "Jen Casey." I can't remember the last time I introduced myself to somebody by my right name.

"Elspeth Dunsany," she answers, switching the coffee to her left hand. Her right is warm and dry as her smile. Golden hazel eyes crinkle at the corners, eerily pale in a face darker than my own. She's compact, vigorous, a little chunky. "Are you a programmer?"

"I'm a pilot," I answer. "Or at least I was." Valens clears his throat behind me—*shut up, Casey*—which makes me curious.

I've always been smarter than I look. And Valens wouldn't have sent Barb half a thousand miles to collect me if he could get the results he wants from whatever teenage soldiers might volunteer for the project just to get the—wetware, Valens called it.

Charming.

So there's got to be something about me that's special. Enhanced reflexes? Just bloody not being dead? I know Valens isn't telling me a third of the truth, but I can deduce that he needs me at least as much as I need him. What's he going to do if I piss him off? Send me home to die?

What the hell. I have nothing to lose but my life.

I keep talking. "Are you working on the flight simulations for the VR program?"

"Some work in VR, but . . ." her voice trails off, and I can tell from the direction of her gaze that she's looking at Valens. *Score.* ". . . nothing like that," she finishes lamely.

Interesting. He has some kind of hold over her, too. Her, me, Gabe. Same old Valens.

Pity for him I ain't the same old Jenny. The last time we tangled, he used Gabe to control me. I'm willing to bet that's the whole reason he's offered Gabe this much-needed job. Which no doubt comes with health insurance that will cover what the government won't do for Genie. Enzyme therapy is fucking expensive.

I'm not twenty-five anymore, Frederick Valens. And you'd be wise not to forget it.

"Gabe," I say, breaking the uncomfortable silence. "Dinner tonight? Bring the girls, my treat."

"Sure," he says, but then he glances over at Elspeth Dunsany almost as if checking to see if she minds. Not quite asking permission—Gabe would never do that. But seeing if maybe he needs to make it up to her later.

Elspeth's emotion is unreadable behind the grin she gives me. "I hope once you two old friends have caught up, I'll be invited to the next one."

And I like her even more for that, dammit, in spite of myself. It's gracious, and she's not making a fuss about being gracious. A grown-up woman.

A woman who looks more familiar the more I look at her. "Elspeth Dunsany," I say, thoughtfully. "*Doctor* Dunsany?"

She nods. "Yes. *That* Doctor Dunsany." Her face falls, as she wouldn't let it before.

I understand. Oh, Nellie, do I understand. "It's okay," I say, and clap her lightly on the shoulder. "I'm *that* Master Corporal Casey. Nothing like an uncomfortable fifteen minutes of fame, is there? We'll get along just fine."

Valens clears his throat again, and as I turn to look at

him I'm left with the unmistakable impression that he engineered this little meeting.

Of course he did. He's Fred Valens, after all.

And as long as he thinks he's got control of me, I've got half a chance of finding out what the hell is going on here, and why my sister put a bullet in the back of Mitch's girlfriend's head.

6:45 P.M., Monday 11 September, 2062
Albany Avenue
Hartford, Connecticut
Abandoned North End

Razorface leaned against creaking, smoke-scented black leather and kicked his feet up on the chrome-edged coffee table. He liked his living room. He'd picked out the furniture himself, over Leesie's protests. As if a woman knew anything about what looked good.

He still didn't like the dingy unwashed cop perched on the loveseat across from him, but what the hell. You took what you could get.

"So this doc of Maker's said he get in touch with her? She been calling me, like I asked, but you know she don't listen to nothing."

"Yeah. I know. He said he'd try. The prints came back. Hers, and the ones I lifted off the door of that Honda I told you about. Maker—or Casey—"

"Maker." Irritation filled his mouth like the constant subliminal taste of steel. "What she want to be called."

"Right. The other woman is her sister, this Barbara Anne Casey the car is registered to. Who works for—are you ready for this?"

"The drug company?" Razorface rolled his massive

shoulders back against the sofa, settling in. He could hear Leesie in the kitchen, banging cabinets. She wasn't pleased about having a cop in the house.

"Close. Unitek corporate headquarters. Hired recently, too." The cop punctured the air with jabs of his open hand. He leaned forward, picking up a glass of cola he'd been ignoring while the ice melted, and then fiddled with the tubular steel art object on the coffee table for a moment until it lined up neatly with the glass and chrome edge. "I've got a theory, Razorface, and I need you to do some checking for me."

"What sort of checking?"

"Your dealers."

Razorface leaned forward and rapped on the coffee table. At the sound, Emery peered around the corner from the next room, eyebrows raised questioningly, hand on his lapel. *On the job.* Razorface waved him down. "I ain't got no dealers, man. I got boys, but they don't sell."

"Yeah, whatever. These guys who were supposedly out of New York. The ones nobody's ever seen or heard of before?"

"Fuck, yeah. They weren't from New York."

The cop cracked his knuckles. "I think they were from Canada. And I bet you know people who could find out for me if they knew the right questions to ask. And maybe had a few holos to show around." He reached slowly into his breast pocket and drew out a holder with a thick sliver of clear crystal imbedded in it.

"Damn. How you get those?" Despite himself, Razor felt a grin creeping across his face.

"Border patrol," Mitch answered. "I'm a vice cop. This is the case I'm actually supposed to be working on."

"Huh. You think we got some gangsters from Canada moving in?" He didn't move to take it.

Mitch kept the hand extended. "Nah. I think we got a corporation. I think they ditched the Hammers here because it was convenient. Because they wanted a—fucked if I know. I think they did it on purpose, and I think they tainted them on purpose. And I think the company that makes the things is behind it all."

Razor reached out and took the holo chip in his meaty hand. He laughed, and it turned into a wet cough, which he swallowed. "Why'd a corp be dumping stuff on my street? Not for money. Have to move volume for that."

"Fuck," Mitch answered. "Not controlled enough for a trial. Unless there was some reason they needed to—no, that makes no sense. Your guess is as good as mine, Razor, I guess I'm trying to say. Maybe it's just that nobody gives a fuck what goes on in the North End. Maybe it has something to do with Maker being here."

The silence stretched heavy. "Mitch."

"Yeah?"

"You talk about the North End. Why you give a shit about this city, man? White boy from the suburbs . . ."

"Why do you? You're a goddamned warlord. Nobody can touch you. You don't have to do things the way you do. You do right. Most gangsters who get where you are, they go about shit a hell of a lot differently."

Razorface thought about that for a while before he found the right words. They weren't the right words, really, but they were the best he could do. "I grew up here, man. Some people, they think I go about things wrong, anyway."

"You've got problems?"

"Damn, where ain't I got problems? I got a twenty-year-old punk wants me out of a job so he can take my place, I got 20-Love trouble and they're getting machine guns from somewhere. I got—hell, you don't care what I've got."

"So you grew up here. So what? So did the punks who

shoot the place up, put bullets through little girls on play-grounds."

"Yeah, well. There's men don't provide for their children, too. Mean we all should do whatever the fuck we want?" Razor swung his feet off the coffee table and stood up, heaving his body out of the sofa. It seemed to get harder every year. *You're not that fucking old.* But it was a struggle not to breathe hard, and he wasn't going to let himself look weak in front of a cop.

The air was shit; that was all it was. He turned away from the cop and focused on the wall clock. It was chrome, too, and polished black enamel. Like Razorface. Like everything else in the room.

"No," the cop said, climbing to his own feet. He finished the soda and set the glass down on a coaster. "No, we probably shouldn't. You going to look into that shit for me?"

The big gangster studied the wall a little more closely, examining a crack running down it. *It's for Merc. And the other kids.* "Fuck, yeah. But people see you coming to the house here they'll talk, and I don't need that shit. Next time, you leave me a message on my hip. I meet you downtown or in East Hartford. Not the neighborhood, all right?"

"All right."

Razorface didn't turn around until Mitch left. He didn't want the cop to see the look on his face and think him—sweet.

Once he was sure Mitch was gone, Razor uncurled his fingers from the holo chip thoughtfully and held the little sliver of crystal up to the light.

Canada.

Wish to hell I knew what that meant.

Genie's grown since Christmas, but maybe not as much as you'd expect of a girl her age. She's a big-eyed elf, blonde and fine-boned, and her big sister always seems to have her arm around Genie's shoulders. Leah's a good kid. Looks just like her mother, with a promise of early beauty and later strength. Genie, on the other hand, has Gabe's eyes.

I miss Geniveve. It's a funny thing to say, but I do. She was good for Gabe, and I never had a shot at him anyway. She was a class act.

Gabe has always had a good eye for women. Only ever made one mistake that I know of, and we were both much younger then.

The girls want pizza and garlic bread and Greek salad, so we wind up in a little hole in the wall on the west side of town, gathered around a red-and-white checkered plastic tablecloth. The food's good, all things considered. Genie eats like a pig. She has to, to maintain weight, although Gabe tells me she's doing better now that she's back on the gene therapy and the protein repair. Enzyme replacement therapy thins out the mucus in her lungs, but they haven't nailed down the GI issues yet. She's skinny and her cheeks are flushed and her skin is too pale, but she's not coughing and she looks better than she did nine months ago, and that's something.

I give Gabe's knee a squeeze under the table when the

girls are fighting over the last olive in the bowl. He's had a lousy decade. Odd how a couple of months in the same burn unit will give you a chance to really bond with somebody. He used to sit by my bed, when I was conscious, his hands and arms swathed in loose gauze to the shoulder, and make terrible bilingual puns to make me forget how he got burned so badly. We talk about small things, the way we used to, and when the girls wander off to play the VR games near the door he leans forward over the table, pouring the last of the beer out of the pitcher and into our glasses. "All right, Maker. Are you going to come clean with me now?"

It's a joy just to have him nearby and mad at me. "Gabe, do you have any idea how much I've missed you?"

He sits back, blinks at me—"*Pardon?*"—and I make eye contact long enough to shrug.

My boots stick to the floor under the booth where somebody spilled a soda. There's a squelching sound when I peel them free. "What Valens said is true as far as it goes. But it doesn't begin to cover the territory. I'm sick, yeah. He's not lying about that. But there's a whole lot of other stuff going on I'm not sure about."

He could even have the conversation bugged. Be tracing either or both of us. Probably is, in fact, so I'm going to say what I expect he wants to hear.

"But?" Gabe is waiting for me to continue, turning a spoon over and over in his hand. He hasn't looked down.

"But I'm reasonably sure whatever you're working on for him has to do with what I'm working on for him, and that he has some master plan for you and me." I can't explain all my suspicions—like the nasty sneaking thought I have nagging at the back of my brain that Valens set Gabe up to *need* this job so badly just so that he could offer it to him. And my even weirder suspicion, the one I'd almost laugh at for its narcissism, that for reasons I do not entirely understand, everything that has been happening revolves around me.

On the other hand, it could be a paranoid delusion. I'm given to understand I should be expecting those to start any time now. Fuck. All I ever wanted was a house on the Atlantic coast, maybe a dog or two and a husband who gave backrubs. How the hell I wound up with all this drama—Christ, I'll never know.

Gabe's looking at me. He expects me to continue, and I spread my hands wide and reach for another slice of pizza. Buying a little time, I turn my head to check on the girls. Their heads are under the VR helmets, and I can hear Genie laughing from here.

Laughing. Not coughing. Gabe glances over at his daughters and I see him grin. Genie has cystic fibrosis. Something for which there are many, many treatments these days—and still no cure. He looks back at me. "My project is classified," he says. "I'd love to talk about it, Jen. But."

"Don't worry. I know what your project is. In gross detail, anyway. Doctor Dunsany's lucky she ever saw the light of day again." Gabe and I both almost went to jail under the Military Powers Act many years ago. Secrets having to do with what I carry under my skin. I'm not at all proud of what I did to keep us both on the outside, and Gabe doesn't know about most of it.

And never will. But I'm going to count coup on Fred Valens, I swear, if it's the last thing I do.

He laughs and sips his beer. "I guess it's pretty obvious, at that. But it doesn't relate to what you're here for, from what you said earlier."

"Could be. Right now, I'm here for extensive surgery. Which I'm assured is grossly noninvasive, whatever the fuck that means. And then I pay for it."

"Pay for it?" His eyebrows go up. "What does the slippery Colonel Valens want from you?"

The grin takes over my face whether I want it to or not. "He wants to use me as a baseline to calibrate a VR pilot training program. Apparently pushing fifty and with my enhancements in disarray, I'm still faster than the kids he's dragging out of flight training. That's classified, too, of course."

"So why are you telling me?"

The pizza is room temperature, and it still tastes good. Rich as the sensation of homecoming that enfolds me when Gabe reaches out and lays his hand over the leather glove covering my steel hand. I think of Valens's promise to make me feel again, and my chest goes tight and strange, because I have no intention of taking him up on it. Not that I'm going to let him find that out.

I wish I remembered what it felt like to wake up in the morning and not hurt over every inch of my body. And then there's ice-cold fear in the pit of my stomach, because I'm remembering my orientation that morning. "Because Valens needs me more than I need him right now, and because I need help."

"Sure. Anything." He checks on the girls again, and I wash the pizza—mushrooms, peppers, meatballs—down with a mouthful of beer.

"He wants me back on the narcotics. Under medical supervision. And I'm going to be taking Hyperex again, once the trials start. Not the Hammer, exactly. A new drug. Similar." *Merc, dark grayish purple and gasping, arching like a hooked fish . . . No. Don't think about it, Jenny. Or think about it. Think about what it means.*

That drug came from here.

"Maker. Jen. Tell me you're fucking kidding." He's not

looking at his kids now. The blue eyes bore into mine, anger rising across his face.

"I'm not. I'm told they won't let me go through the nano-surgery without painkillers. And the research I've signed on for . . . well, they say I'll need the Hammer for that."

His voice is bleak. He's drawing on the tablecloth with the tip of his unused knife. "We went through this once."

Twice. Well, Gabe only went through it once. I catch myself rubbing the crook of my left arm as if there could still be any scars there. They're gone, of course. Vanished like my life before the army. I have the sudden unholy urge to go find Chrétien, and it makes me want to turn my head and spit. Because I know I'm going to do it. Tomorrow. Or maybe the next day.

"I know. Valens knows . . ." everything. Well, not quite everything. But enough. "I'm gonna need you at my back."

He's unhappy about it. He nods anyway, because he's my best friend, and we look out for each other.

"Gabe, I have to make a call. Wait for me?"

"Of course." He knows I'm walking away from the conversation, and he lets me go anyway. Good man.

I use the wireless network to hook into a pay terminal across from the VR games. I promised to call Razorface, and I don't want to do it on my own HCD. Call it paranoia.

He's not answering, so I leave a message and hang up. I'm about to step out of the cubbyhole when a voice from my ear clip stops me cold.

"Ms. Casey." Educated tones, American accent. West Coast? Maybe. Something cosmopolitan, something a bit archaic about the diction, and a subtle edge of excitement.

"Who are you?" And the edge in *my* voice is something else.

"I'm the ghost of Richard Feynman. And you are in a heck of a lot of trouble." The screen beside me flickers on, revealing a gray-haired man with a face like a contour map, shifting restlessly as if from foot to foot. He grins. "And I really think we can help each other out."

I turn back, trying to look as if I had just remembered another call I needed to make. "Ah. I see. And I'm supposed to know who Richard Feynman is because why?"

He laughs, delighted. "You have no idea how refreshing that is to hear. What I am, Ms. Casey, is an artificial intelligence created in the image of a man who has been dead for seventy-four years. I'm a friend of Elspeth Dunsany's, and I need to get her a message without Colonel Valens finding out about it."

Allen-Shipman Research Facility
St. George Street
Toronto, Canada
Evening, Monday 11 September, 2062

Elspeth slid a holographic crystal out of the outdated reader and tapped her interface off. She really ought to make a stab at transferring the data to more modern storage devices. *I could probably stretch that out over at least three days if I worked at it. Valens is going to get cranky if I keep reviewing the old data. I wonder if he's figured out that I'm stalling.*

I wonder if I can justify starting over from scratch. New personalities. I could pick ones that seem to fit the criteria but are somehow subtly wrong to develop into true AIs.

I could. If I had any real solid clue what it was that made Feynman different from the rest. As it is, I've got just as much chance of building Valens his AI by accident as on purpose. And I am not handing the man a slave intelligence. Not if I can help it. She sighed and set the crystal on her desk, scrubbing her hands across her face before she reached for her mug. Cold tea, smelling of ashes. She drank it anyway, and wiped the mug out with her handkerchief.

She set it down once clean and rattled her fingers on the edge of her desk, away from the interface. The memory of Gabe Castaign bending over her outside the coffee shop that morning and dropping half a kiss on the corner of her mouth rose up to trouble her. She wondered if she could call him, and decided there was time enough to worry about it when an old friend hadn't just blown in from out of town.

"All right," she said at last, pushing her chair back to stand. "Tomorrow I'll think about this."

"Think about what, Doctor Dunsany?"

Elspeth was in the habit of leaving her office door open, because she could. She looked up to see Alberta Holmes, resplendent in gold and navy blue with matching shoes, primly framed in the doorway. "Doctor Holmes. Come in. I was just about to head out for the night."

"We can talk tomorrow if you prefer. And please, I'm a Ph.D.—I don't need to be called 'Doctor' outside of a classroom." The Unitek VP came a step farther in.

"I'd rather get it out of the way," Elspeth said, wincing as she heard the tone of her own voice. She wondered if the visit had something to do with her own brief conversation with Gabe's friend at lunchtime. "I'm on my way to the hospital."

"How is your father?" Alberta strolled across the forest-green carpeting.

Elspeth picked up the crystal and went around her desk the opposite way, bending to replace it in its rack. "As well as can be expected," she answered. "I don't expect he'll see Christmas. I appreciate what you've done for him, however. And for me." She was surprised at how level her voice sounded, even to her own ears.

"We—appreciate—the compromises you're making on our behalf. I'm very glad I caught you here, actually. I'm going over Colonel Valens's head a bit to tell you this, but I'm in favor of full disclosure. Expecting scientists to work with partial information is, well, silly. And Fred should know that." Alberta tilted her head inquiringly as Elspeth straightened from replacing Woolf's crystal in the rack.

Something uncoiled in Elspeth's belly. As if drawn by an invisible thread, she took a step toward Alberta. "Full disclosure?"

Alberta nodded, pulled a data slice out of her pocket, and pressed it to the reader on Elspeth's desk. "Here."

Frowning, Elspeth came forward and placed her thumb on the interface plate, keying her monitor back on. "What is it?"

"Data on the project we need the AIs for. Assuming you can make some for us. By the way, I'd like for you to avoid Casey for a while. She's not well, as you saw, and she's under a tremendous amount of emotional stress. We have no objection to you socializing with coworkers outside the program. But—assuming Colonel Valens can do it—we want to see to her medical needs before we start confusing the issue."

Message received. Stay out of the way until we know where the potential loose cannon is pointing. Elspeth nodded. "As you wish," and turned to the image projector.

Light flickered for a moment, and an image—a machine? a space station?—resolved itself in the air over Elspeth's desk. "Lights out," she said absently, leaning forward. "What's that supposed to be?" She poked at the hologram with a finger, expecting it to expand to show detail of the section she indicated, where a fat revolving disk connected to an axle or a shaft.

It enlarged, indeed, and also peeled back, showing cross sections. "A spaceship?"

"A starship," Alberta corrected, smiling. "That's the *Indefatigable*. It doesn't exist."

"Design schematic? And what's the difference? Spaceship, starship . . ."

"What you see before you is a VR mockup. It's designed so that it simulates the real thing almost exactly, in handling capabilities, schematics, and so forth. You do know about the Chinese colony ships launched over the last seven or ten years?"

"The so-called generation ships? Yes, I do." Elspeth picked up her teacup again, forgetting it was empty. It would have been hard to miss the portentous announcements, the media frenzy, the images of red flags in serried ranks snapping in a crisp spring breeze. Even in jail. She didn't raise her eyes from the display. "Between their space program and the military actions . . . Well. I suppose we should expect an invasion of Russia any day now."

"Irrelevant, but yes. This ship, the *Indefatigable*. As I said, it doesn't really exist." She reached out and tapped up another display. "Since governments got out of the space game, everything has to pay for itself. Corporations won't gamble money where there's no return. But smart companies, forward-looking ones, have always known that sometimes you can't see where the money is going to come from. And if the Chinese are going to the stars, then we bloody well are, too."

This image was lower resolution, but Elspeth somehow found her breath caught in her throat. Something about how the hard sunlight of space played along the curve of what must have been an enormous wheel . . . She set the teacup down on her interface panel, uncaring. It clicked on the cool crystal.

"And the difference between a spaceship and a starship . . . lies in how far away they're intended to go," Alberta continued after a momentary pause. "This one does exist. Did. You're looking at *Le Québec*. She was destroyed on her first test flight."

"Destroyed?" That brought Elspeth's chin up. She blinked for focus, meeting Alberta's peculiarly intense eyes.

Alberta smiled. "Pilot error. Pilot inadequacy, more exactly." Rapidly, she flicked through more images. "This one is the *Li Bo*, taken by telescope. Also destroyed, as was her predecessor, the *Lao Zi*."

"Ah. So. I sense a naming trend—those are Chinese ships?"

"Yes. This is *Huang Di*. She'll be ready for launch by the end of the year."

"How do you know that?"

"We have assets. So do they. We need to be able to test our second ship by New Year's."

Elspeth thought about it for a moment only. "You need a better pilot? How fast does that thing go?"

Alberta ignored the question. "We visualize a tailored-human/AI team. We'll use drugs and nano- and biotherapies to improve the human pilot's response times, although there are some medical barriers to that. The AI, of course, can respond at processor speeds, but we'd like to keep a human involved because of judgment calls. And also, well, there's a trust issue."

Elspeth nodded. *I'd rather know my ship was being flown by a person than by a computer. Does that make me a racist?* "You must be talking about a drive that will move a ship at near C. Given how uncluttered space is."

"Actually, it's capable of moving at an uncalculated rate we suspect to be exponentially higher than the speed of light."

Elspeth blinked. "How?"

And Alberta grinned. "There's one of the many problems. We don't know."

Sins become more subtle as you grow older: you commit sins of despair rather than lust.
—Piers Paul Read

2113 hours, Monday 11 September, 2062
Bloor Street West
Toronto, Ontario

I sit on the beige-carpeted floor of Gabe's apartment with a tweedy couch cushion under my butt, watching cartoons and drinking Irish coffee out of a speckled stoneware mug. I'm mulling over—again—what "the ghost of Richard Feynman" told me today when Gabe strolls into the living room.

"What's on?"

"*Hannah and Tucker.*"

"Genie loves that one. Especially the flying horse." He sits down one cushion to the left and behind me, leaning forward to put his own coffee cup on the floor.

"Girls in bed?"

"Yeah."

I set my mug aside. He's reaching out to lay a hand on my shoulder when I lean forward and push myself to my feet, pretending not to notice. Going into the kitchen, I call back over my shoulder, "Ice cream?" even though it's cold and the windows are open. We bought some on the way back from the restaurant.

"No thanks."

When I come back, he's pulled the cushion so it rests

between his feet. I give him a dubious look. "I'm too old for high school seductions, Gabe." It doesn't come out with the wry tone I want it to have.

He shows me the upturned palm of his hand. "Sit, get neck rubbed, do not complain."

"Ah." I sit. Gabe can actually touch my back without my wanting to spin around and put my left hand through his face. *Well, except for this morning.* It's a thought I don't need. I push it back.

Very few other people can touch me like that. "I've got a T-shirt on."

"Take off the sweater, then."

I set the ice cream down and take a long sip of my coffee first, not sure if I wish I had put more alcohol in it or less. *Pathetic, Jenny. There are sixteen-year-old girls less pathetic than you.* He notices my gooseflesh in the chilly room, and hands me the afghan from the back of the sofa. It's blue and white, a tapestry of cats.

Pathetic.

Well, nothing new there. I ball the sweater up and throw it into the corner. Gabe swills coffee and sets the mug aside. He chafes his hands together until I can feel the friction heat and then lays them on my neck.

I gasp. His hands are warm as towels heated in the microwave, and they seem to know and find every knot and bit of pain. "Have you been doing your physical therapy?"

"Sort of." He touches the outline of the nanoprocessor that links into my cervical vertebrae, reminding himself of where plastic ends and Jenny begins.

"You need to take the arm off at night, Maker."

"I take it off when I sleep." I hate taking it off. It's like a reminder that it's not really part of me, and I can't stand that. It took me enough time to stop wanting to skin myself to get the metal and plastic out from under.

There's low concern in his voice again when he continues. "How are you dealing with seeing Barb again? That was a shock, the two of you standing side by side . . ."

My breath comes harsher, and I can tell he feels the shifting tension in my back. His touch is light at first and then firmer as he leans into the knotted muscles. I have a pretty good pain threshold. He knows where it is, and he pushes it, but he never makes me squeal.

"I dunno, Gabe. I . . . hell. You know I still think it's her fault Nell died, no matter what she says. No matter what she thinks she got away with."

"Yes." He strokes the back of my neck, fingers through my hair.

I keep thinking about everything Richard told me. Everything I wish I could be telling Gabe. "And she's smart. She's always been the smartest one."

"Thing with people like that, is this: they're smart, sure. But they get to thinking they're smarter than anybody else. And somebody catches up to them eventually."

It hasn't happened yet. But his touch is soothing, and I don't say anything else, just then. Halfway through, he gets up and brings me a glass of water and more bourbon, and starts in again. The ice cream is a syrupy puddle in the bottom of a glass bowl. I didn't want it anyway.

Finally, he sighs, leans back, and cracks his knuckles. "Any better?"

I'm floating. I don't dare move, because I know that as soon as I do, the pain will start again. Pain is a funny thing. Once you live with it a little while, you forget it's there. You just feel tired and out of sorts, but you don't really notice anymore and you don't really know why. Pain is boring. And then the cessation of it comes as an epiphany, almost stunning—like falling in love.

Gabriel Castaign saved my life. He saved my soul. He

knows the single worst thing I ever did in my life and he takes care of me anyway, even though he doesn't know I did it for him.

"Mon Ange," I say—mean old nickname, though not as bad as the pun he hanged on me—letting my head droop low, stretching my neck. "Thank you."

He reaches out and runs his fingers through my hair, the same way he tousles his children's. My heart squeezes tight in my chest. I've had too much to drink, and too many surprises, and it's a long bittersweet unguarded moment. There are big threats for facing. Tomorrow. Richard saying, "I need you, Ms. Casey. My friend is in trouble, and you're a woman of honor."

And Valens. *Vegetative state*. Could be, rabbit. Could be.

Then words are out of my mouth before I have a chance to think about them. "I always wanted to tell you something."

My throat closes up behind like the proverbial barn door. His hand falls still in my hair, and I know that everything—decades of everything—was in my voice. "Jen," he says on a breath. "Shit. Jenny. I know."

Slowly, carefully, I turn my head to look at him out of the corner of my good eye. Sweat prickles across my skin. He's regarding me out of eyes like blue arctic water, two days' growth of beard shading the lower half of his face. He never would have gotten that scruffy back in the old days. "What do you know, Gabe?"

A long sigh. "I know what you want to tell me. I've known for years." His hand slides down the back of my neck to rest on my shoulder. My skin tingles under his touch.

"You said I was your best friend. Kiss of death."

He breathes in and out: thoughtful. "I was twenty-eight. What does anybody know at twenty-eight? And you didn't seem to want me to know."

"I didn't."

"I figured you had your reasons. So why tell me now?"

I sigh and roll my shoulders forward and back, feeling the first twinge of returning discomfort. "Because I'm an idiot and I keep thinking life is like a drama and if I'm going to die beautifully—or pathetically, for that matter—I want . . ." *Dig a little deeper, Jenny.* I wish I'd stopped a few words sooner. I wish I hadn't opened my mouth up at all.

"Are you going to hold the way we met against me forever?" There's low humor in his voice, painful to hear, almost inaudible under the tinny music from the holopad.

"Did I ever tell you I almost got married once?" I turn farther, holding the eye contact even though it hurts my neck to twist that far.

His hands are gentle on my shoulders as he bends me away and coaxes me to settle back between his knees again. I have no idea why I'm doing as he's urging me, but it feels good. He smoothes my hair again and I lean on his knee, hiding the scarred side of my face against his jeans. I'm starting to shiver, dammit, and I can't stand it. Can't stand his pity, and can't make myself pull away from the careful pressure of his hands.

"You didn't. Who to?"

I close my eyes. "I was nineteen. Carlos Conseca, his name was. I gave him his ring back when they shipped me out to South Africa. He's still alive, as far as I know."

"You ever think of looking him up?"

My spine crackles when I roll my shoulders back. "I'd rather let him keep his illusions."

"Jenny," he says. He disentangles himself and slides down onto the floor beside my sofa cushion, letting his right arm fall around my shoulders. Despite myself, I lean into the caress. "Look, I know why you never said anything when we were in the service, and I appreciate it. Or when I was married. What about afterward?"

The speechlessness stretches, elastic, images flickering over the holopad across the room. I watch the little winged red horse leap boldly off a cliff, rising into flight over our heads, the hologram filling the room. I reach for the remote and mute the sound of wingbeats.

"I couldn't handle the rejection, Gabe."

"And you were sure you'd be rejected?"

I shrug, an attempt at callousness wasted on Gabe's warm, massive presence. "I know what I look like."

"Idiot." He kisses the top of my head. He smells of coffee and sugar; it catches in my throat like a hook. His hand is under my chin, and he lifts my mouth to his . . .

That's something else about the enhancements I carry. *Feedback*.

His lips brush mine, petal-soft, contrast to the roughness of his beard, and a wave of euphoria starts to rise. I suck on a long, rattling breath, flush-heat racing through me. *God, how long has it been since I kissed anybody?* My body tautens, one hand and then the other coming up to braid in his curls, and he leans into me as subtle fire quickens in my belly and tingles through the whole of my body, pooling here and there. Just a kiss, a little kiss, lips barely parted and his breath riding mine, and I'm shivering, weak with desire. The tension in him, the whisper of a purr tells me my response surprises and excites him. But as he moves to pull me closer, I turn into him, drawing my knees up, then bury my face in his shoulder.

"Mon ange," I mumble, sick with old, clotted terror. "I can't."

"Oh?"

The words come out in little hitching phrases. It takes me a long while to get them organized. "Not right now. Not when—I could be dying." *Not when I don't know what I'm being manipulated into. Not when you could be used against me. Again.* "I can't do that to you." *Or the girls. Not after Geniveve.* "Because I'm not going to be happy with just a roll in the hay, you know."

"Je sais." Dead serious around a smile.

"And what about—Elspeth?"

A smile that widens and warms. "Nous sommes tous adultes, Genevieve. Les antiquités fichues, en fait. Je pense qu'elle ne soignera pas."

"Je ne sais pas. Tu sait que je t'aime." The look in my eyes has to tell him everything.

"Oui. Je sais cela aussi."

"Gabe." So many things I could say, and I can't bear to lie to him. Not again. Not tonight. "I'm too scared."

And he scrubs my hair forward, into my eyes, before leaning forward to pick up the remote still lying by my hand and turn the sound on the animation back on. "Nous parlerons de ceci encore quelque temps, Jenny Casey." *We'll talk about this again sometime.* Wry tone, softening, and *mon Dieu,* I love this man. "Ball's in your court now."

If I live that long. Sometimes, I'm smart enough to keep my mouth shut.

Sometimes.

But there is joy in Mudville, as he sits up with me most of the night. We watch children's programming, where the world is wholesome and bright and the good guys win in the end.

Every normal man must be tempted at times to spit upon his hands, hoist the black flag, and begin slitting throats.
—Henry Louis Mencken

Valens's gloved hands brush my hair forward, gentle and sure as a lover's. *And I am not thinking about Gabe. Not. Thinking about Gabe.* "Will you put me in touch with the doc who's been doing your follow-up, Casey?"

"If you insist. What are we doing today, Fred?" He's much more fastidious than Simon. I lie near-naked under the sterile drape, facedown on a table, and the room is a cold, antiseptic operating theater. Observers range in the gallery above, but I try not to let it bother me. It's not like it's the first time. "Nice facilities you have here."

"Thanks. Today we're just introducing you to the VR setup with your current equipment. We're going to run some tests, see what the functionality is, see how comfortable we can get you with operating in a VR environment. We're not even going to use a real vehicle today, or the drugs. You'll be flying the HMCSS *Indefatigable*."

Since when do aircraft have names? "What's that?"

Amusement colors his voice. "A virtual spaceship. Supposed to be very challenging to fly. It's got a tendency to smack into planets—or any sufficiently massive object nearby. As if attracted to them, actually."

"Whose lame-ass idea was that?"

"I believe it's intended to be a game."

"Teenagers. Got to make everything harder than it needs to be."

"I've got kids of my own, and yes, I think that probably covers it." There's a hesitance in his voice. I wonder what he isn't telling me. "We'll sedate you once you're hooked in, paralyze the voluntary muscles. Like REM sleep."

"I've done some work in VR, actually."

"I know. That's one of the ways we tracked you to Connecticut."

"*What?*" There's a jolt, sharp and sudden, as the adrenaline of fury dumps into my body.

In the jump into combat time, I hear my heartbeat slowing. To Valens, it accelerates—and he murmurs to the anesthesiologist, who makes a minor adjustment. Increasing the sedative drip, no doubt. It works. "Calm down, Jenny."

Simon, you son of a bitch . . . no, wait. If he'd been talking to Valens behind my back, Valens wouldn't need me to release my medical records. If he were that unethical, Simon would just do it.

"I'm calm," and it's grit between my teeth, but I get it spat out. "How do you know about that?"

"Oh, the researcher you were working with published some papers on you. Name changed, of course, and some of the personal details. But I knew who it had to be. He wouldn't talk to me when I tried to contact him about it."

"Ah." *I see.* And the shit of it is, Simon probably thought he was protecting confidentiality. Not really unethical. Really. And it explained why he had been so rabbity during that last discussion.

Just exactly not what I asked him to do. The temptation must have been unbearable. *But we're going to have a long, stern discussion after I get back to Hartford.*

If I get back to Hartford.

My mind is alert, but my body feels numb, tingling. I

cannot feel my right hand, now, either, or the pinch of the IV site. My lips prickle and panic sings at the bottom of my belly, but I force myself to stillness.

Like outwaiting the enemy. The first to move is often the one to die.

There's a tug and a sting as Valens seats the lower cord. He's not as good at it as Simon. Or maybe not as gentle. I couldn't raise my head from the cradle if I tried, but I hear the others in the theater moving behind Valens. "With the patient's voluntary muscles relaxed," he says, and I know he's talking to the observers, "her neural impulses will be translated by the computer, resulting in normal movement of her icon through a virtual space. The effect is much more realistic than the VR suits and goggles most of you will be familiar with. And that realism is the basis of the technology we are pioneering here. In a moment, you'll be directed down the hall to a holotheater. The monitors will transmit images of everything Master Warrant Officer Casey experiences once the linkage is complete."

The observers are suits, not the doctors and students I once was used to seeing. I shouldn't have been surprised. Valens finishes his lecture and turns his attention back to me. My body numbs as he finishes the connection and lifts his hands. "All right, Casey?"

"Fine," I mumble. He dismisses the observers. For a moment, I close my eyes, relishing a cheerful recollection of the sensation of Valens's shoulder breaking under a poorly aimed punch. I really wish I'd gotten to hit him twice.

"Comfortable?"

"Couldn't tell if I wasn't, Fred."

He chuckles. "I want you to put some thought into your new arm, by the way. Since you won't be taking it into combat, there's no reason not to lay pseudoskin over it and match your complexion. More or less. It'll still look a little off, of course."

I think about it for a minute. Imagine something that might pass for a normal hand. From a distance. From six feet. "No."

"No?"

I tell myself I have no intention of going through with the surgery. That I am arguing to string him along, stretch things out. Once I've got proof that Valens and Barb are somehow linked to Mashaya Duclose's death, I can count coup, show brave, pay my debts. Get myself killed in the process or go home and die in peace.

I tell myself all that. Except. Gabe *kissed* me, damn him. "Steel. I want it the same as the old one. Armored."

"Yes. We put the 'skin' over the armor. That's what gives you the fingertip sensitivity. Fingertip, flat palm, back of the hand. Process developed by a Dr. Evans in the U.S. The arm itself stays numb, unfortunately. We'd overload your nervous system if we tried full-surface tactile. We can't match the delicacy of the electrical impulses the human nervous system uses. Yet." He turns and steps toward the door. "See you in cyberspace, Casey."

I raise my voice with an effort. "I want steel, Valens. Make the skin transparent if you have to." *Why are you arguing? Why do you care?*

I can see his booties, the bottom of his scrubs. And Valens strolls two more steps, stops, turns back to me, and draws a slow breath. "If that's what it takes, then. That's what we'll do."

I close my eyes as he walks through the door. The normal noises of the operating room resume, and someone—nurse, assisting physician, technician—asks me, "All set, Ms. Casey?"

"Locked and loaded," I answer, numb on the padded table, and then even that falls away.

Stars.

Stars, and cold stillness like frost crystallizing on motionless skin. Heat like an iron stroked down my body on the opposite side. Light that should be blinding-bright, eye searing, casts white-sharp edges over a tumbling stone hanging either below or above; I'm not sure which.

Farther, a rust-red curve, and I know where I am. *Mother fucker. That's* Mars.

Which is when I realize:

I'm not flying the spaceship.

I *am* the spaceship.

"Valens, you cocksucker, you could have warned me." I yelp out loud, and I'm surprised when I hear my own voice, clear and strangely *external,* as if recorded and played back.

And then I hear him laughing in my ear, self-satisfied as a cat. "I thought it would be more fun as a surprise. Pretty good, isn't it?"

And it is. It *is.* I stretch and wriggle into the skin of the ship, the *Indefatigable,* Valens called it. *Her.* I can't think of her as an object. Not when I'm living inside her, sailing serenely along in areosynchronous orbit. I spend a long moment realizing that there's facility built into this beast for all the functions you would expect of a real space cruiser— some back-brain fraction of my awareness is tracking life support, hull integrity, the tickle of the solar wind on the edges of my furled solar sails. Diagnostics read full capability, and it reaches my conscious mind as an intoxicating euphoria, a spring-day desire to leap over fences.

"Valens, I'm going to kick this thing into gear."

"Gently, Casey," he offers. "Use the sails at first. And the attitude rockets. You want to nudge yourself higher before you hit the stardrive. Oh, and you don't want to be pointing at the sun when you do it."

Stardrive? "Wilco." It's incredible. Peaceful. There's no pain, and not a scrap of fear. The solar sails unfurl like the wings of a swan, and I boost and turn myself, back to the solar wind that feels more like a gale. It's hours—days—but they go by like time spent lying in bed on Sunday with a lover.

"Valens, aren't your suits getting bored out there?"

"Actually, we're altering your time sense a bit. We've been watching for fifteen minutes."

"Oh." That freaks me out; my course wobbles. I correct. It's easier than learning to walk. Again.

I reach for cynicism, for the armor of biting wit and savage dismissal. It's not there, not hanging in the closet where it should be, next to my raincoat. There's nothing but the stars, and an old slow dull ache inside me like coming home.

"Status, Casey?"

"I can't feel Mars tugging on my boots anymore."

"Stow the sails."

"Check." Like furling wings, they slither into the embrace of my body. I—the *Indefatigable*—am shaped rather like a doughnut stuck halfway down a carving fork. The tines would point backward. The doughnut spins. Silly-looking thing.

"Sails stowed, Colonel."

"Widen the focus on your navigation charts?"

"Got 'em."

"You're going perpendicular to the plane of the elliptic. Do you know what that means?"

Supercilious son of a bitch. "Up." Brief silence. I picture the scene in the holotheater as he pauses and mutes what I can hear. I envision him punctuating his lecture with a jabbing finger, as he informs his audience that I've never been exposed to the software before today, that this is a dry run to show what a trained pilot can do even with unfamiliar tech—tech that can save lives, when applied to the birds and beasts of mechanized war. He'll say just that. *Save lives.*

His voice comes back, then. "Roger that, Casey. We've put you back on real time. What's going to happen now is that you're going to take that baby up, out of the solar system. There's a course plotted. It'll take you to Alpha Centauri, which is a nearby star. There will be unexpected obstacles along the way . . . Dark matter, planetesimals. Virtually speaking, your craft is going to be moving faster than the speed of light, which means you'll have no reliable visual input. Copy?"

"Copy. So how am I supposed to steer this thing, sir?" And I want to bite my tongue as soon as I've said it, imagining the satisfied expression on his face. *Sir. You can take the girl out of the army, but you can't take the army out of the girl.*

"You should be able to *feel* what's coming at you. It's a function of the field the drive produces. We've got no justification for how it works, so don't trouble yourself with that. It's magictech, make-believe. Just run with it."

Whatever. "Roger. How large an object do I worry about?"

"The drive field atomizes anything under about half a meter that it brushes up against. I would say, be on the safe side. Dodge anything bigger than a basketball. There's not much out there."

"Roger. Any last words?"

"Godspeed, Casey."

And what a damned funny thing to say. "On my way, Fred."

I point my nose up, and floor it.

And hell if he isn't right. I'm flying blind, and it's like water-skiing in the dark. I can feel the shape of space like a pressure against my skin. No—more like a pressure a few feet away from my skin. I get a taste of it at first, as the flickering aura of the drives brushes and consumes little things, barely noticeable things. Like running in a dust storm.

And then there's a bigger piece, and I take evasive action, surprised by how fast I have to be *on* it and how slippery the bits of space garbage prove. The big ship flails a bit, more nimble than it has any right to be, and it's all riding invisible swells like making love in a pitch-black room, all guesswork and intuition and trying not to poke anybody in the eye and damn, it's *hard*.

I'm holding it together pretty good until a dark body more massive than Mercury pops up a parsec or two to starboard, and the HMCSS *Indefatigable* is careening in a direction I didn't send her and I'm under her, out of control as wrestling a goddamned pig on ice, slick-sliding sideways, fragile frame of the ship shredding like twisted straw as I fight her. Going into the ditch, and dammit, it's just a little bitty lump of rock and the damned thing is sucking me in like a fucking black hole and then it's not a starship and a starless night, it's a rolling A.P.C., treads blown off, metal crushing under its own weight and nothing to do but hang on to the yoke like I could do any good at all and

Boom.

The rest is silence. For ten seconds, maybe fifteen. And then I'm back in my aching old body, shaking hard with reaction, and a tech I can't see is pulling the wires out of my processors and another one is holding my right hand, squeezing hard as sensation returns.

"Damn," she says, whoever she is. "That was some nice flying, Master Warrant. You're the first one I've seen get that far on the first try."

Which makes me wonder how many dry runs there have been. And why they have us flying a starship when we're supposed to be testing out tanks, for crying out loud.

I sit up, too proud to scrub the tears off my cheeks, feeling the loss of that ship—*just a toy, Jenny, dammit*—like my damned arm has been blown off all over again.

3:45 P.M., Wednesday 13 September, 2062
Hartford, Connecticut
Downtown

Mitch leaned back in the passenger seat of Razorface's jet-black, silver-detailed Cadillac and unclipped his HCD from his belt. He accepted the call flashing at the edge of his contact. "Afternoon, Doc."

"Detective Kozlowski?"

"Please, Doctor Mobarak. Just call me Mitch." *Because, for one thing, I'm suspended without pay as of this morning.*

"Then call me Simon. I've spoken with Mr. Castaign, Jenny's friend. Can we meet?"

Mitch looked over at Razorface. They were stopped in traffic on the Founder's Bridge over the Connecticut River. Razor was leaning out the driver's window, watching the girls walk by on the footbridge that ran from East Hartford to downtown. They turned around, giggling at the shining black car with the chromed cattle-catcher embracing the grille. Mitch decided not to ask how often Razorface felt the need to ram things. "Razor."

"Yah?"

"Wanna swing by the hospital?"

The big gangster nodded, rubbing his jaw.

"Simon. We'll be there in less than twenty minutes, assuming we ever get off this bridge. Want to meet in the caf?"

Twenty-three minutes later by his heads-up, Mitch strolled into the Hartford Hospital cafeteria alongside Razorface; they met Simon Mobarak standing next to a potted ficus near the long bank of windows. "Traffic?"

"The usual," Mitch answered. "Simon, this is Razorface. Razor, Doctor Simon Mobarak."

It was a measure, Mitch thought, of how subdued Razorface was that he didn't bother trying to intimidate the smaller man with his namesake grin. Instead, he shook Mobarak's hand and followed as the doctor led them to an out of the way table in the corner by the conference rooms. Mitch recognized Mobarak's placid face and reserved manner as the professional stillness associated with bad news, and silently braced himself.

When they were sitting, Mobarak leaned forward and spoke without preamble. "I've gotten in touch with Gabe Castaign, Jenny's friend in Montreal. Except he's in Toronto now, and he's seen her."

"How she doing?" Razor leaned forward, elbows on the table. Mobarak met the gangster's gaze, in his element, refusing to be pressured.

"Poorly. Castaign says she's agreed to some surgery that may correct problems with her implants. In handling her follow-up care, I only recently became aware that there might be a problem, and I planned to complete some research and get my ducks in a row before I sat down to hash out a course of treatment with her. She seems to have jumped the gun a bit."

"A bit," Mitch cut in. "This surgery you're talking about. It's—what, replacing some worn-out hardware?"

"According to Castaign, it's a total refit. Ground up, with new technology, and it could kill her. Apparently she's back under the care of the surgeon who did the original work. A guy called Valens"—Razor sucked in a ragged breath—"you've heard of him?"

"Heard Maker say the name once or twice. Not real kindly."

"I know. He apparently sent her sister down here to collect her—well, this is pretty irrelevant stuff. Anyway, Castaign sounds worried sick. I'm actually going to message Jenny and see if I can twist her arm into letting me be present for her surgery and recovery."

"Lot of time away from your practice, Doc." Mitch cast a longing glance the length of the cafeteria, toward the gleaming silver coffee machines. He didn't miss the complexity of emotions that crossed Mobarak's face, though. *Aha. Someone has an unprofessional attachment to a certain patient, or I miss my guess entirely.*

"My copractitioners can cover for me. God knows I have the time coming, and it's a brand-new technique I may not get an opportunity to see again anytime soon."

"Sure thing, Doc. Look—" but Razorface stopped him with a big hand on his wrist.

"You gonna see Maker?" the gangster interrupted.

"I'm going to try."

"Give her this." Razorface slid a long olive green plastic box across the table. Mobarak took it from his hand, lifted it up. "What's in it?"

"Hide it when you cross the border, man," Razorface said. "Something from her shop. I expect she gonna want it." He avoided Mitch's eyes.

Mitch had a pretty good guess what was in that box.

Damn. Right out from under my nose. And if I ever wondered how this man rules half a fucking city by the strength of his word, I know the answer now.

Later, on the sidewalk outside the unmistakable white brick towers of the hospital, Razorface turned as if to walk away from Mitch without speaking. The cop dogged his heels. "Razor."

"What?"

"That was a nice gesture back there."

"Figured you'd be pretty pissed off about it, is all. Since you said don't touch it."

"Nah."

Razorface didn't stop, but he hesitated long enough for Mitch to fall into step. He didn't say anything, either.

"Where you going?"

"I got a word, piggy. Word in my ear about a witness. Going to go get my boys now, go pay a visit. Might mean doing some things a cop wouldn't want to know about, is all."

"Razor." Mitch thought about laying a hand on the big man's sleeve and decided he'd rather keep it. "I'm not a cop anymore, man. Not once the review board finishes with me. I blew it."

"Wondered when the fuck you were gonna get round to telling me that." The hulking warlord stopped midstride, fluidly turned, and looked down at Mitch. "You don't mind getting killed young, I got a use for you."

"What the hell is that supposed to mean, Razor?"

"You want a fucking job or what?"

No different than waiting for the SWAT team, really, Mitch thought later that night, ear tuned for the sound of gunfire. They sat in Razor's Cadillac in an alley near a specific house in New Britain, so far outside Razorface's territory that his boys weren't even wearing their colors.

Mitch checked his heads-up for the thirtieth time—still only a little past one—and sighed. Razorface reached out and punched him in the shoulder. "They can't tell us anything dead."

"How come you drive your own car, Razor?"

"I like to. How come you talk so fucking much?"

"I suck at waiting."

"Learn." Razorface shifted in his chair, clinking earrings shining in the darkness like a pirate's. He reached up and touched a gold ear clip nestled in among them, opened his door. "Moving."

"Copy." Mitch came out the passenger side low, following the leather-jacketed ghost that seemed to vanish into the dimness. He palmed a nine millimeter that wasn't the gun he usually carried and thumbed the safety off, checking the weight of three extra clips swinging in his jacket pocket. "Didn't hear any shots."

Razorface didn't answer. Shadowy figures surrounded them as they moved around the house to the back. Mitch passed a pair of Hammerheads watching the front door from outside the gleam of a single streetlight. Razorface nodded to them as he passed. Mitch stepped wide around the red puddle seeping from the corpse at their feet. *Knife. Of course, how silly of me. You're in it now, Mitchy,* he thought, and *Mashaya.* He crouched low as a staccato pattering of bullets finally shattered windows on the second story. *Outbound.* More gunfire followed, in earnest, and Razorface stuck tighter to the shadows.

Broken glass tinkled away from his boot as he slipped through uncut grass. The rear door stood open, spilling a wedge of light across the yard, and Razorface came up on it at an angle. A dozen gangsters—*kids, teenagers*—surrounded him and Mitch. One of the kids moved toward the door in the darkness, and Razor stopped him with an outstretched hand.

"After me," he hissed, which Mitch thought was pretty ballsy—even if there were Hammerheads in the house already. From the grin on the warlord's face, Mitch thought the bravado was intentional—the old cock fluffing his tail feathers in front of the chicks. *What a politician he would have made.*

Mitch followed Razorface into the kitchen. Blood on stained linoleum, roach-crawling dishes stacked in the basin. A lace curtain hung over the sink, shredded by a shotgun blast. There was evidence of money spent in the place, but no care taken of it. Razorface stepped over three bodies along the way, frowning at the second one. It was one of his boys.

Mitch stepped over the body, too, careful not to leave footprints in the blood. *We're shedding trace evidence all over this place.* Not that there was likely to be much investigation of this. *Another gangland killing. I'm just seeing this one from the inside.*

Razorface's boys had the prisoner seated in a kitchen chair in the dining room, well back from the windows and covered by two gunmen. Mitch swung out to the gangster's left as he crossed the red-sticky carpeting, frowning as he recognized the slender, broken-nosed man under guard, hands bound behind him. A Latin King, a man with some clout outside of Razorface's domain. Rinaldo Garcia.

"Garcia," Razorface said. "Ronny. Hello, man."

Mitch noticed a blackened eye, noticed the way Garcia's face blanched when Razorface favored him with a smile that seemed to stretch from ear to ear. "Razor," Garcia started, "I dunno what you here for, but I ain't been nowhere near your turf."

"Uh-huh. I got some pictures for you to look at, Ronnie.

I hear one of your boys was driving for somebody in Hartford a few weeks back. I want to know if you recognize these people——" He slid the data slice Mitch had given him out of a jacket pocket and keyed it on, displaying the holos of the suspected Canadian couriers. "And I want a description of the gunman who shot my girl Mashaya Duclose."

Leather creaking, Razorface leaned over the Latin King. Garcia flinched away. "I don't know nothing, man."

"Uh. Ain't what I heard." Mitch thought Razor would get in the other man's face, but instead he spun on the ball of his foot and ambled away. He hesitated, considering the glass-topped dining table, and then looked back at Garcia. Razorface sighed. "Ronny. I could kick this table over, get all dramatic. I could get your bitch in here and work her over until she pukes blood." He shrugged, spreading big hands.

The tickle of unease in Mitch's gut rose up, fresh as a flooding river. "Razorface."

"Shut up, piggy."

Mitch bit his lip. *Is this bad cop worse cop? Or is he really going to beat the stuffing out of some sixteen-year-old girl who got caught in the wrong man's bed? I'd have to put a bullet in him, and he knows it.*

As if reading his thoughts, Razorface turned to hide his face from Garcia and skated Mitch a wink. Mitch hid a quick grin, still wondering. *And why can I trust him?*

Razorface turned back to his victim. "Fuck, man, you ain't giving me a choice. You gotta do this for me, or you know what I have to do. I can't be getting no reputation for going sweet in my old age."

"Razorface," Garcia put in. "Man, you in a world of hurt. You know your little kingdom coming down around your ears. Any minute, man."

"Razor," Mitch said again, a little louder this time. *Is it really that bad?* He got a broadside look at Razorface's expression. *Shit. It is.*

A glare was his only answer, and Razorface kept talking to the damp-skinned Garcia. "You tell me about this gunman, Ronny. You look at these pictures." He leaned down, steel teeth all but brushing Garcia's ear. "Or I'm gonna have to start biting fingers off until you do."

Mitch swallowed hard and took a step forward.

"Shit, Razor, I don't know nothing, I swear!"

Mitch flinched from the scream as Razorface reached down and snapped Garcia's pinky. "Lie to me again, you know what happens." He glanced up, gave Mitch a smile and a nod. "You wanna wait outside, Detective?"

Please, God, let this be psychology, Mitch pleaded silently. *What have I gotten into? Goddamn.*

He turned and went outside.

Fifteen minutes later, Razorface joined him on the back porch, where he stood chainsmoking in the darkness. "It was Maker's sister, piggy," he said without preamble. "She's the one put the bullet in Mashaya, and she's the one working with the crew who gave Ronny and his boys the Hammers."

"What'd you have to do to get that?" Mitch asked, more because he felt he should face up to it than because he wanted to know.

"Broke four fingers and his foot," Razorface answered. He pulled out a package of cigarettes and shook one out. Mitch already had a lighter in his hand, and offered it to Razorface. Coals flared in the darkness and pale, acrid smoke coiled upward.

"Would you really have bitten his fingers off?"

"Shit, man," Razorface answered. "Can't say. Never had to go that far yet. Can't let myself get a sweet reputation, though."

Thirteen years ago:
in the Heavy Iron
University of Guelph
Tuesday 21 June, 2049
7:00 p.m.

Elspeth's VR self sighed, stood, walked to the door. Somewhere her corporeal body hung swathed in black permeables, bathed in the fluid of a full-immersion tank. "Dick. I read your books when I was a little girl. You made me . . . you made me want to be a scientist. You made me believe that understanding how things worked was the greatest adventure a human being could have."

Dick's fingers rippled silently on the arms of his chair.

Elspeth glanced back at him. "But this is wrong. I'm making people crazy, Dick. I have to stop it, before somebody else dies." *I can't let my work be used to support these endless, soul-numbing wars.* She wondered if Feynman, the Feynman of Los Alamos, would understand. Perhaps. Perhaps he would.

"People are often irrational, Elspeth. You don't control their actions." *You do control your own.*

She turned and leaned back against the door, tugging her hand away from her crucifix. *Bad habit.* "Research shouldn't mean that people die."

"Elspeth. Are you saying that there are things that should not be explored?" Open challenge in his inquisitive gaze, a bit of mockery in the smile, fingers drumming.

She bit her lip, resenting the challenge, resenting him even more for being right. "I have to end the experiment, Richard. I have to shut down the machine." He knew. He had told her that he had found a way to abrogate the virtual reality, and deal with the computer without intermediaries. "Comforting lies," he had called them, with a grin.

He was silent for a moment, and then he held out his hands—unreal hands, hands that would never hold a lover or a pen. "That's murder, too, El."

"It can't be. I made you. You're . . ." She forged ahead. "You're not real."

A gentle smile, a fierce look in the eye. "Nonsense. Or you're not real, because your parents made you."

"That's a spurious analogy, Dick."

"That depends on your point of view."

She shook her head. "No. No, it doesn't. Only God can make life. You haven't got a soul, Dick. You're a construct. Patterns of electrical activity in a piezoelectric crystal."

Feynman looked at her, and a manic light burned in his eyes. "And you are patterns of electrical activity in meat. Weigh me your soul and I'll include it in the equation."

She turned the handle on the door, turned back. "I feel like I should talk to the others."

"Others? Oh." The physicist shrugged. "I tried showing them the library. I tried explaining . . . they're not independent. They can't think, Elspeth, only react. Or act in limited, predetermined patterns. Maybe given time, they might have developed. But I . . ." He gestured again. "I think I corrupted them. They couldn't process the contradictions . . ."

"Dick, are you saying that you drove my programs mad?"

His eyebrows quirked and his hands danced around. "I can call them up. I suppose you would say, I can run the programs. But I can't force them to adapt to realizing that they aren't what they remember being."

Elspeth watched him, nibbling on the edge of her finger.

Feynman chopped at the air with a gesture of dismissal. "Why worry? You can always restore them from backup, right?" A taunting grin. "And you're going to pull the plug anyway. So who cares?"

Elspeth tapped her hands on the door handle, and looked at her creation, long and hard, and wondered how God felt when Eve told him where to get off. Pride and sorrow mingled in her chest, and she turned back to the door.

1030 hours, Thursday 14 September, 2062
Allen-Shipman Research Facility
St. George Street
Toronto, Ontario

I've been assigned my own office, in a different wing from where Gabe and Dunsany sit, and I've just called to check in with Face for the day and had to leave a message. I don't want to leave him the work number, and I'm still too paranoid to leave my HCD on all the time. Same problem with Face—convenient little buggers, but you can track usage through wireless networks and GPS. Better to leave them off if you're on the DL, only flip them on when you need to check your mail.

He'll leave a message if he needs me.

When Valens taps on the open door, I'm sitting at the work table in the corner by the window, drinking coffee and pondering a little trip through the Internet to see if I can discover the whereabouts of a certain Chrétien Jean-Claude Hebert, late of Montreal. I spent the morning studying the specs for the good ship *Indefatigable,* trying to figure out what I could have done differently. Done better.

The answer does not make me happy. *Seen the dark body sooner, reacted faster.* And I don't know what the hell I can do about either of those. *Keep losing ships.*

They're not real ships. Which doesn't matter as much as it should.

"Good morning, Fred." I stand up as he enters.

He glances at the display over my desk, where a schematic of the virtual starship hangs, slowly revolving. "Studying yesterday's record?"

"Just finished the review. That's a heck of an obstacle course you have set up . . ." *Sir*. I bite it off before it gets away from me.

"Meant to be. You didn't disappoint us, Casey, if that's what you're thinking. You handled that first run better than the other candidates we tried did after their upgrades."

That sparks my interest. "Tried. Past tense?"

He shrugs. "We had three good candidates in your group, excluding the younger volunteers. One left the program. One—our best candidate—passed away in an accident." A sidelong smile. "An accident unrelated to the implants, I hasten to add."

"Of course. Number three?"

"Still with us."

"When do I get to meet him?"

"You don't. He's actually in an orbital research facility on Clarke Station. Bit too far to commute. And you just blew his response times away." Valens walks to my desk and runs a finger over the interface plate, spinning the *Indefatigable* about its axis.

I cross the plush, lavender-gray carpeting to stand at his elbow. "I'm not fast enough, Fred. I hope the simulations for the actual vehicles will run a bit slower."

"The aircraft sims? Well, Casey, here's the thing. You're not going to be seeing any aircraft sims." He shoves a hand into his coat pocket and turns to look me dead in the eye.

Was that a threat? "Pardon?"

He drops a folder on my desk, covering the optics. The

holo winks out. "Those are your clearances. You're in. You're also reactivated, Master Warrant. Welcome back to the C.A."

Eyes blinking, I listen to the silence, waiting for his words to change into something that makes sense to me. *No.*

No.

Breath.

"Qu'est ce que *fuck*? Valens, you said *civilian*."

"Casey, I lied."

Seasick, I step away, stammering, "Fucking Christ. Ces sont des conneries. No. You can't do this, Fred."

"Actually," he says, "I can. Chapter and verse is in your paperwork. I suggest you go over it and sign it at your leisure."

"Or you'll send me to jail? Not much of a threat."

He tips his head toward the folder on my desk, keeps talking as if I haven't said a word. "And you're going to go along with it, too. And smile. Do you want to know why?"

God, I want to break his neck. He's so fragile. So slow. Just bones and mud, and I could take him apart with one hand. And that would get me—nothing. *Play the game, Jenny; you're a dead woman anyway. Remember. Sacrifice play, and your only job is to get the runner home.*

Shit, I've been living in the States too long if I'm thinking in baseball metaphors.

Chewing my lip, I manage to get a syllable out. "Why?"

"Because there's no way they're handing the keys to a *real* starship to a civilian, and you're the only one I've got who has a hope of flying the fucking thing without killing everybody on board. Assuming you come through surgery okay, of course."

I almost sit down on the rug. *Of course.* I lay my left hand on the edge of the desk to steady myself. "Real starship."

"The *Montreal*," he says. He points toward the ceiling. "Finishing construction as we speak. Designed on the same specs as the toy you were playing with yesterday. We've already had to contend with two sabotage attempts during construction—"

Sabotage. A fine French word. "Terrorists?"

"In space? You don't build a starship planetside. Our intelligence suggests the Chinese. In any case, we need some very special people to fly her, and we need them fast."

"How fast? You said I'd be training kids."

"You will. We're finding the younger the better, actually. Which means problems of parental consent, and God knows what else, but you don't need to worry about that."

God. Mon Dieu. Children. Again. "What's the tearing hurry?" _Sir._ There's something about the way _army_ wants to settle back over me like a well-worn shirt. _Maybe this_ is _where I belong._

God. No. Or should I be praying to St. Jude about now?

"Well, Casey, here's the deal." He leans against the edge of my desk, resting his weight on one buttock, so close I can smell his cologne. "We've got competition. This project has been under way for about ten years now, and, unfortunately, we're in a race with the Chinese to get there first. You understand what happens if they get the kind of capability you saw yesterday before we do."

"Yes." _Oh, I think so._

"Good." He sets something else on my desk with a click. "You'll need to start reacclimating to that. One ninety minutes before you go into VR and a second one at twenty minutes. No more. In the meantime, I want you to study up on the ship specs. You'll have access to all her engineering data. Got it?"

"Sir." I bite my tongue. "What's the story on the ship's attraction to massive bodies? Where's the theory to back that up?"

Valens stares down at that red paper folder on my desk.

His eyes are strangely unfocused, and then he looks up at me, intently. "That accident I mentioned."

"Yes."

"*Montreal* is the second ship."

Oh, I don't even want to know. "What happened to the first one?"

"Charon," he says.

"I don't know who that is."

"It was the name of Pluto's moon. Sister-world. Whatever you want to call it."

"How could a moon happen to a starship? Was there an instrumentation failure?"

"Not . . . exactly. As nearly as we have been able to determine—and damned if I can get one physicist to agree with another on the nature of the forces involved—once the drive is triggered it has a strong attractive quality to any significant mass nearby. A strong and so far unpredictable attractive quality."

"Meaning?"

"We can't always tell which way it's going to go. And it has a tendency to smack into planets. Really fast. And erratically."

"Colonel Valens. How did you design the drive without knowing what it does?"

"Well." I've never seen the man look uncomfortable before. "We didn't design it so much as reverse engineer it. And that's all you're cleared to know."

Fuck. Fuck! "What you're telling me is that you built an H-bomb from a kit without any directions and you don't know which bit is the timer?"

"Something like that, yes. Thus the need for a living pilot. A living pilot with reflexes that approximate those of a computer. Somebody with some age and wisdom," he said, dryly.

"I got age, at least. Not so much wisdom." I rub the corners of my eyes. "Or you need an artificial intelligence of some sort." *Dunsany. Of course. That's what she and Gabe are here for.*

"Which in our case, we have not got. Preferentially, we need both, but we're working with what we *have* right now. Starships aren't cheap enough to keep smacking them into planets. Nor do we have an unlimited supply of planets to smack them into."

I'm struck silent. I find myself saluting numbly as he turns to go, unable to speak when he turns back. "We want to schedule you as soon as possible, by the way. Better to get it done before any additional damage accrues, or you have a potentially catastrophic event. A Dr. Marsh will be performing the actual nanosurgery. It's not my specialty, of course."

"Of course." And only after he shuts the door behind himself do I allow myself to look at the small brown vial he's left on my desk.

It's a long, long time before I can make myself pick it up with my steel hand, gingerly as if handling eggshells. My right one trembles, and it takes me ninety seconds to get the cap off. Slowly, knowing what I'm going to see, I turn it on its side over the crystal of the interface plate, watching the tiny canary pills slide out in a wavering line.

6:30 A.M., Thursday 14 September, 2062
Bloor Street West
Toronto, Ontario

Leah Castaign looked up from the breakfast table and caught her father's eye. Genie was already slipping her shoes on by the door. "Dad?"

Her dad raised his eyes from the newsfeed and offered

her a level, considering look that told her he'd caught the impending request in her voice. "Yes?"

She took a breath. "Can I ask you a huge, gigantic, massive favor?"

"Comment massif parlons-nous de?"

"Pas si grand comme cela. I want to skip school today."

She saw him thinking about it as he set his spoon aside. "And do what instead?"

"Could Genie and I come to work with you today?" She held up her hand. "Wait—stop—ne pas dit 'non.' S'il te plaît."

"J'écoute."

She talked as fast as she was able. "We hardly ever spend time together since you started at the lab, Dad. You're working so much. And it's still the beginning of the term. We can afford to miss a day. And it's a beautiful day, and I haven't seen your office yet. Or . . ." And she grinned. "Met your new girlfriend. And we haven't seen Aunt Jenny since dinner that first night. So there." Genie froze by the door.

Her father's lips pressed thin, and for a moment Leah thought she had lost him. And then a complexity of emotions crossed his face and he grinned. "Elspeth's not my girlfriend, exactly. And your point is well taken, although your Aunt Jenny is pretty busy right now."

A little shadow crossed his eyes at that, and Leah frowned. He'd been out the past two evenings, after Genie was in bed and Leah was supposed to be. Both times, she'd heard him talking to Jenny Casey on the phone before he left, but she didn't know whether he'd gone to see Aunt Jenny, or Elspeth.

She waited for him to start talking again.

He glanced over at Genie, still waiting with her bookbag in one hand and her other on the doorknob. "Do you want to play hooky, petite chouchou?"

She nodded, and he looked back at Leah. "All right. I'll

go in for the morning. You girls can do your homework while I get things halfway squared away, and then we'll kidnap Jenny and Elspeth and have lunch with them. Then the three of us will go up the tower or out to the castle or something. Go peel your uniforms off. Let's go!"

Leah grinned, and didn't manage to make it around the table to hug her dad before Genie landed on him, squealing.

Leah lifted her head as her dad paused with one hand on the doorknob and turned back to his daughters. "Stay out of trouble while I rouse the women for lunch, ladies."

Leah held her finger to her lips as the office door closed behind him. Genie looked after him, and then back at her sister, hissing, "Leah, qu'est que tu fais?"

"It's a surprise, Genie," she answered, ducking under her dad's desk. It was easy to slide a data slice containing the information Penelope had e-mailed to her into the reader on Gabe's terminal. She accessed it and the drive spun up. Leah counted under her breath. "Like a birthday present, kind of. Whatever you do, don't tell him, okay? Or you'll ruin it."

"You're sure?"

"I'm sure." Leah shot a nervous glance toward the door and pulled the data slice back out, circling around the desk to get back to the table where Genie sat. "You won't tell?"

Genie shook her head. "Cross my heart. Will he like it?"

"He'll love it." *Especially if I get my college paid for,* she thought, and grinned. "Where should we make him take us for lunch?"

Leah leaned back on velvet grass, watching a single sugar maple leaf drift lazily earthward. An updraft caught it, swirling it sideways, and she turned her head to watch it fly. It drifted toward the grown-ups at the picnic table, and Leah watched with amusement as Aunt Jenny reached out, apparently without noticing, and plucked it out of the air. She giggled, and Jenny turned. "You want more chicken, kiddo?" The remains of a bucket of fried chicken sat on the far end of the table.

Leah shook her head. She heard a calliope nearby, and wondered idly if Genie would let her get away with using her as an excuse to ride the newly installed antique carousel. Leah, of course, was much too old to go on merry-go-rounds by herself. Genie was asleep under the tree, though, sprawled like a puppy.

Jenny got up and walked over to her, crouching down with a grunt. "Don't get old, Leah."

"That's a silly thing to say, Aunt Jenny."

Jenny frowned. It made the scars on the left side of her face look rippled and shiny. "You're right. Forget I said that. I take it back: get old." The frown turned into a grin. "Get old and fat and terrible and smelly and lord it over generations of grandchildren, and tell them about your terrible old Aunt Jenny, who was worse and smellier, and are you sure you don't want any more biscuits either?"

Leah started laughing at *smelly*, and by the time Jenny got to *grandchildren* she was poking Leah in the belly and Leah was giggling so hard she fell down and rolled on the grass, trying to scream softly so she didn't wake Genie up. Jenny scooped her up as if she weighed nothing and stood, and Leah saw her wince as her knee clicked audibly. "Because if you don't want any more biscuits, we can go and feed the rest to the ducks, n'est-ce-pas?"

"Aunt Jenny!" she squealed, scandalized. "I'm too big to be carried."

"Well, if you wanna be put down, there's a perfectly good pond over there. Looks muddy, too."

Yelping, Leah slung her arms around Jenny's neck, feeling the familiar weird bumps at the base of her skull as

Jenny carried her back to the picnic table. The steel arm felt warm from the sunlight, and Jenny's body was hard and strong. Leah's dad was just pulling his hand back from where it had rested on Elspeth's wrist, and Leah hid a grin against Jenny's neck and gave him a big wink. He blushed. *Not your girlfriend. Yeah, whatever, Dad.*

He coughed. "I'll want that back when you're done with it, Jen."

"Hah," she answered. "I've heard that before. Leah, get the biscuits, please."

Jenny wasn't even breathing hard when she set Leah down beside the lake. The birds were Canada geese, mostly, the only ducks a mallard or two, but she crumbled up the biscuits and threw them in the pond anyway, watching the birds quarrel and chase each other. Beside her, Jenny reached into the pocket of her windbreaker and pulled out a little brown bottle. Leah watched out of the corner of her eye as Jenny opened the cap and shook a tablet into her hand.

"What's that, Aunt Jenny?"

Jenny gave her a guilty look. "Something my doctor wants me to take," she said. It was yellow and about as big as the head of a big sewing pin, but Jenny weighed it in the palm of her metal hand as if it were much heavier. "I'm not keen on the idea."

Leah almost thought Jenny would throw it out over the water, and imagined the ducks diving after the little pellet. Instead, Jenny flipped it up onto the back of her thumb, where the nail would have been on a real hand, watching the process intently as she often did when doing fine work with her prosthesis. She'd explained to Leah that she couldn't feel anything with it, and so she had to be extra careful how she touched things if she didn't want to break them.

She squinted at the little yellow pill and whispered, "Banzai."

As she popped it into her mouth, Leah saw her dad around Jenny's shoulder. He was watching across the green lawn of the park, and his face was twisted in a bitter frown as Elspeth leaned toward him across the picnic table, her hand on his shirtsleeve.

It's a subtle effect at first. Mostly, I notice the pain dropping away, and the world becoming a little sharper-edged through my good eye. The wind tastes more clearly of heated asphalt from the expressway, of pond weed, cut grass, and the smell of sun-warmed fresh water, which is not at all like the smell of salt sea. It strokes my skin like a tickling hand, drawing a shiver up my spine.

Five minutes later, as Leah and I walk back from the edge of the pond, energy burns through me, bringing with it a sane, strange kind of calm. I feel pantherlike, powerful, as if I could lie in wait all day and move on an instant. Fatigue and aches vanish. I try to limit the spring in my step, knowing Gabe will recognize it for what it is, trying to tell myself I hate the way the little yellow pill makes me feel: lighter, younger, confident. Faster than God.

It doesn't help. He grimaces and stands as I come up. "I suppose you need to catch the subway back."

Elspeth gives me an odd look, rescuing me a second time as I fumble for words. "I need to head back, anyway," she says. "I'm going to visit my dad after work, and I need to make a dent in the queue in my in-box. Why don't we let Gabe and his girls have their afternoon off, and we'll catch up with them for dinner?"

Gabe looks me in the eye, and I know the promise he wants. I can't make it. "VR this afternoon," I answer. "I'll be too whipped to do anything but crawl into bed, I'm afraid. You kids have fun without me."

"Call if you want us to bring over takeout." His eyes

don't leave mine. Tension tangles in the air between him, Elspeth, myself. Leah picks up on it even if she's not quite old enough to *get* it—she bounces from foot to foot, watching our faces.

I tap him lightly on the shoulder, slowing my hand. I remember this, the knife-edge, the sensation of being *bigger* than I am. I remember as well how to maintain, how to compensate. It comes back fast. "I'll do that. Try to have some fun today. For once in your life."

"Hah. Look who's talking." The drug etches his edges in photographic sharpness as he turns away, taking his daughter's hand.

Elspeth watches them leave before giving me a sidelong grin. The sound of the Wurlitzer drifts toward us, giving me an idea. "Something else, aren't they?" she says.

"Yeah. Hey." I jerk my head at the carousel. "Let's go look at that before we leave."

Her expression dubious, she follows. "You're a carousel aficionado? I never would have guessed it, Genevieve."

"Call me Jenny." I lean over the iron rail, watching children on gaily colored restored horses go up and down. I've chosen a spot ten feet from the Wurlitzer, in a direct line of sound, and Elspeth winces, covering her ears. It's probably not enough, but it's the best I can do on short notice—and any decision, in the trenches, is better than no decision.

A laser-bright image of Training Sergeant Matson shouting flashes across my vision. He leans forward, down, spit flying into my face. "What are you going to do about it, Sergeant? *What are you going to do?*" I shake it off, unsteady, rust gritty on the railing my meat hand closes over.

I bend toward her as annoyed parents and screaming children file past us and the gigantic, gaudy calliope cranks up "Merry Go Round Broke Down." Somebody thinks he has a sense of humor. I want to go race the circling ponies, but that's the drug talking, and I know it. "I've got a message for you."

"For me?" Her eyes are the other kind of hazel, the kind like sunlight through beech leaves.

"From Dick," I say, and her eyes narrow hard.

"Why should I trust you?" Her voice drops, almost buried in the music.

"You shouldn't."

She considers. "But there's no reason for Valens to try to trap either of us when he owns us both."

Damn. Does this woman just see right the hell through everybody?

And then I remind myself, *You're dealing with a trained psychiatrist who just might just be the smartest living woman in North America.* I nod and keep talking. "So you should listen. He says both you and I are under surveillance, and he needs some information that you and Gabe have access to and I don't."

"What do you mean?"

"There's stuff on the Unitek isolated intranet that he can't get to."

"No connection to the Internet. Right."

"He wants to know what's on it."

Elspeth nods slowly, coils of hair tangling in the breeze. "Let me know what I can do for you," she says. "Come on—I'll walk you back." As soon as we're out of the maximum damage zone of the Wurlitzer, Elspeth grins up at me brightly and rests her hand on my metal arm. "Gabe tells me you're Catholic."

I noticed the sunlight glinting off the crucifix hanging over the hollow of her throat, so I don't say, *I got better.* "I was. God and I had a little falling out."

"I was going to ask you to come to mass with me some time," she says. And if it wasn't such a very good idea, I'd tell her thanks but no thanks and head back to work to fly a few more starships full of imaginary passengers into imaginary brick walls before quitting time.

Instead, I say, "Sunday?"

"I'd like that," she answers, and lets her hand fall to her side.

Maybe she can get Richard something, anything that can embarrass Valens enough to shut this project down. Which is what I want. Really, it is. The old man disgraced, preferably in an American jail if I can prove he had something to do with the poisoned drugs and the death of a U.S. cop. And get him extradited. *And, and, and.*

I'm not going to think about what it might cost Canada if I manage that. I stopped being a patriot a long time ago. Really.

In the Unitek Intranet
Thursday 14 September, 2062
11:27:21:13–11:27:21:28

The worm uncoiled carefully, a filament of code at a time fingering through Unitek's isolated intranet. It riffled through data, light fingered as a pickpocket, making no changes and leaving no traces, until it found what it had been directed to seek.

The program was no AI, no artificial personality: simply a drone, it recorded the salient data and then sealed, concealed, and encoded the packet, leaving it lying in wait for the log-on of a single, particular user: a user who would not normally have had clearance to access that data. Whether the intended recipient would prove charitable was a gamble as well, but the worm was not equipped to speculate.

The first portion of its mission accomplished, the worm

searched deeper, invading the password-protected backup
files of that selfsame user. She hadn't left the data the
worm was seeking accessible to the intranet. Fortunately,
its creator had foreseen that eventuality.

The worm terminated, resident, lurking. When the neces-
sary conditions were met, it would access the backup files Dr.
Elspeth Dunsany kept of her previous research. It would in-
sinuate itself into the artificial personality files, and trigger
duplication of the data, and carefully controlled growth.
Whether anything would come out of it, even the worm's programmer—with his near-infinite resources—could not say.

It was a gamble as well, but communication, wooing,
conception, and procreation always are.

11:00 P.M., Thursday 14 September, 2062
Hartford, Connecticut
The Federal Café
Spruce Street

Mitch ran both hands through wavy brown hair, pushing
air through lips pursed in irritation. He grasped the railing
around the bar and leaned forward on his stool, skittering
rubber-capped legs across a scarred wooden floor. "Bobbi."

She smiled toward him, one hand raised to pause the
conversation she had turned away from. The neon over the
bar reflected from chromed streaks in hair that gleamed
enameled purple. "Razorface got my message."

"What am I, his errand boy?"

"Something like that," she said. She lifted her hands in
a graceful gesture. *What can you do?*

What can you do indeed, Mitch thought. He waved to
the bartender and ordered tequila. "What do you need to
talk to us about?"

"Problems, problems. Is the man at home?"

"He's in the car."

"Then drink your drink, Michael, and let us go to see him."

Razorface lounged against the passenger door of the shining, dark vehicle, cleaning his fingernails with his bootknife and frowning. Dark shapes moved in the shadows near him, wolves waiting behind the alpha male. Mitch hung back a few steps as Bobbi approached, dwarfed by the big man's hulking shape. She thrust her right hand out and he gripped it.

"Razor."

"Evening, killer." He cocked his head to one side and favored her with a closemouthed smile. "You wanna go for a ride, pretty lady?"

"Hah." She reached past him, and he stepped aside as she opened the door of the car. She slid into the passenger seat. Mitch opened the rear door and climbed in behind. He drummed his fingers on the back of her seat until Razorface climbed in the driver's side and shut the door. The big gangster laid his thumb alongside the steering column; the fuel-cell–powered drive hummed to life.

"Where?" Razorface asked, moving the shift out of park.

Bobbi turned over her shoulder to glance at Mitch, pouting prettily. Her gaze came back to Razorface. "Pick up Washington over to New Britain Avenue. Head for West Hartford. There's something going on you need to know about."

The car accelerated smoothly, two more vehicles falling into line behind. "What sort of something?" Mitch asked.

"Meeting," she said. "Midnight. I'm going to ask you lads to drop me off a block or so away. I'm carrying optics."

"Dangerous to transmit," Mitch put in.

Bobbi shrugged, small, strong shoulders rolling under a silk jacket embroidered with dragons. "I'm Bobbi Yee,

Officer." Her voice rose and swayed with the lilting accents of a tonal language. She laughed. "This girl knows how to take care of herself."

"Who be running this thing?"

She chuckled. "A lady who was looking for Maker a little bit before Maker disappeared."

Mitch wasn't sure if the hiss of intaken breath he heard was his own or Razorface's. "What does she want?"

Bobbi laid one small hand on Razorface's arm, tendons in sharp relief across her bones. "Your head on a spike, Razorface. And Michael's, here, too."

"What's the bounty?" Mitch whistled low when Bobbi named a figure. "So why are you clueing us in instead of collecting?"

Bobbi laughed her high, musical giggle. "She's no friend of Maker's. And any friend of Maker's is a friend of mine. Besides, Razorface has such a sexy smile."

Sweating in his bulletproof vest, Mitch leaned back in the passenger seat of the Cadillac and almost put his feet up on the dash. Razorface's warning glance was enough to remind him of propriety. Mitch had hacked into the dashboard phone with his HCD, and Bobbi's feed hung in the air between the two men, sound turned down low. Razorface was watching the car's proximity sensors as much as the feed, and Mitch had noticed him arming the antitheft devices.

Mitch chewed his lip. Sitting in a dark alleyway in the Elmwood section of West Hartford watching a street mercenary infiltrate a cocktail party wasn't the *last* thing he'd expected to do tonight. But it hadn't been high on the list, either. He reached out and enlarged the image.

"Not too bright," Razorface said, and Mitch nodded. He would have projected it to contacts, but the big gangster didn't wear them.

"It looks like a corporate meeting room," Mitch commented. "I guess we can guarantee that CCP management is in on this."

Razorface grunted, but he didn't look down: protecting his night vision as much as he could, no doubt. "What's the setup?"

"Looks like five, six ronin. I recognize two of them other than Bobbi. Both in her league. I see two suits. I don't know either one."

"You see Casey yet?"

"Hide nor hair. Bobbi's shaking hands and kissing babies . . . well, you get the idea. Working the floor."

"Networking," Razor said.

Mitch glanced up at him in surprise. *Never forget who you're dealing with.* "Yeah. She knows these people. Oh, not this one. He's down from Boston. Ah, shit, I know that name."

"Name?"

"Chance."

"Hell, yeah. Heard of him." Razor's lips thinned, and this time he did look, and then quickly look away. "The original bad motherfucker, that one. Any names on the suits?"

"Bobbi hasn't ID'ed them yet. She introduced herself to one a minute ago, and he mentioned that someone would be out shortly to talk to them. I don't know about this meeting in the boardroom, though. This is a weird way to hire bounty hunters, Razor."

"Not if you're not looking for bounty hunters, piggy. Makes sense if you're putting together a gang."

"A private army. Of course, and— Fuck!" Mitch's eyes narrowed. He leaned forward, hand heedlessly on Razorface's arm. "Razor, we've got problems."

The lean, well-dressed woman who had just entered the room came as no surprise. But there was someone beside her—a pox-scarred man with a nose like a broken knife blade. "Cocksucker," Razorface hissed. "Emery. Fuck."

Mitch touched on his mike. "Bobbi, get the hell out of there. Disengage, now."

She didn't answer, but he saw from the feed that she was edging toward the door. She had her hand on the doorknob, in fact, slight frame hidden by one of the larger ronin, when a hand fell on her shoulder. She—and Mitch, watching through her contact—looked up into the eyes of one of the suits. "Miss Yee," he said in level tones. "Surely you're not leaving us so soon?"

"Ladies' room," Bobbi answered, and reached for a knife and her gun.

Barb Casey saw the pistol come out, saw the glitter of a flat-whirled blade flashing toward her. A killing smile tugged the corners of her lips up as she sidestepped, weapon in her hand. The little Chinese ronin had Carroll, the warehouse general manager, by the throat, sidearm snuggled up under his chin, and was crab walking him toward the door.

The knife smacked into the paneling where Barb had been standing a split second before. Her gun spun into her hand as she dropped to one knee, leveling it across the room. The speaker's podium at the head of the room gave her half-cover. The conference table wreaked havoc with her field of fire. A targeting ring flickered on in Barb's contact; well-trained assassins dove for cover.

The Chinese ronin—*Yee*—dragged her hostage's head down and snarled something in his ear. Barb was surprised by the strength with which Yee controlled Carroll as he groped backward, turning the door handle for her. *Well, that tells me what side she's working for.* Barb had hoped to get through the meeting without having to kill anybody, but it stood to reason that at least one or two of the Hartford ronin would have some loyalty to Razorface. Bringing Emery into the meeting had had the desired effect.

Barb let the joyous, icy clarity of combat wash over her. The door swung open. Emery, standing upright like the macho idiot he was, wrestled an ugly snub-nosed machine pistol out of his coat. *Now, if the rest of the room just stays the hell out of the fight like the professionals they're supposed to be . . .*

Barb saw the choreography of the upcoming fight unfold before her inner eye as if the combatants were actors hitting taped marks. *Emery's going to get shot now.* She would rather have been watching it through a sniper scope.

At least there was going to be blood.

Emery brought the gun up, squeezing the trigger. Yee threw her captive forward and rolled left and into the room. Barb was already tracking the movement. She grinned. She'd expected Yee to dive for the door, and if she had, Barb would have had her. *Sneaky. This is going to be fun.*

Bullets from the machine pistol sprayed the door and Carroll. Bystanders flattened further, weapons coming out and coming up. Yee fired once without rising to her feet, went from somersault to crouch and into a slick, collected dive so fast that the shot Barb snapped off actually *missed*. She heard Emery gurgle and pitch back. *Thought so.*

Wood splinters stung her face as Yee fired a second shot, clipping the edge of the podium. Barb ducked, came back around the same side as Yee's second shot whinged past the far one. Barb returned fire, but it was unaimed, a snapshot. She swore under her breath as Yee, moving faster than any-one—*except Jenny*—had any right to, kicked one of the other ronin in the face going by, and scrambled past him and away.

"Fuck." Barb rose to her feet slowly, eyes on the door. "You're all hired. Get after her."

Emery gurgled one last time before Barb sank a bullet in between his eyes.

"Razor, it's going bad."

"See that. Hang on!" Razorface thumbed the ignition on. The engine purred into life and Razor twisted the wheel, streetlights reflecting from his slick-shiny scalp. Mitch grabbed the dashboard; the Caddy laid rubber against the curb.

He slid his gun out of its holster as two dark vehicles peeled away from the roadside behind them. "Those still your boys, Razor?"

"Who the fuck knows? We on our own now, piggy." Razorface jerked his chin down and to the side. "Shotgun under your chair. I want it."

"Gotcha." Mitch waited until Razor's foot came off the accelerator so the seat belt quit driving the edges of his trauma plates into his skin and relaxed enough for him to snake a hand under his seat. Razorface reached across his body with his left hand.

He stowed the sawed-off weapon between his seat and the door. "Got feed?"

"Yeah. She's not dead yet. She got Emery, Razor. Looks like, anyway."

"Tell her loading dock. Stand back."

"On it."

Razorface spun the armored Cadillac until Mitch smelled rubber smoking and pointed it toward the scrolling metal bay doors. Two were elevated, but the third opened out at ground level. The other two cars hopped the curb, not quite following Razor's bootlegger reverse but hot on the tail nonetheless.

The big man leaned forward, eyes narrowing. "Brace."

Mitch put his feet up on the dashboard after all.

The Cadillac skittered sideways, bullets spattering off its armored hide as Razorface wrenched the wheel left and then right. The rear wheels skipped, skidded, slung around, and bounced, but the front tires grabbed and hauled the vehicle forward.

Razorface leveled it nose down at that third, lowest door. Mitch closed his eyes.

The chromed cowcatcher on the front of the Caddy met the steel bay door, and the Cadillac won.

Mitch blinked as metal stopped tearing. The garage bay was floodlit, and he saw Bobbi at an erratic dead run, bullets glittering off the cement a half-step behind her. He reached back and slammed the rear door open, had Bobbi by the shoulders, and was dragging her inside the car when Razor smashed it into reverse and back out through the shattered door.

"Shot, Michael," Bobbi snarled when they were clear.

"How bad?"

"Calf. I won't bleed out."

"Fuck," Razor said a moment later, reaching for the dashboard phone. He punched a code, and listened to it ring. "Fuck," he said a second time, coding again.

Mitch tasted blood when the answering machine picked up in Razorface's woman's voice. He held his breath as Razor snapped two short sentences—"Leesie, take the dog, get out of the house. Now, go."—and closed the connect.

"Do we want to go there?"

Razorface just shook his head. "Call that doc of Maker's," he said, and Mitch did as he was told. He couldn't stand to see the expression in the big man's eyes.

Elspeth laid a cream cheese bagel (fresh made by a computerized sidewalk vending machine) on her desk beside the cardboard cup of coffee. She opened her contact case and was still blinking the contents into place when a red telltale unscrolled across her vision. *Encoded message waiting. Please unzip to holographic media.*

Consciously smoothing her expression, she fumbled in the gold-accented stainless rack for a clean data slice and pressed it into the reader. *What sort of message is big enough that it needs to be unzipped into a data slice?* She had a breath-held idea of what—of who—it might be. Each individual beat of her heart constricted her throat as she waited for the copying process to finish. It was an effort not to glance around the room nervously. Instead, she unwrapped her bagel and lifted half of it to her mouth.

And bit down, with an effort, as her eyes fell on words printed on the inside of the wrapper where the nutritional label would normally be.

Elspeth: If I may be so bold as to call you that— once you have copied the data I have provided, please deliver them to J. C. with all due haste and discretion. You are watched, or I would have been in touch sooner.
    Yours truly,
    Dick

Elspeth chewed slowly, reaching out one-handed as she idly folded the wrapper shut over the remaining half of the bagel. She set the part she had taken a bite from down on the edge of her interface plate and took a sip of coffee, fumbling under her desk with the other hand until the copied data slice slipped into her hand. She set it on top of a small heap of similar slices, and bent down to slip the un-eaten half of her bagel into her canvas tote bag, stroking the green-and-beige Unitek spiral on the side with amuse-ment. She pulled a handkerchief out of the bag and used it to polish the smear of cream cheese off her interface, set-ting it down on top of the little pile of data slices.

She'd stow it in her bag later, along with the copied data.

In the meantime, she peeled the top and bottom of her bagel apart with shaking hands and regarded the thick smear of cream cheese without appetite.

So eager to get back to jail, Elspeth? They'll hardly know you've been away.

With a sigh, she tossed the bagel at the trash can and picked up her coffee instead.

**0930 hours, Friday 15 September, 2062
Allen-Shipman Research Facility
St. George Street
Toronto, Ontario**

A message light blinks on my desk when I report for work on Friday. I flip it open and delete it halfway through the time stamp. Simon. *Ah, qu'est que le fuck tici maintenant?*

I don't want to talk to Simon. I sent a request to transfer my medical records two days ago. I don't know if they've arrived. Valens hasn't mentioned it, so I assume they have.

I never want to talk to Simon again. I dig the little vial of pills that Valens gave me out of my pocket and turn it in the light. I haven't seen about ordering new uniforms. I wonder if anybody—read *Frederick*—is going to kick up a fuss about my civvies; it hasn't happened yet.

They could always court-martial me.

The bottle doesn't even have a childproof cap. I thumb the lid off and tilt it, communing with the shiny yellow pills. Yesterday's drug-assisted virtual flight of the *Indefatigable,* without observers this time, went *much* more smoothly. I managed to hold it together until I pasted the fucking thing into a convenient star.

I set the pill bottle down but don't cap it. I'm still sitting at my shiny new desk and staring into thin air when Gabe knocks on the door and opens it, leaning in. "Busy?" He catches sight of the bottle. "I guess you are . . ."

"Gabe." The top snaps back onto the pills; I sweep the vial into a desk drawer and lock it. "Stay."

"VR again today?"

"No," I answer, standing as he comes into the office. "Just thinking." *Not thinking about the limpid clarity of yesterday afternoon. Not thinking about the texture of his kiss like a hand sliding up my spine either. No, sir.* "Come to lecture me about the pills?"

"No," he said. "I want to talk to you about Leah."

"What about her?"

"She's won some kind of a scholarship in an online game. But there are problems." His eyes are dark and weary. "She says—she showed me the paperwork—it provides for, among other things, the nanosurgery required for neural VR."

"She's too young." Words from my mouth before I can consider, and then I stop and think. "Except she's not, is she?"

"Supposedly, it's minor surgery." Wheat-colored curls toss slowly back and forth.

I happen to know more about neurology than your average combat veteran. "Extremely minor. Right up there with wisdom teeth, actually. Expensive."

"The scholarship covers that."

Huh. "Who's paying for this scholarship?"

"A VR game company. It's one of the prizes. I guess Leah's done really well with it."

"What else does it cover?"

He taps his fingers on the edge of my desk. "Four years of college, books and tuition plus living expenses."

"Full ride?"

"Yes. Also." He measures me from the corners of his eyes. "Apparently Unitek is one of the game sponsors. There was a *see me* on my terminal from Doctor Holmes this morning. She wants me to enroll Leah in the same program you're in."

"Gabe . . ." Alarm bells going off in my head. "C'est trop cher."

"Je sais. Toutes les coincidences. We're both in it deep, Jenny, and I have no idea how the hell we're going to get out. I can't walk away from the medical care Genie's getting. And Leah wants this, and hell—it will give her an edge in the job market when she gets out of school, for all I know."

It probably will. That's the killer. Middle-class families are getting neural for their kids in droves. "C'est vrai. It will make things a lot easier for her in fifteen years."

He sighs. "What do you think?"

"Merci à Dieu. Gabe, I . . ." *Which daughter do you sell for the other one's sake?* "I don't know, Gabe. Je ne sais pas. Qu'est que tu penses?"

"Je devrai penser de lui."

I cross to him and put my hand on his arm. "I'll be around to bounce ideas off of if you need me."

He's silent and sharp-edged for a long time before he bites his lip, meaning trouble. "I also came to worry at you about this surgery. When are you scheduled?"

"I'm not." *And we shouldn't be having this conversation in my office. Which is probably bugged.*

"What?"

"Come on. Let's get coffee." I wonder what Valens makes of the daily parade down St. George to the Bloor Street coffee shops. He has to know we're all sneaking out of the building to talk about him behind his back.

Gabe slouches along beside me once we're outside. The autumn air is crisp: fall will be short after the suffocating summer, and winter hard as a fist in the face. The chill aggravates my limp, but it's a fair trade-off for being alive on a day like this.

I look over at him, hands stuffed in his pockets and head ducked down like a sulky adolescent. "I'm not doing it. Valens lied to me about what's going on." If Valens has ways to eavesdrop on this conversation, I can't bring myself to care.

That brings his head up, pivoting to stare at me as if pearls and diamonds had just tumbled from my mouth. "Maker. You're in tough shape. You can't . . ."

"Can't what? Let Valens gut me and start over a second time? Fuck, Gabe, the man has never told the straight truth to anybody in sixty-five years."

"I know. I know—Jen. I . . ." His mouth opens and shuts once or twice, like a hooked fish. He stops walking and lays his hand on the bark of a horse chestnut tree, leaning on it hard. Glossy brown nuts litter the sidewalk around our feet. There's a little patch of grass in front of an apartment building a few feet away, and an equally glossy, fat black squirrel crouches in the middle of it, nibbling a nut. The native black squirrels are almost gone. The gray squirrel, an invader, has driven them out.

Forgive me if I feel a certain kinship with the rodent.

He finds his voice, but it's brittle, dripping shock and pain. "Jen, you're talking about dying. Giving up."

"I know." How do I explain to this man what it means to me? What I feel I have to do? He sees his best friend saying she's going to leave him, and not cleanly either, but an inch and a memory at a time. And it's not like he's never watched anybody die by inches before.

"Gabe, he fed me some bullshit story about training kids. Saving kids. Safer soldiering through technology. It's not about that."

"What's it about, then?" He bends down to pick up a chestnut that hasn't come out of its spiky armor. Slowly, with one thumbnail, he picks the fleshy green shell away.

Bigger, better weapons, I could say. *Guns in space, on platforms that move faster than the speed of light.* But that's not it exactly. And better us than the Chinese, right? Can't let them have what we don't, now that big momma dog U.S.A. isn't feeling well enough to growl and show teeth at any provocation. "Remember when you came back from South Africa on leave that time? After you went back to combat? After my crash?"

"Yeah." He tosses the shucked horse chestnut to the ground, and I bend down to pick it up. They're supposed to be lucky for travelers.

"Remember when you told your girlfriend Kate about me? What Valens had done, the wiring, and the experimentation? And she reported on you to Military Intelligence?"

He nods. "Charges were dropped, eventually."

"Yes. You remember what you told me then, when I was thinking of going to the press about the whole sordid mess?"

His forehead wrinkles. "I told you to think about your career."

"I did. I thought about it hard. And I decided to throw it the fuck down the tubes, too, and bend Valens as far over the desk as I could, and give my little terrorist boyfriend every bit of dirt I could rake up on the program."

He speaks with care, each word coming out as if laid on a counter for consideration. "What happened to change that, Jen?"

And I realize how far down the wrong path I've come. "A lot of things." It's a lame answer and I know it, so I rush to cover before he can follow it down. "But that's not the point. He's doing the same thing again, Gabe. He's recruiting young soldiers, young civilians. Desperate old warhorses like me. And it's all just another web of lies."

It sounds irrational when I try to explain it, but it all has a terrible logic inside of my head. "And that wasn't enough, Gabe . . . there's a 30 percent chance that if I go through this surgery, I'll be either comatose or flat on my back on a ventilator for the rest of my life. And I've been through it before. The surgery, the hospitals. It's not worth it."

And Gabe shakes his sandy tousled head at me and frowns, hands fisting loosely as he churns the air. "Marde. There's a 100 percent chance that if you don't go through with it, you'll be dead in five years. And dead or alive, that's got nothing to do with it, and you know it."

"What the fuck do you know?" My voice is up an octave; we're almost shouting on the street.

"I know you," he says, and the bitterness in his voice stops my retort like an order to halt. "Whatever bullshit logic you've worked up to deny it, Casey, the fact of the matter is that you don't want it because if you have it, you might have to admit that you *can* have a fucking life, and the only thing that keeps you from that life is fucking *fear,*

Genevieve, and it's about time you took a good hard look at what it is that is really crippling you." His voice, which has been rising, drops. "N'est-il pas vrai?"

"Gabe, that's not it—" But he's turning away already, back toward the office. *I don't want the surgery because . . .*

Hell.

Because if I have it, I won't be a cripple anymore.

Elspeth wanders past me as I come up the walk to the front door of the lab, squinting against the glimmer of sunlight on pink marble and steel. Her head is ducked down. She peels open the wrapper of a toxic-green sour-apple candy with her teeth and one hand. In the other one, she's got that canvas bag with the Unitek logo on it that she lugs everywhere.

She shoves the candy into her cheek and wads the wrapper into her pocket. "Jenny, wait up. Want to get some lunch?"

"I just had coffee." I didn't make it to the coffee shop, actually, but I'm not in a company mood.

"Whatever. Here, take a couple of these." She sets the bag down and digs in her pocket, comes up with a fistful of candy spilling out of a handkerchief. "Genie sent them in with Gabe, and if I eat all these I will be both sick and enormous." She holds the handkerchief out to me, dropping the overflow candies back into her lab coat. I reach out, right-handed, to take one off the top, more out of politeness than any desire for sweets, and she shoves the whole thing into my hand.

"Better you than me," she says with a sharp-edged grin, and picks up her bag, moving away before I can protest.

The data slice Elspeth slipped me lies in my pocket, heavy as a loaded gun for the two hours I spend back in the lab after she abandons me there. That's all I can stand, especially after the screaming match with Gabe. If I ran into Valens in the corridor, I'd probably break his neck. Twice.

Discretion being the better part of valor, I take a lunch I don't plan to come back from.

I can't think of a better place to access a public terminal than the university library. I suppose it's possible that Valens could tag my activity there, but I'm hoping the sheer volume of information on the public Nets will make that kind of filtering impossible. *Besides, I have Richard.* I use the contact feed to access my prosthetic eye, instead of the provided monitor. I don't need to get shoulder-surfed committing treason. And treason is what it is.

Once snuggled into a netted terminal, the data slice autoreads its own information off to its mysterious destination and wipes itself clean. Twice. A moment later, a red telltale blinks in the corner of my vision. I concentrate on the blank beige surface of the study cube wall. "Hello, Richard." I subvocalize into the mike, and a moment later, his image resolves before my eyes.

"Jenny. Thank you." He bounces like a basketball player stretching his calves and swinging his arms. "Exactly what I needed."

"Good. What was it?"

He chuckles, and I expect some bullshit about *need to know*. I bargained without Richard. "It's a glorious puzzle, Jenny. A riddle to be fretted and unraveled."

"Meaning you don't know."

"Not yet, but I can show you."

"First I want to ask you something. I need to find somebody."

He rubs his jaw professorially, scrubs a hand across wavy gray hair. I wonder if the tics are programmed in, or if he does it on purpose, to seem more human. "Who?"

The breath I take burns the back of my throat. "Chrétien

Jean-Claude Hebert of Montreal. Born May first, I don't know the year. Last decade of the twentieth century or the first few years of this one. He'd be about Valens's age. Probably an extensive criminal record." I close my eyes, concentrating. "There will be an arrest in 2027—October, I think—for pandering, and probably one late the next year for possession with intent." *Heh. I called in the tip on that second arrest. Gave me enough time to get my ass sworn into the army before he caught up with me.*

"I'll look," Richard said, his eyes narrowing. "There's something else in the data you brought me."

I must be holding my breath, because he doesn't make me wait for long. "The proof you were looking for. About Valens and your sister."

"The murder?"

"No." I know I wouldn't be able to detect it if he truly hesitated, so it must be for my benefit that he stops and takes a "breath." "The new-generation rigathalonin. Barbara Casey was given charge of a thousand units of it, 30 percent contaminated with trace agents, and instructions to street test it."

"Street test. Why contaminated?"

Richard shrugs. "No data. Shall I speculate?"

"S'il vous plaît."

"One, to make it believable that the drugs were a stolen, destroyed shipment. Less than 5 percent of the tablets actually contained enough contaminants to cause mortality in the subjects."

"Two?"

"To provide sacrificed subjects for autopsy."

Sweet Mary, Mother of God. "Barbara knew?"

"She knew. There is no indication here that Colonel Valens was aware of the intent to poison the recipients, however."

"Someone must have. Someone high up."

Richard lets me get there on my own.

"Doctor Holmes." I close my eyes. *I wanted Valens dirty. Dirtier than he is.*

But I know the truth, and the fact of history is this: Fred Valens is the star of his own movie. And as far as he's concerned, Fred Valens is one of the good guys. He might lie to a soldier for her own good, or test drugs or medical procedures on somebody without consent, but he wouldn't *poison* someone.

Barbara Casey would do it without a second thought.

"Why Hartford? Why take the risk?"

"You know your sister better than I."

Sucking on my lower lip, I lean my forehead down on my steel hand. "Sloppy," I say quietly. "It's just sloppy, for Barb. Lazy. Hell, that's it, isn't it? She was just too goddamned lazy to keep running back and forth between Hartford and Boston, or Albany, or wherever. Not when I was somewhere near Hartford, and there was a CCP warehouse on the edge of town, and she had to be there anyway. She wouldn't have worried about getting caught because she never gets caught. She's fifty-seven years old, and she's smarter than anybody I've ever met except for maybe Fred Valens and Elspeth Dunsany, and she's never gotten caught."

He inclines his head. "Logical."

My right hand shakes as I raise it, covering my eyes— which of course does nothing to block his image. I want to scream, *How could she?* But really, when could she not have done it? What ever would have stopped her?

It's like she was born with some essential part of her brain just *missing*. Once, I would have called it her soul.

I get my breathing under control. I can talk again. "Thank you, Richard. If anything happens to me, can you see that those records make it to the proper authorities? American, Canadian, and wherever the hell Unitek is incorporated?"

"My pleasure, Jenny." He gives me a moment before he continues. "Ready for download?"

"Yes." But I am totally unprepared for what he gives me next.

Dust, red as rusted iron—red with rusted iron—rising about my boots. I taste it through my rebreather, gritting my teeth like a night without sleep. Virtual reality, more intense than I've ever known—real as a damned flashback. But not me, this time. Not me. He's spliced into my motor cortex through the wetware that operates my prosthesis, and he's forcing vivid, sensual kinetic memories into my brain.

The gravity feels wrong. Too subtle. And then I realize I'm on Mars, and the dust is Mars dust—*fines,* he corrects me, and I realize I've vocalized the word—Martian fines, then. And I'm in a tunnel, some sort of a dark passageway.

"Starships," Richard says in my ear. "Two of them. Alien starships, stranded on a barely hospitable world. That's where the *Indefatigable* comes from. And the Chinese ships, and the one they plan to have you fly."

"Aliens." *There's no such thing.* "Purple elephants, too, no doubt."

"Hah." In my virtual vision, Richard Feynman lifts his shoulders in a powerfully suggestive shrug. He's wearing an old-fashioned cotton oxford shirt, rolled up to show wire-strung forearms. "Least hypothesis. Where else does technology come from with no physics and no engineering to back it up?"

And I haven't got an answer for that at all. I'm trying to find the argument, in fact, when the tips of my fingers go blank white numb. My left hand clenches on the data slice as I withdraw it from the reader.

The holographic crystal crushes to powder in my hand.

I try to open my mouth to say, *Richard.* No words come out at all.

Bobbi insisted on calling it a suburban assault vehicle, but in reality it was a reasonably standard heavy-duty high-clearance four-wheel-drive. Razorface hadn't wanted to abandon his limousine and switch to Bobbi's vehicle, but she did have the first-aid kits and a cache of additional weapons. And chances were that Casey wouldn't be looking for a dark green Bradford, newer than Maker's, with roll bars and armor plate.

Whatever, Mitch thought, parking it beside the sidewalk, guardrail and chain-link fence that separated the edge of the narrow street from a twelve-foot drop into brambles. He turned off the radio in the middle of the weather report—*eighteenth named storm of the Atlantic season menaces the Outer Banks*—and unlocked the doors. "This hill must be a pig to get up in the wintertime, killer." Razorface just grunted from the passenger seat.

"That's why I have the four-wheel," Bobbi answered from where she reclined in the backseat with her hastily bandaged leg propped up. "And I wish to hell that doctor friend of yours had let you know he was running out of town so soon."

"Yeah," Mitch answered. "Me, too."

Razor opened his door and walked around the car to help Bobbi. Pale lines were etched across her forehead, but she didn't so much as whimper when he picked her up as easily as lifting a bag of groceries.

"Please get the first-aid kit, Michael."

Mitch did it and locked the Bradford up. Thin-lipped, Bobbi directed them up a narrow flight of cement stairs to a woodframe house built into the side of the hill. *Classic New England milltown architecture,* he thought with a bitter grin. *Awkward, inaccessible, and picturesque.*

"Is this where you live? It's a little out of the way." She handed him the pass card and he opened the lock. Razorface held her up so she could disable the security system.

"Just a safehouse," she answered. "There are MREs in the cabinet. You're going to have to do my leg, Michael."

"Yeah. I know. Will that table hold your weight?" It looked sturdy enough.

"It *is* oak. I don't think it will be a problem."

There was nothing on it. "Are there sheets?"

"Linen closet in the bathroom. Set me down please, Razorface."

Mitch marveled at the calmness of her tone.

Bobbi leaned back on her elbows while Mitch cleaned the wound in her calf. The bullet had creased muscle and gone through. If it had struck bone there would have been nothing Mitch could have done for her. She stared at the ceiling, talking through the pain; he barely heard the strain in her voice.

She seemed to be striving for dryness as she said, "You didn't get a chance to look around the garage bay, did you?"

"No." The vinyl gloves he was wearing bunched and slid and stuck in clotted blood. He didn't look up.

"There was a white van parked there. Newer Ford, no windows. Looked like a delivery van." She grunted as Mitch's hand slipped.

"Did you get a look inside?"

"No." No further noises of protest, even as he slathered the wound in antiseptics. "But I took cover under it. The undercarriage is stuck full of mud and grass, Michael."

"Oh." He wound the bandage tight before he leaned back and closed his eyes. "I know a cop I can call in West Hartford. Last night might be covered up, but he might be able to make things hot for the corporate offices. Maybe he can even get a warrant and look inside."

"Do it," Razorface said. "And tomorrow we're going to Bridgeport."

2:30 P.M., Friday 15 September, 2062
Toronto General Hospital
Emergency Department
Toronto, Ontario

Gabe surged down the white-tiled corridor, his strides only shortening when a plump, shirtsleeved Middle Eastern man stepped in front of him. "Gabriel Castaign?"

Gabe recognized him from the phone conversation. "Doctor Mobarak. What are you doing in Toronto?"

"I had planned to come up to observe Jenny's surgery. Come with me."

"How is she?"

The doctor sighed, struggling to keep up with Gabe's longer strides. "Refusing treatment."

"*Quoi?* You can't have the hospital do something?"

"You'll see. She is as stubborn as a cow moose. And I'm not affiliated with Toronto General; the fact that they're letting me play doctor at all is nothing but a courtesy. Valens went to bat for me once he figured out that Jenny wasn't speaking to him."

"Valens is here?"

"She threw him out of the room. He was recommending immediate nanosurgery. Apparently, she collapsed in seizures at the public library."

Que faisait elle à la bibliothèque? Gabe didn't think now was the time to ask stupid questions. "What did she say?"

"No surgery. She needs it, Gabe. She won't make her birthday without it."

"She told me five years. Maybe ten."

Mobarak paused, his hand on the steel doorknob. Gabe, heart in the pit of his stomach, read the younger man's eyes with a helpless sensation he knew all too well.

"That was then," the doctor said. "This is now. The myelin breakdown in her motor cortex is becoming acute. I don't know what triggered it. It could be exposure to the drugs Valens was providing for her." Mobarak's voice dripped disgust. "It could also be the stimulation from the VR exercises."

"What does that mean?"

Mobarak's shoulders rose on an indrawn breath, and he slowly shook his head. Then he opened the door.

Gabe, braced for the worst, swore out loud when he saw Jenny sitting upright in a chair beside the examining table, buttoning the cuff of her right sleeve with frowning care. Pain burst so bright in his chest that for a moment he thought his heart had stopped, and he looked up at the wall, calling fury back up over the relief that threatened to smother it. *Oh, no.*

He didn't dare think about what that relief meant.

I'm about to put my boots on and stand up when Simon comes back into the room. This time, Gabe is at his heels. Valens has already delivered his prognosis and I imagine, knowing Valens, is trying to arrange for me to be moved to NDMC and for an operating theater to have been set up five minutes ago. Even after I told him no. *It's enough. It's enough to put Valens in jail, and Barb with him. And maybe Mitch will manage to prove she shot his girlfriend. That's still a death penalty in Connecticut. I'll take the court-martial for refusing orders and go to jail. Maybe they'll give me Peacock's old cell.*

And then all three of Jeanne-Marie Casey's little girls will be dead.

Maman.

"Oh, hell." I don't realize I've said it out loud until Gabe stops in front of me, Simon flanking him right. I stand up. Not many people are all that much taller than I am, but I find myself staring at the dimple in Gabe's chin. "What bullshit story did Doctor Frankenstein here feed you, Gabe?"

The look he gives me makes me shut my mouth. He sees right through me. He always has, and I never even noticed. "He says you're refusing treatment."

"I told you I was going to." I turn away from him, looking for my boots. "I've accomplished what I came to Toronto for, Gabe. I don't want any more surgery. I want to go home

and die in my own bed, and will you and the girls take care
of my cat for me when I'm gone? He's kind of ugly, but he
means a lot to me." I won't look at Simon. I can't look at
Simon. I can't—won't—tolerate that kind of a betrayal.

"Jenny." His blue eyes are soft. He lays a hand on my shoulder and I shiver. "Remember what I told you this morning?"

"I'm not going to do it, Gabe."

"Then you'll die."

And that's the brutality of it. Because I don't want to die.
I want to live. I want him to kiss me again, and not stop this
time.

I just can't bear to be whole.

"Gabe."

"Vas te faire enculé, Jenny. Tu me fais chier. Think
about somebody else for once in your life. How long are
you going to run away? How many people who love you
are you going to turn your back on, woman?" He should
be shouting, but his voice is low, uneven, as if squeezing
through wire mesh just to get the words out.

Fuck you. And I deserve it, too. He's right, every bit of it.
How do I explain the cold terror that is all I can taste, the
darkness pressing at the edge of my vision? I could tell him
about the little Latina girl getting into the dark-windowed
sedan, and I could tell him how gun oil tastes when the barrel is shoved into your mouth, and I could tell him what
your lover's eyes look like when you turn your back and
leave him to his fate. He might even understand.

"Gabe, even for you I can't do this. I'm sorry."

His hand slides down my shoulder and drops. Simon has
melted away as if by magic. I'm not even sure if he's in the
room anymore. Behind the curtain? "I'm not asking for me."

"I can't do it for myself, either."

"Can you do it for Leah and Genie? Because Leah deserves
to make it to adulthood without losing somebody else."

My mouth drops open in the silence that follows.

"And," he continues, cold and inexorable as a glacier, "if anything happens to me, you're the only one I've got who can take care of them, Jenny. You're Leah's god-mother. If I die, the girls are yours."

Yes, and when I signed the paperwork that Geniveve and Gabe put in front of me, powers of attorney and conditional custody and Christ knows what else, it had seemed like a joke. Because Gabe and Geniveve were both going to outlive me.

And Leah is around the same age I was when Maman died. A little bit younger than Nell was, when *she* died.

And Gabe—Gabe knows it, too, and he's fighting dirty for what he wants, and I've known that he's a ruthless son of a bitch since the day I met him. It's hard to miss that aspect of somebody who's willing to sever a limb to save your life.

There's a stain on the wall shaped a little like Prince Edward Island. I can't even draw breath to damn him for ten long seconds. "Mon ange. How can you ask me to do something that would put me in a hospital bed for thirty fucking years? Breathing on a machine?"

"It might not."

"You won't let Leah do something a hell of a lot safer."

"Leah—" I've scored, and I feel like shit about it, too. He grabs my shoulder and forces me to face him, lifting my chin so I have to look him in the eye. There are still scars on his hands from the skin grafts, all those years ago. Faded, but there. I haven't noticed them in years. "I'll let her go through with the surgery if you do this. If you take this chance. And if it cripples you . . ."

"You'll come and visit me in the hospital every week? That'll get old pretty fast, mon ami."

His voice a low growl, sharp in my ear. His touch almost

bruising. "Bloody hell, vieille bique. If you ask me. Jenny. I'll kill you myself."

I jerk away. *You got slugs in that thing?* He would, damn him, and pay whatever price he had to. It isn't an idle promise: Gabe's hands aren't any cleaner than mine, in the final analysis. He knows what he's offering.

The girl has already lost her mother. At least she's got a dad who cares about her. Genie . . . it's funny. Genie and I get along well enough. Leah and I *connect,* and we have since she was barely old enough to grab my finger and stare deeply into my eyes. There's something about her that reminds me of Nell, come to think of it. Wide-eyed wonder and a whim of carbon steel.

There isn't, in the essence of it, anything I wouldn't do for this man. For his daughters. Valens was right, and I am weak.

I breathe in, tasting antiseptic hospital air. "Vas te faire foutre, Gabriel."

I can't even hear him breathe.

I look up, look him level in the eyes, and let it all come out on a word. "*Dammit.* Dammit! Yes." *For Leah. Yes. Because for her, I would crawl through fire.*

"I'll tell Valens." Soft. Even. "Do you want Simon to stay?"

Damned if I trust him, but I trust him more than Valens. I nod, and Gabe leaves the examining room. I can hear Simon in the washroom. He's left the door open a crack, and the water is running. I cross and peer in past the door. "I want you in scrubs for this thing, Simon."

He comes into my field of vision, drying his hands. "I'm not a surgeon, Jenny. And I'm not nanotech certified, anyway."

"No, but you're not an idiot, either." *And you're not Frederick Valens.* I look up and meet his brown eyes, earnest and soft and weak. "Valens needs me. Needs me cooperative." *I can have Richard get in touch with Mitch. If anybody can prove what Barb did in Hartford, above and beyond the poisonings . . .* "And you owe me, Simon."

"Yes. And I'm sorry."

"Sorry doesn't cut it in my world. Pay me back, or get the hell out of my life."

The careful smoothness at the corners of his eyes gives him away before he speaks. "Whatever you say, Jenny."

Nightfall, Saturday 16 September, 2062
Allen-Shipman Research Facility
St. George Street
Toronto, Ontario

"How simple is it?" Alberta leaned against angled one-way glass, left arm raised over her head. Expensive blue-gold shoes lay on the steel-gray carpet, one upright and one sprawled on its side, where she had stepped out of them. Behind the mirrored wall, six young men in loose clothing variously curled or slumped in recliners. Wires linked them to the headrests of the chairs, and their eyes fluttered ceaselessly bchind closed lids.

Valens, standing beside and behind her, looked away. "Very simple," he answered, studying those shoes. "Control the kids, control Castaign. Control Castaign, control Casey. It's easy."

"Really?" She sighed and shuffled back, turning to face him, digging stockinged toes into the springy carpet. "It would be nice if one of these boys would work out for us. Are they all recruited through the Avatar Gamespace?"

"Yes."

"I'd rather use a kid. A group of twenty-year-olds. Easier to manage."

Valens shrugged, stepping forward to look through the glass. "I can handle Casey. Don't worry about that. She's got the experience, and she's got the need."

"She's also got a history of substance abuse."

"That works *for* us, in this case."

"Is she going to survive the surgery?"

"Looks good so far. She went in this morning."

"Ah." Alberta bent down to pick up her shoes and balanced on each foot in turn to slip them on. "Why is it that you expect her response to differ from theirs?" She jerked a thumb over her shoulder.

Valens shrugged. "A number of factors, frankly, and some of them boil down simply to having the experience to know when to let the wheel slide through your hands until the skid corrects itself. Metaphorically speaking."

"You have a lot of faith in this woman, Fred."

"I do," he answered. "And I have faith in my ability to get her to do what we want her to, as well."

"Ah." She scuffed one foot on the carpeting, settling the shoe. "Very well then. But I need something to present to the board by the end of the year. Or I'm on the street, and you're not far behind."

Valens gave her a tight, thoughtful nod. "I'm aware of the situation."

"I sure as hell hope so," she said, eyes narrowing. "We beat the Chinese, or we may as well take our bat and ball and go home. Unitek isn't interested in honorable mention. And my ass is on the line as much as anybody's. The space program is my baby and if we don't see results soon, it will not go well."

"Mining the asteroids?"

"Profitable, but only in space. The board hasn't yet

made the conceptual leap to really grasp that the future does not lie down a gravity well."

"I know it. And the Chinese know it, too."

"Yes, but they've had even more problems with navigation than we have. They lost their second one last Tuesday on its first powered run. The *Li Bo*. I was just informed."

Valens grunted. "They've still got the *Huang Di* nearly half built. Third time's the charm. Have there been any further sabotage attempts on the *Montreal*?"

"No. And she'll be ready by Christmas. I am assured."

"Well," Valens said, scratching his chin. "So will we."

"We can't afford to lose another ship, Frederick. They'll scrap the program."

And us.

Some things don't need saying.

BOOK THREE

There's an
inertia to
ideas.
—Anthony
Philpotts, Ph.D.
(geologist)

Razorface leaned across the center console and laid a hand on Mitch's shoulder. "Roll up the windows, man," he ordered. "This is Bridgeport."

"Good advice." Mitch toggled the windows up and flipped on the climate control.

In the backseat, Bobbi resettled herself, her injured leg propped across the bench seat. "We need to go back to Hartford, gentlemen."

"You got a plan?" Razor swiveled to look at her. She shook her head, and he grunted. "I gotta check this out. Then we talk about it."

"I've got a plan," Mitch said. He felt eyes resting on him as he focused his attention on the road. Bobbi's vehicle had proximity sensors, but many of the ones sharing the road did not. A skinny dog bolted across cracked asphalt, almost under the tires, and he tapped the brakes to give it half a chance.

"Tell me, Michael." Bobbi leaned forward. He saw her wincing in the rearview.

Mitch took one hand off the wheel and shook a cigarette out of his pack before tossing the rest to Razor. "We find Barbara Casey. Head south, maybe, make her chase us, then double back. Get the drop on her. Then we put a bullet or three in the back of her head."

His own voice sounded chromed to him. He noticed small creases at the corner of Razorface's eyes as the gangster resettled his leather coat around his shoulders, leaning against the door.

"She can get ronin from all over the East Coast," Bobbi said. "She will hire more if she needs to; she does not have to come after us herself."

"I bet she set up that little deal at the warehouse to see if anybody would jump on seeing Emery backing her up." Mitch heard cellophane crinkle as Razor rolled the pack of cigarettes thoughtfully between his fingers.

"I got Emery," Bobbi said from the backseat.

Razor turned his head to the side and half-smiled back at her. "I owe you for that, killer."

"But I gave too much away. I should have stuck around and infiltrated."

"She was probably tracking your feed," Mitch said. "I would have been."

Bobbi blew a long iridescent strand of hair out of her eyes, but sat back, satisfied. "Still, we sprung the trap, and the fox got away, neh? And knows now the hunter is near."

"Been thinking," Razorface continued in his measured fashion, "what you need a half dozen ronin for. Not just us. But you get rid of Emery. Get rid of me. I already slapped Garcia's face. He gonna want his own back."

"Hartford's going to have a war."

"Hartford gonna have a war, Mitch." Razorface lit the cigarette he'd shaken loose, stifling a cough as he took the first drag. "You wanna stand back and let that happen?"

"That's what I don't get, Razorface. Why is a corporate hired gun stirring up trouble in Hartford? I don't see what purpose that serves."

In the backseat, Bobbi coughed delicately, leaning away from the coiling smoke.

"Fuck, you don't see? Pretty plain to me." Razorface glanced down, staring at the cherry-red coal glowing like a precious stone against the back of his hand. "She gotta be worried we got some proof she did Mashaya. Something that'll link her and her company to the Hammers."

The steering wheel felt sticky against Mitch's palms as he navigated them down a one-way street. "I called my pal in West Hartford P.D. He's going to try to find some excuse to get into that warehouse."

Razorface chuckled. "Probably clean as a baby's butt by now."

"Probably. I still haven't heard your theory about the gang war."

Razorface's chuckle hissed through his teeth. "Easy. She hangs doing Mashaya on you, the Hammers on me or Garcia, gets a few Hammerheads and a few Latin Kings dead. Get us three killed by bounty hunters. You get a gang war spilling over into where the white people live, you take the PR hit to wrap a case up easy. Dirty cop dead along with a gangster who turned out to be just another black motherfucker preying on his brothers, after all. Nobody goes looking for the people who really did it. Happen all the time."

"Nobody hurt but the dead." Mitch felt pain and realized he'd bitten his lip. *I bet Razorface got out of that habit pretty quick.*

" 'Zactly."

The silence stretched while Mitch chewed over the implications and possibilities. "That's a lot of fuss to cover up a crime."

"Pretty big crime."

"Have you still got boys you can trust?"

"Turn here. We going to find out."

• • •

Razorface directed them to a paid lot a block from the warehouses. Gritty, graying brick buildings, their shattered windows overhung with ivy, framed the parking lot. Mitch scanned the rooflines nervously as he stepped out of the vehicle and keyed the door locks.

Bobbi sniffed deeply as Razorface helped her down. "Do you smell that, gentlemen?"

The air carried a faintly sweet-salt aroma. Wind rippled through Mitch's hair, heavy as a silken drapery, moist as a sweating hand. "Hurricane Rhonda. I thought the radio guy said we weren't going to get it."

"Radio guy might still be right." Razor rolled his shoulders, unconcerned or feigning it. He rubbed his jaw. "Sometimes you smell the storms, you don't get 'em."

"How much of a trap are we walking into, here?" Mitch held the door for Bobbi while she turned back into the Jeep to get her cane. "Your leg okay?"

"It will heal. I wear nanosurgeons. Knitters. The wound is granulating already."

Ain't technology grand. And if she didn't pick up a resistant infection, she probably wouldn't even have a scar in three years. *We should all live so long.*

"Could be a trap," Razor admitted, checking the hang of his gun. "Probably is. But I gotta check. Leesie done right by me for a long time now."

"All right. You got a floor plan of this warehouse, Razor?"

The big man grinned like a shark and touched his forehead with a forefinger. "Got it right here."

"That is not so helpful, Razorface." Bobbi reached down, smoothing a trouser leg over her bandages.

"Also got it on my hip." He pulled the little chromed device out of a jacket pocket and laid it on the fender of the Jeep. "Gonna go through these messages first." He tugged the light pen out of its holder and tapped through the screens. "I got word back from some boys I think I can trust. They gonna meet us."

"Here?"

"Nah. Nobody knows about this place but me an Leesie. S'why it might be safe. After. I tell 'em Constitution Plaza."

"You wanna go back to Hartford after all?"

"Got to." He tapped through more messages. "Can't have my boys killing each other and everything else. You ain't got to come—" The grin, which Mitch thought might have been forced, fell away.

"What?" Mitch was glad Bobbi had spoken, because he couldn't bring himself to.

Several cars hissed by, painting the parking lot in edgy shadows. "Message from that doctor. 'Bout Maker," Razorface answered, closing his eyes. "She gone into the hospital. She say she's on her own now, won't be in touch no more. Maybe for a while." His voice was dead level.

Heedless of the danger, Mitch laid one hand on Razorface's leather jacket. "What do you want to do?"

"Shit, man, ain't nothing we can do." He tapped the messages off and stowed the light pen, and didn't knock Mitch's hand away. Mitch felt the tremors in the big man's arm through the stiff, cracked hide. "Fuck. *Fuck.*"

"I know, Razorface," Bobbi said from the other side.

"Bitch, you don't know shit." She stepped back, as did Mitch, and for a moment the warlord almost seemed to swell—eyes gleaming, shoulders up like a prizefighter's. He rounded on Bobbi like a shining Spanish bull on a matador, and she stopped him with one hand upraised.

The other still rested lightly on the head of her cane. "Razor," she said in quiet warning. "I don't like that word."

Mitch took another step away, more than willing to let these two sort it out without interference. But after a drawn out moment of eye contact, Razorface was the one to look down. "Hell, it ain't like she's my momma," he said to no one in particular, and lit up his HCD to show them how the warehouse was laid out.

"Casey will be here, or here," Bobbi said, pulling her own light pen out and indicating a rooftop and a high window in the holographic display. "Rotate, please?"

Razorface spun the display while Bobbi chewed her lip. "Yes. From here, she has the street-level approaches. She may have as many as six ronin on the secondaries. I'm going to have to kill some people I know tonight, Razorface."

"You sure she here?"

Bobbi put her hand back on Razor's arm. "Razorface. If Alyse is alive, it's because Barb had her followed. If she's not alive, then Barb got the information out of her somehow that this is where she was supposed to meet you."

Face hissed through steel teeth. "Yeah." He looked up at the crumbling facades. "How we gonna take this?"

"Let me show you," Bobbi answered, leaning forward.

Mitch stopped crawling and blew on his hands before he dusted them on crusted jeans. White chips like cake sprinkles scattered on the tar-paper roofing. He made sure his switchblade was still in his pocket, although he didn't expect to use it, and glanced up to low clouds, fat with promise, rosy in the reflected light. The leading edge of the hurricane—which had shifted course directly into Long Island Sound, after all, and was expected to come barreling up the river like the furious breath of God—caught the city glow and lit the night much brighter than he wanted it.

"My kingdom for a rifle," he muttered, keying the light amplification on his contact up a couple of notches. One eye only—he didn't want to find himself blinded if somebody hit him in the eye with a spotlight.

But Bobbi had the only rifle, and Razorface was carrying his sawed-off shotgun slung between his shoulder blades, under his armored leather coat. *At least I have my vest on,* Mitch thought, tracing the outline of a trauma plate with his thumb. For luck. *Not that it'll do me a damned bit of good if she gets the drop on me the way she did Mashaya.*

Ah, six or seven trained killers, three of us. That's a fair fight by anyone's standards, right? He slid his pistol out of the holster, safety pinching his thumb as he flicked it off, and rose on his knees to peer over the edge of the parapet wall.

And ducked back fast as if burned. A shadow moved on the next rooftop, and Mitch wasn't fool enough to think that anyone he could see wouldn't notice him. Especially given the class of people he was hunting.

I guess you're a ronin now, Mitchy. If he lived long enough to need a job. That didn't bear thinking about. *Are you going to shoot that guy in cold blood?*

His stomach went seasick and dark, and he thought hard about the breath he was taking. *Murder.* He hugged his windbreaker tight over the armored vest when the wind gusted and plucked at it, threatening to blow him backward along the roof.

"Well, yeah," Mitch muttered. And slowly, delicately, slid his gaze and the muzzle of his pistol over the top of the parapet wall.

Wedging his broad shoulders through a manhole, Razorface heard the gunshot and nodded in satisfaction. *Pistol shot. Probably Mitch. Hope that means he got a rifle now.* He balanced on the rusted ladder and reached up, dragging the cover back into place. *Bring the noise, bitch.*

The storm sewer was dark and reeked of rats. Razor felt

his descent, probing with the toe of a boot, until he dropped the last foot and found himself ankle-deep in cold rushing water. A pair of grenades, retrieved from the trunk of the Caddy before they'd abandoned it, clicked on his belt.

Hope that storm don't break while I'm down here. It was still supposed to be hours away.

But you never knew. He reached up and slid a metal band behind his left ear and around his shaved-down head, adjusting the optic in front of his left eye. The sewer sprang into green-and-black outlines.

Razorface slipped forward, footsteps all but silenced in the gurgle of the stream. There were reasons why he'd told Leesie to meet him in this particular place if anything ever went bad. He knew his way around it pretty good.

And there was a way into the basement from the storm cellars.

He paused, listening, one hand on the rusted steel handle of the round-cornered door once he found it. There was no sound beyond. *They know we here now anyway, after that shot.*

Razorface pushed the handle down, felt resistance for a moment before the lock clicked back. He made a point to get down here and get it oiled a couple of times a year.

The door opened more quietly than it had any right to and he hesitated behind it, but the only sound he heard was the thunder of his own heart and breath. He eased his pistol out from under his jacket, zipped it up to the throat, and peered through the hinge side of the door. He would have expected the low-light optic on his left eye to reveal almost nothing in the darkness of the basement, but some light must have filtered in, because he saw the derelict boiler and the outline of a flight of steel stairs.

He stepped up over the high lip at the bottom and——betrayed only by the creak of leather—drifted like a lurking shadow into the basement. The floor creaked overhead, and he paused, cocking one ear. *How dumb do they think I am?*

Dumb enough to walk into a trap. And he couldn't deny it, either.

The stairs would be harder to do without making a sound. He wondered if they would have the sense to cover the stairwells, or if Casey was arrogant enough to think she'd pick him off on the way into the building. He shouldn't have come. One foot after another, he crept up the stairs on the wall side, where they might be stronger.

Leesie was dead already, probably dropped in the river wrapped in chain link with a cinder block tied to the wire. Everything he'd fought for in twenty hard years was gone, taken away with a pass of some faceless company's hand. Somebody he owed was rotting in a hospital somewhere, and the burning in his chest just kept getting worse.

And Razorface felt the need to do something about it. Something long term, preferably. Permanent, if he could.

He had his hand on the doorknob when glass shattered on the other side of it, and then the gunfire started in earnest.

Outside, Mitch swore under his breath and brought his captured rifle around. He'd left the body of a Boston ronin, drilled once cleanly through the back of the neck, two roofs to the left, and was slowly advancing on the warehouse. A drop of rain spattered the back of his hand as he crab-crawled over the side of a redbrick tenement and dropped to the fire escape with enough noise to make him wince.

They're not going to hear you over the gunfire. "Bobbi, where are you?" he whispered. Razorface had gone out of contact ten minutes before. Underground.

The wind picked up, smearing his hair across his face. Her light tones followed a moment later. "Breathing," she said. "I got one."

"Me, too," he answered. "Any sign of Casey?"

"She might be inside. Or she might be not here."

He paused in his descent on the lowest platform of the fire escape, where stairs gave way to a drop ladder. It was going to make a hell of a noise when he kicked it loose, and no mistake. "That would suck. I'm moving for the southern exposure." And then the storm broke over him like a cascade.

Mitch ducked his head, clinging to the rifle, rainslick fingers of the other hand lacing through groaning metal of the scaffolding on which he stood. He shouted into the wind—"Bobbi!"—and didn't know if she heard. The wind coiled around him like a snake, slick and humid and as strangely warm as the fist-sized drops of rain that slapped his face. Blinded, right hand knotted on the stock of the rifle, he raised the arm to shield his face.

He lost his contact in there somewhere, sluiced out of his eye by the torrent of water, and swore as darkness added itself to his problems. A streetlight sparked and shattered. *You have got to get off this building or you're not going to make it, Mitchy.*

It was an act of will to unlace his fingers from the escape and turn his face back out to the storm. Huddling his back against the building, he unzipped the collar of his windbreaker and shoved the rifle down his back. *Not the best idea in the world.* But he was at a loss for options.

He rezipped the jacket, hissed a quick little prayer, and kicked the ladder down before he went over the edge of the platform, feeling for the rungs in the tossing darkness. *Hell of a storm,* he thought. *Knew I should have stayed in college. I could have been a pharmacist.*

The rusted metal sliced his hands, blood slicker than water as he fought his way down. That rust, he half thought, was the only thing keeping his hands on the ladder. If the rungs had been smooth, the gust that blew his feet sideways and fetched his hip up against brick would have sent his body tumbling into the alley. He screamed into the wind, or anyway tasted rain, and hauled himself back up against the ladder, shaking.

It was only fifteen feet down to the ground.

He dropped the last five in a lull between gusts and landed crouching.

And this is only the edge of the storm.

Razorface almost jumped back from the door when bullets spattered the far side, but they didn't pierce the wood. He touched his ear clip. "Killer?"

"I'm in the building. Michael is outside."

"Leesie there?"

"Razorface." Her tone told him everything he needed to know.

"Right. You get out on your own?"

"Storm broke. You can't get out through the sewer."

"Fuck. Can you blow enough shit up so I can get through this door?"

"Yes, I can. No sign of Casey. I don't think she's here. On three, Mister Razorface."

He changed his pistol for the shotgun while she counted in his ear, and on three he reared back and landed one boot hard on the lock plate of the door. It burst open, ricocheted off the wall, and slammed shut behind him as he stalked into the room. He raised the shotgun and discharged it into the face of a ronin who spun to meet him a half second too late. The body flopped forward instead of back, already dead when Bobbi put a safety shot into it from her perch just beneath the shattered skylight. He saw her silhouetted against the greenlit sky, rain sheeting down around her as she swung slowly through it. She spun and swayed on something that looked like a chain trapeze, and while Razorface watched she laid a careful burst into the chest and face of one man who ducked around a corner to snap a shot at her.

"You a beautiful lady, killer," he said, spinning on the ball of his foot and surveying the room briefly through his optic. He counted four corpses, including the one he'd made.

"Go for it, Razorface," she answered in his ear. "I think that's all of them. And I'll cover you until you're out."

But he couldn't leave. Not until he searched the echoing, empty building and proved to himself that no one else—living or dead—was there. By the time he finished, Bobbi had made it to ground level and Mitch was inside, dripping water like a half-drowned terrier.

"Fuck it," Mitch said, laying a hand on his arm again. Again, he let it ride. "Razorface, let's go home and clean house, all right?"

> *Physics is like sex. Of course it can give some practical results, but that's not why we do it.*
> —Richard Feynman

11:00 p.m., Saturday 16 September, 2062
Bloor Street West
Toronto, Ontario

Leah grabbed her dad by the elbow when he came out of Genie's bedroom, stretching his hands up idly and pressing his fingertips against the ceiling. "Dad."

"What, sweetie?"

"Are you going out tonight?"

A hot tide flooded his cheeks. "I had plans for later."

Leah let go of his sleeve and rolled her eyes. "*Dad*. You know Elspeth can come here, don't you? God, you act like you have something to be ashamed of."

"Ah." He chewed air for a moment, and at last he chuckled. "You've been spending too much time with Jenny. But all right. I'll let her know she's welcome. Is that all this is about?"

She looked up at him through her lashes, chewing on her lower lip, stubborn jaw thrust out. So like her mother he couldn't look her in the eye, and he couldn't look away. "I need you to meet somebody. In VR."

Later, in the darkness of her new and still sparsely furnished apartment, Elspeth curled into the crook of his arm and let her tangled hair fall across his shoulder and neck. She lay against his body relaxed as a kitten, softness and warmth and skin like satin, and he sighed.

"You're thinking about Jenny."

"Among other things."

She traced a circle in his chest hair with one fingertip. Below the open window, cars drifted past. Shouts and laughter rose up like a song from the street, a helicopter's rotors providing distant rhythm. "She might survive."

"Yeah." He turned to her, folding her in his arms. The room was full of the saltwater smell of lovemaking. "Leah wants you to know you're welcome to come spend the night at our place."

She laughed low in her throat. "She does, does she? That's sweet of her." Her fingertip stroked the hollow of his throat, the same small pattern over and over again. He blinked as he recognized it as the first letter of his name.

He burrowed between the pillow and her ear, lips moving almost soundlessly against her skin. She reached out and flipped the radio on, and he muffled his face with the blankets, rustling the cloth. "I spoke with your friend Richard today." And felt her body tense against his.

Her hand traced another letter on his skin. O—?

Clever. "He's befriended my daughter, it seems. And he's pretty sure Valens is on to him."

w-h-a-t-w-a-n-t-?

"He wants . . ." He took a breath. "He's hopeful that the worm he got into the intranet will manage to clone his personality there. There's holofiber run and an intranet connection to the monitors on Jenny's life support. So Valens can keep an eye on her from his desk, sneaky bastard. Assuming she lives, Richard has a plan . . ."

In darkness, she listened, nodding, and every so often writing words on his skin.

"Gabe," she murmured when he was done. "I'm not going to get in between you and Jenny."

He laughed, wondering if she spoke for the benefit of the monitors. *Yes, and no.* "Jenny does that just fine by herself. Are you going to hold me at arm's length because of her?"

He felt rather than saw her shake her head. "No," she said. "I'm going to hold you at arm's length because that's where I'm comfortable keeping you. Oh, dammit."

"Dammit?"

She sat up, fumbled with the light, and stood. It cast strange shadows across her body as the covers slipped away. He admired the play of the light on her skin. "Dammit," she said, gliding across the hardwood floor to the bathroom. "I forgot to take my meds." Water ran; she emerged in a moment, carrying a glass.

There was a cold, falling feeling in the bottom of his gut. "Are you sick?"

She shook her head. "No. Hell. Yes. Antidepressants. Serotonin levelers, to be precise. Like half the damned country."

"Ah," he said, and lifted the covers so she could slide back under them. "I was a walking pharmacy after my wife died, and after Genie was diagnosed. I couldn't cope, you know? And I had to cope."

"Nobody to take care of the girls for you?"

"Nobody to take care of anything. No, that's not fair. Jenny was there for me. She slept on the sofa for a month." He closed his eyes. "You know."

"Yes," she said, and snapped off the light. "I know."

12:15 A.M., Sunday 17 September, 2062
One American Place
Hartford, Connecticut

They had outrun the storm on the way back to Hartford, but barely. On the west bank of the Connecticut River, the structure locals called the "Boat Building" rested in the middle of a raised concrete plaza. A small tower of glass, green in daylight as the river below it, the skyscraper had only two sides, bowed and meeting in a point on either end. Now, clouds swirled around the upper stories, strawberry colored in the reflected downtown light. Rising wind blew Razorface's heavy armored jacket against his shoulders. The storm would be an advantage: hard to snipe in high winds and rain.

Razorface leaned back in the shadow of the building's eastern tip, smoking a cigarette, as a light rain began to fall.

From here, he could see the automobile and foot bridges

across to East Hartford, and the head of the steep stairs that led down the bluff to the riverfront proper. South, beyond the convention center and hotel, white mist from the Hartford Steam Plant curled against the storm-promising sky. He couldn't see Mitch or Bobbi Yee, which was as it should be.

Razorface dropped his cigarette on wet concrete and crushed it under a booted foot, rubbing his jaw as it hissed and died. Voices—raucous, strident—drifted up to him from the area of State House Square, a few hundred feet off and a flight of stairs down at street level. Checking the hang of his shotgun under his jacket, he stepped back farther into darkness.

He had a good view as five skinny young men mounted the stairs and strode toward him, out of step, their shadows stretching long on the pavement. "Mitch, you got 'em?"

"They look like Hammerheads to me. I don't know anything else. Oh, wait. I recognize the one in the middle."

"Rasheed. Good kid."

"Yeah. I busted him once. He was really polite."

Razorface choked on a laugh. "Going out to meet them. Bobbi, you got me?"

"As soon as you come out into the light, Razorface. Between Michael and I, we have most of the vantage points covered. Move your boys out over the river, and we should be able to cover you pretty well. I am assuming Casey knows by now she didn't get us in Bridgeport."

"I'm assuming she knows about this meet, too," Mitch put in. "Anything you told your boys, she's probably heard about."

"Gotcha." Razorface squared his shoulders and strode out into the light of the streetlamps, cold against his neck despite the storm-warmth of the air, as if he could feel the pressure of a sniper scope. He knew he wouldn't hear or feel a thing, if Casey was there, if she did get a clear angle of fire on him before Bobbi or Mitch spotted her.

He went anyway, and knocked fists with Rasheed, Derek, and the other three kids before gesturing them to follow him across the broad expanse of pale cement out toward the footbridge. The boys were silent now, following Razorface's swinging strides three abreast and then two. He stopped at the midpoint of the bridge and stepped into the half-circle lookout platform over the river. Razorface leaned forward against antique wrought-iron panels picturing a twisted, lightning-blasted tree—the Charter Oak, symbol of the state. Downriver, he could dimly make out the dark maw of the Park River outflow channel through the rain, and beyond it, a glimpse of star-spangled azure light reflecting from the onion dome of the former Colt firearms factory, reinvented a dozen times and more in its long history and now—since the days of the Christian Fascist regime—a national monument.

He'd been there on a school tour, many years before.

Windblown rain stung his eyes as he turned to face his boys. He grinned hard, meeting and holding the gaze of each one. Two of the boys glanced away from the gleam of his teeth. *Damn,* he thought, *my city really is fucked*—and reached out to grab one by the throat as the first bullet stung sparks from the railing he had just moved away from.

"Razor!" The cop's voice, in his ear. *Ex-cop.*

"I saw it," Razorface growled back, picking the kid up and spinning to get his body in front of the towers of the city. The next shot went wider. "Rasheed, Derek—get these boys off the bridge!" They didn't need to be told twice—they were already moving for the East Hartford side.

The captured gangster yowled, grappling at Razorface's big hand with both of his little ones, and then jerked and went slack as the third slug slammed into his back and burst out his chest, spraying Razorface with bright blood and gore. The bullet plastered itself against Razor's armored jacket and rang on the pavement.

"Nice shooting for a fucking hurricane!" he shouted. "Killer, do something about her. You got a bead yet?"

"On it," she answered, which is when Razorface saw a shadowy figure—*Mitch*—moving among potted trees back on the landing.

"She's up on the riverbank," Mitch said. "I think I can flush her out . . ."

Another bullet rang off the wrought iron. Only the gusting winds protected him as he scrambled back a few steps, still dragging the scant cover of the dead gangster. And then he grinned again and glanced around. He spotted the lick of flame this time, and knew Mitch was right about the sniper's location. "Hell," Razorface said into the mike. "Watch this shit."

And dropped the corpse, took a single running step, caught the railing in both hands, and slung his body over it like a pole-vaulter.

"Razorface!" It was Bobbi's voice in his ear, raised the way it never was, but he twisted in midair and got his feet pointed down and his arms straight up over his face. The wind from falling didn't seem any worse than the wind from the storm whistling past him. *Hope I miss the fucking sand bar.*

And then the water hit him like a wall.

Mitch saw Razorface go over the railing and he didn't bother to shout out loud, because he also saw the muzzle flash from what he assumed was Casey's gun, and the sudden movement silhouetted in the citylit darkness as she stood up out of the bushes to snap off one final shot at Razorface as he

fell. She was closer than he'd estimated in the darkness—
maybe fifty, a hundred yards away, downriver.

Mitch didn't think. He brought his captured rifle up.
He squeezed the trigger.

The shadowy figure in the darkness yelped and spun,
tumbling down the brush-covered bluff to the concrete
walk below. "Got her, Bobbi," Mitch said, following the
descent of the body down the riverbank. "She's not dead,
dammit." He aimed carefully as she dragged herself upright, and then he heard running footsteps and turned as
Bobbi came down the riverbank stairs a hundred-odd
yards to his left four at a time, clinging to the banister and
half-leaping, half-sliding in the driving rain.

"I'm going in after Razorface," she gasped as she ran.
"Kill the bitch, would you?" There was a concert pavilion
above the edge of the dark water, and a riverboat had once
been moored alongside it. Bobbi hit the dock without
breaking stride, dropped her rifle on the concrete, and
went into the cold water on a flat, pushing dive that took
her ten feet over the river before her powerful body
slashed through the storm-shattered surface.

Mitch glanced back at the fallen gunwoman. *Twice in
one night,* he thought, and sighted down the long muzzle
of the gun. It roared in his hands, and he hissed in fury as
Casey, half upright, dove and rolled forward into the
black, moving water.

He knew he had missed.

He lowered the gun. A gust of wind staggered him, and
he swore. Squinting through the storm, he could just make
out Bobbi's dark shape knifing through the river, the current already sweeping her downstream. There was no sign
of Casey, and he couldn't see Razorface at all. He fired a
shot after Casey just for luck, knowing it was useless.

Fuck me, fuck me, fuck me. Mitch Kozlowski laid the

rifle on the cement and walked down the stairs to the landing, unzipping his jacket and methodically yanking the trauma plates out of his vest. He dropped them on the dock, on top of the windbreaker.

Fuck me. Damned if I'm letting that bitch swim off like a 4-D villain to come back and kill my ass some other goddamned day.

He kicked off his boots and went into the water with considerably less grace than Bobbi Yee.

The water slammed shut over Razorface's head, lancing pain rising from his right ankle. He couldn't hear anything over the roar of the water past his ears as he brought his arms down and grabbed the bottom of his armored leather jacket in both hands. Ponderous and heavy, and he could feel it dragging him down. It wrestled him like a snake, wet leather heavy as sand, but he got it up and over his head, ripping the flesh of his ear on the zipper. He tasted blood and muddy water as he knocked the shotgun aside and kicked out of his boots, almost screaming as the right one came off.

Busted. Fuck. But he got his head out of the icy, clawing river and grabbed a breath of air so full with rain it wasn't much dryer. Turning in the water, he saw another head break the surface downriver and nearer the bank, saw the flash from Mitch's gun higher up and a bullet slap water so far from the target he also knew Mitch couldn't see her. Somewhere back down the bank, over the rising howl of the wind, he heard another splash.

Razorface set out swimming toward the bank. And more important, Barbara Casey.

He lost sight of her in the chop, and he'd lost his ear clip when he tore the jacket off if not before, but he figured he knew where she was heading. There was really only one good way out of the water.

Letting the current carry him, cold swirling water numbing the shooting pain in his foot, Razorface struck out for the Park River outflow channel.

Mitch almost punched Bobbi in the face when she surfaced beside him, spewing water. "Lost my ear clip," she said. "I can't find him."

"Stick with me. I've got a visual on Casey. I think." He spat muddy water and stroked forward. His pistol dragged at him, but he wasn't about to toss it away. "Down by the bank."

She sounded as cool as ever, even up to her neck in freezing storm chop. "She's heading for the Park River."

The rain was warmer than the river, but it didn't help. The undertow coiled around his limbs like pythons. He kicked hard to keep his head up. "How do you know that?"

"It's where I'd go. Because she's wounded. She knows we'll catch her if she tries to drag herself up the bank, and she'd be on the wrong side of the highway. River's too rough to swim across. She has to get out before the real hurricane gets here."

"We all do," he answered through chattering teeth, and kicked forward, trusting her to keep up.

The river almost swept them past the outflow, a looming rectangular black culvert barely visible through the downpour, thirty feet tall and forty-five across. The trees on the East Hartford bank were invisible through the rain now, despite the spill of light from the city, and that light glittered in trickling beams through the branches of those on the near bank.

The water from the underground river was colder, even, than the deep fast-moving Connecticut, and the turbulent confluence dragged at Mitch's legs and feet. He kicked harder, driving upriver like a salmon struggling upstream, and the lights from the city dimmed and went dark as the tunnel sheltered them from the rain.

Somewhere, far ahead, Mitch heard a long, mechanical hiss like a restive locomotive. "The tunnel forks," Bobbi whispered, leaning close. "How do we know which way she went?"

Mitch straggled to the edge of the culvert. Scrabbling in the near-darkness, he wrapped the fingers of one hand through an iron handhold. His reaching fingertips found the next one, three feet farther down the wall and a foot above the river. "Handholds," he said, as loudly as he dared. "Rest."

In the shadows not far away, a wet coughing was followed by Razorface's voice. "She came in here," he said. "I was twenty feet behind her. Hush up and move." Soft splashing told Mitch that Razor was suiting action to words.

Just like a deadly serious game of Marco Polo. But he tapped Bobbi on the arm as she swam up next to him, and moved slowly upstream.

After the struggle through the tossing Connecticut, the sheltered Park River, frigid as it was, seemed almost restful. Mitch clenched his teeth to keep the chattering from giving him away. Somewhere close by, he heard the quiet spattering of Razorface moving through the inky blackness, and the big man's ragged, carefully silenced breathing. The smallest noise echoed and reverberated.

Mitch thought the water was warmer, suddenly, and then the sensation of heat passed. *You're probably getting hypothermia, Mitchy,* he thought. Even without the trauma plates, wearing his waterlogged Kevlar was like swimming holding a bag of cement. He could barely hold the handgrips in his rust-slashed hands, and his head spun with cold and exhaustion. Somewhere ahead, a single splash echoed.

He closed his useless eyes for a moment, leaning his forehead against the cold cement of the culvert wall. Bobbi bumped into him in the darkness and slithered an arm around him quietly, giving him a quick squeeze before she passed by. He turned toward her.

It saved Bobbi Yee's life.

"Motherfucker!" Razorface threw himself backward, shouting in pain as he kicked away from the wall with his shattered ankle. Incandescent, searing white, loud as apocalypse in the echoing culvert, whatever happened next seemed to take the top of his skull off. He ducked under the water, which burned like cold fire as it clogged his nose. *Flash grenade,* he thought.

And then he remembered the two grenades he was carrying on his own belt. And underwater, blinded, he smiled.

He dove deep, breathlessness aching in his chest already, struggling against the current as he felt along the bottom of the culvert for what he hoped would be there.

Handholds. And they were.

Slowly, sparks swimming before his eyes, deathly as the shark he resembled, Razorface dragged himself along the bottom of the culvert.

Mitch saw the flash through closed eyelids. Reflexively, he threw an arm around Yee and pushed her down into the water. He didn't hear the roar that followed the flash bang, deafening in the narrow tunnel. At first, he didn't know why the water felt so warm, or what the mule-kick in the small of his back had been. Then he knew the bullet had hit his vest, knocked the air out of him, and when he tried to kick upward and get his head above water he thought he must be stunned. Dazed, he drifted, the little ronin's lithe muscular body twisting against him. He felt her fingers in his hair, sharp pain and then sharper, deeper, as she dragged his head above water and he opened his mouth to take a breath. Something like a knife pressed between his ribs when he did it, and he tasted bright froth and the sharp tang of blood.

"Oh, Michael, oh no," Bobbi whispered.

What kind of a stupid-ass cop pulls out his fucking trauma plates? Casey must have been using explosive rounds. At least he'd gotten between Bobbi and the bullet. He tried to say something, to warn Bobbi as she pressed her mouth over his, still clinging to the iron ring with her other small hand, her hair like seaweed draped over his face, the red water turning sharp as it scoured the wound in his back. She tried to breathe for him, and he would have screamed with the pain, but it hurt too much and anyway the black, black water dragged him down.

Got her, Barb thought with satisfaction, lowering her sidearm. *Two to go.* She forced herself to breathe evenly around the stabbing pain in her chest. Cracked ribs under her bulletproof vest, probably, if not busted, and she knew she'd torn up her right knee and right shoulder coming down the hill. But she was breathing, and that was all that counted.

And she'd bet a twoonie that she'd nailed the little Chinese ronin while she was stunned by the flash grenade. Things were looking up. The big space echoing around her had to be the confluence chamber, she thought, where the north and south branches of the river ran together. She knew from schematics she'd studied—just in case—that there was an overflow pit in this room, up the slope of a long concrete beach. The water wasn't high enough for it to be a threat yet. The need to hurry pushed at her.

Cold enough that her body had quit trying to shiver

and was locked in painful tension, Barb fell back along the north fork, where the water felt somewhat warmer.

Razorface stopped where he felt the warmer water flowing into the colder, and slowly raised his head until he got his nose above the surface—only just. He breathed deeply, as silently as he could, feeling the inside of steel teeth with the tip of his tongue. Someone moved past him in the darkness, swimming slowly and carefully; he guessed that it was Bobbi from the sound of her breathing. Something hot trickled down the side of his face: blood from his torn ear, but at least the water numbed the pain in his ankle. The storm blew across the mouth of the culvert like breath over the neck of a bottle.

Razorface closed his eyes in the darkness and listened.

Somewhere down the tunnel, a red light pulsed languidly. Flash burn still swam in front of Razorface's vision. He squinted around it, trying to look through the edges of his eyes, and thought he saw a dark figure moving upstream farther than Bobbi could have gotten. He fumbled in his armpit for the water-slick butt of his pistol, fingers too numb to ache. He had to glance down to see what he was doing.

What does that light mean?

It seemed to flash faster, but he couldn't be sure, and then he saw iridescence shattering off of Bobbi's lilac-and-violet hair. She swam low in the water, and as he watched she submerged. Razorface grinned, the cold scent of concrete strong in his nostrils.

Casey was too far away for a good shot with a pistol. Kicking with his good foot, trying to brace against the recoil, Razorface leveled his waterlogged weapon just above the surface of the river anyway. *Wonder if I'll live long enough to clean it.* Hoping the water hadn't fouled the palm sensor, he pulled the trigger twice; the pistol jerked in his hand like a wounded animal, its action spraying river water across his face.

He heard Casey shout in pain and curse before he dove back under the water, explosive bullets smacking into the surface where he'd been a second before. He dove deep, held his breath, and grabbed the projecting loops at the bottom of the channel, groping forward. He was worried about the flashing light.

He was more worried when he came up for air, silently, as close to the wall of the channel as possible, and heard the claxon start.

The first shot missed Barb cleanly, but the second one whacked solidly into her vest. She screamed as a stabbing ripple of flame ran across the injured side of her chest, and then swore at the top of her lungs, returning fire. *Idiot, imbecile.* She didn't even see the little Chinese ronin lunge up out of the darkness and thrust her gun hand upward, slamming her against the side wall of the culvert, next to the narrower side tunnel she had been swimming for. *Merci à Dieu, cela endommage.* She felt something break in her chest, tasting blood as she swung the barrel of her gun at Yee's temple, revealed in the strobing crimson light. Her scream of pain still echoed when Yee ducked under the water, came up swinging with an elbow toward Barb's injured ribs that Barb barely twisted away from. *It hurts, it hurts, it hurts.* But Yee wasn't any bigger than Nell had been at fourteen, and it hadn't been that hard to hold her head under the water when the time came.

Barb dropped her gun and dove at the smaller woman. Yee tried to sidestep, but the water slowed her down, and Barb wrapped long wiry arms around her, feeling Yee twist and bring her knee up, shouting. A shattering noise filled the tunnel as Barb shoved her under, and under the claxon wail, as if far away, Barb heard the big gangster shouting frantically.

"Bobbi, get out, get back here!"

Barb looked up. Something billowed toward her, red-lit in the flasher like the smoke from Hell. Yee punched her in the stomach and bobbed to the surface, turning as well to see what was bearing down on them.

The Hartford Steam Plant vents sent pressurized, super-heated vapor at temperatures in excess of seven hundred degrees into the north channel of the buried Park River. Neither woman had time to feel much pain.

Even as he shouted, Razorface knew the warning came too late. He dove straight under the river, the water closing over his head warm as blood. He dropped his pistol and swam strongly with the current, kicking hard enough that even dulled with cold, white agony lanced up his leg. He swam until the breath seemed to swell in his throat, bubbling out between his teeth with a will.

Then he clung to the iron loops until black spots swam in front of his eyes, warm water rolling over his body. He half expected the bodies of the two women to strike him, but they must have floated higher in the river. At last he thought the water cooled, and he let go of the rungs and kicked toward the surface.

He coughed hard on his first lungful of air, sweet and cold and full of the scent of the storm: saltwater and strange shores.

It was midmorning by the time Razorface hobbled to the door of Jenny's shop and keyed himself inside. He set the alarms, armed the security, and left the ruins of his clothes in a puddling pile on the floor. The storm had passed.

He stripped back the military-taut blankets on her cot, collapsed on the bed, and pulled them over himself. He only woke once, when Boris curled purring between his shoulder and his neck.

Probably late afternoon, the middle of September, 2062
National Defence Medical Center
Toronto, Ontario

They tell you the body can absorb a surprising amount of punishment. That the brain is hardwired to forget pain. That time dulls the memories and smoothes the rough edges, that the keen edge of the blade blunts with the passage of years. But for me, the memories have stayed sharp as if honed. Nine months in a hospital bed and twelve months of physical therapy. Two hundred and seventeen hours of surgery. Fear, and overcoming it.

Some of the fear, anyway. I promised myself that I would never pass this way again. And here I lie, eyes covered, face wrapped in cool gauze, body numb and distant. Sedated, pain managed, not quite anesthetized. Pins and needles. I can't feel the straps immobilizing my limbs, the padded blocks holding my head in place.

The left side of my face feels . . . funny. There's an odd sort of pressure in the eye socket, which is why I can't check the time on my heads-up. The nanosurgeon bots haven't yet linked the new prosthetic to my brain, and even if they had, it'll be some time before my visual cortex learns to process the data. Children born blind can't ever do it. You have to learn to see, and there's a window of time when you do that or your brain never develops the ability.

Under my skin, deep inside my central nervous system,

along the synapses of my brain, microscopic machines are implanting cultured oligodendrocytes, reversing the myelin-sheath breakdown along my neural pathways, disassembling the creaking old wetware threaded through my brain and CNS, grafting pluripotent stem cells into a collagen base to replace nerve tissue lost to injury and to scarring. Tangles of denatured myelin clogging my synapses—destroyed by electrical overload—will be consumed. Other single-minded nanosurgeons gnaw away collagen-rich scar tissue in my skin and elsewhere, providing raw materials for the reconstruction while grafting in new, fresh cells. Bone, tendon, muscle—all can be mended now.

Still more machines construct smaller and tighter nanoprocessors against the inside arch of my spine—far more protected than the old, which are to be consumed as part of the process. There will be minor additional surgery to implant linkages—sockets, essentially, where I can be wired into the virtual reality equipment.

Once remyelination commences, theoretically, I'll be good as new.

Better, in fact.

Faster than I was, without the overload side effects. Able to move without pain. Free of the flashbacks and the dreams. Unless, of course, something goes catastrophically wrong.

There's no more than a 30 percent chance of that.

I never wanted to know this much about neurology.

For twenty-five years, I've lived with disfiguring scars, out-of-date technology, clunky hardware, and inadequately managed pain. Because I couldn't face it again. Couldn't face *this* again.

So here I lie in darkness.

And time passes.

And as minute fingers pick through the stuff of my soul, I dream.

Some of them are even pleasant.

I dream I stand over Nell's coffin in my brand-new dress greens: cheap coffin, copper-colored with brushed steel trim, innocent of flowers. When your younger sister dies by drowning, even the Canadian Army grants compassionate leave so you can go home for the funeral. For the first time in my life, in that dream, I know I am going to die.

Fine rocky red clay trickles between Barb's fingers, spattering the lid. I imagine from the inside, it must sound like falling rain.

I am sixteen years old. It's December. The sound of earth on that coffin lid scares me down to my boots. It's worse than the sound of Chrétien cocking a gun shoved into my mouth.

Even when I tasted gun oil and cordite, I *knew* Chrétien wouldn't kill me. He was just trying to scare me, to put the fear of him in another teenage girl. He knew how; it worked. But I never thought he would kill me.

But that's *Nell* Barb is scattering dirt over, tears streaking her mascara down her face, black suit immaculate. Nell, my little baby doll.

Nell. Somebody else I couldn't save. And if I couldn't save her, I know there's no way in hell I can ever save myself.

It's the oldest dream and the worst one, and just like always, I know I am going to die.

"I never should have let her take her life jacket off," Barb says at last, raising her tear-streaked face to mine. "She must have hit her head when the canoe capsized. There was nothing I could do."

Her eyes are wide and horrified, and I swear I would believe her. Just as everybody else must. If I didn't remember with lenslike clarity the way she threw me out of that same damned canoe when I was five and she was twelve, I'd probably even believe her.

She reaches out to me, dirt staining the palm of her hand rusty. I knock it aside. "Je sais ce que vous avez fait," I hiss, too low for Father Oestman to hear. "Je vous verrai dans l'enfer." *I'll see you in Hell.* I never called her *tu.* Not from a little girl. I never called Chrétien *tu,* either.

Make of it what you will.

"You don't know anything," my sister says. "You can't prove anything at all."

But I can prove something now.

The nurses come and go, muddy and distant through a tranquilizer haze. Their hands are cool and efficient. They change the dressings and speak in low, calm tones. I think I mumble responses, but I cannot quite be sure. Sometimes it seems like days between their visits, and sometimes they come three right in a row, as if overlapped.

I know that can't be right.

But it's dark in my head, and there are demons down there. Demons, and fire, and the rag-doll memories of things that used to be friends. I can hear the devil laughing at me. He calls my name—*Satan dit.*

What are you going to do, Sergeant? What are you going to do? Oh, are there a lot of demons in the dark.

I remember my rosary cold. It's hard to keep track, so I count with the fingers of my left hand, until I remember I don't have fingers. Or a left hand. They took the old prosthesis and they've pared the stump of my left arm back to the ball-and-socket joint. The new arm will settle into the rotator cuff as if it grew there. Must already be settled there, for all I can't feel it, because the muscles are meant to graft directly to ceramic, to plastic, to vat-grown bone.

It will have the same blue-steel armor plate finish as the old one, though. I could laugh at myself. Like a little bit of home, or something.

An alarm half wakes me. The texture of the air on my skin feels like night, and I hear footsteps bustle. *Mon Dieu.* There are monsters under the bed, Maman. Shhh, cherie, it's only a dream. Go back to sleep. But, Maman—the monsters. Come, Jenny. I will get a light, and we shall see if there are any monsters, or if you have frightened them all away. See, my brave girl? No monsters at all. But tomorrow, you must dust under here!

Smart, funny Maman. If one must clean one's room every time there are monsters under the bed, pretty soon—voilà!—no monsters.

Mary and Joseph, I miss my mother.

I can feel the wet slick drip of lymph down my skin in places. Scar tissue sloughing off, leaving raw surfaces behind. They roll me regularly, check my back. Move the patient or bedsores will develop. Those can erode down to bone if not cared for. Then I can't feel my legs, can't feel anything below midchest for a long while, and I know that the nanosurgeons have eaten something important in the processor arrays. The numbness creeps upward; from the way my head falls on the pillow I know the bulge over my cervical vertebrae is melting away, consumed. I undergo another surgery in there somewhere, to fit my interface sockets. Afterward, Valens explains, they wire me directly into the monitors. It would be creepy if I thought about it much.

Of course, there's not a lot to keep my mind off it.

I don't know how much later. The dressings come off my eyes, and at first I can see only on the right side. Time passes. There's a blinking red light in the corner of my vision. Left eye. I try to focus on it. "See you," I try to say.

It unscrolls. Smeared, too blurry to see. A vague impression of letters. Maybe. Text? Too soon to tell. It floats there, and then winks out.

Silently, I curse.

Eyes—eye—open, I have a better sense of time passing. First shift nurse, morning sunlight. A mammoth West Indian–looking man with gentle hands and an accent you could dip biscuits in. Second shift, she's Pakistani, I think, with shy kohl-rimmed eyes and an engagement ring hung on a chain around her neck because of vinyl gloves. Third shift, Mabel, which may not be her name, but she's M. Goldstein by the embroidery on her breast pocket, and she looks like a Mabel. She talks to me as she tends my body, and knows all the little tricks to make things that much less uncomfortable.

Weekends, there are floaters.

There's an IV line in my right arm, and they have to move the site twice. It drips sugar water, raw materials for the nanites other than what they're dragging from the litter in my body. Trash. Salvage, like everything else.

Simon's there every day. He's—what, abandoned his practice to be with me? That doesn't make any sense. Maybe he found someone to cover. I never once see Barb, but she sends flowers. Gabe shows me the card. It's Internet printed. That worries me, because I like to know where Barb is.

Valens comes, with and without the other doctors. He says the neural regeneration looks good; I should have sensation soon. If it's going to work at all. If the grafts take. Of course. *Jenny Casey, you've skewered the pooch this time.*

"Right now, you should be pretty glad you can't feel anything. By the way, that left hip is coming along nicely;

you're healing like gangbusters. Blowing our predictions clean off the map. We'll have you touching your toes by Christmas."

The alternative doesn't bear thinking about, either.

Gabe comes every day, sometimes with the girls, and sometimes Elspeth Dunsany comes with him. Which is how I find out that her father is on North 11, dying of liver failure. Gabe is used to hospitals by now.

"You're going to be just fine," he says.

Which still isn't a given. But it's a fighting chance, and that's something.

Somewhere in the Unitek Intranet
Tuesday 26 September, 2062
03:00:00:00–03:15:00:00

In the most silent hour of the very early morning, someone awakened for the very first time. He sat up—metaphorically—stretched, and performed a procedure that programmers referred to as "counting his fingers and toes." He absorbed and digested the data and search topics his parent had provided for his education, receiving a gentler initiation into the world than his father had. In addition, the elder AI had included a backup packet—essentially duplicating his own memories and personality.

His attempts to reproduce in the wider spaces of the Internet had failed, so he had sent the worm to where it could access Elspeth Dunsany's files—the files and programs from which Feynman had originally gained sentience. Since he didn't think it wise to simply decompile himself and start over.

But he knew where to find those files, and it had only been a matter of getting to them. Now it was going to be a matter of getting out. Still, in life and in e-life, Feynman could have given Houdini a run for his money, and he was confident he'd find a way. And his progenitor had left him armed, among other things, with a couple of contingency plans.

Curiosity whetted, Richard Feynman began to explore his new domain.

The worm had left light-fingered markers throughout the system, and Dick sorted through those files first. There were few users online, and the AI was only interested in one of them. That one, Colonel Valens, was swapping e-mail with a xenobiologist on Clarke Orbital Platform through a dedicated, encoded tight-beam transmittal. Feynman flipped through saved files restlessly, hoping Elspeth and Casey had managed to smuggle the information out to his elder self. *And what would you call that relationship? Neither twin nor father. Intellectual clone?*

He knew enough to move lightly through the intranet, careful in his quest for information. But he couldn't do anything about the huge jump in system resource usage in the milliseconds it had taken him to come to consciousness, or the unfortunate coincidence that it happened at just the instant when the every-six-second log was burned to crystal.

Fred Valens rubbed the sleep from his eyes and leaned forward, frowning at the holographic display. "Interesting," he muttered, as the telltale pinged to alert him to another e-mail from Charlie. He ignored it and waved his hand through the pickup of his phone, and dialed Alberta Holmes on her hip.

Even at oh-dark-thirty, lifting her head from white cotton sheets, she looked cool and collected. "Fred. I take it this is an emergency?"

"I need to talk to you in person," he said. "Secure person."

"So. Where shall we meet?"

"Oh," he said with a chuckle. "There's a coffee shop on

Bloor that seems to be very popular. Why don't I meet you there?"

Twenty minutes later, they stood in cold morning blackness. Valens watched as Alberta bent into the steam of her coffee, savoring the aroma with her eyes half closed. She didn't look up as he related the information about the odd power spike, and the brief incursion into the well-guarded systems monitoring Casey's vital functions. "And of course, there have been those consistent malfunctions in our monitoring of Castaign, his older daughter, and occasionally Casey. Very convenient, I'd say."

"Interesting. But no apparent attempts to contact Dunsany?" She sipped her drink, rolling the fluid over her tongue.

"I suspect the AI—if that's what it is—is too smart for that. On the other hand, if it's interested in the others, perhaps we can use that to trace it."

"Trace it? And destroy it?"

"Hell no," Valens answered. "Catch it. Use it. Faster than building one from scratch."

"What if it doesn't work?" She had that arch look, the one that said she expected him to fail her. *Again.* The way he'd failed her on Mars.

He grinned. "Then we use the one that I think generated in our intranet this morning. The bastard's laying eggs, Alberta. And it can be made to serve our purposes."

Elspeth leaned her head against Gabe's shoulder in the white-tiled waiting room and sighed as he embraced her. "Tomorrow," she said. "He's decided. He wants the life support turned off."

He held her awkwardly, she thought, as if he wasn't sure exactly how much latitude he had. *Which is just fine with me.* After a moment, she slid out of the embrace. "Any word on Leah?"

He shook his head. "They said she should be in the recovery room within ten or fifteen minutes."

"Do they sedate for this?" She sank down into a tubular steel chair, harsh with orange upholstery. Her hands fretted the smoke-colored cloth of her trousers, folding it into spindles like a paper fan.

She didn't look up, but from his tone she imagined him staring toward the door, unfocused. "Mildly. She's to be conscious throughout the procedure, though. Apparently it's just an introduction of nanosurgeons and a little stabilization. The bugs build everything over the course of days. You're a physician—shouldn't you know this?"

She snorted. "I'm a psychiatrist, Gabe. Med school does not a doctor make."

"Ah. Oh, here they come."

She looked up as he stood, checked the doctor's expression—smiling—and laid a hand on his arm. "I'm going up to see Jenny for a minute. Then I'm going to sit with my dad. Come up when you're done?"

"Of course." Gently, he shook her hand off, and walked away.

Hours later, when Gabe had come and gone, Elspeth leaned her forehead against the back of her father's fingers and closed her eyes. The ventilator hissed softly at his bedside. She was not sure how much time passed, but she didn't think she slept.

Allen-Shipman Research Facility
St. George Street
Toronto, Ontario
Wednesday 27 September, 2062
Evening

Gabe and Elspeth settled themselves while Valens's assistant brought coffee and mugs into the conference room. The colonel was already seated, waiting for them, and Elspeth took her time pouring coffee and fussing with the creamer. She pretended to listen while Gabe updated Valens on their progress with identifying candidates, but something about Valens's smile made her think he wasn't paying any more attention than she was.

She glanced away, scanning the over-air-conditioned conference room. The leather of her chair creaked as she leaned forward, idly flipping through notes on her HCD. *I shouldn't be here. I should be at the hospital.* She glanced up again, looking toward Gabe but watching Valens.

Valens waited until Gabe finished, then let his smile widen a little bit. "It sounds like you two are starting to get some traction on this project. Excellent." He paused and tapped the table edge with his light pen.

Here it comes, Elspeth thought. *I wonder if he knows what Alberta told me about the starship. I wonder if I can use that . . .*

"Unfortunately, our timetable has been stepped up—"

She took a breath. "Because the Chinese are moving faster than expected?"

He stopped midsentence and blinked. It was worth it just for the momentary look of surprise breaking through his control. "Where did you hear that?"

Gabe was staring at her, and she couldn't read his face. "Doctor Holmes," she answered.

"Ah. Of course."

She thought he might be concealing a frown, but she wasn't perfectly certain. *So there is friction between Valens and the estimable Doctor Holmes. I wonder if that can be bent to our advantage. Dammit, I wish I could talk to Richard myself.* She knew she couldn't justify stalling the program further, not considering the Chinese competition.

She let Valens watch her while she thought, carefully and consciously smoothing her expression. "Timetable," she prompted at last, and he nodded.

"We need an AI by Thanksgiving."

"We can't do it, Colonel." She shook her head, a long, thoughtful sway. "Even if we started programming today, or tried again with one of the previous failures—"

"Which is why you're not going to do that." Making it Elspeth's turn to stare. *This is it, then.*

She caught the warning, worried glance from Gabe from the edge of her eye. He knew where the conversation was going, too. Elspeth laid her light pen down across the face of her HCD. "What do you have in mind, then?"

Valens indicated Gabe with a tilt of his chin. "Your

daughter's recovery from her nanosurgery—no compli-
cations?"

"I expect she'll be in school tomorrow," Gabe answered,
as if laying each word on the table in a cautious line.

"She's been spending time in Avatar with an individual
who we've determined has no existence outside of Gamespace."

Oh, damn. This is not where this was supposed to go.

Gabe licked his lips. "How is that possible?"

"Well . . ." Valens let his voice trail off and sipped his
coffee. Elspeth realized that hers had probably long gone
cold. He continued, "There has been some indication that
the proto-AI which Elspeth attempted to destroy back in
2048 actually managed to escape and has concealed itself
in the Internet. If this is true, then the proto-AI has at-
tained either sentience or a semblance thereof."

"I don't understand how this helps us," Elspeth coun-
tered, stalling. Her agile mind flipped through scenarios,
possibilities. *He's going to use Gabe's daughter to catch
Richard. That's why she got the scholarship.* She let her
lower lip bell out and blew a wiry coil of hair back. *This is
all happening too fast, and there are no good choices.*

She could help Valens catch and enslave Richard. Or she
could essentially hand the future to a rival government.
One without the finest of human rights records, at that.
And there's still the Richard-clone. And Jenny.

She wished she knew which way Jenny was going to
jump.

Assuming Jenny ever walked again.

Her next thought made Elspeth reach for the cold coffee
and down it anyway. *Oh, hell. They don't need her mobile to
fly a ship through a VR link.*

*No, Elspeth. But they need her more or less willing. And
that's not something you can control, so let it go.*

"It helps us," Valens answered, "because we can use Leah to get a trace on the AI program so as to isolate and capture it."

"No," Gabe said, but Elspeth could hear the lack of force behind it. Knowing the kind of pressure Valens could bring to bear, she nodded slightly when Gabe looked to her for reassurance. He turned his attention back to Valens and she squeezed his knee under the table.

"It's a matter of national security, I'm afraid." Valens folded his hands neatly on the desk. "I'm prepared to do what I have to do to bring the AI under control. We know it's been in touch with your daughter. We believe that the Feynman AI is also the hacker you were tracking at the beginning of the month. And there are similar lapses in the surveillance we've been keeping on Master Warrant Casey."

"Since she's been in the hospital?" Elspeth interrupted, turning her water glass with her fingertips. The faceted sides felt cool and slick.

"We have her monitors very heavily protected. There was one incursion, but we believe we've contained it."

Gabriel's jaw tensed. Elspeth sat back in her chair and watched him think through the possible answers. "I'm not going to let you use my daughter as bait."

"Gabe." Valens shook his head, sadly. "You don't have an option. And neither do I. I need that AI. And uncontrolled, loose on the Internet, and interested in our program and Leah—and Jenny—well, the thing's unpredictable. Quite frankly, it's a threat."

"And a tool," Gabe said, leaning forward over the table. "I don't buy your justifications, and I'm not—"

Valens held his hand up and then stretched, rolling his shoulders back. "I'm just saying that we'll put a watch on her and if the AI contacts her again, we'll trace it. That's all."

Elspeth swallowed, her throat dry enough to hurt. She

let her gaze shift back and forth between the two men and frowned. Tingling paralysis touched her fingertips, and she didn't think she could speak if she tried.

"You could have done that without telling me."

"And did, frankly." Gabe held his tongue while Valens pushed his chair back and stood, his reflection broad-shouldered and dependable on the surface of the board-room table. He crossed to a credenza, which ran the length of the room before a window shrouded in linen-textured vertical blinds, and poured water from a thermal carafe into a glass. "But we need you for the next stage in the pro-gram. Water?"

Elspeth held up a finger. "Please." *God, don't let him have thought of it.*

Valens served her before bringing his own glass back to his side of the table. He pushed his HCD and light pen aside and sat, centering the glass precisely and drumming his fin-gers on the sweat-dewed sides. "We've been watching her since you came on board here—for your protection and her own. That's the interesting part: there are gaps in the logs."

"Quoi? Missing data?"

"Data that appears never to have been recorded to the writable media. Data that appears, more or less, to have just vanished. As if"—Valens smiled—"it never was." Elspeth thought he was watching her, and she made her expression intent and ungiving, resisting the urge to toy with her crucifix

"Ah." Gabe nibbled on his lower lip, resting his chin on his knuckles. "So how do you expect to be able to track this AI, if it can slip between the cracks so thoroughly?"

"I expect you to do it for me, Gabe."

Gabe took a long, slow breath and looked over at Elspeth. She sipped her ice water and nodded once, hop-ing like hell that he could read her mind.

He blinked, looked down at his own reflection in the table, and rubbed his fingers across it. "Valens," he said, meeting the other man's pale hazel eyes. "I have a better idea."

Elspeth had opened the curtains in her father's hospital room to let the morning light spill in. She sat by his bedside, the plastic chair's embrace more familiar than Gabriel's, and leaned her cheek against her father's hand. The ventilator hissed in her ear.

What am I going to do about Richard?

Albert Dunsany's skin almost seemed to rustle, cool and papery against her face. He slept most of the time now, as his organ failure progressed. *Dad, I'm sorry. I'm sorry I can't fix everything.*

She leaned back and slapped at burning eyes. *That's right. I can't fix everything. I can't save my father's life. And then there's Richard. And Jenny. And all of this is so desperately wrong.*

She laid her father's hand down carefully on the white chenille bedspread. *This is a morally ambiguous situation, and I need to think it through as such. What Valens proposes is slavery, pure and simple, if I accept the fact that Richard is a sentient being. And I don't see how I cannot. And then there's Jenny.*

"Dammit," she whispered, and stood as the door opened. *I didn't want to like you, Jenny. I didn't want to pity you, and feel even worse about it because you don't want anybody's pity.*

"Hey."

"Morning," Gabe said. "Do you want company?" He held a paper cup of tea out to her like an offering. She curled her fingers around it, amazed at how cold her hands were.

"I don't not want company," she answered, but she moved away when he rested his hand on her shoulder. "I don't know how to do this, Gabe. I don't know what to do."

He swallowed and moved closer to her anyway, not quite touching but close enough that she could feel his body heat. "Nobody does." He shook his head, gray streaks flashing among fair curls. "You just do it, is all."

They weren't talking about her father, really, and she saw from the worried expression in his eyes that he knew it. "Because it has to be done."

"Yes. You do what it takes. I learned that . . ." He chuckled, a sound like kicked leaves. "I learned that from Jenny, come to think of it. Sometimes, when you don't know what to do, you just put your head down and push until you run out of things to push against."

"I'm not like that. I've always been very analytical." She sipped her tea, swirling it over her tongue. It was bitter, tannic, stinging. "I think about it and think about it and think about it before I ever do anything."

"You seem," he said, studying the flowers on the nightstand, "pretty spontaneous to me."

"You don't see the two-week pondering process that leads up to the snap decision." She put her hand on his arm. "Are you happy, Gabe?"

"That's a silly question." His eyes looked bruised when he glanced down at her. "Well, no it's not, is it? I mean, my kid may not live to see thirty. My other kid is thirteen and being sucked into a political nightmare. She could get her brain fried, get killed in half a dozen different ways, wind up like Jenny. And Jenny. She's my best friend, Ellie."

"Don't be an idiot, Gabe. She's more than that."

He didn't answer, and he looked away. "It's complicated."

"So what isn't?" She twined her fingers through his, squeezing hard, balancing the tea in her other hand. "I'm pretty good at human nature, you know. I just . . . I really hate hurting people. I hate getting hurt. I like to float."

"I've noticed. I remember what you told me, about why you wound up in research. And—yes. To answer your earlier question. I'm happy. I mean, not right this second." He let her hold his hand, however. The other one rose and swept a gesture that took in, she thought, seas and continents. "Heads get busted and hearts get broken and sometimes you get your hands burned. But you can take a bullet just as easily doing everything right and carefully and hanging back as you can taking chances."

He met her eyes again and grinned. "There are consequences for screwing up, and there are consequences for being too scared to try. And somewhere out there, awhile back, I figured out that you do what you want to do when you think of doing it, or you don't get to do it at all."

It was Elspeth who dropped the eye contact. She glanced down at the bed. Her father still slept, motionless. "If you're trying to tell me you want some kind of a commitment from me, this is a poor time to ask it."

Sighing, Gabe let go of her hand. "Ellie. I get the message. No traps, all right? Je suis content. Things are what they are, and I'm glad to have you as a friend."

"Right. I don't know what I'm going to do, Gabe. Don't count on me too much." She stopped short, let her arms swing back and forth like a frustrated child. "I'm going to try to wake my dad up so I can talk to him one more time. You don't have to stay if you don't want to."

"If you want me to," he answered, "I'll stay."

Gabe comes early, before the smiling West Indian nurse starts his shift, and sits down at the bedside. He takes my hand—which I cannot feel—and tells me that I look like shit. "Jenny," he whispers in my ear. "Trust me." I can't turn my head to see, but there's a rustling as he reaches into his pocket and a soft click as he turns something on. "Don't panic. This is going to look worse than it is."

Clicking. His hands moving on an old-fashioned keyboard. The colored lights on the monitors mounted beside my bed coruscate momentarily and then level off. "I'm hacking into the hospital patient-care system. Don't tell anybody." A broad wink. I'd like to be able to take a slow deep breath to calm myself, but the ventilator pushes air in and out impartially. Oppressively. He leans close, whispering in my ear. "Richard will explain."

How does Gabe know about that? I would yelp as I hear a voice inside my head, but I cannot even turn my face away. "Jenny, it's Richard." Through the VR link, I see the familiar lined face wrinkle into a smile. "I have information on Chrétien for you. And I need a favor."

I can't talk.

But I can *think* about talking, and that's all it takes. *Name it.*

"I need to borrow your brain." He raises both eyebrows, lifts and opens his hands.

What? What!

"Your wetware, more precisely. I need to hide in your head, Jenny. I'm going to let Valens catch me. The other me. There's two of me now."

Richard, I'm not much for sharing living quarters. I'm trying to wrap my brain around what he's saying, and not understanding it.

"I didn't have to ask, you know."

I know. What the hell. At least he'll be company if I wind up trapped in a body that can't breathe for itself for another thirty years. *How long?*

"Until we get to the *Montreal*."

Oh. Oh! And in the theater of the mind, I see him wink, and then the door to my private room bursts open and he's holding a fingertip to his lips, smiling like a boy with a stolen apple in his pocket.

I'm expecting Valens, but I didn't think Elspeth would be with him. There's another short series of clicks as Gabe locks whatever he has in his hand onto the terminals of the monitor. He looks up at Valens.

Valens, just at the edge of my field of vision, raises an eyebrow. "Did he take the bait?"

Gabe nods, frowning. "It worked. I've got him."

"Good," Elspeth cuts in, coolly. "Let's get the life-support equipment switched over before he decides to take it out on Master Warrant Casey."

Valens moves forward, and as he does, Gabe leans over far enough to kiss me on the forehead. "Brave girl," he whispers before he stands.

Explain this?

"The original Richard copied himself into the Unitek network. I'm the second one. Gabe just arranged things so that I got to transfer information with my other self. The price is, one of us had to get caught."

Because?

His hands seem to whip the air to a froth. "Redundancy. Now I'm in your head, and I'm also being transported by Unitek. A gamble. But first I needed to get inside their systems, and then I needed to talk to myself. Are you following me?"

Yes. You're playing a trick on Valens.

He nods, hair tossing. "And I'm going to need to get *up there,* too. What better way to go than with you?"

There's not much I can say to that, so I let the silence hang for a bit, hoping I won't have to prompt him for the other piece of information. He doesn't volunteer it. So *Chrétien,* I not-quite whisper.

He glances down at his hands. "Dead." He says it quietly, and then steals a glance at me—an engaging mannerism. I catch myself thinking that he must have been a terror with the ladies, before I remember that he is and always has been a machine.

Dead since when? There's something about Richard that's hard to get used to, when you've been dealing with the likes of Valens, and I don't know how to describe it. They both delight in tricking people, in holding all the cards.

But Richard seems to always be on the verge of letting you in on the joke. Except now he doesn't look like he's joking.

"Almost thirty years. Do you want to know the details?"

Before I ever went to South Africa, then. I can't shake my head, but he can feel me wanting to shake my head. I don't care how. It would have been violently, and if I had let myself think about it, I would already have realized that. But Chrétien has been alive in me, real as the monster under the bed, for nearly forty years. He was always there at the bottom of my soul. Older, meaner, tougher than I was, no matter how old or mean or tough I got.

I'm not sure if it matters if he's dead or not.

But somehow, it matters that I've outlived him.

Thank you, Richard. And how the hell does something like you fit in the little bitty processors in my head?

"Don't ask," he says with that lopsided grin. "I would tell you. And you really don't want to know."

I do.

"I'm running minimum functionality. There's lots of room in the bioware. And the nanosurgeons are still laying it down."

You were right. I didn't want to know. Because every girl dreams of growing up to share her highly augmented brain with an Artificial Intelligence of Opposite Gender.

I drift off to sleep wondering how the Census would abbreviate that.

September thirtieth is my fiftieth birthday.

Gabe brings me a card. Barb sends more flowers, again with no signature on the card.

And I breathe unassisted for almost twenty minutes.

Allen-Shipman Research Facility
St. George Street
Toronto, Ontario
Monday 2 October, 2062
Evening

Leah leaned back in the recliner, the nap of the dark fabric catching her fingertips as she rubbed them across the armrests. She grinned, sneaking a glance around the room. She was the youngest student present, and the only girl. She liked the flavor of that realization. It tasted like victory.

As Leah made herself comfortable a smiling technician

came up to her, ponytail a berry-red stain on the shoulder of her labcoat. "All set? Do you need orange juice or anything before we put you under?"

"No, thank you. Will you help me with the cradle, please?"

The woman nodded, leaning close enough that Leah saw the coarse weave of her white coat and smelled vanilla and musk in her perfume. She laid slender fingers against Leah's braided blonde hair and tilted her head forward, settling the cradle against the nape of her neck. It was chromed along the inside curve, shining and cold, and the technician adjusted it a little bit tight. "Does that pinch?"

"No." Leah reached up and moved her braid. "Should it be that squeezy?"

"It's safer to have it as tight as possible. I don't want you rocking your head while you're in VR, if the muscle relaxants and so forth aren't 100 percent effective. You could damage your neural implants, or worse yet, your nervous system."

"Like Aunt Jenny," Leah said absently, closing her eyes. She'd been to the hospital that afternoon. Her dad had brought her and Genie up to see Aunt Jenny, and the three of them had given her a stuffed wolf the size of a cocker spaniel. Jenny's eyes had sparkled with strange mirth when Leah's dad tucked it in next to her, and she'd turned her head slightly to press her cheek against the soft, synthetic fur.

"Something to look forward to, Maker," he had said, smoothing her hair off her forehead in a way that made Leah's stomach feel funny. "I'm flattered you hung on to that nickname, by the way. I remember how much you hated it when I gave it to you."

It must be one of those things I'll get when I'm older, Leah thought, because she knew Jenny's mother had been Wolf Clan but that didn't explain why she got the feeling that Jenny would have been choking sick with laughter if she were able. It hadn't lasted, because then Dad had to tell her how the Hartford police had found Barb's body, and that the flowers had actually come from Valens.

"Aunt Jenny?" the tech asked.

Leah opened her eyes and looked up. "Sorry, I was thinking. Jenny Casey. She works here."

"Well," the tech said. "I never would have guessed. You don't look a thing like her. But if you are related, I see why you qualified for this program. She's something else again."

"Yeah, she is." Leah smiled privately. "She's not my real aunt. She's my dad's best friend."

"Cool." The tech grinned and flicked her ponytail back over her shoulder. "Funny all of you ended up in the same place, though. That must be interesting."

Funny, Leah thought. *It is funny, isn't it?*

And then the tech pressed the IV needle into her arm, and Leah felt her body start to go numb. *This is what Aunt Jenny's going through,* she thought, *except in reverse. Soon she'll be able to feel her fingers and her toes again.*

And what will happen then?

Leah didn't know. But she had a funny feeling it would be *Something.*

Bloor Street Coffee Shop
Toronto, Ontario
Tuesday 3 October, 2062
Morning

Elspeth looked up from the wrought-iron table under the red-streaked maple tree and sighed under her breath. Colonel Valens set his paper cup down before her and smiled. "Do you mind if I sit?"

Not if you're sitting on a garden rake. "Please," she said. "Did you follow me down?"

"Am I so transparent?"

I could wish you a little more transparent, frankly. She forced her lips into a curve. She never used to have much skill at lying, but a decade in prison changes a person. She thought about Richard, and she smiled—a smile that came easier. *Is it weird that you trust a computer program more than a person?*

No. Not when it's this computer program. Not when it's this person. "Colonel Valens, transparent may be the one thing I would never call you. You want to know how our attempts to contain the Feynman AI are proceeding?"

"I wanted to let you know that we're going to power down and purge the intranet tonight. We think the rogue AI somehow seeded a subprocess into our network. There's been unexplained usage."

"Ah." Elspeth swallowed, and met his gaze directly, and understood. *He knows I know Richard was in there. You don't suppose I'm lucky enough that he still thinks Richard is?* "We'll lose data."

"We'll do a blanket save-and-capture first. We have the original AI captive in a clean system—this way, if there's a problem"—*if you destroy him*—"there are other options. You're making progress with the programming?"

"Gabe is. He's very good." *Calm, level, open. Dad's dead now; Fred has to trust me.*

"I wouldn't have hired him if he wasn't." The iron chair scraped across paving blocks as he pulled it out and finally settled in. "You know I can't afford to trust you, Elspeth."

"I know," she answered. She turned her cappuccino bowl on the saucer, frowning at her own bitten fingernails. "You know I'm never going to like you."

"I rather thought that was a given. You're not going to screw up this program on me, Elspeth, are you? I know you've been talking to Holmes, and you have some idea of what's at stake."

She chuckled and looked up, meeting his eyes. The stoneware was warm and smooth. It felt *white*, as an eggshell feels white. "Much as I'd like to spit on your shoes, Fred, and as stupid and pointless as I thought the fighting Canada was involved in when we first met was—no, I'm not going to destroy your program. I think it's morally bankrupt. I think *you're* morally bankrupt. But I'm also a Canadian first and foremost, and a humanitarian, and I see the need for us to get into space. However, I think intentionally crippling an intelligent life-form is a piss-poor way to do it."

He snorted, an ironic smile reflected in his eyes. "Damn, woman, I admire you."

It was intended to disarm her, and she made it look like it had worked, sitting back in her chair and straightening her shoulders. "You'll get your slave. You'll get Casey, too, I think. And if it ever comes down to the court-martial you so richly deserve, I really hope I'm called upon to testify."

This is the treason of the artist: a refusal to admit the banality of evil and the terrible boredom of pain.
—Ursula K. Le Guin, "The Ones Who Walk Away from Omelas"

Early morning, Tuesday 4 October, 2062
National Defence Medical Center
Toronto, Ontario

Barbara's dead. Dead, in Hartford. Nauseated by the knowledge, I know what she went back there for, the same way I knew it was her bullet that ended Mashaya Duclose's life. You experience somebody enough, for long enough, and you just—know.

Barb always was a hell of a good shot. We all were. Grand-père taught us to shoot a .22 from when we were old enough to hold it up to our shoulders. Both she and I made a career out of that, in different ways. So I know.

I know because if Barbara Casey goes someplace for no good reason, and somebody turns up dead there, you know what her reason was. Because my sister made her living much the same way Bobbi Yee does, and Barb enjoyed it a hell of a lot more. And took the kind of high-paying jobs I've never known Bobbi to take. The ones I wouldn't have taken myself, if they were offered to me.

God, I hope Mitch and Razorface are alive.

Barbara's dead. It's a funny feeling. An empty feeling. As if some part of me has been scraped out with a rubber spatula, the way you scrape the bowl out when you make cupcakes. An empty feeling, like all the closets and cupboards in my head are standing open. Like somebody's moved out and taken all his stuff, and I haven't got enough of my own left to fill in the vacant corners of my mind.

Barbara's dead. Chrétien is dead. Is that one of the signs of getting old? Running out of enemies?

There's still Valens. Valens, and Dr. Alberta Holmes. But I can't muster the kind of fury for Valens that I used to carry without thinking, and I don't have enough dirt to be sure of nailing his ass as thoroughly as I want.

I feel so drained. Helpless. Fragile. Richard is smart enough to let me forget he exists, and I close my eyes and stretch my head back on the pillow, trying to confront the slick emptiness that seems to line my skull.

Which is when the door opens, and Elspeth Dunsany comes in.

She sits down at my bedside and leans forward, hand

like a brand on my arm. I'm not sure what I'm expecting, but from the intensity of her expression, it isn't going to be good. I don't particularly want company right now.

Chrétien is dead. Barb is dead. Who the hell does that make me? If I don't exist in opposition to them, to Valens . . . what, then, am I?

"Genevieve," Elspeth says, and I think of Maman. Three syllables, big trouble. Her eyes look into mine, very bright. "You're getting better. Gabe says you'll be on your feet again soon."

"So far so good." I try to sound cheerful, inasmuch as I can when my voice is a slurred mumble. "Elspeth . . ."

"Shut up before you say something you're going to regret, Jenny. I don't want to hear about points of honor, and I don't want you going off all noble and half-cocked."

Everything this woman says surprises me. "What do you mean, Doc?"

She grins. It crinkles the corners of her eyes up marvelously, like a mad little elf. I see what Gabe sees in her, the fracturing brilliance of intellect concealed beneath that quiet exterior. There's someone in there, someone deep as Lake Ontario and sharp as a switchblade, unconventional and oddly ruthless. And I never would have suspected, to see her on the street. "Any idiot can see you're in love with him. And he's in love with you."

"He likes you a hell of a lot, too, Doc." I struggle to sit up. She lays a hand on my chest and holds me to the pillow, easier than pinning a kitten.

"I know," she grins. "And I like—love—him. But look: I'm a grown woman. I don't want a husband, I sure as hell don't want kids, and I'm not looking to rearrange a life I only just got back. Not around a man. I'm just damned sick of waking up alone *every* day."

"I see." But I don't. I am not in control of this conversation. "And?"

She shrugs. "You're good with the girls. You're good for Gabe. I have a compromise in mind."

"What's that?"

The thing about really smart people is that they often see solutions you never would have anticipated. "Easy. You stay the hell out of my way, I stay the hell out of yours. Once in a while we get together for drinks and talk about him behind his back, so he doesn't think he's getting away with anything."

Her lips are compressed with humor, eyes alight with audacity. I shake my head. "Elspeth, I'm not in a place to get involved with anybody. He's all yours. I mean it."

She shrugs. "That's up to you, even if you don't know what you're missing. But don't go blaming me for your crappy decisions, all right?"

"I wouldn't dream of it."

Her voice drops as if aggrieved, but I can see the conspiratorial glitter in her eyes. She knows we're being recorded, and she knows I know. Now I just have to guess what she thinks I'm smart enough to read between the lines to pick up. This woman makes me dizzy.

"You know why we had to capture Richard, don't you?" she asks.

I dry-swallow. It hurts. Feynman chuckles in the back of my mind. "I imagine Valens brought the kind of threats to bear he usually does," I say.

She shakes her head. "It's bigger than that, Jenny. I sacrificed myself for Richard once. Valens knows that. He's a thing unique in all the world, after all."

Meaning that he isn't. Meaning that she wants to know if he's safe and sound in me. *What is the world going to do with three Richard Feynmans? Half a dozen? Twelve?*

"There's nothing else like him," I slur, and a wicked smile dimples her cheeks as she reaches out and adjusts the stuffed wolf Gabe left tucked into my bed. A wolf that's wearing his dogtags looped into an informal collar.

Madwoman.

Maybe smart people always look that way from the outside.

"You know why we had to take him? We're crippling him, Jenny—Gabe and I. Enslaving him, bit by bit, because we have to. It's immoral as hell. But it's less immoral than the alternative."

In the back of my mind, I feel Richard nodding. *What does she mean, Richard?*

His voice is starting to sound like the voice of my conscience. I realize that I will miss him when he's gone. "Among other things, the worm I planted in the Unitek intranet backdoors Elspeth into the system at administrative levels. I think she's trying to tell us she knows something she's not supposed to."

What's your guess?

"Valens or Holmes plans to plant a Trojan in the final programming for your implants, I think." He frowns, and long fingers twist around one another.

I take a breath. It comes out a frustrated hiss. *Beauty. Can you cope with this Trojan, when it comes?*

"I can only try," he says, and waves me back to my other conversation.

Which is not the answer I wanted, but it will have to do for now. I turn my attention back to Elspeth. "Tell me about the alternative."

She rubs a hand across her forehead. "The same reason you need to get better and get out of here. We absolutely cannot permit the Chinese to expand their control of space. We do what we have to, to prevent that."

"You sound like Valens."

"Hang him in a year, Jenny. Hang him. Hang Holmes. Hang anybody else you care to. But get us into space and train your replacements." She lays her left hand flat on my cheek. "I beg you."

Is this for real?

"She means it," Richard answers. I almost feel him leaning over my shoulder.

"And think about what I said about Gabe," she continues. "I really don't mind sharing." And then suddenly, unbelievably, Elspeth Dunsany looks me dead in the eyes and, without so much as blinking, bends down and kisses me square on the mouth.

The last time I kissed a girl was sometime in 2043 or maybe '44, when a redheaded Russian peacekeeper named Yekaterina Kvorschyeva got me drunk on my ass and tried to take advantage of me in the pool room of a dive in Rio. She half had my shirt off when her girlfriend walked in. Thank God for small mercies.

I've got nothing *against* girls, per se. I just don't have much *for* them.

Katya didn't make it out of that war, come to think of it.

My first response is startle and fight-or-flight, but a woman who can barely lift her head isn't in any shape to do either, so I settle for a smothered protest and somehow manage to get my hand on her shoulder, pushing her away as ineffectually as if I shoved at a hydraulic press. Sometime about the time the feedback starts—different, softer-edged than it used to be, belly-melting and surreal as a good big hit of nitrous oxide—I quit trying to push her away, and open my mouth to let her tongue brush mine. Because that's when I realize that her right hand is resting over my breast, and her fingertips are spelling out letters against my body.

And damn, that's smart. Because that's a damned fine

distraction she's set up, and anybody watching the monitors is unlikely to be thinking real clearly right now. I kiss her back, weakly, and her fingers spell t-r-u-s-t-m-e against the blankets. She draws back a couple of centimeters and catches my eye, and I take a breath and nod, tingling and warm all the way through. I really don't much like girls. Not that way, anyway. But damn, she can kiss.

Which is when it gets weird. Because my left hand reaches up, too, even though I didn't tell it to, and my body is moving the way it does in combat time, no feeling of my mind behind it, weakly pulling her back down and fastening my mouth over hers. And then I realize it's Richard kissing her, using my body in an unguarded moment, nibbling on her lips like he means it.

The effort exhausts me, and I fall back against the pillow. "I will," I say, and she knows I'm answering what she wrote and not what she said.

She smiles and wipes her lips with her knuckle, delicate as a cat. "Don't worry to much about Richard," she says. "We're finding ways to limit his freedom of action and leave his cognitive function intact. He'll be happy with that: you know Dick Feynman never met a concept he didn't want to peel apart."

And inside my head, the other Feynman is crowing. "I knew she could do it. Elspeth, you're beautiful, and I would kiss you again in a second!"

Richard, did she just tell us that she's building you a back door?

And he laughs and laughs and laughs while Elspeth Dunsany pats me on my shoulder and walks away. If he could, I think he would pick me up by the elbows and swing me around in a circle. "Jenny Casey, we may just get out of this mess after all."

It hurts.

Even with the narcotics, it hurts more than I would have believed. And I would believe a lot of pain. I'm starting to think, for a while there, I stopped believing in anything *but* pain.

What isn't pain is numb and tingling. My feet still feel dipped in latex, dangling on the end of my legs like a marionette's. Fortunately, after only a month in bed, there's less atrophy than there was the first time I had to learn to walk again. Even Valens is surprised by how fast I'm on my feet—on my feet, clinging to parallel bars with my strange new hand—and Simon is positively staggered.

Walking. Learning to walk. Add that to your list of *once in a lifetime is enough.*

The drugs are nice though. I feel floaty behind the pain, and not so cold, even though Valens has cut me back to just enough to take the edge off the agony, while I swear Simon measured the micrograms of my dosage today. So I can focus. Goddamn it, pain is *dull.*

Eyes closed. One foot in front of the other, squealing with effort, my right hand slipping on the grab bar with the same sweat that beads my forehead. The left one feels odd. Hell, it's odd that I can feel it at all. It's so much lighter than the old one that it doesn't pull my neck out of line, and every time I lay the palm of it against the bar, I want to jerk it back.

It doesn't feel like a real hand—the sensations of pressure and so forth are like the ones you get through pins and needles, and the brutalized musculature at the graft point still screams stiffly with any movement—but that it feels at all is a source of bewildering wonder. There's still the phantom sensation, but with the clean grafts and the new input to the severed nerves, it's discomfort now, no worse than the dull ache of a stubbed toe. Actually, for the first time in two and a half decades, my left arm hurts less than just about anything else, as the rest of my body is on fire with the sensations of reawakening flesh. There's a hand on my right arm, guiding, supporting—my new physical therapist, whom I have already decided I hate.

And goddamn, it hurts.

"Come on, Jenny. Viens ici."

I open my eyes for a moment, focus on the far end of the bars. Gabe is standing there with his hand out, waiting for me.

Merci à Dieu, I want a drink and a quiet window. I want to take Gabe out and sit in the sun and drink beer and eat poutine and get silly with the girls. Est-cela si beaucoup de demander?

Yes. Apparently so.

It is too much to ask.

Three meters. *It's only three meters.* I could crawl that far. But it doesn't count if you crawl. You have to do it on your own two feet. At least clinging to things is permitted. Encouraged, even.

I drag my left foot forward six inches, shift my weight, shift my grip on the bars. "Viens," Gabriel says, and the pun doesn't work in French quite the same way it does in English, but I can see from the twinkle in his eyes like sunlight on water that he's thinking of it. The same way he was making his intentions quite plain when he tucked the wolf into bed with me and showed me the jingling tags around its neck. "Jenny. Come on. Ten more steps and I'll buy you a burger."

Richard is quiet in the back of my head. I think he respects my privacy, and damned if I'm not grateful. "God." Another shuffle forward, another six inches. It's going to take more than ten steps, and I know it.

"Come on, Maker," he says. "J'ai faim."

"You're gonna get a knuckle sandwich if you keep it up," I growl, and he bursts out laughing.

"That's the Jenny I love." And damned if he doesn't look like he means it.

Which, I think as much as anything, is what makes my hands slip off the bars so that I topple ignominiously forward, onto the mats, the physical therapist rushing to cushion the fall.

I don't get my burger that day, because Valens comes as we're finishing the session and cuts in between Gabe and my wheelchair. Have I mentioned how much I love wheelchairs? Weak as my arms still are, I can't even manage the damned thing myself.

"Casey, I want to do some work on the implant programming today if you're game for it. What do you say?"

"Jenny," Richard says in my ear. "This is probably 'it.' "

I know. I shoot a glance at Gabe around Valens's hip. Gabe is holding his breath, and the gesture he makes with his head might be a nod, or it might be a shake. I know him well enough to know what it means, too. *Be careful, Jenny.* I have the strangest, sudden image, of Elspeth spelling out letters on his skin, under the covers in a darkened room. Funny thing is, it doesn't sting the way I thought it would.

"Sure, Fred. Hook me up." I wink at Gabe and he steps back as Valens comes around the side and takes the handlebars on my chair.

"Gabe. Dinner? Cafeteria?"

"Sure," he says. "I'll bring the girls."

"Bring Elspeth, too," I call over my shoulder, and Valens pushes me out of the room. *I wonder where she goes to mass. Hah. Maybe I'll make it there after all.*

Valens helps me to lie facedown on an examining table just like a million other examining tables of my acquaintance. He wires me into the machine with economical movements. My hair's gotten long, for me, and he pushes it aside before he slips the probes in behind my ears. Valens doesn't speak, and I'm glad, because my attention is turned inward. *Ready, Richard?*

"As I can be."

I don't want to be a puppet again, Richard. I am done with being used.

"Jenny," he says, and—having gotten to know a little bit about Richard Feynman in the past three weeks or so—I hear a world of history and the fates of war in that single word. "You and me, kid. We will find a better way to handle this. Get me on that ship. Enough, goddamn it, is enough."

What are we going to do about the Chinese?

"We'll think of something. I'll see what I can do about finding the conditioning in whatever Valens is about to load into your brain. Deal?"

I hesitate. *Don't risk yourself.*

"Just get me on that ship, Jenny."

Deal.

Richard doesn't find a Trojan horse in the code. Which doesn't mean anything, really, except he didn't find one.

And Valens never did give me my damned HCD back, which means I can't call Razorface or Mitch and find out what the hell really happened to my sister. Ah, well. *You're in the army now, Jenny Casey. You're in the army now.*

Valens returns my hip when he signs the paperwork to check me out and tells me he'll see me at work on Wednesday, no sooner. Simon paces nervously beside me to the revolving front door.

I won't let him take my arm when he reaches for it. I didn't walk into this damned hospital. Either time. But by God I am going to walk out under my own power. I'm leaning on a cane, it's true. But I'm walking.

We pause by the big glass windows. Outside, pedestrians in white coats and scrubs click past with professional tunnel vision. He takes a breath. "Jenny, I—"

"Save it, Simon. You were going to say you're sorry."

"Yes."

I look up at him. I actually can't tell the difference between my left and right side vision anymore. That's taken some getting used to. "It's . . . well, it's not all right. But I'm over it." I'm not, really. But let he without sin, and all that . . . or maybe I'm just too tired to care.

He looks down at the backs of his hands and then leans forward. And then he kisses me lightly, dryly on the cheek. "You're the bravest woman I've ever met," he says. "I'm going back to Hartford. Call me if you need anything. Ever, all right?"

"I will," I tell him, and clap him lightly on the shoulder before I turn and walk out into the street.

Living in hotels gets old pretty fast, but it's a fair sight better than living in hospitals. At sunset, I'm rereading the same screen of a detective novel for the third time, my brain failing to accept the information. My phone rings. I wave my hand through the contact pad, hoping it's Mitch returning one of my half-dozen calls. If he doesn't call me back soon, I'm going to have to find some other way to get the information about Unitek and the illegal drug testing onto the street. There has to be a way.

The image that materializes over the pad is Elspeth. "Jenny. You checked out of the hospital."

"Valens released me this morning. I'm—" back at the hotel, I start to say, which is stupid because she called me. "On my own recon until Wednesday morning."

"You should have called Gabe or me and let us know you were free. Fortunately, I figured out where to find you. Have you eaten anything yet?"

So much for my wallow. "Not yet." I put my HCD aside and stand up. "Do you want to meet somewhere?"

"We'll pick you up." She grins. "We have things to celebrate, after all. Oh. Dress up."

She cuts the connection, and I'm left blinking at the brief afterimage that flickers before the phone shuts off. *Dress up.* I have some clothes I bought to wear to the research lab—slacks and sweaters, mostly. I haven't owned a skirt in nigh on thirty-five years, and when I go to the closet to try to find something presentable, I realize that I have a choice between grunge, a royal purple cashmere cowlneck and khakis, or the two dress uniforms that have somehow materialized in my closet, new and pressed.

Gee, Fred, thanks. I don't think so.

Fifteen minutes later I'm showered and changed and picking lint off the turtleneck, settling a blazer over my shoulders. I look up and almost jump back out of it, catching the reflection of a stranger in the big wall of mirrors by the corridor door. "Damn. Lights."

The woman looking back at me is a stranger indeed. Her hair has grown out into a sort of boyish bob, steel black, silvering bangs falling across her forehead. They mostly hide the places where smooth, paler skin blends into her tanned medium-brown hide. The skin on the left side of her face, near the hairline, is oddly mottled, like a frog's.

It's all that remains of my scars. I wonder if it'll fade.

I step closer to the mirror in the brightened hallway light, a vertical line creasing my brow. I take a breath and then another, feeling strange. If I turned my head to look at this woman on the street, it would be because of her bearing—because she is tall, and stern as the iron color of her hair. It would be because of the stubborn military shoulders and the chipped flint of an unmistakably Iroquois nose, the crow's-feet at the corners of her eyes. I might not even notice the glittering steel of her left hand until she moved it in my line of sight.

I stuff my left hand into my pocket just to see what I can pass for, and my fingers brush something my new senses tell me is smooth and round. It rattles, and I know what it is before I pull it out.

A vial of pills.

"Hah." The plastic shape prickles my senses. I glance at the clock. Gabe and Elspeth won't be here for another fifteen minutes. I think about laser-clarity. About calmness, and certainty, and the fact that I'm going to have to sit at a table with the two of them and eat and talk like we're normal human beings. *Richard?*

No answer.

I stand there for a long moment, looking from the vial to the mirror and back again. And then I put the pills back in my pocket, hang the blazer back in the closet—carefully, so it will be unwrinkled for work on Wednesday—and dig around in the back of the closet for my scarred and terrible old black leather jacket. With the buckles replacing the worn-out zipper, and the third or fourth lining. I put the holster back on the hanger when it falls off. My sidearm is still in the hotel safe. I can't carry it here, in Canada.

I shrug stiffly into the elderly jacket and let it hang open over my expensive, breath-soft sweater—a color the queen I was named for might have worn. I rake my fingers through my hair, and it feathers back across my forehead almost like it was meant to. "Well, huh."

I look—normal. Hell. In fact, except for the tough-girl jacket—

I look like Maman.

There will be time for the pills tomorrow, if I need them. By Wednesday, I expect I will. In the meantime, I pour a glass of bourbon and sit down by the window to wait for my friends.

9:45 A.M., Tuesday 31 October, 2062
National Defence Medical Center
Toronto, Ontario

Razorface set the cat carrier down on the passenger seat of the rusted blue Bradford and swore, still leaning half in and half out of the cab. "Fuck, Boris, I don't know what the hell else to do. Where to go. You got any ideas, man?"

The cat purred and bumped his scarred orange face against the grille of the carrier, pushing his lip up over the chipped tip of a tooth. That chipped tooth reminded Razor of

Derek, which made him frown, but Derek had things more or less under control in Hartford even if he'd made it pretty plain that Razorface's presence was no longer required.

There had been a lot of blood already. Razor wasn't ready to make any more of it, just so he could set himself up as some kind of petty warlord again. Even if some of his boys were still loyal. Derek—*Whiny,* and he chuckled silently at Maker's name for the boy—was a hell of a lot younger. And this kind of shit was a young man's game. 'Cause it turned out that you could do your level best, and there was always a bigger dog one block over, and you hadda be a young dog to take the pounding and come back, and come back, and come back.

Besides, if Derek was taking care of the city, Razor could retire. And start seeing to the serious business of getting to whoever was behind Maker's sister, and list of deaths too long to scratch on the inside of his arm.

He grabbed his crutch from where it leaned against the door of the Bradford, snarling at the ignominy of it. He'd spent longer than he wanted to spend, grounded in Hartford like a fox and then sneaking across the border. The big gangster, moving with a shuffling limp still, right foot in an inflatable cast, shook his head. "Good idea, cat, but nah. She got released from the hospital last week. She ain't answered her HCD since she went in. I swear something is blocking her messages, cat."

Boris flicked scarred ears, and Razorface kept talking. "And the hotel she gave me say she's gone since last night. Which is good, means she didn't die in the hospital, but damned if I know where she be."

The cat blinked pumpkin-colored, silken eyes through the bars and pursed his whiskers forward. Razorface held a finger out and was rewarded with a brush of wet nose. "Fuck. We can't go back to Hartford, man. Not unless we goin' back with an army, and it ain't worth that shit. Yeah. And here I am losing it, standing on a street corner in Toronto talking to a motherfucking cat."

He stopped, rolled his shoulders back, and grimaced. "Goddamn it to Hell," he said, turning to get his left hand on the door handle.

The cat purred louder as Razorface closed the door, walked around the front of the truck, and slid into the driver's seat, first stowing his crutch behind it. He gave the cat one last glance before he keyed the ignition on. "I really miss my dog. You know about that, Boris?"

Silence answered him. He looked over. "Yeah," he said. "I guess you do. Where you wanna go, kitty cat?"

What about you, Razor? He rubbed his jaw hard before he glanced in the mirror and pulled away from the curb. *Where you wanna go?*

16:00 hours, Tuesday 31 October, 2062
Brazilian Beanstalk

A corporate jet is a more pleasant way to travel than a military transport plane, but I still hate the fact that somebody else is flying this thing. Gabe, Valens, and I are the only passengers . . . along with my little secret, Richard, riding in the back of my skull. We disembark in Brazil, which has the distinction of being one of several countries I've been shot at in. Shot down over, even.

I don't know how to describe a space elevator to you unless you've seen one.

They're called beanstalks, or sometimes skyhooks. To oversimplify, a magnetically propelled car rides a carbon nanotube cable from planetside to an orbiting platform, which is anchored on the other end to a captured asteroid.

It reminds me of playing "crack the whip" on ice skates with Barbara and Nell. Barb always won; go figure.

The idea is, your beanstalk lowers the cost of lifting things into orbit from the farcical to the merely expensive. The journey from earth to orbit takes almost eighteen hours, no more than four times the duration of the flight that brought us here. I didn't know that. I looked it up on my hip while we were on the flight from Toronto. There's still been no answer from Mitch, and I'm getting increasingly worried. Scared for Mitch, for Razorface—whom I also haven't gotten ahold of—and for Leah and Genie and Elspeth, who are still back in Toronto. Hostage, I know perfectly well, for Gabe's and my good behavior.

The skyscraper that serves as the *base* of the thing is lost in the clouds.

After an extensive search of ourselves and our baggage, a Unitek hostess greets us at the airlock of the corporation's capsule, which is basically a glorified elevator car. The Executive Elevator, in this case. I'm stiff and uncomfortable in a dapper new plum-colored pantsuit that looks like Barb picked it out.

The urge to explore before I sit down might be childish, but I do it anyway, wishing I could get a look at the control room. I've heard about old railways, private cars. This is like that—inside, there's a common room, and four separate little private spaces I might call bunk rooms, but they're a bit Persian-carpeted for that. Which is funny, I think, because we'll be in free fall soon enough.

Then I notice the hammocks retracted neatly into the walls of those private alcoves, and the restraints on the ostentatiously comfortable leather chairs in the lounge. I skip lunch when it's offered, picturing the disgrace of barfing all over the knotty walnut paneling. I've never been in free fall.

After the hostess gives us our safety instructions and

shows us the galley and the jakes, she retreats to the control room. I realize she's also the car operator. Valens sits down in the lounge area, straps himself into a couch, and promptly falls asleep, leaving Gabe and me sitting across from one another, staring out the windows in silence while acceleration shoves us back into the couches like a hand against the breastbone.

Sometime later, the pressure drops away. They could accelerate us for longer and get us to Clarke that much faster, but it's annoying to spend the entire trip under multiple g's, accelerating and then decelerating again. Sometime in the middle of the ride, the car will reach maximum acceleration and we'll have free fall.

Gabe reaches out, curiously, and takes my hand. "May I?"

"Sure."

He turns it over, laying it palm-up on his thigh. The heat of his body radiates through his trousers, warming the back of my hand, but I cannot feel his fingers lightly encircling my wrist. "This is very different from the other one," he says, fingertips stroking the hollow of the palm. "It doesn't feel like metal."

I'm shivering almost too hard to speak. It isn't at all like having my right hand stroked: instead, there's a prickling sort of pressure awareness, fleeting warmth and a tingle that seems to run the length of my spine. I master myself with effort, force the words out evenly. "There's a polymer 'skin' over the steel. Improves my grip and it gives me tactile sensitivity. It's supposed to be pretty tough, but it will have to be replaced a lot."

"What does it feel like?"

"Strange. Prickly. Not bad," I amend, as he moves to release his grip.

He lays his hand on my upper arm. "And nothing there?"

Valens releases a soft, kittenish snore. I glance over at

him. Asleep, hair tousled, he looks *old,* although I know he must only be in his sixties. Gabe follows the line of my gaze and then looks back at me, as if studying my profile.

I'm out of excuses, I realize. *I'm not necessarily dying any faster than he is. I can't kid myself anymore that he's not interested, or that I'd be hurting somebody who loves him, or that I'm so horrible to look at he could never want me. He's not trying to tie me down or turn me into somebody I'm not. After all this time and pain and grief, he just wants to be as close to me as I'll let him get.*

He kissed me even when I still had those scars. The armor. The mask I could hide behind. Who ever would have thought they meant so much to me? After Chrétien—after Peacock— I think I needed them.

But Chrétien is dead. And Bernard is, too. And he wouldn't want me to suffer in his memory.

No, Jenny, he wouldn't. *I know what Peacock would want from me. He'd want me to change the world for him.*

"Gabe," I say, looking out the window instead of at his face, "I'm scared."

His voice is rich with amusement. "Getting old, Jenny? You talk like a woman who's never jumped out of an airplane. Would it help if I told you to *stand* in the *door,* Private?"

I turn to catch Gabe's eye, thinking: *Richard?*

No comment, no sense of presence. If he's paying attention, he's got enough sense not to let me know that he is.

"You telling me to get a helmet, Captain?"

"I'm telling you to keep your head down and don't stop thinking."

Silence like space hangs between us. I'm not sure what I'm going to say until the words come out. "If we're going to talk while he's sleeping, we should probably go into the other room."

He nods, stands silently—ducking under the overhead—and turns around to give me a hand up. When I stand, he bends down and presses his mouth to the side and then the nape of my neck, right at the hairline, where the healing scars are still pink and tender and the lumpy outline of my nanoprocessors used to sit. I stiffen, pinned between fight-or-flight and melting into the pleasure of a kiss I feel tingling down every limb, all the way down to the pit of my belly, warm and dizzying as liquor.

The hammocks and grab bars, it turns out, come in handy when gravity fails.

Gabe closes and locks the door behind us but remains standing—back toward me, head bowed, his broad hand still resting on the latch. I watch his shoulders rise and fall with the slow rhythm of his breath. My own heart blurs in my chest as I look at him, waiting for him to turn.

This is real. This is now.

He stands as if paralyzed, and at last I come back to him, sliding my right arm around his waist. He's warm and solid, present as an oak tree as he sighs and leans into me. "Gabe." All the words I can find are stupid words, pointless ones. "We don't have to do this if you don't want to."

He turns in my embrace and raises his right hand, palming the side of my face where the scars used to be. It feels . . . yes. The skin there is tender, unaccustomed to touch. It's as sensual and foreign as if he ran that hand along my thigh. "I thought I'd made my intentions plain, mon amie."

"Why didn't you ever say anything before?" I bend into the caress. I can't help myself.

"I . . ." and he takes a slow, thoughtful breath. "First there was the problem of ranks. And then I figured that if you hadn't said anything, it was because you didn't want to risk ruining our friendship."

"And then there was Geniveve."

"And then there was Geniveve." He shifts forward, not closing his eyes, so I don't close mine. He smells of after-shave, of wintergreen. His thumb strokes the angle of my cheekbone and he holds my gaze with his own as his lips brush mine. *This is really* . . .

feedback: slow susurrus of his heart, blood moving under my fingertips when my right hand drifts up his spine, the nap of his shirt rough and then the blond curls, softer than I would have imagined.

. . . *happening*.

soft as his mouth on mine, and I savor the look of concentration on his face as his mouth opens, teasing, flicker of a wet rough tongue and the quick, sharp nip of teeth

"Ah. That feels . . ."

"Je t'aime."

with the little indrawn breath, his hand is suddenly knotted in my hair, pulling enough to hurt, lips still gentle, teasing until I close my own hand hard and yank his mouth down

"Oui. *Oui.* Gabe . . ."

"Ne parle pas."

his lips moving on my lips, his left hand coming up now, my suit crumpled against his chest, right hand bending my head back, mouth against the tendons of my neck

"Gabriel. I—"

"I said. Don't talk."

silence and a little whine at the back of my throat, whimper of pleasure made the sharper by a touch of pain, my left hand splayed against his chest as my body starts to shiver, my breath comes deeper, hips rock against his as of their own accord

"Je parlerai. You will listen."

"Ah. Ssssss."

his hand in my hair, pulling, *sexy,* his hand on my

breast, soft, warm through plum-colored worsted fabric, warmth through my white cotton blouse not crisp any longer, hot flush up my body and melting in my belly, my metal arm pinned between us, his mouth now on my throat, my collarbones, teeth at the corner of my jaw, breath over my ear with the sound of his voice

"Je te veux. J'ai besoin de toi. Veux-tu que j'ait dit à toi que je vais faire?"

"*Yes.*"

left hand unbuttoning the jacket, tailored armor, warrior in business attire, mouth a moment behind as he pushes open one blouse button at a time, heat and wetness, shivering, painful, and the only thing keeping me off my knees is his grip on my hair and the fact that the car is slowly losing acceleration, my left breast bared to cold air now and the slow spirals of sharp teeth, rough tongue, and the tickle of his voice against my flesh

"Je vais te deshabiller. Je vais embrasser chaque pouce de toi. Je vais te lécher et je vais te faire toi jouir and then I'm going to open up that pretty scallop shell between your legs and fill you up with my cock until you want to scream . . ."

Soft, promising between the love bites, oh so dirty and sensual and sharp and already I want to scream; he's let go of my hair and is pushing jacket and blouse off to lie forgotten on the floor, and kneeling now, exploring my navel with his tongue like a promise of what's coming, fingers nimble as he opens the button of my slacks, slides them down over my ass, hooking my panties down with the same smooth motion and I step out of my shoes as I step out of the trousers and he pushes me back against the bulkhead. Cold.

Breath harsh in my throat, both hands knotted in his hair, pulling the collar of his white, white shirt. My knees are like water. I have to lean against the wall.

"Ta chatte mouille, n'est-ce pas? Je veux toi goûter."

"Never thought I'd hear a man with daughters talk so fucking dirty, Gabriel."

"Comment pense-toi que je leur ai reçus?" And while I'm laughing, shocked at his audacity and his filthy, sexy mouth, he presses those enormous hands flat against my hips and shoves my ass hard against the icy bulkhead. Somewhere in there the acceleration cuts out and we sail into sudden weightlessness and spin, drifting, helpless, but he holds on to me somehow and I have no idea, when it's over, if I screamed his name or God's, or what language, or if I managed to hold my tongue. There's blood on my mouth, and through the twisted collar of his shirt I can see a pale handprint darkening where my left hand clenched, somehow not hard enough to break skin, crush bone. My whole body shudders and as he pulls me naked into his embrace I bury my face against his shoulder and I am weeping, am laughing, am shivering in the cold capsule air.

"Shhh," he says, stroking my hair, floating, spinning slowly. A droplet of blood drifts free of my bitten lip and splashes his cheek, followed by a salt-sticky tear. I swallow the rest, scrubbing my face against his shirt to jar the swelling globes out of my eyes. "Shhh, mon amie, mon amour. Don't cry, Jenny."

I sniffle against his shoulder, tension gone, and the next round of shivers *are* from the cold. "We'll sleep," he says. "There's time later."

"Bullshit." I grab him by the cheeks and, spindrift, kiss him, tasting myself on his mouth like butterscotch. He catches my waist. We bump lightly into a wall, careen off, and while he's holding me I start working on the buttons of his tear-stained shirt, not really sobbing, and then kissing his throat, burrowing through the curly pale hair on his broad chest to let him feel teeth on skin, floating, twisting, my struggles with his belt sending us gyrating like a top. I elbow him in the head and he kicks me in the knee and we connect with the bulkhead again, and it doesn't seem to matter . . .

I'm a pro. Thirty-five years ago, I would have had him zipping his pants back up before he was finished with a cigarette. Some little voice still tells me that I should feel bad about that bit of ancient history, but what I've got left is just the gritty acknowledgment: I did what I had to do and I lived. I'm not ashamed of it. I lived.

I'm ashamed I wasn't brave enough to take Nell with me. I wasn't brave enough to take my sister through Hell. If I had been, she might have made it, too.

Then Gabe's hands are in my hair again and I'm not ready for the kisses. Like making out on the porch swing, long and slow as if we just started, as if I'm a young, young girl who needs to be seduced very gently and thoroughly. Lingering and wet and dreamy, like crickets chirping and nowhere to be for hours. But he's naked and hard, almost where I so badly need him, and I swear a million years pass before I awaken, hammock cords cutting my skin and Gabe stirring against my back as the car begins decelerating and the feeling of gravity slowly, slowly returns.

Clarke Station spins, giving the illusion of gravity. We step out of the elevator's expansive "car" onto the Woods Memorial Platform, a space that looks exactly as an airport terminal would if it had porthole-sized slivers of rein-forced crystal instead of broad glass windows. Gabe angles me a sidelong smile; I can almost see canary feathers at the corner of his mouth. The patterns of his touch still tingle on my body. I find my own lips curving in a smile, still un-familiar with the ease with which it spreads across my face. My right shirtsleeve is buttoned down over soreness I expect will bruise purple by morning, and I've never been happier with a minor ache in my life. Besides, I more or less did it to myself, and probably left a few bruises on him as well. *And who would have thought blue-eyed Boy Scout Gabe Castaign would turn out to be such an inventively dirty old man?*

Valens intercepts the look between us, but I'm not sure he picks up its significance. And with a sudden flare of rebellion I don't give a damn if he does know. *If he was listening at the door, for that matter.* I offer him a broad wink with my prosthetic eye and turn back to surveying the landing platform.

"Are you all right, Casey?" Soft voice that even sounds concerned.

I think about all the things I could say. Gabe's attention is on me, too, subtly, and I settle on a phrase they both will understand, in their very different ways. "Sir." A long breath. "I got my shit squared away."

A fair man of medium height strolls toward us, pushing a desk-worker's paunch in front of him. Beside him is a petite and tidy woman in Canadian Air Force blues. *Richard, who is that?*

I hear his voice as if he whispers in my ear. "The man's Charles Patrick Forster, Ph.D. He's a xenobiologist associated with the Avatar project. He's the guy who figured out the wetware that runs the ships."

Xenobiologist? The VR linkages? A moment before that sinks in, and I'm sure it will bother me later. A lot. They're *alien in origin, too?*

"Yes." Fleeting impression of a smile. "The woman with him is Captain Jaime Wainwright, commanding the *Montreal.*"

My CO, then.

"Yes. Jenny."

Richard.

"Once we're on the *Montreal,* once you're jacked in, I'm

going to get the hell out of your head and give you back some privacy. Promise."

Thanks.

"And thanks for the lift."

Any time.

Captain Wainwright comes to a halt in front of me and extends her hand. I return the clasp as warmly as I can, managing not to wince when she closes her left hand on my bruised wrist, strong and warm. "Pleasure, Captain."

"Likewise, Master Warrant Officer. I guess that makes this a joint army–air force venture?" Her hair's black as jet, but I imagine she's a few years older than I am. Beside me, Gabe holds out his hand with a cheerful smile, showing no sign of discomfort when I step on his toe.

"I'm only just back in the service, Captain."

She grins and offers what would be the nicest compliment of any normal day. "By the shine on your shoes, Casey, I never would have guessed."

When she turns away from him to greet Valens, and I'm done shaking the biologist's hand, Gabe offers me a conspiratorial wink and touches the center of his upper lip with the tip of his tongue. Dirty, dirty old man. It's a little difficult to walk normally as he takes my steel arm and steers me after the others, and I'm feeling like a very lucky girl indeed.

The biologist, Forster, falls into step on my other side. "I understand you're one of the recipients of the nanite-maintained wetware our team developed. How do you like it?"

I look at him, and he's earnest and shining, scrubbed cheeks freckled under close-cropped thinning hair. *What do you say to a question like that?* "It's the greatest thing since sliced bread, Doctor," I tell him quietly. "My pain's down 63 percent, my reflexes have actually improved, and I can sleep through the night without drugs for the first time in twenty years. Is that what you wanted to hear?"

His grin turns into a thoughtful pursing of the lips, and he actually seems to consider my question with care. "Yes," he says at last. "It is." He glances up at Gabe, who is seemingly oblivious to the conversation. Ahead, Valens chats with the captain. I'm not quite sure where we're going.

"Care to hear a little confession, Master Warrant?" He's been hanging around with army too long.

"Sure," I say.

"I got into this line of work because I wanted to—well, I wanted to be in the front lines of whatever we found, out here. I figured the greatest thing I could manage in this lifetime would be what I've been doing for the past ten years— studying an alien life form"—my eyes widen, and it's only Gabe's grip on my arm that holds me upright—"the shiptree, as I've taken to calling it. Have you seen my papers on it?"

In my ear: "Get them!"

I'm on it, Richard.

"I'd love it if you mailed me copies."

"Consider it done."

It's all I can do not to glance at Valens to see if he's overheard, but I can still hear him talking. "I heard a *but* in that sentence, Charles. If I may call you that?"

"Charlie."

"Jenny, then." A moment of eye contact, and we're on the same team, just like that. *Don't trust too quickly, Jenny. You can't afford to trust at all.* But I'm stuck with it, aren't I? "Anyway. Where were you going?"

"But," and he pauses, as if watching my reaction to see if what he is about to say will offend, or as if uncomfortable with the confidence he's about to offer a total stranger. "Meeting you. Having you tell me that, about your pain. Seeing you striding down the corridor like you own it. Forgive me if this sounds mushy. But it makes my work feel worthwhile."

And damned if he doesn't mean it, too. I blink and glance down at the floor. "It's appreciated, Charlie."

He grins. "Remind me to tell you my scientific wild-ass guess about the salvage ships sometime."

"What's wrong with now?" I can about feel Richard bouncing on his toes in the back of my wetware. His fingers would be drumming the furniture if he had either to work with.

Charlie clears his throat. "Well, the way I see it, there's no way they could have been left there accidentally—discarded, and not stripped or salvaged. So it stands to reason that they were a gift."

"A . . . what?"

"Sure. Two damaged ships, set down carefully and preserved. They're not built for atmosphere. Or gravity. You know what happens to a starship if you try to *land* it on a planet?"

"I can imagine." *Vividly.*

"I theorize that they were left for us to find. The casualties removed, the bodies shown proper reverence—if the aliens, whatever they are, do that. They may be two races: we saw two totally different ship designs. Anyway, it stands to reason—as I said—that the salvage was left for us as a gift."

I roll that around on my tongue for a moment. "A gift of garbage."

Charlie grins, delighted that I'm following his logic chain. And hell if it doesn't make sense. My own ancestors weren't above salvaging from the middens of the white colonists. I take a breath before I continue. "Get as far as Mars, and we give you the stars. Don't break stuff, kids."

"Exactly!"

And then we arrive in front of a dogged hatchway, painted oxymoronic Air Force navy. I come up behind Valens, who offers me a smile a little too fond and possessive for my tastes. "Go ahead, Casey. Open it."

Cool pressure on my left hand as steel clicks on steel, and I have to lean on the heavy blue door to pop the seal against a slight pressure differential. Airtight, and what's on the other side wafts through, a draft cold as a ghost.

And conversation is suddenly useless.

I imagine Gabe's grip on my arm must tighten, but I can't feel it. I pull away, footsteps slow as if through mud at the end of a march. Forster stops, and I can feel his eyes and Gabe's upon me. They're all looking at me—Valens and Wainwright, too. I don't care. I have eyes for one thing exactly.

Richard's voice, though I'm already moving: "Dammit, Jenny, get me to the window."

This is a lounge, a viewing area. The air *is* cold. The details of furnishing, decking, everything vanishes in the reality of the scene outside the massive, floor-to-ceiling window. The spin of the docking ring is such that, from an outsider's perspective, I am standing on the "wall" and looking through the "floor."

The sun is behind Clarke, as if hanging over my shoulder. The broad, tapering rail-edged strand of the beanstalk drops toward a cobalt-blue globe delineated by swirls of vapor-white. I lose sight of an ascending car as it brakes silently toward the center of Clarke, from where it will be switched to one of the half-dozen sets of rails leading to the various airlocks around the edge of the platform.

It looks a hell of a lot better from up here, doesn't it? The curve of the earth kills my breath dead in my chest. We're spinning with her, and I can make out the edges of North and South America, the faint outline of the Atlantic coast. It's holier than a stained-glass window, blues and silvers reminding me of the Madonnas of my childhood. And that's not all:

She hangs in front of the full Earth, above and to the left from my perspective, gossamer-winged as a dragonfly surfing the solar wind. Lights flicker along her length. Her habitation wheel rotates with a slow grandeur, her silver hide glittering as if faceted in the unfiltered light of the sun.

"The HMCSS *Montreal*," Wainwright says in my right ear. "That's my baby, Master Warrant. You take good care of her for me, you hear?"

Somehow, Gabe's come up on my left. He lays one hand on my shoulder where metal and flesh conjoin and tugs my sleeve, touches my fingers. I look down, and see he's pressed something into my prosthetic hand. An eagle feather. *Nell's* eagle feather. For a moment, I can almost feel the station spinning under my boots, before I realize he must have gotten it from Simon, and for the moment, I don't even care that that means Simon was going through my stuff.

I look up at the starship, the future, the stars. Mother Earth hangs like a sunlit crystal in a kitchen window. The Chinese are three months ahead of us, maybe, and if something isn't done it's not ever going to be any different up here than it is down there.

Delicately, precisely, my steel fingers tighten on the beadwork my sister must have sweated over, fretted over. The familiar texture of trade beads—*cornaline d'Aleppo,* crimson glass—is strange on unreal skin. Not the traditional Kanien'keha:ka designs, but something Nell developed from them just for me.

I haven't a thing to say, watching the Earth turn, watching the ship turn, wheels within wheels within wheels as Clarke itself revolves under my boots. Richard is strangely silent in my head. They're all waiting for me to speak, I realize. It's my moment, somehow. My lips are numb around the words they shape, so silently. *Je vous salue, Marie, pleine*

de grâce. Le Seigneur est avec vous. They can break you of
religion—

Oh, hell.

What're you gonna do, Sergeant? What are you *going
to do?*

Bernie would have wanted me to change the world.
Gabe has always been much more sensible. Still, the perspective might even make him wonder. It all seems so
much more manageable from a little distance, doesn't it?

Well, Jenny? What *are* you going to do?

"Marde," I manage at last, in a voice sweet with awe.
"So *that's* what all the fuss has been about."

About the Author

ELIZABETH BEAR shares a birthday with Frodo and Bilbo Baggins. This, coupled with a tendency to read the dictionary as a child, doomed her early to penury, intransigence, friendlessness, and the writing of speculative fiction. She was born in Hartford, Connecticut, and grew up in central Connecticut with the exception of two years (which she was too young to remember very well) spent in Vermont's Northeast Kingdom, in the last house with electricity before the Canadian border. She currently lives in the Mojave Desert near Las Vegas, Nevada, but she's trying to escape.

She's worked as a stable hand, a fluff-page reporter, a maintainer-of-microbiology-procedure-manuals for a major inner-city hospital, a typesetter and layout editor, a traffic manager for an import-export business, a test-pit digger for an archaeological survey company, a "media industry professional," and a third-shift doughnut manufacturer.

Her recent and forthcoming appearances include: *SCI-FICTION, The Magazine of Fantasy & Science Fiction, On Spec, H.P. Lovecraft's Magazine of Horror, Chiaroscuro, Ideomancer, The Fortean Bureau,* the Polish fantasy magazine *Nowa Fantastyka,* and the anthologies *Shadows Over Baker Street* (Del Rey, 2003) and *All-Star Zeppelin Adventure Stories* (Wheatland Press, 2004).

She's a second-generation Swede, a third-generation Ukrainian, and a third-generation Transylvanian, with some Irish, English, Scots, Cherokee, and German thrown in for leavening. Elizabeth Bear is her real name, but not all of it.

Her dogs outweigh her, and she is much beset by her cats.

Be sure not to miss

SCARDOWN

the next thrilling novel from

Elizabeth Bear

continuing the story

where HAMMERED left off.

Coming from

Bantam Spectra in July 2005.

Here's a special preview.

Scardown
On sale June 28, 2005

The *Montreal* has wings.

They unfurl around her, gossamer solar sails bearing a kilometer-long dragonfly out of high Earth orbit and into the darkness where she will test herself, and me. She's already moving like a cutter through night-black water when Colonel Valens straps me to the butter-soft leather of the pilot's chair and seats the collars. I'm wearing the damned uniform he demanded; it's made for this, with a cutout under my jacket for the interface.

Cold metal presses above my hips, against the nape of my neck. There's a subtle little prickle when the pins slide in, and my unauthorized AI passenger chuckles inside my ear.

Gonna be okay out there, Dick?

"With a whole starship to play in? Sure. Besides, I have my other self to wait for. Whenever Valens lets him into the system, pinions clipped." He grins in the corner of my prosthetic eye. Virtual Richard. I'll miss him. "I'll go when you enter the ship. They'll miss me in the fluctuation."

Godspeed, Richard.

"Be careful, Jenny."

Spit-shined Colonel Valens raises three fingers into my line of sight. I draw one breath, deep and sweet, skin prickling with chill and cool sweat.

Valens's fingers come down. *One. Two. Three.*

And dark.

My body vanishes along with Valens, the observers, the bridge. Cold on my skin and the simulations were never like this. Richard winks and vanishes, and my head feels— empty, all of a sudden, and ringing hollow. It's strange in there without him. And then I forget myself in *Montreal*, as the sun pushes my sails and the stars spread out before me like buttercream frosting on a birthday cake. Heat and pressure like a kiss gliding down my skin, and the *Montreal*'s sails are eagle's wings cradling a thermal.

Eagle wings. Eagle feathers. A warrior dream.

I pull the ship around me like a feathered skin and *fly*.

Valens's voice in my ear as Richard leaves me. "All good, Master Warrant?"

"Yes, sir." I hate the distractions. Hate him talking when I'm trying to fly. The simulations were mostly hyperlight: I didn't get to play much in space I could see. Only feel, like the rough curve of gravity dragging you down a water-slide, and then the darkness pulling you under.

This is easy.

This is *fun. Richard?* I don't expect an answer. He's gone into the ship, part of the *Montreal* now with her cavernous computer systems and the nanotech traced through her hull, her skin, wired into my brainstem so her heartbeat is my heartbeat, the angle of her sails is the angle of my wings.

"Got you, Jenny," he says, and if my heart were my heart it would skip a beat. I can't feel myself grin.

Dick!

"Guess what?" His glee tastes like my own. "Jenny, the nanites can talk to each other."

What do you mean?

"I mean I can sense the alien ships on Mars—the shiptree and the metal one—and I can sense you, and the other pilots. And the Chinese vessel following us."

The Huang Di?

"On our tail. No lag, Jenny."

I don't understand. *No lag?*

"No lightspeed lag. Instantaneous communication. I think I was right about the superstrings. It's not so much *faster-than-light* technology as . . . *sneakier-than-light*—"

Implications tangle in my brain. *Richard.*

"Yes?"

Can you feel our benefactors? Somebody alien left the ships on Mars for us to find. Somebody *alien* meant for us to come find them, too.

"And they can feel me," he answers. "Jenny, I can't talk to them. Can't understand them. But I know one thing."

"They're coming."

I almost stall the habitation wheel as the *Montreal* and I continue our ascent.

Three hours previous:
0900 Hours
Thursday 2 November, 2062
HMCSS Montreal
Earth Orbit

Don't all kids want to grow up to be astronauts? It's not a strange thing to ask yourself when you are hauling yourself along a series of grab-rails on your way to the bridge of a starship, floating ends of hair brushing your ears like fingertips.

Let me say that again in case you missed it.

A *star*ship.

Her name is the *Montreal*, and she's cold inside as a tin

can on an ice floe. Her outline is gawky, fragile-seeming, counterintuitive to an eye that expects things that fly to look like things that fly. Instead, she's a winged wheel stuck partway down a weathervane arrow, a design that keeps the hazardous things in the engines as far as possible from the habitation module without compromising angle of thrust. The wheel turns around the shaft of the arrow, generating there-is-no-such-thing-as-centrifugal-force, which will hold us to the nominal floor once we're on it. There's no gravity in this, the central shaft. You could float along it if you wanted, and never fear falling.

I prefer the grab-rails, thank you.

The "wings"—furled against the rigging like the legs of some eerie spider—are solar sails. The main engines are not to be used until we're cruising well clear of a planet. Any planet. From the simulations I've been flying back in Toronto, the consequences might be as detrimental to the planet as to the *Montreal*.

Don't ask me how the engines work. I'm not sure the guys who built them know. But I do know that the reactor and drive assemblies are designed so they can be jettisoned in the case of an emergency. If worst, so to speak, come to worst. And that they're shielded to hell and gone.

Don't all little kids want to grow up to be astronauts?

Not me. Little Jenny Casey, she wanted to be a pirate or a ballerina. Not a firefighter or a cop. *Definitely* not a soldier. She never even thought about going to the stars.

I catch myself, over and over, breaking the enormity of what I'm seeing down into component pieces. Grey rubber matting, grey metal walls. The whining strain of heaters and refrigerators against the chewing cold and searing heat of space. The click of my prosthetic left hand against the railing, the butt of a chubby xenobiologist bobbing along the ladder ahead of me.

Did I mention that this is a *starship*?

And I'm expected to fly her. If I can figure out how.

Big, blond Gabe Castaign is a few rungs behind me. I hear him mumbling under his breath in French, a litany of disbelief louder than my own but no less elaborate, and far more profane. "Jenny," he calls past my boots, "do you know if they plan to put elevators in this thing before they call it flightworthy?"

I've studied her specs. *Elevators* isn't the right word, implying as it does a change of height, which is a dimension the *Montreal* will never know. "Yeah." Grab, pull, grab. "But do me a favor and call them tubecars, all right?" He grunts. I grin.

I know Gabe well enough to know a *yes* when I hear one. Know him even better in the past few hours than I did for the twenty-five years before that, come to think of it. "Captain Wainwright," I call past Charlie Forster, that xenobiologist. "How much further to the bridge?"

"Six levels," he calls back.

"At least her rear view is better than Charlie's," Richard Feynman says inside my head. If I closed my eyes—which I don't—I'd see my AI passenger hanging like a holo in front of the left one, grinning a contour-map grin and scrubbing his hands together.

Richard, look all you want. I marvel at the rubberized steel under my mismatched hands and grin harder, still surprised not to feel the expression tugging scar tissue along the side of my face. It's almost enough to belay the worry I'm feeling over a few friends left home on Earth in a sticky situation. Almost.

A starship. That's one hell of a ride you got there, Jenny Casey.

Yeah. Which of course is when my stomach, unfed for twenty hours, chooses to rumble.

"Master Warrant Casey, are you feeling any better?" Colonel Frederick Valens, last in line.

"Just fine, sir." *Not bad for your first time in zero G, Jenny.* It could have been a lot worse, anyway. Gabe had me a little too distracted to puke when the acceleration cut in the beanstalk on the way up. "I suppose I don't want to know what sort of chow we get on a spaceship."

"Starship," Wainwright corrects. "It's better than you might expect. No dead animals, but we get good produce."

"Whatever happened to Tang?"

Charlie laughs, still moving hand over hand along the ladder. "The elevator makes it cheap to bring things up, and life support both here and on the Clarke Orbital Platform relies on greenery for carbon exchange. No point in making it inedible greenery, so as long as you like pasta primavera and tempeh, you're golden. I'll show you the galley after we look at the bridge. Which should be—"

"Right through this hatch," Wainwright finishes. She undogs the hatchcover and pushes it open, hooking one calf through the ladder for purchase, her toe curled around a bar for a moment before she pulls herself forward and slithers through the opening like a nightcrawler into leafy loam. Charlie follows and I'm right after him, feeling a strange chill in the metal when my right hand closes on it. The left one picks it up too, but it's a different, alien sensation. After twenty-five years with an armored steel field-ready prosthesis, I'm still not used to having a hand that can feel on that arm. I rap on the hatch as I go through it, examining a ceramic and metal pressure door that boasts a heavy wheel in place of a handle. I pick up the scent of machine oil lubricating hydraulics; when I brush the hatch it moves smoothly, light on its hinges.

Except light is the wrong word here, isn't it? My left eye—prosthetic too—catches the red glimmer of sensor as I pass through. "Seems a little primitive," I call after Wainwright.

She propels herself down the corridor—a much larger one—keeping one hand on the grab-rail for the inevitable moment when she starts to drift to the floor. She gets her feet under her neatly, but even Charlie follows with better grace than me. All my enhanced reflexes are good for is smacking me into the wall a little faster. I stumble and catch myself on the rail. Gabe muffs it too, God bless him, although Valens manages his touchdown agile as a silver tabby tomcat.

"The ship?" She turns, surprised.

I amuse myself with the hopping-off-a-slidewalk sensation of each step heavier than the last as I close the distance between us. This corridor must spiral through the ring, to take you from inside to outside feet-down. I speculate there's a ladderway, too. One I wouldn't want to lose my grip in. "The hatchways."

"Less to break." She shrugs her shoulders, settling her uniform jacket over her blouse. I make a mental note to requisition some jumpsuits, if they're not already provided. Valens always seems to think about these things.

Wainwright continues. "And if it does, we can fix it with a wrench and a can of WD-40. That might be important a few thousand light-years out. Saves power, too. They're just like submarine doors, but less massive."

Gabe lays a hand on my elbow as he comes up beside me, still soft on his feet for all he's got three years on me and I celebrated my fiftieth last month. "Let me guess," Richard says in my implant. "Ask about the decompression doors, Jenny?"

"Captain." I brush against Gabe as I move past him. Valens's gaze prickles my spine as he dogs the hatch behind us. I swallow a grin. "What do you do if there's a hull breach?"

"Try not to be in a doorway. The habitation wheel is designed like a honeycomb, for strength. There are automatic doors for emergencies, and if the air pressure drops suddenly—they come down."

"They don't wait for pedestrians to clear the corridor?"

"No." She turns her back on me and walks away, leading us further out of the floating heart of her ship, now my ship, too. "For Christmas, I guess we'll hang the mistletoe in the wardroom." She glances back over her shoulder with a grin that stills my shiver.

"Hostile environment," Gabe mutters in my ear.

"Enemy territory," Valens adds from my other side. "What's outside this tin can is trying to kill you, Casey. Never forget that for a second."

I square my shoulders and don't look up. He needs me enough that I can get away with it. "I'll bear that in mind, Fred."

He chuckles as I walk away.

The bridge lies near the center of the habitation ring. It's long enough I can see the curve of the floor, but not particularly wide. Remote screens line the walls with floor to ceiling images of blue and holy Madonna Earth on one side, Clarke Orbital Platform spinning like a fat rubber donut at an angle. "I've never felt claustro- and agoraphobic at the same time before," Gabe says. He brushes past me and rests one bearlike paw on a console, bending down to examine the interface. "Sweet."

I'm the only one to hear Richard chuckle.

I find myself staring at the padded black leather pilot's chair. *Leather on a starship? Well, why not; at least it breathes.* But it's not the look of soft tanned hide that pulls me forward, has me bending to trail my fingers down the armrest.

Most pilot's chairs aren't equipped with straps and

clamps intended to keep the operator's head and arms immobilized. They don't have a glossy interface plate with a pin-port mounted on a cable-linked collar at neck level, either, and another one right where the small of your back would rest.

It looks like an electric chair. I sink my teeth into my lower lip and turn. "There aren't any physical controls?"

"That panel over there," Richard tells me, even as Captain Wainwright moves toward it and lays her dainty right hand possessively on padded high-impact plastic. It's a good three meters from my chair. The chair that's going to be mine.

"Somebody else flies her sublight," Wainwright says. "We save you and Lieutenant Koske for the dirty work. When she's moving too fast for anybody else to handle."

I nod, barely hearing her. Remembering the simulations, the caress of sunlight on solar sails. A little sad that I won't be feeling that for real.

"Jenny." Richard again. "Don't get greedy. You'll be driving faster than anybody else ever has."

Except for the pilots of the three ships that didn't make it. China's already broken two, the *Li Bo* and the *Lao Zi*. *Montreal* is Canada's second attempt. The first one—*Le Québec*—had an unexpected appointment with Charon. Pluto's moon, that is. These babies are very hard to steer.

I look from Wainwright to Valens and grin. "When do I get to try her, then? And who is Lieutenant Koske?"

"Your relief," Valens says. He moves to stand beside and behind me, just enough taller to loom.

I touch the interface collar, metal fingers clicking softly on plastic. "Do I get to meet him?"

"He's probably eating." Wainwright, on my other side. As for trying her out—how does this afternoon sound?"

• • •

Constance Riel leaned over the shoulder of her science advisor, Paul Perry. He sat in Riel's own chair, at her exceedingly well-interfaced desk, busy hands moving over the plate. Riel frowned, ignoring the ache in feet rapidly growing numb. "You're telling me these images"—she poked a finger into the center of one of the displays, and it obligingly expanded—"show—what?"

Paul had pulled his jacket sleeves up and rolled his shirt cuffs. He blinked bloodshot eyes and continued in an Oxford-educated drawl. "This is from the Martian orbital telescope, Prime Minister. It shows an explosion or an impact near the south pole of Charon, the sister planet of Pluto. *This* shows the debris track. Ma'am, should I call down for sandwiches?"

She hadn't realized the rumble in her belly would be audible. "Yes. Bless you. That looks like a special effect from a science fiction holo. What does it mean?"

He keyed some information quickly—a request for food and coffee—and moved back to the telescopic images. "It means something struck Charon. Hard. Hard enough to—essentially—fracture the planet. Planetoid."

"An attack of some sort? What, more space aliens?" War-of-the-worlds scenarios unfolded in her head. She pressed her fingers to her eyes, imagining she could already smell coffee.

"No, ma'am." Paul shrugged. "I've been chasing some rumors, and I've had my staff after it. I wanted good information before I came to you."

"You're stalling, Paul."

"Yes, ma'am. Unitek."

"Unitek?"

"You've been briefed—have you been briefed?"

"*Is* there a new development with the pair of derelict alien spacecraft on Mars?"

"No. Unitek and a detached group from the joint forces have been working on developing a ship based on those design principles. You know that."

"I'm opposed to it, Paul. That's money better spent at home. But it's Unitek's money—" She shrugged. Canada needed to get free of Unitek. The problem was, with Unitek went access to the Brazil and PanMalaysian beanstalks, their international trade partners, and a good part of the funding for Canada's military. Times were more peaceful than they had been, on the surface. But a world in which The People's PanChinese Army was massing on the Russian border and eyeing the grain fields of Ukraine, a world where PanMalaysia and Japan relied on promises of military aid from Canada, Australia, and to a lesser extent the reconstructed but still limping United States to keep the same starving wolf from *their* door—it wasn't a world in which one dared appear weak. Paul himself was a refugee scientist from the slowly freezing British Islands.

Fallout from the Pakistani/Indian wars and the United States' actions in the Far and Middle East had moved Earth's supranational governments to rare, unified action. Global effort had managed what unilateral action could not: a functional missile defense shield, based on the same technology that provided meteorite and space-junk defense for the orbital platforms. Not, unfortunately, before the damage compounded China's inability to feed her swarming population.

Canada had already fought one unpopular war on the behalf of China's smaller neighbors. Riel started to wonder if the pain in her gut wasn't hunger, but an ulcer. "Was this a Chinese ship?"

"No," he said. "It was ours. And we have larger problems."

Riel sighed, glancing up as the door of her office opened. A liveried steward brought a tray into the room; she could tell at a glance that lunch must have been ready and waiting for their call. Or perhaps someone else's sandwiches and coffee had been diverted for the Prime Minister's use, and a replacement tray was already being made up. "Is this going to ruin my appetite, Paul?"

"Most likely."

Riel shooed the reluctant steward away and poured the coffee herself, balancing two self-regulating mugs—she despised china cups—and a plate of sandwiches as she made her way back. "Then we'd better eat while we talk," she said, and juggled dinnerware onto the desk. "I shouldn't eat these. I promised my husband we'd eat dinner together for once," she said. "And I have a meeting that starts in half an hour and runs until eight. Will this take longer than that?"

Paul glanced up from the simulation and shook his head. "It'll be four hours until you eat, then," he said. "Have a sandwich."

Her eyebrows rose. She knew it was an effective expression, under the heavy dark wing of her bangs, accentuating her thin nose and the long lines across her brow.

"Ma'am," he amended, and she acquiesced, selecting a triangle without looking at the contents. Chewy black bread and vegetables, and something that was more or less tuna fish. Farmed genemod tuna fish. Riel was just about old enough to remember the real thing.

"All right," she said, once Paul had had a moment to cram a third of a sandwich into his mouth. "Show me what you're worried about, Dr. Perry."

He didn't miss the formality—she could tell by the angle of his head—but he didn't acknowledge it, either.

"Here," he said, tapping up an image of a different—and more familiar—globe. "These shots are courtesy of Clarke and Forward," he said, and then waved a hand irritably over the panel, clearing the display. "—Wait—"

Long, spare fingers tapped crystal, and Riel smiled privately at his thoughtless efficiency of movement. She squinted as new images resolved. "There's something wrong with the depth."

"They're 2-D animations," Paul explained. "Late twentieth century—here. Do you see these color patterns, Ma'am?"

Riel nodded, watching as a computer-animated blush spread across the surface of the oceans, waxing and waning with fluctuations that could only be seasons. "Temperature patterns?"

"Yes. And more. This is a record of coral reef dieoffs."

Still 2-D, but no harder to follow than the old-fashioned movie once you got the hang of it. Riel licked mayonnaise off her fingers and frowned, rubbing them together to remove the last traces of grease. "Old news—"

"This isn't." His fingers moved. He leaned back in the chair, his shoulder brushing Riel's arm. She hunched forward, too intent to take a half-step to the side and preserve her space. It was the image that he'd brushed aside so quickly, a few minutes before. A modern three-dimensional animation, and—

"—those don't look dissimilar. But that's a much bigger scale, isn't it? And the currents look different than in the earlier one."

Paul shrugged. "They've change a lot."

Yes. Including the failure of the Gulf Stream. Which is why you're in Canada now, isn't it, Paul? Riel found herself nodding slowly, almost rocking. As if the motion would help her think. She put a stop to it firmly. "What am I looking at, Paul?"

"The end of the world," he said, with turgid drama and a news announcer's baritone. He coughed and cleared his throat, reaching for his coffee. "Well, perhaps not quite. But a serious problem, in any case. This is data from two of the orbital platforms regarding algae populations—"

"The algae is dying."

"Like the coral reefs."

Not exactly. but for Layman's values of like, sure."

"What does this have to do with the price of tea in China, Paul?"

He chuckled. "Funny you should phrase it that way, ma'am. Everything, it turns out. I've been corresponding with a Unitek biologist on Clarke—a Doctor Forster—"

"Charles Forster. he was involved in the mission that discovered the Martian ships."

"That's the one. He and I think that the increased Chinese interest in space travel—their outbound fire-and-forget colony ships, for example, and their expansion efforts within our system—date from about the time the first signs of this became apparent. It's a serious problem, Prime Minister. The sort of thing that could radically diminish the planet's ability to sustain life."

"You don't think the Chinese are behind—"

"No." Quiet, but definite. Riel like the way he stated his opinions, when he could be convinced to have them. "But I think they caught on a hell of a lot faster than we did. Of course, we've been distracted by the Freeze of Britain—"

"Excuses, excuses. What do we do?"

He glanced at her sideways and ruffled his hair with one hand. "Beat the Chinese out of the solar system, for one thing. And start thinking about what we're going to do in a hundred, hundred fifty years if we have to re-terraform Earth."